CHAOS

LUNA MASON

CHAOS

LUNA MASON

Title

CHAOS

Beneath The Secrets Series, Book One.

By Luna Mason.

Copyright © 2024 by Luna Mason.

Cover Design: Coffin Print Designs

Cover Model: Clever Huller

Photographer: Bryan Santos

Editing: Indie Proofreading

Formatting: Cruel Ink Editing + Design

A NOTE FROM LUNA MASON

CHAOS is a dark, stand-alone, mafia romance.
It does contain content and situations that could be triggering to some readers. This book is explicit and has explicit sexual content, intended for readers 18+.
This book follows the MMC's battle with his mental health and the **MMC does attempt suicide in chapter sixty-six.**
I urge you to protect your own mental health when starting this journey with Jax. So, chapters 65-70 can be skipped if you feel like you need to.
A full list of triggers can be found on my website: www. lunamasonauthor.com

If you or someone you love needs help, it is out there. Particularly for men, it can be difficult to open up, to show their emotions. There is a stigma around men's mental health that needs to change.
One man dies by suicide every 13.7 minutes in the U.S.
Although in this book, there is a happily ever after, sadly, that is not the case for so many men.

MANUP!
https://www.manup.how/
MOVEMBER:
https://us.movember.com

PLAYLIST

want me, Ex Habit
Kool-Aid, Bring Me The Horizon
Bite Marks, Ari Abdul
Formaldehyde Footsteps, BertieBanz
Lose Control, Teddy Swims
High Enough - RAC Remix, K.Flay, RAC
Limits, Bad Omens
love me, Ex Habit
Sugar, Sleep Token
Dark Signs, Sleep Token
Give, Sleep Token
on your knees, Ex Habit
I Found, Amber Run
RIDE, Chris Grey
The Apparition, Sleep Token
Never Know, Bad Omens
Like A Villain, Bad Omens
Home, Good Neighbours
don't worry babe, Ex Habit
I Get to Love You, Ruelle
Numb, Linkin Park
In the End, Linkin Park
NUMB, Ryan Oakes
Make Up Sex, SoMo
The Best I Ever Had, Limi
I Want It All, Cameron Grey

Paralyzed, LANDMVRKS
Shelter - from the room below, Sleep Token
Half A Man, Dean Lewis
PLEASE, Omido, Ex Habit
Telomeres, Sleep Token
Distraction, Sleep Token
When The Party's Over - from the room below, Sleep Token
Mine, Sleep Token
Can You Feel My Heart, Bring Me The Horizon
lovely (with Khalid), Billie Eilish, Khalid
Slow Down, Chase Atlantic
Godzilla (feat. Juice WRLD), Eminem
Home, Good Neighbours
Hypnosis, Sleep Token
Hold On, Chord Overstreet
My Home, Myles Smith
More songs can be found on the Spotify playlist.

All of Ex Habit's songs have clickable links at the start of their chapters. So you can click, play, and enjoy the smut with the full experience. His songs have been a life-saver in getting these spice chapters as hot as they are. So, @ex_habit, thank you and please keep feeding our addiction to your music. Xo

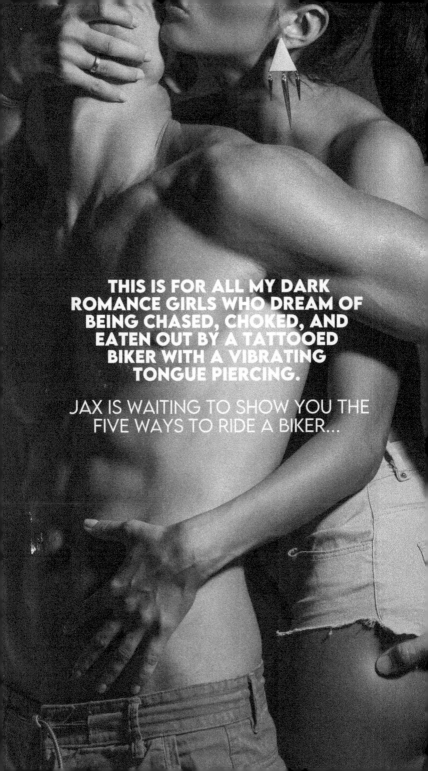

THIS IS FOR ALL MY DARK ROMANCE GIRLS WHO DREAM OF BEING CHASED, CHOKED, AND EATEN OUT BY A TATTOOED BIKER WITH A VIBRATING TONGUE PIERCING.

JAX IS WAITING TO SHOW YOU THE FIVE WAYS TO RIDE A BIKER...

CHAPTER ONE

JAX

Song- Hear You Me, Jimmy Eat World.

THE GEARS ON THE PULLEYS SCREAM THROUGH THE MISTY air as the casket lowers.

It's almost like Kai is nagging me one last time before he disappears into his grave.

Fuck, I'm going to miss him.

Grayson gives me a slow pat on my shoulder and a sympathetic look before he walks past with a teary Maddie huddling into his side.

Frankie gives me a small nod before taking Zara's hand and following the rest.

Everyone is in black. They fade into a haze as I stare at the gaping hole in the ground.

Of all the people to go, why Kai?

My first and only friend. He found me as a lonely kid and showed me that there was more to life than the empty halls of my father's estate.

I couldn't have made it past my dad's death without Kai. He kept me company every time my dad left on business. After Dad died on one of those trips, Kai was the one who pulled me away from the grief to find a new sense of belonging as a boxer.

Channeling the rage and loss into my fists, it opened up all the opportunities I never knew I wanted.

A new life, a new group of people that accepted me as one of theirs. Like a family.

But it still feels hollow without Kai.

I wish he was here. He'd love this adventure I'm starting.

All the girls in Vegas are waiting for me.

The lights of the Strip will never hit the same without him.

Clicking my tongue piercing against my teeth, I step forward and stare down at the top of his coffin.

His last place.

My best friend.

"It hurts so fucking bad, Kai. I don't want to leave you here." My knees land in the soft mud, soaking through my pants.

The heavy mist darkens into rain, just like my mood.

I've held his motorcycle helmet throughout the entire funeral. It's a piece of him.

The scratches have dulled on it from the time we were barely eighteen. I had just gotten the news about my dad, and Kai made me leave.

Shit, we found so much trouble that day. Going to the biker bar and finding the two hottest girls in there pissed off their boyfriends.

He used his helmet to beat down the biggest motherfucker, who was trying to use me like a punching bag.

I trace the long gouge on the side that still shows where the asshole gang member hit it with his fist full of rings.

Better than my face.

Water mixes with my tears to drip off my nose and chin.

With blurry vision, I toss down his black helmet.

It lands near the end of the mahogany box, right where his head rests beneath.

Pretty sure I just dropped my last give a shit down there with it.

I thought that when we killed Romano, this wouldn't rip me apart so bad.

But it does.

I can't bring him back.

The cold rain soaks through my suit and sends a shiver through my body.

Goddamnit, when did it get dark?

A clanging sound draws my attention to see two men folding the chairs and rolling up the fake grass ground cover.

It's time.

"See you on the other side, Kai. I hope I make you proud."

CHAPTER TWO

JAX

"Hit him again!" Grayson's voice booms over the din of the crowd.

Dodging a left hook, I duck and give a hard uppercut to 'Hurricane Hunter', landing a solid blow to his chin.

The big man teeters, his eyes glass over, and his arms drop.

Slack jawed, he stumbles backwards and falls against the ropes. Sweat sprinkles off of his hair under the harsh lights before he sinks onto the mat.

"Knock out by the King of Chaos, Jax Carter!" The thin referee jumps in front of me and yanks my arm above his head.

My ears ring from the roar of the packed seats. Thousands of people cheer behind a wall of flashes and confetti falling from the ceiling.

Hunter got in a couple of jabs that make the room blur around the edges. Or maybe it's the fading remains of my anger that lets everything come back into focus.

It's been hard not to hold back in the fights.

Channeling the pain and emptiness in my chest into every punch seems to help for a little while.

"Jax! Jax! You did great, kid. Come on, let's go." Grayson's large hand lands on my shoulder as he guides me out of the middle of the ring.

The high of the win fades as each step takes me farther into the bowels of the building to my changing room.

I feel nothing again. Like I need to go out and get wasted or get laid.

"You let him get too close again, Jax. Why are you dropping your guard when you know he's telegraphing his every move?" Grayson's blue eyes watch me as he unties my gloves. "Do you want him to hit you?"

"I don't care if he does." I don't want to tell him there's a part of me that wants to tap out. To get hammered so hard I can't remember my past.

Kai's empty chair mocks me from the other side of the room. It's the spot he always sat, so he could reach the little fridge stocked with beer.

Grayson's palm smacks against my cheek, startling me.

"Jax! What the fuck? Pull your head in, straighten your shit out. Go shower and change. I'll see you back at the gym in the morning." He jerks the towel from around his neck and throws it into the basket near the door. "Can't stay in the past," he mutters. "Learn from my mistakes; look forward."

Silence weighs on me after he leaves.

The cold shower doesn't shock me out of my daze. Grabbing my bag and my motorcycle helmet, I take a last glance at the worn seat and its echoes of the past.

Maybe Grayson is right.

Splashing through a shallow puddle, I cut around the dark corner to where my Ducati is parked when I hear footsteps.

"Jax Carter?" A man about my age approaches from the wall near my bike.

"What do you want?" I have no interest in fans unless they're carrying a fifth of whiskey and boast a pair of tits.

"Jax? It's me. Brody." He steps into the dim light of the street lamp, revealing dark curly hair and chestnut colored eyes.

"I don't know you." My duffel finds its place on the small rack over the exhaust where I strap it down. I want my hands empty in case I have to beat the shit out of this guy before this is done.

My heart beats a little faster at the thought of knocking someone else down.

Fuck or fight. What a great purpose to life.

"Brody Leary? Ring a bell? I'm your brother, man." His palms turn up as he inches closer.

"I don't have a brother." Fame has its drawbacks. All the crazies find their way out from under the rocks.

His voice drops to almost a whisper. "Carine."

Before I can stop myself, my hand wraps around his throat and pins him to the bricks. "The hell did you just say?"

He has an air of cheap cologne with a tinge of vodka aftershave. "She's my mom, too. Was. She passed this last spring," he chokes out.

This close, I can recognize the look. I see it every morning in the mirror.

"I don't have any money for you. If that's what you're here for?" I lighten my grip so he can breathe, but still keep my palm against his neck until I'm sure he isn't going to lash back.

"Keep your money." The whites of his eyes flash and a drop of sweat catches a glint of light.

His nostril flares as he battles with the obvious panic

7

lying just beneath the surface. I can feel it in his racing pulse.

"My mother left when I was young. How old are you?" I hate how much he resembles me. I only know her from photos, but I know we both favor her.

"Twenty-four."

Timeline works.

Jesus Christ.

A roll of every emotion cascades through me. Backing away, I find the seat of my bike to lean against and dig out a cigarette from my bag.

Grayson would kill me if he saw me smoking right after a fight, but I don't care.

"Why are you here?" The nicotine calms my nerves, but doesn't stop the knotting in my stomach.

A brother.

"I'm getting married. I want to invite you, as family." His shaky hand sticks out in a silent plea, holding a small card. My eyes flick between his crumpled note and his lips, flattened in doubt.

I grab the paper from his hand and toss it onto the damp pavement. "I already have a family."

And the only brother I ever knew, I buried just a couple of months ago.

That place is taken.

His brow furrows, and his hands close into fists. "I thought I was extending an olive branch. I didn't know you were really the asshole you portray in the ring. Seems like there was a good reason Mom left you." He turns on his heel and his boot grinds the slip of cardboard into the asphalt before he stomps away.

I don't need this.

I just want to be left alone. Everyone's always pushing me to get back up, go out, to do shit I don't want to do.

Even Grayson, tonight, said to look forward.

The white of the card glares against the dark ground in front of me.

A sibling?

Nah. I'm leaving for Vegas soon. It's already arranged. Why start a friendship with someone I don't know so close to leaving New York forever?

He's blood. He knew mom.

More than I ever did.

Fuck it.

Picking up the invitation, I knock some of the water from it, hoping it didn't ruin it.

It's the day before Frankie's baby shower. I'm stuck in the city until then. I promised I'd be there.

Hell, weddings always have desperate bridesmaids. Maybe I'll get laid one last time before starting over in Vegas.

CHAPTER THREE

SOFIA

"Brody, you can't come in here!" I shove the door closed, pushing him out.

"I need to see you, boo. It's important."

I frown as his serious tone fills the room. Today is supposed to be a happy day, our wedding day. Why does his voice crack and quiver, as if he's holding back tears?

"Is everything okay?" I ask, holding my breath.

There is a thud as he rests against the door, and I hear him let out a deep exhale. A few moments of silence pass, and my heart rate speeds up. Our wedding is the sole thing that keeps my mind active following the loss of my parents. A distraction from my grief that stops my heart from shattering.

Even though it was four years ago now, it still seems like yesterday when I got the call. The cops called it a freak accident. They never got to see me graduate. My dad won't be here to walk me down the aisle today. I'm lucky I had Brody. We met at college and he proposed shortly after their deaths. As soon as his own career took off, we moved back to New York. I was unable to focus on anything, so I made the decision to pause my schooling and prioritize his job.

And here we are.

I hold on tight to my mom's diamond around my neck. I've worn it every day since she passed. Call me strange. It makes me feel like she's here with me.

"I just needed to hear your voice, Sof."

"You still aren't coming in. It's bad luck." And I don't want any more of that. Not today, at least.

"I just want you to know I love you."

I stiffen at his words. I can't get past the grief in his voice. I know him. I've spent the last four years living with this man. I'm a psychology major. I know when something is up.

My fingers press against the thin barrier of wood between us. "I love you, too, B. Are you sure everything is okay?"

The last three months, I've hardly seen him. He's so busy with work, I'm asleep by the time he finally gets home. I'm hoping after the wedding is out of the way, we can go back to normal. He hasn't even touched me in weeks. Every time I bring it up, he reminds me of the wedding we have to pay for.

"It will be, I'm sure. I'll see you at the altar." He pushes away. I can just hear the echoes of his steps.

"See you soon." It comes out in almost a whisper.

"What the hell was that about?" Anna asks as she waltzes out of the en-suite into the bedroom. With her hair beautifully curled and resting on her shoulders, she now has a full face of makeup that includes blush lip gloss to match her bridesmaid dress.

My shoulders shrug on their own. "I honestly don't know."

She shakes her head. She's never hidden the fact she

isn't a fan of Brody. It goes both ways. Which only makes it awkward for me. That's why I haven't told her what's been going on over the last few months. How I've basically lived on my own.

"As much as I despise him, he loves you, Sof. He's probably just nervous."

I bite down on my lip and nod. I've never known Brody to get nervous. He's cocky and knows what he wants. Much like his father, Knox. Except Knox is a complete creep. I shudder at the thought of having to even be in the same room as him again. I'm just glad he lives in Vegas, so I don't have to see him.

"Yeah, he probably is."

With a smile, she grabs the champagne from the dresser, pours us each a glass, and hands one to me.

"Well, here's to your last moments as Miss Garcia."

As I take the drink from her, I can't help but notice my engagement ring sparkling in the light, which brings a smile to my face. Everything will be fine after today.

"To becoming Mrs. Leary."

Anna snorts out a laugh. "I think I prefer your last name. Drink faster. I have some best men to size up for later."

I laugh, shaking my head. "Apparently, Brody's half-brother is coming."

Anna's blue eyes widen, and a little smile creeps up her lips. "Oh, interesting. What does he look like?"

"Not a clue. Brody's only met him once. He started looking for him after his mom died."

Her finger traces the rim of her flute. "Same mom?"

I nod. Brody hasn't grieved his mother's passing. It's like it never happened. I wonder if that's what's bringing up his emotions today?

"Hey, maybe he's less of an asshole," she says.

With a glare, I lock eyes with her.

She breaks into a burst of laughter, the sound mixing with the clinking of her empty champagne glass.

"Be nice, just for today. Please." I pout at her, batting my lashes for effect.

"For you, anything," she says as she drapes her arm around my shoulder.

CHAPTER FOUR

JAX

RESTING BACK IN MY CHAIR, I TAP MY RINGS AGAINST MY glass of whiskey. The collar on my shirt digs into my neck, and I want to rip it off already.

"Shouldn't you be leaving? You're already late, and I have to go deal with the next shipment with Nikolai, and then I gotta get back to Zara and Leonardo," Frankie says from my left with a grin.

He knows I don't want to go to this wedding. Seeing the family my mom created after she tore ours apart. I'd rather be with him and Nikolai, heading straight back to my new life in Vegas with the Volkovs.

"You got a curfew now, boss?"

"Zara needs me. What can I say? You'll understand one day." He shrugs.

I scoff, picking up my drink.

"Doubt that, Frankie."

I've been working for Mikhail Volkov in Vegas since Kai's death. I will always have my home here in New York. I just need something new. I need to be away from the reminders. And I certainly don't need a woman. I prefer the variety.

"Couple more drinks first," I reply, letting the last swallow of bourbon burn down my throat.

I need a few to face this. Maybe Brody isn't a complete asshole and is nothing like my mother. Even so, after today, I won't be seeing him again.

"One more. Then go to that damn wedding, show your face and don't get too smashed. It's the baby shower tomorrow." Frankie's finger wags like he's my father.

I nod, catching the attention of the pretty waitress with bright red lips.

"What can I get you?" she asks, twirling her blonde hair around her pen, eye fucking me as she speaks.

"Two whiskeys and a shot of tequila."

I feel Frankie's disapproving stare on the side of my head.

She leans over, her hair brushing against my jaw.

"How about saving the shots for after I finish?" she whispers in my ear.

I bite down on my tongue as Frankie clears his throat beside me, causing her to pull back.

"I've got plans. Maybe I'll be back after." I wink at her.

She blushes, giving me a knowing nod before she waltzes off with a sway in her hips.

I watch her take every step until she disappears behind the double doors to the bar.

"Maybe tonight won't be so bad after all," I mutter, rubbing my hands together.

CHAPTER FIVE

SOFIA

I TAKE MY PLACE AT THE HEAD OF THE TABLE AS BRODY pulls out my seat with our hands intertwined. Glancing up, his bearded dad smirks suggestively, showing off his gold front tooth, making me swiftly avert my gaze.

"Here you go, wife," Brody whispers in my ear as I take my seat and he sits beside me.

"Your shithead brother didn't turn up then," Knox says from beside Brody. Apparently, he wasn't too happy with Brody searching out his long-lost brother.

Brody's best man, Ash, clears his throat beside me. He's forcefully pressing his fingers into his thigh while keeping his jaw clenched.

Resting my head on Brody's shoulder, he wraps a protective arm around me. He's tense, too. Maybe they had an argument. They've been friends since they were kids, so I doubt it.

Ash stands beside me. The excited chatter of our guests gradually fades away as he taps his knife against his glass, capturing their attention.

"I thought your speech was first?" I whisper to Brody, and he stiffens beside me.

"Welcome to the beautiful wedding of my best friend, Brody, and his stunning bride, Sofia," he says, holding his drink up to the cheering crowd.

"I've been best friends with Brody for as long as I can remember. We've been through everything together."

"Aww." I nudge Brody.

He remains expressionless, clenching his fists.

"And, apparently, it seems like we share everything now, too." Ash pauses, turning to face me and Brody.

"Isn't that right?" Ash presses, his hand shaking around the glass.

"Stop it, Ash. I'm warning you. Not fucking now," Brody hisses.

Ash bursts out into laughter. "What? You don't think she deserves to know?"

"Know what?" Blood hammers in my ears, what the hell is going on.

"Ignore him," Brody whispers.

"Well, I fucking think she should know that you've been sleeping with my fiancé for the past year. You bastard." Ash waves his arm out in a grand gesture, like he wants the entire audience involved.

As I release my hand from Brody's, his grip around my shoulders tightens. I shake my head frantically. In the silence of the room, my heart pounds relentlessly in my chest.

He's fidgeting, scratching the back of his neck, and his cheeks are turning a rosy shade.

Panic rises within me. "Tell me he's lying, Brody."

He won't look at me.

My throat squeezes shut as a sob threatens to escape. "No," I whisper, my hand tightening around the wine flute.

"Congratulations, Brody. You've ruined two people's lives today. Some best friend you are." Ash's words echo through the silence of the assembled guests.

I flinch as the microphone drops to the floor. I can't even see straight. The room starts to blur.

How could he do this to me? With who? I start to wrack my brains–Ash's fiancé, Lisa. Where have I seen her before? She's drop dead gorgeous.

The realization dawns on me. Lisa from accounts at Brody's firm.

I feel a fiery anger building up inside me as I stand, forcefully jabbing his arm.

"Fucking look at me," I hiss.

His watery eyes meet mine, and the full weight of the truth hits me. All the sacrifices I've made for his career and this is how he repays me.

That's why he's pulled away from me. Not to pay for our wedding, but so he can stick his dick in Lisa.

"You piece of shit."

In an impulsive moment, my fist flies through the air and connects with his cheekbone.

He jerks back, and his palm covers his cheek. "Fuck, Sofia."

With trembling hands, and ignoring the pain radiating up my arm, I swipe up the wine bottle.

I can't even bear the sight of him. My heart breaks in my chest as I barge past him, feeling the heat of everyone's gaze on me as I storm through the marque.

"Sofia, wait." His call is punctuated by the sound of his chair shoving away from the table.

I stop in my tracks at the door, and with frustration building, I stomp my foot for emphasis.

"Stay the hell away from me. We're done. Over. Have a nice fucking life."

He steps forward to grab hold of me, and Anna barrels into him.

"You piece of shit! I knew you were an asshole. But this?" Her painted nails lash out and rake down the sleeve of his suit.

"Back off." He turns, squaring up to her.

I can't deal with this. Their arguing all melds into a deafening noise. I run my hands along my dress, trying to regain some sense of reality.

Turning on my heel, I dart for the exit. I need some air before I pass out. How could he do this to me?

With tears streaming down my face, I feel the cold breeze against my flushed skin. He's been cheating on me for a year.

Once safely in the parking lot, I collapse onto the hood of his car. The cool metal soothes the heat of anger burning through me as I finish off the remains of the champagne.

Fuck him.

In a moment of frustration, I wipe away the tears on my cheeks using the back of my hand, then forcefully toss the bottle to the ground, savoring the chaotic symphony of its destruction.

My breathing becomes suddenly heavy, each inhale feeling labored. None of this was real. He never loved me. I gave up my career to help him. I did everything for that piece of shit.

The parking lot is shrouded in darkness, with only the faint flicker of festival lights illuminating the surroundings.

Shit.

As I head towards the iron gates, the sound of my heels clicking along the pavement echoes in the quiet street. I need to get away from here.

With headlights getting closer, I squint, and the sound of a rumbling bike fills the air.

I keep walking. Whoever it is, they won't be any of my friends or family.

I have no one.

CHAPTER SIX

JAX

My palm squeezes the throttle, amplifying my frustration through the deep rumble of my Ducati clenched between my thighs.

I slow down as I approach the iron gates, blinking a few times to make sure I'm not hallucinating. I know I had a couple of whiskeys on hardly any sleep.

My foot lands on the pavement as I try to make sense of what I'm seeing. I'm not imagining this. A woman in an unmistakable white wedding dress stomps towards me, her veil billowing in the wind. Her tiny frame is accentuated by her dark maroon hair, cascading down and stopping just above her waist.

Bringing my bike to a stop, I switch off the engine and prop it up with the kickstand.

Pulling off my helmet, I shake out my dark curls.

"Are you okay?" I ask, striding towards her.

Her beauty is illuminated by the soft light of the street lamp as she comes to a halt.

"Do I look it?"

Woah, okay. Holding up my arms, I step in front of

her. I can't help but notice the hoarseness in her voice and the bloodshot look in her eyes.

"The wedding's the other way, isn't it?" I tilt my head to the side, taking her in.

A burst of laughter escapes her lips.

"Exactly why I'm heading in the opposite direction. I'm getting the fuck out of here."

With that, she steps around me, her footsteps clicking loudly as she continues stomping into the darkness.

What the fuck.

"Hold up," I call out, catching up to her easily and stopping in front of her. "Where are you going?"

As she shrugs and turns away.

I can't resist the urge to grab her elbow and swing her around to face me, getting lost in her mesmerizing forest green eyes.

"What does it matter to you? Who the hell are you?" she says, shrugging away my touch.

"I'm Jax. Pleasure to meet you." I grin at her, holding out my palm. She raises an eyebrow, studying me.

"Sofia. I would say the same back, but you're related to that asshole. So have fun. I'm sure you can all have a good laugh at my expense." Her chin juts out defiantly.

Stepping closer to her, I notice her eyes widen.

"What did he do?"

She sucks in a sharp inhale. "He's been sleeping with his best friend's fiancé."

She chokes on the words. Instinctively, I put a supportive hand on her upper arm.

"Stupid man," I whisper. He is no different from my mother. Maybe it runs in the blood.

Her warm palm rests on my forearm. "Yeah, he really is," she replies, her hot breath hitting my chest.

The rapid beating of my heart pounds in my ears.

She pulls away and I already miss her touch. What the hell is wrong with me? I bring the helmet up, sensing her hesitation and creating a physical divide between us.

"I can take you home."

At this point, I don't know what I'm saying or why. All I know is I want her away from my brother. And far away from here. I can already tell she deserves better than him.

"On your bike? How the hell do you suggest that will work in this?" She dramatically tugs on her puffy dress.

"We'll make it work, don't worry."

Ignoring her doubts, I swiftly slide the helmet over her head, muffling her complaints, and take her hand.

As soon as our fingers touch, I feel a jolt of electricity course through me.

I walk us towards my bike, the sound of our footsteps echoing in the air. She stops, her arms crossed, and flips open the helmet that she tilts to the side. "I don't want to go home."

"Then where to? It is your special day, after all."

With a casual shrug, she casts her gaze downward.

I watch as her body shivers.

"Just take me to a bar. I need to forget that today ever happened."

I let out a laugh. There is absolutely no way I'm letting her walk around New York, wearing a wedding dress, in the feisty mood she's in.

"You wanna get hammered?"

One of her small fists props into her canted hip. "Why? Are you offering to join me?"

"I know just the place." I pull off my leather jacket and thread her arms into it.

Sliding back down her visor, I bend down and push up her dress, revealing her smooth, bare legs as I help her up over the bike.

This might be a mistake. A big one. There's something about her that has me questioning what the hell I'm doing.

But, as I slide in place in front of her, and her thighs hug my hips and her arms wrap around my waist, I know this night is just beginning.

She wants to forget. That's something I can help with.

CHAPTER SEVEN

SOFIA

As soon as the bike comes to the stop in some fancy underground parking lot, I feel like I can breathe again.

Why I'm doing this, I don't know. He seems more interested in me than going to the wedding. He promised me drinks. And that's all I want.

To forget the utter embarrassment and hurt of the last few hours.

I tug Jax's jacket tighter around me.

I don't realize how firmly I'm gripping onto his muscular chest until he physically has to remove my hands to stand.

He slides the helmet off of my head, letting my tangled hair fall around my shoulders.

Instinctively, I use my fingers to run through my knotted locks. There's a strange little feeling that I want to look better around him.

Probably because he's so handsome. I shouldn't be thinking about that. I got married to another man less than two hours ago.

"All good?" His deep voice grabs my attention.

I look up at him, holding his hand out to me.

"Yep." I don't trust myself to say much more.

He could be an asshole, like his brother. Hell, this could all be a setup and Brody is upstairs waiting for me.

Not that it matters. I'll happily punch him again. Harder this time.

Placing a shaky hand in his, my body buzzes to life as his other palm lands on my hip and he helps me off the bike. Snatching free from him, I shuffle down the dress so it covers my legs again.

He pauses and watches me. "Sweetheart, I don't bite."

My mouth parts, ready with a quick retort. But the way his dark eyes burn into mine before a smile erupts on his face, revealing his perfect white teeth, tells me he's clearly a joker.

"Come on." He chuckles and gestures for me to walk beside him to the elevator. When he jabs the button with his ring-covered fingers, I notice the tattoo ink patterned across his knuckles and disappearing beneath his sleeve.

Seeing him in real light, he's something else to look at. Tall, a dark scruffy beard that doesn't disguise his chiseled jaw. And, damn, the way that shirt clings to his arms, he's ripped.

Again, nothing like his brother. The only resemblance really is the curl in their hair. Except Jax's is way darker, and his skin is more tan.

He turns his head to the left, sporting a boyish grin.

Great. He's caught me checking him out. Luckily, the elevator pings and the door opens. I follow him in and position myself in the opposite corner, trying to put some space between us.

I'm clearly not thinking straight.

He leans against the mirrored wall and crosses his thick arms, making his biceps bulge. "You okay, Sofia?"

I give him a small smile and a nod.

I'm not. Deep down I'm hurt, I'm furious. I want to scream.

He was right earlier. I have nowhere to go. I let out a gasp as his hot palm touches the small of my back and the silver doors slide open.

"Hey, come on, let me get you that drink?" The softness in his voice catches me off guard.

I cautiously step inside the massive apartment. Before I can take in just how beautiful it is, I scan the room. Almost waiting for Brody to pop up from somewhere. As a few moments pass, I relax slightly and step out of Jax's reach.

He watches me move around the room, peeking through the open doors. "Trust me, he won't be here. He doesn't even know where I live, and he never will."

Tugging hold of my hand, he leads me through the living room, complete with a theater-sized TV screen up on the wall and black leather sofas.

As we get to the kitchen, he pulls out a bar stool and heads straight to the refrigerator, picking out two bottles of beer and opening the caps with his teeth, making me cringe.

"Here, I have plenty more." He offers one of the drinks to me.

"Thank you." My fingers wrap around the cold glass, and I watch as he tips back his head, downing the contents in no time.

Hell, maybe he's had a crappy day, too.

As he goes to grab another, he stops. "You don't like beer? I have harder stuff if you want it?"

"No, it's fine," I reply, taking a sip. It's like an instant relaxer.

He takes a seat beside me and his muscular thigh

brushes against me. His close proximity makes my body heat.

"So, what do you need?" His words are low, but they feel like they're burning into me.

I spin to face him. "What do you mean?"

His teeth flash over his lower lip before taking another sip of his beer.

"Well, we can sit in silence, you can tell me to fuck off to another room, or, I don't know, play a game?" He spins the bottom of his drink in the wet circle of condensation on the table.

"You'd just leave me here in your house to drink your booze? Why?"

He shrugs, twisting in his chair.

He's right, I normally wouldn't want to talk. I'd retreat and try to fix myself on my own. Yet, for some reason, his company is kind of comforting. He's actually relaxing to be around. Even if he seems to carry a tension in his shoulders like a coiled snake.

"You had a shitty day. I've promised you a drink. If you don't wanna talk, you don't have to."

I blink at him a few times. He isn't like his brother. Brody is a control freak, an uptight one, who always needed to press everything.

Jax, however, seems to understand what it's like to be hurt. To not want to talk. Maybe he's like me? We suck it up and get on with life.

That's how I dealt with my parents' deaths. That's why it didn't break me.

"A game? What do you have in mind?"

His face softens before I'm given one of those sexy, lopsided grins.

"Never have I ever?"

I let out a laugh. I haven't played this in years.

"Well, that's a blast from the past," I reply. "Count me in."

"How old are you?" he asks, raising a brow.

"Twenty-four. You?"

"Twenty-six." He looks deep in thought. "What the hell are you doing getting married at that age?"

"Clearly, I didn't have a clue. Now, that, I don't want to talk about."

He salutes me with his beer and pairs it with a wink. "Got it." He stands and grabs us two more drinks, dropping a freshly opened one in front of me. "Ladies first…"

I tap on my chin, I'll start easy on him. "Never have I ever broken a bone?"

He tips his beer and I leave mine on the counter.

"Many. I like to fight too much."

"You any good?" I bite the inside of my mouth to hold back the smile.

"Haven't lost yet." He grins.

I doubt he has. He's huge, jacked, and has that slightly crazed look in his eyes that tells me he would thrive on it.

"Your turn."

"Never have I ever moaned the wrong name during sex."

I take a drink and then burst out laughing.

"I don't believe you." I eye him suspiciously and he bites down on his lip. Clearly, we aren't playing the usual rules.

"Is that where we're going with this?" I ask, feeling the heat spread to my cheeks.

"The naughty version is more fun. Unless you want me to start listing my felonies or broken bones?" He holds out his left hand, palm down, showcasing two crooked fingers.

"I'm sure that's quite the list." I look closer and see small scars dimpling both of his eyebrows and jaw.

His lip turns up in a wry smile. "You have no idea."

"Okay, my turn." I straighten my back, resting my hands on the counter. "Never have I ever had a threesome?"

He stiffens beside me, looking straight past me at the wall, his fingers tightening around the neck of his bottle.

I can't help but lean forward and place my hand on his thigh. It's almost like he's seen a ghost.

Without averting his gaze, he lifts his drink and empties it in one long swallow. His tongue bar clicks against the rim before he lowers it.

"I'm guessing it wasn't good?" I ask, trying to lighten the mood. He snaps his eyes to me, a darkness flashing over them that has me jerking my hand back. He shakes his head, snatching my fingers and placing it back on his thigh. The warmth of his touch sends tingles up my arm.

"It was pretty damn great," he says, looking at me with a crooked smile.

The change in his expression puts me more at ease.

"Well, you're free now. Maybe you can try one." He leans in and nudges me with his shoulder against mine.

I almost choke on my drink, and my cheeks start to burn.

I never thought I'd be sitting here laughing this evening. I have Jax to thank for that.

He leans closer, invading my space. His musky after-shave lingers in the air. I close my eyes to fight the woozy feeling. It has to be the alcohol. I wouldn't be getting this hot and flustered over him otherwise.

As I open them, I find him searching my face, tilting his head slightly to the side. Assessing me. And suddenly everything is too much. This dress is so damn tight it's hard to breathe.

I pull at the corset trying to give myself some room, but it does nothing.

"If you go in the top cupboard, you'll find some better drinks for this. Let me go get you something," he says in my ear. I simply nod. I watch as he strides out of the room, running a hand through his dark curls as he does.

I bet he's feeling this, too.

CHAPTER EIGHT

JAX

Song- Desire, MEG MYERS

I PACE THROUGH MY LIVING ROOM, STOPPING JUST SHORT OF the bedroom. I feel like an ass, almost losing myself in memories of Kai. Initiating the game is supposed to be fun, a way to lighten the mood. But all that's happened is my dick is hard as fuck, and every time she blushes, my heart pounds. She's a perfect everything.

With my steel piercing caught between my teeth, I lean back against the door, my eyes fixed on her as she energetically searches the cupboards. A smile spreads across her face the moment she lays her hands on the tequila. I can't help but notice that tiny dimple on her left cheek.

I stay fixed in place. She really shouldn't be here. Nor should my cock be twitching just watching her.

Kicking myself back up, I head to my bedroom, rummaging around for an oversized top and rolling up my sleeves. The temperature is soaring in here.

If she wants to forget today, she needs out of that wedding dress.

"For you," I say, handing her one of my black shirts.

"You know I'm technically your sister-in-law right now? I shouldn't be here, should I?" she teases, taking the fabric from between my fingers.

I swallow past the lump in my throat. That's what makes this so damn hot. She's the woman I can't have. That I shouldn't want. I've never been one to play by the rules, and now, there's no one to keep me on the straight and narrow.

I can't focus on anything but her slender neck as she tips her head back and drinks the tequila straight from the bottle. My hard on is twitching against my zipper. It's almost painful at this point.

"I just thought you'd want to get out of that dress." I bite back a grin as the lie rolls off my tongue.

"So you didn't even contemplate the fact you might sneak a look?" She looks up at me through her thick lashes.

She's got me. We both know it.

"You could have just dropped me at a hotel, you know?"

She leans back against the counter, tapping her nails against the bottle with a grin. I can't stop myself from closing the distance between us, our noses almost touching.

"I could have. What kind of man would that make me?"

One that doesn't want to bend his sister-in-law over the counter and fuck her senseless.

She sucks in a breath, tipping her chin up to me with a fire behind those beautiful green eyes that sparks something deep inside me back to life.

"I think you're one of the good ones, Jax. You're a rule follower." She runs her tongue along her lips and I can't tear my eyes away. I want this woman, probably more than I've ever wanted anyone.

She captivates me. For the first time in a long time, I don't feel empty. Fuck it. I'm going to hell, anyway.

"Do you want to get naughty with me, sweetheart? Break them with me?" I whisper against her jaw, smiling as she shivers against me.

"How badly?" she asks in a sultry tone, trailing her hands up my abs and landing on my pecs. She can probably feel my heart pounding against her palm.

Clicking my tongue piercing against my teeth, I lean in closer so she's pressed tight against me. My hands squeeze the countertop, the only thing stopping me from tearing that dress off her like an animal.

"I think we can shatter just about every fucking rule that exists, baby. Tonight, I'm all yours."

A moment of silence feels like hours as I wait for her reaction to my words. I've never hidden who I am or what I want. And right now, she's the prize I've set my sights on.

She gathers up her maroon curls in her hands and spins so her back is to me, brushing against me as she does. "Help me out of this dress."

I clear my throat before cautiously stepping behind her. As I trail my index finger along her smooth skin, I feel her chest rise and fall.

Undoing the bow, I begin the task of gradually loosening each string, taking my time. With each passing second, I swear my body heat rises.

Watching her let her hair down, I can't look away as she awkwardly maneuvers out of the sparkling white dress. Only a thin, white thong remains.

"Fuuuuck," I groan.

Those perfect curves and fine ass make me want to grab hold and never let go.

While she slides into my shirt, I nonchalantly run my

fingers through my hair, turning my attention to the tequila bottle beside me.

I need to get my head back.

She isn't mine. She isn't meant to be here. Even if I've wanted a taste since the moment I first laid eyes on her.

"Where are your glasses?" she asks. Her soft voice knocks me back to reality. As I glance upwards, I see her on tiptoes, attempting to reach the cupboard, her top revealing enough to showcase her toned ass.

There is only so much restraint a man can have, and the last of mine just disappeared.

"Here." I click my tongue piercing against my teeth. Her plump, shiny lips curve into a mischievous smile as she spins around to face me.

I grab up the bottle from the counter and tilt my head back to pour tequila into my mouth, sealing it shut to hold the liquid inside. I grip her throat, pressing her body against the cabinet.

Towering over her, she bends her head back and opens wide for me. I spill the contents from my mouth into hers and my dick nearly explodes in my pants. I feel her neck bob as she swallows. Her eyes meet mine, full of desire.

And I can't move.

She slowly wipes the excess away from her lips and then licks her finger clean. A groan escapes me. I take a step back, running a hand over my face, letting out a ragged breath.

She takes a small step towards me, grabbing hold of my tie, and tugs me back towards her.

I want her so fucking much.

"Do it again, Jax. This time, kiss me." Her words come out in a breathy whisper.

I don't hesitate in crashing my lips over hers, letting my

tongue explore her mouth. She tastes like strawberries and mint, mixed with tequila. Hot as sin.

"This is so fucking wrong, Sofia," I mutter between kisses.

"Just shut up, Jax." She tugs on my hair, deepening the hold she has on me. The fact that she knows what she wants and doesn't hold back is even more of a turn on.

"Keep talking to me like that."

In one swift movement, I lift her onto the counter and position myself between her legs. My fingers find the hem of her top, and I slowly peel it over her body, admiring every inch of her as I do.

"So beautiful, Sofia."

A blush creeps up her chest. I can't help but lean in and run my tongue between her breasts and all the way up to her neck. She tips her head to the side, giving me better access.

"You taste so sweet. I bet your pussy is even sweeter."

CHAPTER NINE

SOFIA

Song- don't worry babe, Ex Habit.
https://lost.exhabitmusic.com/dontworrybabe

I STARE AT HIM, MY HEART ACCELERATING, AND MY SKIN IS on fire.

Do I want tonight to replace any memories I have of my disaster of a wedding day?

Absolutely.

"Never have I ever slept with my brother-in-law."

A grin forms on his lips.

"We gotta change that, baby. You in? Fuck the rules?"

I blow out a breath, but don't hesitate in my reply.

"Yes——"

He cuts me off with a kiss, a ferocious one. His tongue explores my mouth as he effortlessly lifts me into his arms, carrying us through his apartment to his bedroom. I drop down onto his plush gray bed with a bounce.

Sitting up on my heels, our eyes lock as he gets to work removing his tie and shirt. The muscles in his forearm bulge as he does. His whole body is covered in dark ink. It's hard to make out what they are.

He licks his lips. The way he eats me up has me on the edge. I've never experienced this pull before.

"Gorgeous," he mutters before kicking off his boots and pants.

I blink a few times, looking at his huge dick straining against his boxers.

"You wanna see?" he says with a mischievous grin.

I prop myself up onto my elbows and lick my lower lip suggestively. "Show me the goods."

He slowly pulls down his boxers, his huge cock standing to attention.

"Wow," is all I can say.

He kneels onto the bed and pushes me onto my back, his arms resting on either side of my head.

"Yeah, I'll take that. Keep the compliments coming," he whispers against my cheek.

He wedges his hips between my thighs, resting on his forearm as his other hand slides down my body until his palm reaches my pussy. With his soft strokes, I inch my legs open further and let out a moan.

"Close your eyes, focus on how good it feels. I've gotta get you nice and stretched so you can fit in *every. Single. Inch.*"

My eyes flutter shut as he slides his fingers in as deep as they can go.

"Fuck, Jax. It'll fit, right?"

With his thumb circling my clit, he starts to kiss and bite at my neck. Each one erupts sparks inside of me.

"Hear how wet you are for me? That tells me your tight pussy is going to take me perfectly, sweetheart."

I can. It's the only noise in the room.

"Mmm, yeah. Keep doing that," I reply.

With his tongue exploring my collarbone, he quickens the pace of his fingers, and my back arches off the bed.

"I'm close, fuck."

I've never gotten off this quick in my life. But, it has been months.

"Good, now be a good girl and come all over my fingers. I want to lick it all up after."

His words have my eyes opening, and I find his face just a breath away from mine. All I can focus on is his grin.

"Kiss me."

He runs his tongue along his teeth before crashing his lips over mine, and I wrap my arms around his neck, pulling him even closer as he tips me over the edge, my body shuddering against his. I moan into his mouth and he doesn't let up, taking what he wants from me.

Even as I'm riding out my orgasm, he keeps kissing me.

He pulls back with a smile on his face as I try to calm my panting.

"Happy with the service so far, sweetheart?"

I run my fingers through his dark curls.

"It's a pretty good start. What else have you got for me?"

He dips his head into the crook of my neck and bites down on my sensitive flesh, curling his fingers inside me, right on that sweet spot that has me ready to go again.

"Jax," I moan.

He runs his tongue along my throat, all the way up past my jaw, his piercing heightening the feeling.

"We can do better than 'good', baby," he says, sliding his fingers out of me and stroking my hair away from my face.

"I didn't have you down as a kisser," I say.

"Oh, I'm not. I told you, the rules are out the window today."

"I think I need your mouth somewhere else." I bite back a grin, unsure where this confidence is coming from. But, when his eyes light up with desire, I stop doubting myself.

He rolls onto his back, his arms resting above his head.

"Get your ass up here and take a seat. It's the best one in the house."

Sitting up on my forearm, I trace the tattoos on his hipbones, inching closer to his cock, swiping the liquid from the tip with my index finger.

"Trust me, baby. You'll be getting enough of my cock tonight. Get your ass up here and ride my face."

Before I can even consider moving, he sits up, grabs me by the waist. I let out a squeal as I land on top of him.

"Much fucking better."

Pushing my body up, his fingers dig into my hips as I settle myself on his face. My hands splay out on his toned chest.

"Oh, shit," I pant out. The metal ball of his piercing hits my clit and he starts to play. Sitting myself up higher, my hands trail up his chest and I grab the sides of his throat for support, causing him to groan beneath me.

CHAPTER TEN

JAX

Song- don't worry babe, Ex Habit.
https://lost.exhabitmusic.com/dontworrybabe

She can choke me as hard as she wants. As long as I have that pretty pussy smothering my face, I'll die a happy man.

The weight of her body rests against my neck, making me dig my fingers into her fine ass even deeper. I'm starving for her, and that sweet taste on my tongue. I can't get enough.

Those little breathy moans she lets out only spurs me on further. Every time my tongue bar hits against her clit, her legs clamp around my head.

"God, yes, Jax."

Oh, she's close.

I slide one of my hands along her toned stomach, cupping her full breast in my hand, and pinching the nipple. Her hips start to roll, and her pussy rubs against my face.

Fuck.

I suck on her, at the same time slapping her ass hard enough to have her completely trembling above me. Her hand tightens around my throat, and her nails dig deep into the skin. Blood rushes to my head as I feast on her, taking every last drop of her climax onto my tongue. I want to taste her on there forever.

She slumps herself forward with her breasts squished on my abs and her ass in my face. I can't resist sitting up and sinking my teeth into the flesh of her thigh and she cries out.

"Oh, shit," I groan as her lips wrap around my cock.

"I need to see you." As good as my view is, I want to look into those enchanting eyes as I throat-fuck her.

With her mouth still on me, she shuffles around, positioning herself between my thighs. Her eyes don't leave mine as she starts to lick up the shaft. I clench my fists, trying to regain some control over myself.

"Keep doing that, and I'll come all over your face. Is that what you want?" I ask, sitting up on my forearms.

She shakes her head, taking my dick as far down as she can. I can't hold in the moan that slips from my lips.

As she leans back, she sucks on the tip and my whole body tenses.

"I'd rather have you come inside me," she says with a smirk. My heart almost explodes out of my chest.

I splutter on a cough, taking in the filth coming from her mouth. Damn, she is perfect. When she starts to climb up my body until her dripping cunt is rubbing on my cock, I don't know how I don't come on the spot.

Her hair flows over her shoulder, tickling against my face as her nose presses against mine.

"Be a good boy and fuck me, Jax."

It's like she's managed to unleash a feral beast inside of me. I let out a growl and my hand shoots out, grabbing hold of her throat. I squeeze tight, claiming my lips with her own as I roll us over so I'm positioned between her legs.

"If it means I get to sink inside your soaking pussy, then I'll be such a good fucking boy for you, baby."

As my dick teases her entrance, she pulls on my hair, burning my scalp. Which seems to knock a little bit of sense in me.

"Condom, shit."

Laying her down, I keep kissing her and fumble around, pulling out the nightstand drawer, not wanting to ruin the moment. This is one rule we need to keep.

I keep feeling around for the foil, but nothing.

"Jesus fucking Christ." Why now? Why, of all times, does this shit happen to me?

"You've run out?"

It's clear she's unamused by her tone.

"Screw it."

My whole body is on fire. I need to be inside her.

"I'm clean. I don't do this with anyone, ever," I say, trying to gauge her reaction.

Her teeth nibble on her lower lip. "So am I. I'm on birth control. I've never gone without one, even with—"

I cut her off with a kiss. That's enough. I said fuck the rules. Looks like I really meant it.

Sitting back, I spit on my hand and stroke my dick. She gasps, that perfect blush spreading up her neck, matching the color of the marks from my hands.

Hooking her legs around my waist, I grab a pillow from behind us and prop it under her hips.

"I want to see you take every inch of me, tigritsa."

Her eyes go wide as I sink into her.

"So tight. Jesus," I hiss.

With one arm above her head, I lace my fingers

through her other and lean over her, her hot breath hitting against my lips. With every thrust, the feel of her warmth surrounding my cock is pure, electrifying pleasure.

I've never done this raw before. And, holy hell, it's worth the risk.

She was right. Kissing isn't my thing. Yet, with her, I can't get enough.

"Kiss me, baby."

She moans into my mouth as I pick up the pace, slamming into her and slowly retreating out, over and over again, until I can barely see straight.

"Oh my god, Jax."

"Keep saying my name, baby."

She clamps around my dick, and I can't hold back. The second her teeth sink into my neck, pain sears through my skin, and I erupt with the most violent, all-consuming orgasm I've ever had. As my hand finds her neck and I squeeze, she shatters around me.

Holy fucking shit.

Resting my sweaty forehead against hers, I have no words. We just lay there, her nails tracing small circles on my back, sending tingles throughout my entire body as my cock twitches inside her.

"Better than good?"

She lets out a laugh and my heart hammers.

"I don't know my own name right now, Jax. Yeah, five star service."

I smile against her hot skin.

As I push myself up, she links her arms around my neck, pulling me back to her.

"I'm going to get you cleaned up," I whisper against her lips.

She shakes her head.

"No?"

The corner of her mouth turns up in a teasing smirk. "What's the point? We're going again, right?"

I bite down on my tongue.

My brother seriously fucked up letting this woman go. I'm kinda glad, since she's in my arms and I get to experience this. Damn shame it will only ever be once.

———

I wake up, immediately aware of the strawberry scent invading my senses. Sweet Sofia. Her back is pressed up against my chest. And I'm lying here with a handful of her breast and an already hard cock poking her ass.

What a way to start my last day in New York.

"Morning," I whisper against her shoulder and follow it with a kiss.

"Hmm, good morning." She stretches out, rolling onto her back. With the morning light streaming through my windows, I can see the full array of beautiful red marks scattered on her body.

She smiles at me, reminding me of the last rule I had that we broke. No sleepovers. Not that we slept much.

"And how was the bed for your stay? Comfortable enough?" I tease. Playfully, she hits my chest. Before she can pull away, I hold her hand in place.

"Pretty damn good." Her fingers trail through my tangled hair before she lets her arm fall to the pillow.

I don't know what to do with a girl the morning after. This is completely unchartered territory. "What's your plan now?"

She pulls the covers under her chin and I yank them away, positioning myself between her legs.

She sighs, relaxing her knees against my ribs. "I honestly don't know."

"You want my advice?" My palms work up and down her thighs. I don't know what will happen later, but I can't stop touching her.

Her eyes narrow in a look that tells me she doesn't, but I'll give it to her, anyway.

"Get as far away from my family as you possibly can. They're toxic. All of them." Brody has proven to be no different from my mother. I'd take bets on my 'step-dad' is a complete asshole, too.

Her lips thin, and her gaze drifts to a spot on the wall behind me. "Easier said than done. I don't have anything in my name."

I tip her chin up. "Start with nothing and build an empire then, sweetheart."

I grab her left hand, studying the rings on her finger. There's no way he spent more than five grand on these. Fucking cheapskate.

"I'll give you fifty-thousand for these. Think that's fair?"

She blinks at me a few times. I turn her palm over and drop my lips softly on the delicate skin of her wrist.

"No. We both know they aren't worth anywhere near that. I've got a little of my inheritance left from my parents." She lets out a long breath like the words hurt to say.

I don't think I should ask about her parents. That would be crossing a line that we both silently agreed to place. "In a joint account?" I pull back and study her features.

She frees her hand from my grasp to rub her temples. "Yep."

Fucking bastard. A money grabber like Mom.

Anger boils in my chest. "How much did you have in there?"

Her maroon hair fans out as she shakes her head. "I don't know, probably twenty?"

"Wait here." The air is cold on my naked body when I crawl out of bed, but I'm on a mission.

I head into my office and open up the safe, and start shoving bundles of cash into a bag. There is something telling me to help her get away from them. I don't ignore my instincts. She deserves better than them, anyway.

As I return to the bedroom, she's sitting up, watching me cautiously. I drop the duffle on the floor.

"Jax. What the hell are you doing?" The sheet falls from her, exposing her perky nipples, tightening in the chill.

I bite back a groan as my eyes roam her naked body, rubbing a hand over my face to try to concentrate for a minute, then I hold out my hand. "The rings."

"I'm not taking your charity, Jax." She folds her slim arms over her chest, obscuring my view.

I step towards her and grab her chin. "You are. I've got far too much of it. I'd just spend it on another fucking bike that I've got no use for. Take it and run, baby."

"Why are you so certain I can't stay in New York?"

If only she knew just how dangerous this city is, and how hard Frankie works to keep it under control, she'd want to leave. Plus, if I knew where I could find her again, I would.

"You got any good reason to stay here?"

She shakes her head, so I point down to the black duffel bag. "This is a fresh start. A clean break."

Gripping her slender shoulders, I push her back on the bed, her deep maroon hair splaying out above her head.

My nose is inches from hers. "Tell me you'll take it."

She sighs.

"Sofia," I growl.

"Fine." She wraps her legs around my waist and pulls me towards her, making my cock press against her soaking pussy. "One last time?" She bites down on her bottom lip.

I lean forward, taking it between my teeth. "Is that your way of saying thank you?"

I could do this again and again. Possibly forever. I know I can't. I'm telling her to run as far away as she can. I'm heading back to Vegas in the morning, anyway. My life here is done.

Her nails rake down my back. "No. I just want you once more."

CHAPTER ELEVEN

SOFIA

Two years later...

"I NEVER SAID I WOULD HAVE TO FUCK THEM ALL." ANNA rolls her eyes dramatically as her hands plant on her hips. "It's a *dancing* job, Sofia. Not a prostitution gig." The cupboard slams as she pulls out a glass and pours herself wine to the brim.

"It's not a lifestyle I want to be around with Maeve." Picking up a pink elephant and a babydoll, I toss them into the toybox before turning back to Anna. "That isn't the best environment for her."

Anna flops onto the couch, her long lean legs draping across the tattered arm. "You know what's good for her? Food. Housing. Clothes. Clean water." She waves her arm around our tiny two-bedroom apartment. "This is becoming unsustainable. They're jacking the rent. Again. Do you have another idea?"

Chewing on my lip doesn't magically pop anything into my mind. "No. If I could finish my degree, it would help.

But my scholarship money ran out." Every penny disappeared into medical bills.

Who knew having a kid would be so expensive?

Anna's long blonde hair splays out over the stained cushion as she stares at the peeling ceiling. "Maybe you should find that Jax asshole and make him give you more money. That sounds like the only solution." Her fingers balance her drink on her flat belly.

"He isn't an asshole," I say quietly. He's the best memory I have from the last few years. I see him in Maeve's eyes every time I look at her. "Besides, I have no idea where to find him." I've looked. A lot. I don't even know his last name.

But what would he say? I bet he has girls all over. Even other kids.

He wouldn't care.

That's what I keep telling myself.

"All I'm saying—" Anna waves her hand in a lazy circle, "—is Vegas, baby. It will be good money. I'm even getting a moving bonus. You're welcome to come with me, but I think, either way, I'm going." She props herself up onto her elbow and takes another long swallow before batting her big blue eyes at me.

"Maybe I'll find some rich gambler and he can be my sugar daddy." Her white teeth flash as she falls back into giggles.

Glancing at the stack of overdue bills on the coffee table, I think I know what the answer needs to be.

"I'll start packing."

CHAPTER TWELVE

JAX

"Are you sure you don't want to go with? We could blow off some steam at Viper's." I carry the feet while Nikolai carries the shoulders.

Between us hangs a very dead, small-time dealer who thought he could get away with cutting Mikhail's drugs and passing them off as his own.

It wouldn't have been so bad if he hadn't been talking so much shit and trying to turn some of our own guys to work for him.

"I can't, man. I'm sorry. My babysitter said she had to bail early." Nikolai wipes his sweaty face against his own shoulder before hoisting the stiff higher into his grasp.

This isn't the first time we've had to do this. Since Nikolai and I started working closely together two years ago, we've gotten into a rhythm.

He slams the trunk shut over our deceased cargo. "I'm looking for a new one. This girl thinks she wants to start singing at that new jazz club that opened up. I've heard her sing to Lily–the girl would sound better with a cock in her throat." A touch of his Russian accent comes out as he gets agitated.

"What, like yours?" I've seen her. It'd take a lot of vodka.

"Funny. Not even close. There are lines you don't cross." Nikolai pauses as he shifts the car into drive to look at me over his sunglasses. "Well. You cross lines. I do not." The corner of his mouth turns up in a sarcastic smile before he slams on the accelerator, pushing us both back into our seats.

He's never going to let me live down messing around with my brother's wife.

Half-brother.

Brody sounds like he's kind of an ass, anyway, from what Sofia told me.

Fuck, she had the most amazing—

"*Idi na khuy!*" Nikolai yells in Russian at the windshield as he slams on the brakes.

A stumbling group of college age guys bump into the front of his Hellcat. Their half-full plastic glasses of alcohol scrape against the gray hood before they navigate to the sidewalk.

"If you want to tell them to go fuck themselves, English gets through their drunk noggins a lot faster." I slump down against the window and turn the air conditioner vent to blow on my forehead.

It's still over a hundred degrees. The heat won't be doing any favors to the body in the trunk.

"I get tired of how simple they are. Don't they know that my father's men are coming?" Nikolai's large fist bunches over the steering wheel.

"Are you sure they are? I mean, things have been pretty quiet lately. Except for the occasional little fish." I jerk my thumb towards the back.

"It's always this way with him. Silence before all hell breaks loose." His teeth grit and his hand twists on the leather.

With a sigh, he slumps back.

The buildings thin and disappear as we drive further into the desert. Reds and golds are bursting across the dusky sky when he turns us onto the secluded dirt road.

Raking my tongue bar across my teeth helps to vent out some of the nervous energy bouncing through me.

I just want to get this shit done.

"We need to hurry. We'll just leave him for the buzzards and coyotes." Nikolai opens the trunk.

I can smell the guy already.

Vegas has a lot of perks, but keeping a body fresh isn't one of them.

"Nasty. Did he shit his pants?" I hope this smell doesn't linger. "Next time, we load them alive, *then* bring them out here." My stomach rolls as bile rises in my throat.

Nikolai shakes his head. "They'd just scream the whole way." The tattoos on his knuckles stand out as he locks his hands around the chest.

We drop the body in a small ditch. Someone would have to walk right up to it to find it.

"Good enough." He wipes his hands across his thick thighs and climbs back into his vehicle.

My rings catch the glint of the fading light as I open and close my fingers. The last hit left a twinge, but I've had worse.

It's dark by the time we get back to the lines of casinos.

An ache in my chest tells me tonight is long from over. It's hard to want to just go back to my suite and deal with the silence.

"Are you sure about Viper's?" I duck my head as I lean against his window. "Just a couple of drinks?"

"Next time. See you tomorrow. Don't forget, we got a date with the boss in the morning." Nikolai takes off, leaving me in front of the Luxor pyramid.

Walking distance to Viper's Pit. They have the best bands and the hottest waitresses I've found.

I need both today.

The bass from the speakers vibrates through me as I step through the heavy doors before the wall of sound tries to push me out.

Fuck yeah, SACRED is playing tonight. I can tear some shit up in the pit.

"Hello, handsome. The usual?" A short, bouncy blonde saddles up to me with an empty tray propped under her arm.

"Hey, Rhonnie. Yeah, make it a double." I just want to lose myself in the music for a while so I can pass the hell out tonight.

"Sure thing. Hey, you sticking around for a while?" She chews on her bottom lip and twirls the end of her hair around her finger.

"Yeah, but going home alone. I got shit to do in the morning." Mikhail would kill me if I showed up late. He doesn't have a lot of rules, but he demands respect.

She pouts, then shakes her head. "No. I was just hoping us girls could hang tight tonight. There's a rowdy bunch in." Her chin juts toward a group of tables near the back.

Four big guys sit in a shadowed booth, loudly calling out to her.

I can hear them yelling over the screaming of the lead singer.

"I'll watch your back. Just keep the drinks flowing." Working my way through the thick push of people, I find a spot near the wall where I can see the band and watch the guys at the same time.

Rhonnie shows up with a red-headed waitress in tow. Both of their trays are loaded with beers and shots.

"Here, hon. Thanks for keeping tabs." She leans over far enough for me to see her nipples poking out over her low cut shirt. Her mouth twists into a seductive smile and she gives me a slow wink.

"Not tonight." I have no interest in her level of drama.

"Well, I am still glad you're here." Her shoulders draw back, and she takes her partner with her into the den of thugs in the back of the room.

Whistles and catcalls break up the lyrics, but I do my best to ignore them.

It's only when one of the girls cries out that I rip my eyes off the stage.

One of the bald gorillas against the wall has the redhead pinned across his lap and she's struggling to get up.

"Hey, fucknut! Leave her alone. She doesn't want your ugly ass." I throw one of my empty bottles in his general direction. The shattering glass makes him lift his head and meet my stare.

He stands, letting the waitress slide off of his thighs and land on the hard floor.

"What the hell did you say to me?" His long beard ripples with every word.

I knock my chair back as I jump to my feet.

I'm always ready for a fight.

"Do I need to sound it out for you? Or leave a row of bumps across your forehead so you can read it in braille?" One last swallow of my drink gives me another possible missile to launch at his sweating dome.

The large man takes a deep breath and his fists rise in front of his chest.

"Wait, wait. I got this." A smaller guy with curly dark hair jumps between us, holding his palms up to the pissed off brute.

When the shorter one turns to me, he flashes a big smile. "Jax Carter. Never thought I'd see you here." His light footsteps carry him closer.

Is that who I think it is?

No way.

"Brody?"

What is my half-brother doing in Vegas? I haven't talked to him since his wedding.

That whole thing could have gone better.

Is he going to hate me for fucking his wife?

Well, I assume ex-wife by now.

I still wonder where she is and if she found someone new.

Sofia.

I should have left my number. Or got hers.

It's one of my biggest regrets, but my head was so fucked up at the time, I didn't know what I had until she was gone.

Losing her is always a double whammy when the anniversary of Kai's death rolls around.

If I hadn't been an idiot and let her go, she might have been the one to help fill this hole in my heart.

"Look, no hard feelings about the wedding, okay? I get it that you didn't want to show." He holds his hand out for me to shake it.

The big bearded, bald man grunts as the waitress scurries past us.

Does he know why I didn't make it?

"Yeah, sorry, I got sidetracked. How is she?" I still

wonder if she stayed away and took my advice to start a new life.

After a long drink, he smiles. "She bailed. She was a good piece of ass, too. But I found a better one. This one is a keeper; she knows better than to run out on me."

I bet that means he's beat her harder.

His eyes tighten and he tilts his head, the smile still dancing over his lips. "I'm having a bachelor party next week. Maybe you can be the perfect test for her. I mean, we do kinda look alike. If she still chooses me over you, I know she's loyal."

The empty bottle makes a thump on the table as he sets it down.

"You want me there as some sort of test?" My opinion of him sinks another couple of notches.

He laughs and slaps my arm. "Worst that could happen, we can spit roast her cheating ass together."

"Sounds like love," I say sarcastically.

He shrugs. "I'd like to get to know my big brother. It's at The Sinners, next Friday at seven. I'll make sure you get the VIP treatment."

Brody turns away and talks low to the big bald guy.

As a group, the men stand and start working their way out of the club.

"It was lucky to see you again, bro. We always seem to be meeting over a girl." Brody laughs and throws his arm up in a wave before disappearing into the Vegas night.

CHAPTER THIRTEEN

SOFIA

"Why is it so hard?" I slump against the wall and bring my feet up onto the lip of the counter. "This is the fourth interview today. Is it really that impossible to find a job in Vegas that *isn't* stripping?"

Anna stops putting on her mascara to meet my gaze in the mirror. "Quit knocking the only thing paying our bills. You should just do it. I can get you in tonight."

"I can't. Who would watch Maeve?" I'm just getting used to being here, but don't know any babysitters.

She finishes and switches to a bright red lipstick. "Brittney told me there's quite a few twenty-four-hour daycares here, since there's so many night gigs in town. I'll text her and find out where she takes hers."

"Wait, I didn't say that was the hold up…" I chew on the inside of my cheek, weighing my options.

There aren't many choices.

Anna snaps her clutch closed and fluffs her buoyant blonde hair before turning to me. "You need to shit or get off the pot. We've been here almost a month. I can't afford to take care of you by myself."

All I can do is nod.

I've exhausted every possible lead I can find.

But I have to feed my little girl.

I'll do anything to make sure she's taken care of.

She's my world. The thought of her going without the things she needs makes my chest ache.

"Okay. Set it up."

Anna squeals and wraps me in a hug. "It's going to be so much fun getting to work together!"

In less than two hours, Maeve is dropped off at a very nice-looking facility, and Anna is helping me prepare for my audition.

Except, I hate this outfit. It shows too much and pinches in all the wrong places. The silver sequin bra does make my boobs look great, though.

"You'll be fine, Sofia. Just flip your gorgeous maroon hair and bat those big green eyes. Gil would be crazy not to hire you." Anna slips on a ridiculously high-heeled pair of thigh-high boots and zips them up.

Tassels hang from her nipples. It's hard not to glance at them every time she moves.

I never thought I'd have a job wearing pasties.

My phone background picture has my adorable baby with a big toothless smile.

I'm doing this for her.

One last look at it before I toss it on top of my bag and shut the door on my locker.

Gil's office is every bit the dingy room I'd expect in a strip joint.

Pin ups of naked girls cover the walls surrounding a desk piled heavily with papers and a broad open area of worn carpet that highlights a bronze-colored pole attached to the ceiling.

I guess that's my dance floor tonight.

"You're every bit as hot as Anna said you'd be." Gil rubs his thick hands together over his desk before reaching over and pushing a button on an old cassette player.

Scratchy music with a deep bass line fills the suffocating space.

He leans back and pushes his thick glasses up on his nose. "Make me horny."

This isn't what I expected.

I should have.

Swaying my hips to the music, I do my best to stick out my tits and shake my ass. Bending over and then tossing in some exaggerated hair flips.

I'm halfway into the song when he hits the button and silence fills the room.

"Half-chub. Maybe three quarters. You have potential, but you're starting on the bar line running drinks. Keep practicing and you'll clear four figures a night. Talk to Christine about scheduling. You're on B rotation." He digs a cigarette out of his sweaty polo shirt pocket. Pointing the smoking ember in my direction, he waves me towards the door. "I dig the hair."

"Thank you." This has to be one of my most embarrassing moments.

Well, nothing beats leaving Brody at the wedding reception, but this is a close second.

CHAPTER FOURTEEN

JAX

Dust rolls from the tires of the trucks as they pull into the abandoned quarry north of Vegas.

Nikolai and I sit in his black Hellcat, waiting for them to roll up next to us.

The air conditioner barely keeps up with the sultry one hundred and ten degree sun.

I can feel the heat radiating through the roof into my head. At least he has cooled seats that keep my balls cold.

When they're sweaty, I get cranky.

"How many crates did Frankie send?" Nikolai asks me without looking up from his phone.

"Enzo said a fuck ton. This is going to suck ass." Mikhail sent us with a small fleet of cargo vans to move the guns through the city without bringing suspicion.

But it means we have to move every single one of them from one rig to the other.

"It used to be we would be here to protect a shipment from the Reapers. Now, we're here just as extra workers." Nikolai slips his phone into his pocket and checks the chamber on his pistol. "Gun fights were more fun. But peace is good."

The only time I get to rumble lately is in the boxing ring.

When we open the doors, the wave of intense heat almost knocks me back into my seat. "Damn, can it get any hotter?" My curly hair lays limply across my forehead.

"Just wait until we're in the back of those containers. Like an oven." Nikolai shakes his head as he hoists me into the cargo bay of the first truck.

Enzo made it easy with his inventory app. I scan each crate before dragging it over to Nikolai to load into the smaller vehicles for distribution.

Like a regular big box store for weapons.

I'm sweating so badly, my eyes are blurry when I finally get to the last box. Nikolai pulls it out as I jump down onto the dry dirt.

My junk is sticking to the inside of my thigh, and it makes me want to punch something.

"Viper's tonight? Alexei said he could meet us there." Nikolai wipes his palm through his short brown hair, making rivulets run down the back of his neck. "I could use a cold drink."

I glance at my Rolex.

Shit.

"Sounds good. Let's blow off a little steam since I have that bachelor party thing tomorrow." There's a part of me that really doesn't want to go, but it's not every day I get the opportunity to get to know a brother I didn't know I had.

Nikolai's blue eyes narrow. "Are you sure you can trust this guy?"

I can't help but laugh. "Yeah, 'cause we're upstanding

citizens and all. I gotta give him a chance. Blood should count for something?"

Maybe.

It's too hot to think clearly.

"Is this because of the anniversary?" Nikolai walks ahead of me and doesn't look back when he asks.

"Fuck off. I just think I outta give him a chance." I don't want to tell him that there's a part of me that misses having a brother.

And that it might be because the date of Kai's death is rolling up on me.

It still isn't fair he's gone.

One day, I'll find something to fill this hole in my chest.

In the meantime, it can't hurt to get to know my own brother.

We load back into his car and I bask in the cool air as he peels out of the gravel pit.

By the time we get back into the city, I'm not as cranky.

Alexei is already inside with Enzo when we get there. Alexei always has a wild look in his eyes, the tattoos stretching up either side of his neck help give him an old school berserker vibe.

Most people don't know he's actually pretty chill.

"The birthday boy!" Alexei smacks me on the shoulder as I sit at the table.

Rhonnie steps near his side with her empty drink tray pinned beneath her elbow. "Birthday? First round is on me!" She gives me a slow wink before patting Nikolai on the top of his head.

She doesn't see him scowl in response as she heads back to get our drinks.

"Next time, I pick the bar," he grumbles. "I dislike how handsy she gets."

"Ah, it's because she hasn't touched the right spot yet."

I grin as I push my sweaty hair back and prop my sunglasses on the top of my head.

Alexei laughs loudly, tipping his chair back to let his feet dangle between the legs. "Niki, you need to get laid. How long has it been?"

"I don't know. When was the last time your mother visited?" Nikolai stretches his arms and lets a small smile play across his lips. "Put your chair down, animal."

Alexei rolls his eyes dramatically before dropping it down. "Fine, *Dad.*" His palms fly up in a sign of surrender as Rhonnie returns with our drinks.

It wasn't that long ago that Kai and I were joking just like this. He was the quiet one, always trying to keep me in line.

Now, I have no one. I didn't realize I wanted a tether until he was gone.

Why did he have to die so close to my birthday? It makes this shit so tough when all I can think of is that it's one more he isn't here for.

We used to get a new tattoo every year and see what kind of trouble we could find.

Now, it's hard to want to do anything but my job.

And even that is getting harder.

Boxing used to be my outlet. Until I was suspended for three months because I didn't stop swinging after my opponent went down.

Any sense of self control I once had is laying in the ground in New York.

"Don't you think, Jax?" Alexei interrupts my thoughts.

"What's that?" I have no idea what he was talking about.

"I said, Enzo mentioned something about opening a new branch to his club here. I offered for us to try out the girls he wants to employ there." Alexei grins like the Cheshire Cat with his boots propped on the table.

Enzo laughs.

Fuck, I missed him coming in, too.

His black hair falls forward over his eyes that his smile never touches. "I'll need lots of girls. I don't think you boys could keep up." The ice in his glass clinks as he sets it on the table.

The diamonds in his rings reflect the light like the cubes in his cup. "Besides, you have things to do. I don't need you at the club standing on your dicks all day long. You'd die of dehydration."

"There's worse ways to go," Alexei says before he takes a long swallow of his beer.

Enzo wags his finger at Alexei. "You, little boy, would be a flash in the pan."

"That's why I have this." I click my tongue bar against my teeth. "If I'm in between nutting, I can always keep them happy."

"The only thing you know how to do with that is make annoying noises." Nikolai taps his finger against the table in a mocking rhythm of my piercing. "All day. Like a clock that doesn't keep time. Is that why you're late most of the time? Your timer is broken?"

I don't want to tell him that the person who used to keep me in line isn't here anymore. That I feel like I'm numb and wandering and lucky when I do remember to show up.

"Nah, man. I'm just late to give your mother-hen ass something to do, keeping tabs on me."

CHAPTER
FIFTEEN

SOFIA

"I DON'T SEE HOW THIS IS MY RESPONSIBILITY." ANNA'S brows furrow as her fists dig into her hips.

Maeve whimpers on my lap. Her small cheeks are flushed with a low grade fever. "Please? I can't stay home. I just got the job." I wipe back her curly dark hair that's plastered to her warm forehead.

Anna sits with a sigh next to me on the couch. "I don't know if I can? I was supposed to dance for a bachelor party tonight. I almost had to promise Gil a blowjob to get the chance. They're always big money." She takes Maeve's tiny hand and strokes it. "She's never this quiet."

"She's getting better. The meds the doctor prescribed are kicking in. They'll keep her comfortable." I grab the red bottle and dropper from the end table. "It says you just have to give her a dose every four hours. I can probably get back before three?"

The club almost always slows down by then. I've only been there a couple of weeks, but it's becoming predictable.

"God, you're killing me, girl. But I get it. I'll tell Gil I have cramps and can't make it." Anna pulls my sleeping Maeve onto her lap and props her head with a pillow. "It's kind of creepy he tracks our cycles, but luckily mine is due to start in two days."

A shudder runs through me. That guy is strange, but he pays well. And his advice for what kind of moves to do really is an improvement.

I've never had someone tell me to thrust my pelvis in such a clinical way before.

If I was still working on my psychiatry major, I bet I could learn all kinds of things about his kind of debauchery.

When Maeve shifts, her chocolate colored eyes open and flick from Anna to me. "Momma?"

"Shh, baby girl. I'll be back soon." When I kiss her temple, I'm glad to feel it's already cooling.

She looks so much like her daddy. It sends a pang through my chest.

I'm glad I get this reminder of him every day.

He saved me and made me realize that there are some nice guys out there.

I wonder what kind of dad he would have been?

Not like I'll ever know, but it's a dream to have. One day, I'll meet someone who will accept her and me as a package deal.

I'm just not sure if that will be anyone I meet at the club. But, if I keep getting better and bigger tips, I should be able to afford to go back to college this fall part time.

A bachelor party would go a long way to helping with that.

As soon as I get to the club, I head straight to Gil's office.

"I swear I can do it." I've got my best outfit on. My hair is perfect, in a sensuous wave down my back.

"Do you have a gimmick? Because at the moment, you're still just a three quarter chub." He smooths a wild hair back into his dirty blonde ponytail. "I mean, you're hot, but men aren't gonna come in their pants watching you. Yet." He gives me a finger pistol with the last word.

"What do you mean by 'gimmick'?" I know I can dance better. My tips have skyrocketed in the last couple of weeks.

"Carrie can pop a ping-pong ball out of her pussy and catch it in her mouth. Emily can sink a whole traffic cone into her black hole of a cunt. Can you do anything like that?" Gil sits back in his squeaky chair, his thick arms fold over the pooch of his belly.

I shake my head. I don't know what to do, I just could really use the money. Especially when Maeve's hospital bill arrives.

Gil sighs and pushes up his glasses. "Yeah, fine. I had two girls call in today. You and Brittney can cover the bachelor party in Suite D." He doesn't look at me as he scribbles something on his notepad in front of him. "Do that hip thing. It's your best move."

The back of his fingers wave me out of his office.

A giddy feeling takes over me.

This could be my big break.

CHAPTER SIXTEEN

JAX

WHY IS MY STOMACH ROLLING ABOUT SPENDING TIME WITH my brother? I don't think he knows I ran off with his wife on his wedding day.

Hope like hell he doesn't find out.

A pair of wiry men in slick leather jackets and crisp fedoras stand outside the door of The Sinners club. They both look like card sharks from the fifties, but keep the lines moving.

"Hey! Brother! You made it. I wasn't sure if you'd actually show this time." Brody claps me on the shoulder and leaves his hand as we approach the entrance. "This place has the hottest girls. For the right price, they do anything you want."

I'm penned in by his friends. "I'm happy for you, man. Yeah, I figured I better show. I'd like to get to know you a little more." All I know about him is what Sofia told me that night.

But, I don't remember much of what we talked about. Every memory I have of her is how she tasted, how her hips moved against mine, the way her mouth formed an 'o' when she came.

Why can't I stop thinking about her?

Maybe it's seeing Brody again that triggered those thoughts.

I'm lying to myself. I know more than once a week for almost two years I've woken up with my cock in my hand and her name on my lips.

We step into the dark building and are directed to a back room.

"Suite D. Guess that means the dick place," Brody snickers.

One of his guys laughs and pushes us from behind. "Hell yeah, the girls are getting all of it tonight!"

Several dancers line the hall in skimpy clothes. String bikinis and pasties bounce against our arms and their fingers trail over us as we head to the private area.

"Oh, aren't you the King of Chaos?" One perky brunette wraps her hands around my neck and pushes her body tightly to mine.

"I am. You wanna be my queen for the night?" I give her a lopsided grin as my palms find her hips, tugging her closer.

"Baby, I'd love to. Can I find you after the show?" Her tongue pokes out and licks my bottom lip.

She tastes like cough medicine and cheap cigarettes. Whatever blood had started rushing to my crotch cuts off in a hurry.

I pick her up and move her to the side so I can continue through. "Maybe next time."

Her bright red bottom lip sticks out, but she quickly turns to the next man in line to hang off of.

After having a taste of the finest wine, vinegar just doesn't seem as appealing.

How long am I going to hold Sofia as the standard?

Why do I?

There's a polished brass pole in the middle of a circle of overstuffed chairs. Two large crystal decanters of some sort of dark liquor are sitting on a silver tray lined with glasses filled with ice.

The set up is top-notch.

"Boys, we're gonna get fucked up!" Brody yells loud enough to fill the room.

Hell yeah. This might be a fun night after all.

CHAPTER SEVENTEEN

SOFIA

"I'LL TRADE YOU." FANCY'S EYES ARE WIDE WITH excitement as she grips my arms. "The King of Chaos is here! Please, let me swap and work the party. You can have the floor."

Despite my nerves, doubt prickles through me. "Why?"

"Have you seen him? He's sex on a stick. I watched him win a fight in less than twenty seconds. He brought home almost half a million dollars. In *twenty* seconds. Do you know how much that is?" Her fingers dig into my skin.

"Five hundred thousand?" I can't tell if she's being serious or if it was a rhetorical question.

She blinks slowly and stares at me for a moment. "Yeah! That's a lot! What do you think?"

I'm not sure how her telling me that there's a rich, sexy boxer in my bachelor party is supposed to make me *not* want to dance for him.

"Sorry, I can't. Gil sets the rules." I shrug her hands off and head to the dressing room to check my makeup.

Brittney rushes in behind me. "Did you hear? The

King of Chaos? Oh my god!" She bends over my shoulder to use the mirror next to me, fluffing her big blonde hair.

"We better go. Gil said they're here and waiting on us!" She grabs my wrist and tugs me with her down the musty hall to Suite D.

I stumble into the room, and immediately, my body goes into overdrive. A rush of fire courses through my veins. The first thing that hits me is a familiar musky aftershave.

"Oh my fucking God, look who it is, Brody." An unfamiliar voice echoes across the dim room.

I stiffen, my heart almost beating out of my chest.

Shit.

It's like all the air has been ripped from my body.

It can't be.

All I can hear is the sound of deep chuckles filling the room. I can't move. I can't see.

When I look up, I lock gazes with a familiar set of dark, brooding eyes. Almost identical to the ones I look into in my daughter's eyes.

Jax.

I swallow down the bile rising in my throat as my cheeks burn. What the hell is he doing here?

The room goes silent. I can't tear my focus away from him.

After all this time, I'm still drawn to him.

Another man jeers from the corner. "Only you could have your ex-wife at your bachelor party, man. What's the fucking luck?"

Jax stiffens in his seat, playing with the rings on his tattooed fingers.

In that moment, seeing him again, I'd forgotten about his asshole of a brother. I can feel Brody's cold stare on me. I don't even want to give him the satisfaction of a glance.

He doesn't deserve anything from me. I ran out of New York so quickly he didn't even get a chance to grovel. That's how I used some of Jax's money—to pay for that annulment and never see Brody again.

The girls all get to work on the guys. The music pounds in my ears, yet all I can hear is my blood rushing.

Shit, am I going to pass out?

I swallow, taking a step forward. I can't pass up on this tonight. I need the money to pay for Maeve's treatments. She deserves better, and Brody sure as hell isn't taking this from her.

"Hey, bro, you finally get to meet Sofia." Brody's deep voice cuts through the air and chills run down my spine.

I finally settle my gaze on my ex-husband and feel absolutely nothing. However, as I peer left, taking in Jax, I notice that he has only gotten more fine in the last two years. More ripped and even more rough around the edges. The way his tight black tee is hugging every bulging muscle, the black ripped jeans and boots, give him a bad boy aura that makes my knees weak.

A wave of anger washes over me. Since the last time I saw him, I've been struggling with bringing up our daughter on my own, and he's been befriending Brody. Clearly, I meant nothing to him. Why else would he do that after fucking me?

He got what he wanted.

Screw them both.

I scan the room and kick my ass into gear. I can avoid those two—they have plenty of friends here I can make a chunk of cash from. I beeline in on the one I don't recognize. Tatted, with a grin on his lips, while watching me with amusement.

He's not like the other suited guys with Brody.

Resting my arms on his chair, I get to work, swaying my hips and biting down on my lip.

"Well, hello, gorgeous." He winks at me. His rough fingers brush against my chest as he stuffs a bill in there.

I swear I can feel the daggers from Jax behind me. The guy leans forward, his black hair brushing against my jaw.

"This just got interesting, didn't it?" he whispers. I nod, brushing myself against his thigh, and letting my hands slide down the front of my body. He has no idea.

"I'm just here to keep you guys happy." I give him a broad, fake smile.

He leans back in his chair. "Turn around, then. I'm more of an ass man."

I flick my hair over my shoulders and spin on my heel, pushing my hips out further for him. Holding back a grin, I cast my gaze over to Jax.

His jaw is tight, and his fists are clenched. So I put an extra sway in my movements, grinding on this guy's lap with as much fake desire as I can muster.

Darkness flashes across Jax's face as I cup my breasts. It makes me give him a pouty face and stick my tongue out towards my own nipple to tease him.

The guy clears his throat behind me, so I turn to face him. I resist eye rolling as he stares at my tits. He holds a wad of cash in his hand and gestures for me to lean closer.

As I do, his hot breath, laced with whiskey, hits against my cheek.

"Take this, go and dance for that guy." He points behind me. I know exactly who he means.

I follow his finger and land on Jax.

It's a lot of money.

When I turn back to him, he has a knowing smirk on his lips. Enough to tell me he wants to cause trouble.

I snatch up the wad.

"Coming to me, boo?" I recoil at Brody's words. Like hell am I going anywhere near him.

But, Jax, I can play games with.

I can imagine he doesn't want his brother to find out what he did.

Ignoring my irritating ex-husband, I head towards Jax.

With each step closer, my body ignites.

"It looks like she'd rather fuck your brother, man!" one of the guys calls out.

I look to Jax to see his reaction.

But he's too busy looking at me like he wants to devour me.

Shit.

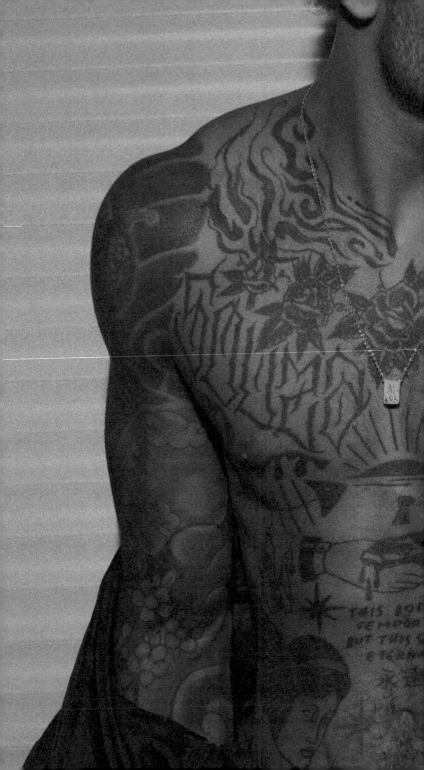

CHAPTER EIGHTEEN

JAX

Song- want me, Ex Habit.
https://ffm.to/wntme

HOLY FUCKIN' SHIT.

Sofia.

Electricity shoots through me the closer she gets, with a fire in her eyes.

The woman who I've fucked my own cock dreaming about for two whole years. The rhinestones on that black mesh bra, that pushes up those beautiful breasts perfectly, catch my attention for a brief second.

But it's her eyes that captivate me. The ones I see in my dreams when I do sleep.

I clear my throat, the silence in the room almost deafening. You could cut the atmosphere with a bloodied knife.

She stops in front of me, that sweet strawberry scent washing over me. I keep my hands gripped to the chair to resist touching her.

I rake my eyes up her body, the knee-high black leather boots covering those slender legs I remember tightly wrapped around me. Her panties match the black, sparkly bra. I shift uncomfortably in my seat, thinking about how good her ass looked covered in my bite marks.

"Oh, fuck," one of his asshole corporate friends shout. As I look over, the other is too busy snorting a line of coke from the table in front before slamming his palm on the table, looking up at Sofia with a sleazy grin.

I lean back in my chair, gripping onto the arms, spinning the rings on my fingers. I need to distract myself, keep my ass firmly in this seat, so I don't pick her up and take her home.

She shouldn't be here. This isn't her. What the hell did she do with all the cash I gave her?

I tense as I watch Brody rubbing his hands along his thighs, watching his ex-wife like a feral animal.

"Hey, Sofia. Five hundred dollars to dance for B. He's always going on about how he misses your ass. Go on, give him the send off he needs," one of the dickheads calls out, and I grit my teeth.

With a wicked look in her eyes, she spins on her heels, so her ass is facing me. I do everything in my power not to groan out loud, and my dick is immediately standing to attention.

As if on perfect timing, two girls get busy entertaining Brody beside me. She backs up, and I open up my thighs. With every brush of her skin against my leg, I lose more and more control.

"Turn around," I say under my breath, loud enough for her to hear.

She shakes her head subtly, sweeping up her maroon locks, giving me the perfect view of her tanned skin, now glistening.

"Look at me, Sofia." I say it under my breath, keeping my tone dangerous.

I can sense her reluctance, but she does as I say. Slowly turning and leaning over me. Fuck. I can't breathe.

Now, it's just me and Sofia in the room. Her eyes lock with mine. She fucking consumes me. Forgetting who I am, where I am, I lean back, and my hands roam up her smooth thighs.

Her hands now resting on my shoulders. That contact is enough to have all the blood rushing to my cock and my heart racing in my chest.

"Much better," I mouth to her with a grin, and I don't miss the small smile that tugs on her lips, nor the blush creeping up her neck.

Every time she brushes against my thigh, electricity bolts through me. I'm almost fucking panting watching her.

It's hard to keep my eyes on her face as she dances on me, as she leans in, her plump lips brush across my beard.

"Keep dancing like this for me, I'll give you every dollar to my name," I whisper in her ear and feel her shiver against me.

"Go on, get those tits out, Sofia. Charlie here's always wanted to catch a look, haven't you?"

I let out a growl, and she subtly shakes her head, giving me a warning glare.

That gets Brody's attention. I feel the heat of his glare on the side of my head, and I drop my hands from her.

"Don't you think it's time you gave me a dance, like old times?"

I stiffen at my brother's words.

Sofia looks to me, then at Brody, plastering a fake smile on those beautiful plump red lips.

"I'd rather cut off my own hands than ever touch you again. You're probably riddled with diseases." She flicks her hair, turning her attention fully back to me, turning the heat up on her moves.

Jesus Christ.

Her fingers run down my chest.

Brody scoffs next to me.

"Go on, boo. One last dance I can remember before I get married again."

She doesn't falter at his words, and relief washes over me. "If I get any closer to you, I'll stick my stiletto straight through your teeny weeny dick." She holds up her little finger and wiggles it. I have to cover my mouth in an attempt to hold back my laughter.

The tension is thick in the air, her eyes now firmly back on me.

"You look better, Sofia. I always said you needed more weight, too boney before. You're more womanly now with those hips."

She goes still and rage burns through me; the room falling to complete silence for the second time.

Sofia pushes herself up off me, straightening her spine, and steps towards Brody.

"What the fuck did you just say?" she spits out, her fingers twitching at her side.

"I said, you look better with some weight gain. Suits you," he replies with a smug grin. One I want to beat right off his face.

"Fuck you." She pulls back her hand, and he catches her wrist. I jump out of my seat and step behind her, towering over the both of them.

"Hit me. I'll have you arrested and fired." Anger flashes across Brody's face and her hand trembles.

Who the fuck does he think he is talking to my Sofia like that?

Wait.

Mine?

This possessive beast comes from nowhere with her. I don't think I could stop myself.

"Let go. Now." I punctuate each word.

He drops his grip and holds his arms up.

"Jax, calm down. She's my ex-wife. I can do and say whatever the fuck I want. She deserves it. She ran out on me."

I take a step forward, grabbing him by the scruff of the neck, and pull him to his feet as Sofia scuffles out of the way.

"I fucking wonder why," I sneer.

"I didn't hurt her. I stopped her from hitting me."

I scoff. Pathetic excuse of a man.

I look over to Sofia and already see the angry red mark forming on her wrist as she rubs it.

"You can't get me fired." He looks up at me, confused, realization settling as I pull back my fist and launch it straight into his nose.

The girls all erupt into screams, but that just spurs me on further.

"Speak to her like that again, I'll rip your fucking tongue out."

He collapses on to the chair, blood spilling down his face.

"What the hell are you doing? You really going to do this over that whore?" He wipes his nose.

I shake my head, white rage taking over. Lunging forward, I grab him by his brown hair and smash him face first into the metal table in front of him.

His friends stand. I puff my chest, looking between them and their now unconscious friend on the table.

"Sit the fuck back down, unless you want to take a nap with him?"

They back away, slowly sitting back down, their faces pale.

The girls are all huddled in the corner, all except Sofia. The door clicks shut, and I don't waste a second in following her. I stride out of the room, searching the busy room for the maroon hair I'm desperate for.

I've let this woman invade my mind for two years. Some kind of divine intervention landed her back on my lap tonight.

I'm not letting her go a second time. I've regretted it every day since.

CHAPTER NINETEEN

SOFIA

Song- Sugar, Sleep Token.

SLAMMING THE DOOR SHUT TO THE DRESSING ROOM, I STEP in front of the full-length mirror.

I look hot. I've worked hard to try to get my body back after Maeve's birth.

Clearly not hard enough.

My body changed. I have faint stretch marks on my hips. I hate them. That's why I wear these high waisted shorts. My ass is still out, but my hips are covered.

Wiping away a stray tear with the back of my hand, I can't go back in there. I need to go and find Gil and see if I can get on the main stage instead.

Tossing the notes from my bra onto the table, it's not enough.

I need the damn money. Especially with the hospital bills coming my way. My daughter needs a roof over her head, and I have to do what I need to.

I just need a second to clear my head.

Seeing Brody and Jax together threw my mind into turmoil.

The man who I've dreamt about finding for two years. The eyes I stare into every morning when I pick up Maeve for a cuddle.

The man whose strong hands I can still feel on my body. That one night altered my life forever, not just with Maeve, but my heart.

When I walked into that room, it hurt. Seeing them together. Brody got to have a relationship with him. I didn't, nor did his daughter.

But even then, he still consumed me. When our eyes locked, it was as if two years had never passed. There is no way I can let him back in. I don't think I can take it. How do I tell him he's a dad? That could ruin everything for him. He could be married or dating someone. He could have more kids.

I am no one to him. Just his ex-sister-in-law, who he happens to have fucked. A mistake.

Why the hell is he here with Brody? And why did he knock him out for me?

My eyes snap up in the mirror as I hear the lock click behind me. Chills run down my spine as Jax's dark eyes meet mine and he stalks towards me, stopping just behind me.

I suck in a breath, the room now fizzling around me.

I don't know what to say, so I keep my lips sealed shut. I glance down at the blood covering his knuckles, and it's hard not to smile.

Seeing Brody get knocked out is a highlight of my life. The asshole deserves it.

Without a word, he brushes my hair away and exposes my shoulder. Without thinking, I tip my head to the side and he rests his chin there.

Eating me up with his eyes in the mirror.

"Don't listen to a word that asshole said, sweetheart."

I slowly nod, not trusting myself to speak. My body sparks alight as his index finger trails up my side, leaving tingles in its wake.

"You are, and always were, fucking gorgeous. Way too beautiful to be here."

I swallow past the lump in my throat.

With his finger now stroking my neck, he tips my head back. Blood thumps in my ears as I wait for his next move.

"You need to leave, Jax." It comes out in a whisper.

He shakes his head, running his tongue along his lip.

"We were meant to break rules together. We aren't done, tigritsa."

I blink a few times.

"We are. We were done two years ago. One night. A mistake, clearly."

He tuts, his lips now brushing against my neck.

"Is that what you think? That I don't replay that night on a loop in my brain?"

My mouth falls open. He's lying. He has to be.

"I doubt that. I bet I haven't even crossed your mind. How can you be friends with Brody otherwise?"

He chuckles, his chest rubbing against my back.

"I just smashed his face in. He's irrelevant to me."

"Oh, right, how could I forget? The King of Chaos."

Something flashes across his face, almost like hurt.

"You knew who I was the entire time?" he says with a frown.

"Yep," I lie, feeling the warmth spread along my cheeks. He doesn't need to know I found out less than an hour ago.

"You're a bad liar, aren't you, sweetheart? Because if you did, you would have found me."

I swallow, I can't say I haven't tried.

"Nope. There was no need. Once was enough."

He takes a step back, and I immediately miss his body pressed against mine.

"Was it? It wasn't for me."

I turn to face him, a spark lighting inside of me as I'm met with a smile.

He takes a step forward, and I take one back, until my back is up against the cold floor-length mirror. His nose just a breath away from mine.

"There are plenty of women out there to entertain you," I say, needing some distance. He's too much.

"Not interested. The only woman I want is right in front of me."

I roll my eyes and he grips my chin.

"Don't do that. I'm serious."

"So am I," I bite back and he leans in.

"You left your claws in me for two years, Sofia."

"What do you want? Another quick fuck so you can go laugh about it to your new friends?"

"Oh, sweet, sweet, Sofia. You have no idea, do you?"

He leans in closer, his lips brushing against the shell of my ear.

"You can play hard to get all you like. I fucking love the chase."

"And I love to run."

"Let the games begin, sweetheart." He winks and steps away, tossing notes by my feet.

"What's that for?"

It's enough for me to get out of here for the night. To pay her medical bills.

"Clearly you need more money. This isn't you."

"You don't know me."

"I know enough, Sofia. Now dance for me, baby. Make it worth every single dollar."

I keep looking between him and the notes. He can't be serious.

"Strip for me, tigritsa."

As he says that nickname, the one I've had playing on repeat in my brain. Tigress. And he isn't offering this as a question.

"What? No," I stutter.

I feel empty as he steps back, a darkness flashing across his eyes as he shoves his hand in his pocket and throws another roll of cash next to my feet.

"I can't get caught doing private dances." I spin to face him, looking up at him through my lashes.

"I locked the door. No one is stepping foot in here." He smirks and pulls a chair across and takes a seat in front of me.

"I've just thrown thousands of dollars at your feet. Dance for me."

I blow out a breath. What's once more, anyway? It's the last time I truly felt alive.

"Fine. I have strict no touching rules, though."

He scoffs, pushing himself back up, and I cross my arms across my chest, holding my breath as he leans down.

"Tell me, was the 'don't fuck my brother-in-law' rule high up on that strict list?" he whispers in my ear.

"We had a break from rules that night, remember?" I bite back a grin.

"There are never any rules when it comes to us, sweetheart. I shouldn't still be dreaming about fucking you after all this time. Yet, I do, often."

My mouth falls open, and he laughs.

"I got to you, too, didn't I?" He strokes my cheek.

He has no idea. Which is why this can't happen. I have Maeve to think about.

I place my palm over his hand, leaning into his touch.

"Sit down, gorgeous."

He pulls back and his eyes light up. As he sits himself down, his legs spread. I can't help but admire my view. Going back to my table, I pick up a couple of thongs from the drawer and walk over to him.

"What are you doing?" he asks, raising an eyebrow as I start to tie his wrists as tight as I can to the arms of the chairs.

"One rule," I reply with a grin.

"You honestly believe that is enough to keep me from you?" He chuckles.

No. It won't. But it'll give me a head start.

He tips his head back slightly. I lean forward and run my tongue along his throat.

"Do you think you can be a good boy and follow my rules?"

He groans in my ear, and my pussy is throbbing. I want him.

"For you, you know I can," he replies in a low voice, almost a growl.

"Good."

Running my hands down his chest, over his abs, I keep going all the way down his thighs.

"Are you an ass or a boobs man?"

"I'm a Sofia man. I want to see all of you."

"I wanna try something. I think it will be hot," I say, eyeing one of my sparkly belts.

He raises a brow. "Close your eyes."

He does as I say, and I snatch up the belt, positioning

myself behind him, running my nails through his dark curls, before placing the belt over his eyes.

"Sure you don't want to choke me with that first?" he says with amusement in his tone.

Visions of doing just that invade my mind. Jesus, why is everything he says so hot?

"Maybe later, you could even do that to me, too," I whisper in his ear, tightening the belt.

"Fuck, baby," he moans as I run my hands along his broad shoulders.

Placing wet kisses along his jawline up to his ear, he's already tugging at his restraints.

"Let me go grab one more thing." I place a kiss on his cheek and retreat.

Collecting all my cash from the floor, shoving it in my purse and stopping just before the door.

My heart wants to stay, to give him the show of his life and remind me of how good he makes me feel.

My head is screaming at me to leave. Him and Brody, he's Maeve's dad. He's a thug. He won't want me. What if he rejects her?

It's all too much. I need time to process. When the time is right.

As silently as I can, I steal one last glance and open the door.

"Sofia?"

Shit.

Stepping out, I close the door behind me and run as fast as I can.

CHAPTER TWENTY

JAX

THE DOOR CLICKS SHUT AND I LET OUT A LAUGH.

She really thinks she can run from me? That I won't chase her? Wrong.

With ease, I rip off the flimsy little thongs binding my wrists and tug the belt from my eyes. I'll give her points for creativity.

If anything, she's just fueled me further. She's hiding something from me. How the hell did she land herself here, and why is she running?

I can tell from her reaction to me that she feels this as much as I do.

My heart skips a beat as I make my swift exit.

Where the fuck did she go? Wandering through the dark hallways, filled with groping hands and couples fucking in the shadows, I look in every door that isn't locked.

All these years of dreaming of her, just to have her slip through my fingers?

Not a chance.

She will probably be in her car by now. I need to think outside the box for my little tiger.

When I push into the office of the owner, I know I've stumbled on the right spot.

The schedule is hanging on the wall.

Perfect. Now I know exactly when she'll be back.

I take a quick picture with my phone and slip back out.

Working my way past a dressing room and some sort of prop storage, I finally find the exit.

A dark sedan speeds by, but I catch a glimpse of the driver in the yellow streetlight.

It's her.

She ducks her head and doesn't hit her brakes before peeling out into the road.

If Sofia thinks she's going to get away from me again, she's going to learn just how stubborn I can be.

My bike is parked against the far curb. Racing over, my helmet is barely on before I'm gunning the engine to follow her through the darkness.

All of my lights stay off until I catch up.

If she wants to run from me, I want to see where she's heading.

Twisting and turning through the streets of Vegas, it isn't hard to hang back far enough and still keep her in my sights.

She finally slows down and turns into an older subdivision filled with Spanish villa apartments.

The lights are already on in the room she enters.

Who the hell is that with her? Another shadow crosses in front of the window. Tall, thin, and long-haired.

A roommate.

I know where she lives and her schedule.

There's no getting away from me this time.

CHAPTER TWENTY-ONE

SOFIA

Maeve pulls her arms up to frame her face in a big yawn.

"I feel ya, baby girl." It's a perfect morning to stay in bed late and wish that yesterday didn't happen.

Of all the clubs in the entire world for Jax to end up in, it had to be mine. But for him to be there with Brody confuses everything.

Slumping back against the pillow, I try to fit everything together, but none of it makes sense.

If Jax and Brody aren't friends, how did they both wind up at the club? If they are friends, why was Jax so quick to knock Brody out?

That will forever go down as one of my all-time favorite memories.

Well, second to the moment Maeve was born. I scoop up my sleeping baby and lay her in her crib before heading to the kitchen to make coffee.

"Morning. Your phone has been going nuts. Gil texted me to see if you were around. I told him you were sleeping." Anna hands me a steaming cup with a half-frown.

"You came home early last night. Is everything okay?" She pulls her yoga mat from the rack and unrolls it while watching me.

"Everything that could go wrong, did." I slide onto the high stool and wrap my fingers around the hot mug. "They were both there." My sigh ruffles a maroon lock of hair.

"Who?" Her long legs fold and the soles of her feet meet.

"The two people I never thought I'd see again. Jax and Brody." I drop my head to my arms.

This is the last thing I want to deal with.

Anna leans over her paired ankles, and her brows raise. "Maybe it's a good thing. Did you ask Jax for some child support?"

I groan against the cool countertop. "It isn't like that. He knew I was on birth control. It wasn't his fault Maeve beat all the odds." She's my little miracle baby. With the heart of a tiger.

"You didn't tell him, did you?" Anna's voice drops.

I can tell she's disappointed.

"Did you at least throat punch Brody for general assholishness?" Her arms twist her torso around in another pretzel looking stretch.

"You'll never believe this. Jax did. Well, not in the throat. But he did punch him!" It's still the highlight of the evening.

"Maybe that's why Gil is trying to get a hold of you," she says, facing the wall. "You better call him."

"Fine." I don't move, though. The froth on my coffee flattens as I take a sip.

There. Now I can get back to him.

Shit. Fifteen missed messages.

Gil: Whatever the fuck happened last night, you need to call me.

Gil: Call me now.

Gil: Whoever this guy is that broke my desk getting your contact info owes me a new one

Gil: YOU OWE ME A NEW DESK

Gil: Never mind. You're just fired.

Are you kidding me?

Did he just fire me over text?

Would Jax do that?

My stomach twists at the thought of how hard he hit Brody.

There's no doubt he's huge and strong. He would be terrifying to be on the wrong side of.

I must have made him mad the way I left him.

Unknown: I know where you are now. I'll be there in the morning.

Oh my god. He's coming here?

A cold wave of nausea goes over me.

"Anna?"

"Hmm?" Her feet and palms are on the floor. All I can see is her ass sticking up in the air.

"I think Jax is on his way. Can you keep Maeve

distracted? I don't want him to meet her. At least, not yet." I have no idea how he will react. What if he's angry?

She flips over and sits on her mat with a confused look. "Wait, you don't want him to know?"

"Please? Just until I know for sure." Rushing to the bedroom, I change out of my baggy t-shirt and shorts to jeans and a long-sleeved blouse.

The thought of Jax thinking he can just waltz in after getting me fired makes me furious.

Who does he think he is?

He can't just take over and ruin everything that I've built.

By the time the doorbell rings, I'm fuming.

Flinging it open, my jaw drops in shock.

Brody.

"What are you doing here?" I push the door almost closed as he wedges his foot in the gap.

"I felt bad about how things went down. It was a surprise seeing you last night. You still look good. Nothing a few workouts wouldn't fix." He gives me his best lopsided grin.

It used to make me giddy.

Now I want to kick him in the balls.

"What do you care? You gave up any say over me, or my body, a long time ago." My heel finds its way onto his toe.

He grunts and his lips thin, but he doesn't move his wedge.

"That isn't what I meant and you know it, Sof. Things in the past can stay in the past. We all make mistakes. It's important that we move on from them." His palms open as he steps closer and his voice gets husky. "You did moves last night I've never seen. I want you to do them again, but for me."

"Mistakes? Like 'oops, I tripped and fell into my best friend's fiancé's vagina with my dick?' It's not like you misspelled a name on a piece of paper, Brody. That isn't something you can just erase." I try to shove his shoe out again. "Go away."

"You know I didn't love her. She didn't mean anything." His fingers thread around the edge and he starts putting his weight behind his push.

"I don't care. We're so—"

I'm cut off by Maeve screaming from the back room.

Brody's eyes widen. "Is that a baby?"

"Yes. Now go."

His knee digs against the wood, and I lose ground. "Who's is it?"

"Not fucking yours." I grab my keys laying on the table and dig the sharp metal into his knuckles.

He lets out a yelp before stumbling backwards.

His swearing is muffled as I slam the door closed.

CHAPTER TWENTY-TWO

JAX

IS THAT BRODY? WHAT THE FUCK IS HE DOING HERE?

The fact that he's walking away cradling his own hand kinda tells me that things didn't go so well.

I'm not surprised she rejected him, but why is he here?

Why am I sitting down the street in my blacked-out Bentley, watching her?

She took my money and left me tied up at the club.

Sofia couldn't hide that fire in her eyes from me, though. The moment she locked her gaze with mine, the same heat returned. Two years vanished, and it was just her and me in a room alone.

I want that again.

She was the only thing that kindled any emotion in me. I've been hiding that flame within me since the day she left.

Seeing her ignited an inferno I can't put out.

"Enzo? I need a favor." I know he has eyes and ears everywhere.

"Did you get in another fight, Jax?" He sounds bored.

I *may* have asked him a time or two to help me clean up messes.

"Not this time. I want to trace a car. Can you set it up to send me updates? And I need you to send me that pairing app so I can get a phone number." It's been handy. We use it to find out secrets for Frankie.

"Easier than sending out the cleaning team. Send me the license plates."

It doesn't take long to get both requests taken care of.

I don't think I'm ready to knock on her door quite yet. Apparently, she knows how to keep it shut.

Good girl.

I'm in the gym working one of the heavy bags when the tracking app dings through my earbuds.

The velcro of me taking off my gloves almost drowns out the next notification.

"Where are you going, my little tigritsa?" Popping my phone out of my duffel, that sexy little red dot shows me she's parking in one of the nearby casino parking lots.

"Hmm, gambling?" Lucky me, it's one of the places under our protection, so we have access to the cameras.

White blouse, black skin-tight pants, and heels. My girl is dressed for success, and it makes me hard, thinking of pulling those high-class clothes off of her.

I'm just about out the door and climbing on my bike when I find her on another view, sitting on a bench near the office door with a piece of paper clenched in her hand.

What is she doing?

That place has a great taco bar, and I'm suddenly hungry. Purely a coincidence that I'll be able to see the office door from the booth there.

It only takes a few minutes to make my way to the

motorcycle parking near the main doors. The chilled air makes my scalp goosebump as it hits my sweaty head.

A cold beer and a bowl of chips and salsa help to kill the time until I see her walk out of the office behind an older woman with graying hair.

Sofia nods enthusiastically to whatever her guide is saying before they disappear into the kitchen area of this very restaurant.

I'm on my second Dos Equis when they reappear.

Fuck, she's beautiful when she smiles. And she's absolutely beaming.

I have to figure out how to make her grin like that when she looks at me.

When they shake hands, I watch my dark-haired beauty until she leaves.

The parking garage cameras catch her doing a happy dance next to her car before she climbs in.

It seems that burritos might be on the menu a lot more now.

CHAPTER TWENTY-THREE

SOFIA

THE COOK SQUINTS AT ME. "ARE YOU SURE THAT'S WHAT they ordered?"

I let out a long sigh, blowing a strand of purple hair away from my face. "No, sir. Let me go confirm."

He always makes me feel like a fuckup, but I know I'm getting better at this waitressing gig.

Dolores told me so when she gave me a small raise at the end of my first week.

When I return from the very cranky family regarding how well to cook their steak, Gigi is dancing excitedly near the register.

"Sofia! You have a table of hotties in booth eighteen!" Her pink pigtails bounce as she hops from foot to foot.

"Oh?" I don't care, as long as they don't change their minds ten times regarding how rare they want their meat.

"Girl, their tats barely can cover all of those muscles." She licks her lips and hands me a stack of menus.

I recognize the laugh before I see him.

Those wild curls and his broad shoulders are a dead giveaway as I arrive behind him.

"Why are you here?" I hope none of my coworkers hear me, but I'm not in the mood for the 'correct' welcome.

He leans forward on one elbow and turns to face me, that sinful tongue piercing popping against the back of his teeth.

"I'm here to eat, sweetheart. What are you gonna feed me?" His wide grin flashes as he winks at me.

There are two other huge guys with him, both covered in patterned ink. One even has it up the sides of his head. When he smiles, one silver tooth reflects the dancing lights.

"Jax, I—" What can I say? I can't kick him out.

I hate how wet my panties are, seeing him.

"Fine," I huff. "What can I get started for you?" Sugar oozes from my words.

I'll just kill him with kindness.

"Hold on a sec." He fiddles with his phone, then holds it up and it makes a snapshot noise.

Anger bubbles in me. "Did you just take my picture?"

He shrugs. "I gotta have something to look at tonight when I think about you. Unless you want to join me and give me the real thing?"

Fuck. I'm tempted.

I can't stop dreaming about him.

"Funny. How about you? Are you here to give me a hard time, too?" I point the end of my pen at the biggest of the three, sitting silently with a flat expression and his arms crossed across his chest.

"*Niet*. I want to get the number eleven and a beer." His heavy Russian accent takes me a moment to decipher.

The leaner one leans back on two legs in his chair. "I'll have a number one and eleven beers." He laughs as he throws a piece of his napkin at the quiet man. "Nah, make it just a single for now. Maybe a shot of tequila, too."

"I like that idea," Jax says as he hands me back the menus. "A round for all of us. You should be rich enough to pay, since you took all my money the other night."

Our fingers brush, sending sparks up my arm.

"You were the one who broke into my dressing room. Let's call that a finder's fee." When I playfully push on the bare skin of his shoulder, it's hard to resist wanting to keep touching him.

"Tigritsa, I'll be happy to be the X at the end of your treasure map." His hand clasps over mine, holding my palm against his sweltering heat.

The leaner guy laughs loudly. "Jax, that has to be one of the cheesiest lines I've heard."

My cheeks burning, I turn away and hurry back towards the kitchen. I can hear Jax yelling behind me.

"Stuff it, Alexei. You wouldn't know a good woman if she came up and kicked you in the balls."

I bite my knuckle to keep the giggles down.

Hiding isn't an option. My heart races as I carefully place their drinks down.

Jax grabs my wrist and pulls me close as I try to leave.

"You know I was joking. I'd be happy to be your over-flowing money chest, sweetheart." His warm breath hits my neck and his dark eyes brim with sincerity.

I don't know what to say, so I back away on weak knees.

He's all talk. He has to be.

A guy like him probably flirts with every girl he sees. Famous boxer, rich, hot.

Oh, man, is he fine.

And the way he can use that tongue keeps me awake at night remembering it.

He's a wild ride, but can't be anything more. He wouldn't want to be a father, it'd just cramp his image.

With a firm resolve, I make my way back with their food.

Despite the fire burning within me, and the urge to straddle his lap right here amongst the fake cacti and his friends watching, I keep my composure.

"Sof, what do you say? Sit with me after your shift? Have a drink?" His fingers sit lightly on my arm.

My pulse pounds in my ears. I want to so badly.

"I'm afraid I can't. I have plans."

His piercing clicks. "Break them, tigritsa. I want to spend time with you."

The big man in the back stops with a taco halfway to his mouth and stares hard at Jax. His serious blue eyes flick between us and one dark brow raises.

"Jax, are you sick?" he asks before taking a large bite. "I can have Mikhail bring in the doctor."

Jax scowls at him. "No, Niki." He reaches across the table to the shot of liquor still sitting in front of his friend and takes it.

After swallowing, he looks back up at me. "I'm serious."

Alexei laughs, leaning back in his chair with his cell poised. "I gotta get a pic of Jax getting denied for posterity."

"Send it to me," Jax says to him before turning to me. "I'll make it my wallpaper as a reminder of when you broke me."

This is too much.

"You can pay with Gigi. Maybe next time." I run into the back of the kitchen. My shift ended three minutes ago.

Clocking out, I dart through the back entrance.

Any time I'm near him, my body wants to do things my mind tells me not to.

But Maeve owns my heart. I need to stay strong for her.

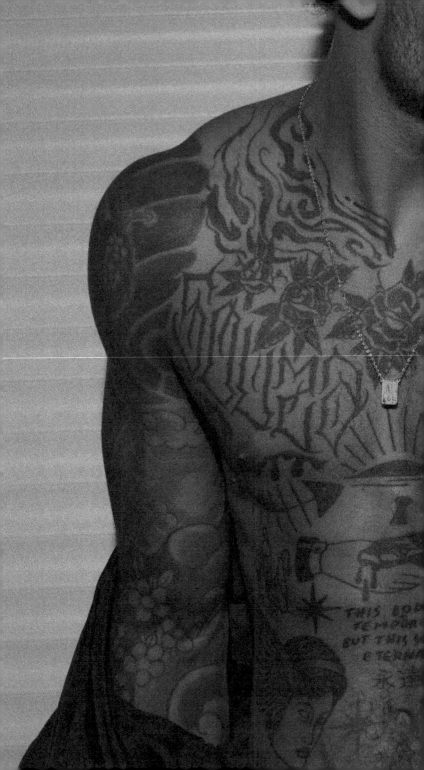

CHAPTER TWENTY-FOUR

JAX

WHY DO I KEEP FINDING MYSELF SITTING DOWN THE STREET from her house? I can't stop thinking about her.

Seeing her at the restaurant yesterday nearly did me in. Getting that intoxicating scent of strawberries nearly drove me wild.

She's fighting it, too. I saw it in her eyes, felt it in her touch. That lingering palm still burns into my skin.

There's a fire in me that's getting harder to keep at bay.

But how do I show up on her doorstep without revealing I've been watching her?

My thumb twitches as I rotate my rings around my fingers.

I'm always the first one to jump into a situation, running at the front of the pack, jumping the bell in the ring.

Yet, here I sit.

Frozen.

"Kai? What the fuck should I do?" I wish he was here. He always had some deep answer to every problem.

The low growl of engines grows from behind me.

Three big Harleys rumble past me and stop in front of her house.

It has me sitting up a little straighter in my seat.

They're all wearing backwards baseball hats and I can't see them clearly from this angle.

One of the smaller guys jumps off and saunters up to the door.

Brody.

Again?

My knuckles pop as I squeeze my fists. He doesn't take a hint, does he?

As soon as the door opens, it's flung shut.

His arm raises as he beats on it. I can hear him swearing at her from here.

When he turns back and gestures for his two companions to join him, I see red.

My engine roars to life and I nail the gas, leaping me forward.

Tires squeal, and my car fishtails until it gains traction and guns straight for them.

Both of the leather vested men jump backwards, falling to the ground as I slam on the brakes.

My Bentley hasn't stopped moving before I'm leaping out and barreling towards Brody.

He's my brother, but now he's no better than dirt to me.

His eyes only have a split second to widen before my ringed fist finds his jaw, knocking his head backwards, followed by his body.

Another punch lands to his ribs before he hits the sidewalk.

I grab up his shirt, lifting his shoulders so his nose is only inches from mine.

"I thought I told you to never fucking speak to her

again? Did you think I'd forget?" My next hit lands on his cheekbone. I can feel it splinter from the force.

His hands fly up, trying to block my blows, but he's no boxer.

Heavy footsteps distract me just long enough to see the two goons cutting around my still running car and heading for me.

I drop Brody like the piece of garbage he is and come up swinging.

The first catches the full force into his nose and blood sprays all over his chest. My fingers claw into the jacket of the next, tearing the fabric off in a chunk before my knee slams into the soft meat of his belly.

He doubles over with a grunt, falling to his knees while the other still whimpers, holding his nose.

Brody groans and rolls onto his stomach. "You're gonna pay for this, brother. This isn't your business."

"When you fucked with Sofia, you made it my business. She's mine."

Is she?

At least, as far as he's concerned, she is.

"Why the hell do you care about her? You don't even know her!" Brody coughs out.

I step forward, towering over him with a smirk.

"That's where you're wrong. I know her *really* well. In fact, I have since the night of your wedding."

His dark curls plaster to his forehead as he shakes his head, his face paling as he realizes what I mean.

"You motherfucker." He spits out as he pushes himself up to his knees.

Before he can launch himself at me, I forcefully kick him in the chest, knocking him back down and stamping my foot on his throat.

"I think you mean, *wife-fucker.*"

His nostrils flare as he claws at my calf, and I laugh. Pathetic.

"I won't let you hurt her again. *Brother.*" I spit out the last word. "Now, get out of here and don't come back, or else next time, you won't be getting back up."

I release my hold on his neck, kicking up dust into his face.

Brody pushes himself unsteadily to his feet. Blood runs down his face, and one eye is already swelling shut.

He tugs his vest tighter over his chest and helps his buddy to his feet.

Their bikes spit up gravel as they rally away.

My hand is sore where I hit him, so I flex my fingers to work out some of the pain. That's when I notice the other is still clenched around the tattered piece of clothing.

A scythe.

Fuck.

Reapers.

I drop the patch on Mikhail's desk. The beast of a Russian stands with his back to me, his massive hands gripped behind his broad back.

"I may have fucked up, boss." Leaning back in the stuffed leather chair, I wait to see just how bad it is.

He faces the window in silence. The slick edges of his black hair catching the glimmer of the Vegas Strip lights below.

His jaw moves in silence beneath the thick fabric of the balaclava that covers his lower face.

He's the only person I've ever met that makes me feel nervous to be around.

"Did you kill him?" The deep rumble of his voice fills his penthouse office.

"No, but I wanted to. He was trying to attack my girl." I should have hit them all a dozen more times.

His face turns and one of his dark eyes stares through me. "You? Have a girl?"

I shrug. "I dunno, boss. She's special. Maybe."

He strides from the window and his broad palms grip the back of his chair. "So, she doesn't know she's your girl? Is it worth starting a new war over?" He leans over and picks up the scrap of clothing and rubs it slowly between his thick finger and thumb.

His muscles flex under his snug suit as he sits. "They've been getting too brave lately. When I was a boy, my uncle would tell us of the *Baba Yaga*, who would feast upon troublesome children to make the others behave."

He tosses the patch to me. "Perhaps it is time to teach them some manners."

CHAPTER TWENTY-FIVE

SOFIA

It was terrifying huddling inside with Maeve in the back room closet when Brody showed up yesterday. It sounded like he was going to break the door down.

But, after a while, I didn't hear anything. This morning, I could swear that there was blood outside on the concrete.

"What the hell are you going to do about him?" Anna lays out four slices of bread on the counter and folds the bag closed. "This is the second time? Third?"

"Second. I don't know what he wants. He was mad at the club when I wouldn't dance for him, and it's just gone downhill from there." He's been angrier each time he showed up.

"I thought he was there for his own bachelor party?" Anna drizzles mayo, then smears on a thick layer of guacamole. "And you have Jax showing up at your job? Geez, Sof. You really have your hands full."

Funny she says that as I'm changing Maeve's diaper. "Yeah. I do."

"Are you ever going to tell Jax?" she asks quietly before

adding the last few layers of our sandwiches and cutting them diagonally. "He's going to find out if you start seeing him." She takes a large bite and disappears into her bedroom.

I don't know if I want to see him.

Well, a big piece of me does.

"What do you think, baby girl?" I coo against Maeve's chubby foot. "Would you want to see him?"

I stare back at his eyes on her round face. His dark curls fanning around her head.

Could I handle seeing his rejection of her?

Maybe it will just be easier to deal with explaining to her once she's older why he isn't around. It would be better than her knowing that he didn't want her.

It makes my stomach roll.

What if I'm wrong?

Could there be a piece of that wild, sexy man who would want to be a dad?

My phone vibrates where it's wedged beneath her elbow, making her giggle.

> Unknown: I'm outside. Want to say hi?

My stomach tightens. I scoop up Maeve, run to Anna's door, and knock in a panic. Flinging it open before she replies, I rush to her bed.

"What the hell, Sof?" She's stretched out, her cell in one hand and the last of her sandwich in the other.

"I got another no-name text. I know it's not Brody, he's saved under 'Asshole'. Can you keep her back here until I figure out what's going on?"

She rolls onto her side, tucking her shoulder under her ear. "Over a message? What did it say?"

"That they're outside."

Her blue eyes widen, and she sits up in one motion. "Yes, of course!" She pulls a squealing Maeve onto her lap and wraps her arms around my baby protectively. "Do I need to call the cops?" Her thumb hovers over her phone.

"Not yet. But, be ready." I pull the door around behind me.

I wish I had a baseball bat.

Or a gun.

I've never had the urge to fight back, but that was before I had a child.

Slowly pulling the curtain back, all I can see is the dark form of a motorcycle parked in the street.

Shit. Brody rode one here yesterday.

The knock reverberates through the living room and makes my heart nearly stop beating.

It isn't the same forceful pounding he used last time.

Grabbing my keys in my hand, I thread them through my knuckles.

I really need to get a better weapon.

Or maybe a big dog. I bet Maeve would love that.

When I slowly open the door, a dark shirted figure is leaning over my small handrail.

"What do you want?" I hiss through the narrow gap.

"Oh!" Jax turns around. "I was starting to wonder if you were home." His broad smile is highlighted by a big bouquet of lilies and yellow roses clutched tightly in his hand. Just like my mom used to have scattered around the house. Yellow was her favorite color.

My absolute shock at his presence has me forgetting to be guarding the house. "What the hell are you doing here?"

He holds out the flowers to me. "It's later."

I must have a confused look, because he laughs.

"You said you'd go on a date with me 'later'. Well, that's now." He starts to step inside, but I shift so I'm blocking him.

"This isn't how that works, Jax. How did you get my number?" I toss my keys back on the table. I can think of better ways to punish him if he gets out of line.

Like sitting on his face.

Oh, man. The way his eyes work over me makes my thighs rub together.

"I called in a favor." He gives me a crooked smile and leans closer so his lips nearly brush my ear. "Well? Gonna get ready?"

Maeve cries from Anna's room.

Jax's eyebrows raise as he glances past me.

Fear courses through me. I'm not ready.

"I'm babysitting, Jax. I can't go." I rest my hand on his chest. "I'm sorry."

"We could stay in?" His finger runs lightly across my shoulder and down my arm, leaving a trail of goosebumps behind. "I like kids. My friends back in New York are popping them out so fast it's like a daycare when I visit."

God, he's making this hard.

There's a part of me that wants to pull him to show him Maeve.

But I also know that guys always say things they don't necessarily believe. It's one of the biggest things I learned at the strip club and my ex-husband. Empty words to fulfill their own fantasies for the night.

I can't play with my daughter that way. I need to be sure.

"I don't think so." My palm tingles where it rests against him. So, I push him back a step. "You can't just show up at my house like a stalker, Jax. Trust is to be earned, not taken."

It's funny, I don't want to stop touching him.

But I do.

He catches my hand and brings my fingers to his mouth, lightly kissing the tip of each before letting go. "You can trust me. I'll prove it. I can even follow the rules, if I have to." His teeth flash in a wide grin before he skips off of the concrete step and heads back to his motorcycle.

Straddling the racing bike, he pauses with his helmet above his head.

"I will get that date, tigritsa. I'll give you some time to get used to the idea that you're going to be mine."

His beard disappears beneath the dark visor. The rumble of his exhaust barely reaches me before he speeds away.

Pushing the door shut, I hug the flowers to my chest and fall onto the overstuffed couch.

Why does he have to be so damn perfect?

CHAPTER TWENTY-SIX

JAX

TODAY IS AN EASY DAY. I JUST HAVE TWO PROTECTION payments to pick up, then I'll be able to hound Sofia for that date.

She didn't scream and try to stab me in the hand, so I'll call that a win.

"You're early." The owner wipes sweat from his bald forehead when he sees me. "I have my wife coming back from the bank. I swear I'll have your money in just a few minutes." He paces behind his bar nervously. "Here, have a drink on me while you wait."

I haven't had to threaten him. He's always complied with our rules.

But he's also never been late before.

"Fine, next time plan ahead, huh?" I hate having to strong-arm on people.

Mikhail was clear, though. Everyone in this city is on the take. If they want to stay safe, they need to hire someone.

It might as well be us.

His lower lip trembles as he slides my tequila out. "I just, well, I didn't expect I'd have to make a double this week." He shifts his beady gaze towards the tables near a bank of big screen TVs.

The seats are crowded with a bunch of men wearing the leather vests that Brody's buddies were wearing at Sofia's house.

Wait.

I recognize the dark mop of curly hair, so similar to my own.

He's here.

They all groan in unison as the team they're watching scores a goal. A bald, bearded asshole stands up next to Brody and yells at the television as he throws a beer bottle at it, shattering the glass in a spark of colors.

"Dad! What the fuck? That was the best one." Brody throws up his hands as he yells at the towering figure.

I know that bald fucker. He's the head of the Reapers. We've had a few heated exchanges with him and his crew, but he's fallen off the radar for a while.

He's Brody's father?

I sneak a picture so I'll be able to show Mikhail later. He'll want proof.

Drifting back over to the owner, I try to keep the wall between me and the group. There's too many to risk an exchange.

"Are they the ones hitting you up?" I ask quietly.

He nods, his bald head gleaming under the fluorescent lights.

Shit.

"Keep this month's payment. We'll get these bastards cleaned out of here. Keep your head." He needs to play it cool or they'll ruin him. Or kill him.

The Reapers aren't exactly known for their gentle ways.

If Brody is affiliated with them, that means Sofia might not be safe, either.

Pushing my way back into the sweltering Vegas afternoon, I call Nikolai as fast as I can bring his name up.

"Come on, answer," I mumble into the phone.

"Jax? Problems at Vox's?" Nikolai's thick accent comes through the tinny speaker.

"Yeah, but not what you'd think. Where are you?" I need to get out of here before a lingering Reaper sees me.

"I'm on the south end. I'll be there in five." The line goes dead.

I can hear the growl of his Hellcat three stop lights away as he gets closer. When he stops at the corner, I jump in.

The cold air conditioning feels good.

"What is the problem? I find it hard to believe you need help breaking an old fat bartender's legs." Nikolai doesn't look at me as he accelerates through the next intersection.

"Brody was there."

When he takes a hard turn, it pulls me to the left before he stops in a shadowed parking lot.

"Why does that matter?" He turns and faces me with a frown. "Sibling spats should not come before business. Miki and I just fight and move on."

"Thanks, oh wise one." I pull out my cell and bring up the photo of Knox and Brody before handing it to Nikolai. "See? That's the problem."

Nikolai takes my phone in a large hand and swipes the image larger. He moves his finger across the screen, but it disappears, revealing the blurry picture of Sofia I snuck at the restaurant.

"Jax." He rubs his temples and tosses my iPhone back to me. "Why is that girl your background? What kind of tacos is she feeding you?"

With a groan, I fall back against the seat. "Man, she has the best kind."

He holds up his hand, palm facing me. "*Niet.* Women are a distraction. We have work to do. I don't care if her pussy cures cancer. If Knox is back, I need your head in the game."

Nikolai grips his steering wheel, twisting his big knuckles and making it creak. "I will tell Mikhail."

"They made the owner pay them. Isn't that an incursion?" It's like Knox spit in Mikhail's face.

Nikolai nods, his jaw clenching as he stares out the window.

"I will take you back to your bike." He revs the engine, tugging us in reverse and the tires squeal as he shifts into first.

As he pulls up to my Ducati, the flat of his hand shoots out and smacks me across the shoulder. "And, Jax. If you're going to have a girl on your phone, get a better shot. That one makes you look like a fucking pervert. Ask her for a sexy pose. If she likes you, she'll send one." His broad palm shoves me out as I open the door.

My feet barely find the asphalt before he's speeding off.

I still have one more stop, but his words eat at me.

> Me: Nikolai saw my phone. He said the pic of you was blurry

> Sofia: You have me as your wallpaper?

Me: Yeah. You're beautiful. It's all I got until you go on a date with me.

By the time I get the last payment and load up on my motorcycle, I still haven't heard back.

Maybe I spooked her off.

I chew on my tongue bar as I walk into the penthouse over Mikhail's casino.

He isn't here, but his accountant is.

"All but Vox." I drop the duffel of cash on his desk and slump onto the leather couch.

The last update on her car tracker has it sitting at her house.

He's been there twice that I've seen.

What if he goes back when I'm not there?

I can't protect her there.

Here would be better. Mikhail's security is better than anyone else's in Vegas.

If Kai were here, I know he'd help me keep watch.

Fuck, I miss him.

My throat tightens, then a wave of guilt washes over me. I haven't thought about him in a couple of days.

I've been too distracted by her.

It's like she's the cure to this dark hole inside of me. My light.

If I need to be persistent, I will.

My notification pings.

When I click on it, big forest green eyes are framed by her luscious hair that looks almost burgundy in the soft light.

But, below her sly smile, her fingers hold the fabric of

her deep red colored blouse out just far enough I can see the top of her black lacy bra.

Blood rushes to my cock so fast it pinches in my jeans.

Careful, Sofia. You're making it very difficult to follow the rules.

CHAPTER TWENTY-SEVEN

SOFIA

Song- I Want It All, Cameron Grey

I KNOW I SHOULDN'T TEASE HIM, BUT HE'S IMPOSSIBLE TO resist.

There's a tiny part of me that doesn't want him to stop when I tell him to. Well, maybe a bigger portion.

The way he looks at me, like he's seeing through me to my innermost thoughts, it's unnerving and addictive.

I want to be seen, wanted, and even loved.

Can I have that with him? Or will he turn out to be like his brother?

Maeve changes everything I thought I knew. She's a huge factor in every decision I make.

Why can't I stop thinking about him? All day at work, I kept hoping he'd saunter in and take a seat.

He makes me feel beautiful when he watches me, as if I'm the only person to exist.

Driving home, my mind wanders to his tattoos and piercings. I wish he would make me feel like he did that night years ago.

Lost in his touch and the intensity of the moment.

I almost don't notice him leaning against his motor-cycle outside of my house.

No. My hair is a mess and I've been running all day. I don't know if I'll have the willpower to deny him again.

Why should I?

Maybe I should just give in.

Unless he's not serious. And I'm just a game. The prize at the end of the chase.

I bet if I give in, he'll get bored and move on.

It's a chance I don't want to take.

He looks up as I drive past. His eyebrows raise and fall when I don't turn into my driveway.

I give him a small wave and a smile before hitting the gas. Taking the corner a little fast, my tires chirp across the pavement.

My heart pounds in my ears at the thrill of his expression.

"Joke's on you, Jax." I grin at the windshield as I speed past the houses.

There's a park just ahead. If I hide the car behind the pavilion, he shouldn't be able to see me.

When I turn off the engine, I hold my breath, listening for the rumble of his bike.

Hugging myself in excitement, I hear him drive by.

I did it! I feel like a master prankster… who has to pee.

If I go straight back home, he's probably going to double back.

The public bathrooms aren't far, just to the side of the big empty lot and nestled between some trees.

As I'm washing my hands, I catch my own reflection. My cheeks are flushed and my eyes are the brightest I've seen them in months.

I guess I just needed a sexy biker to chase me around.

When I push the door open, I freeze.

He's leaning against my car.

Shit.

What do I do?

The tree line extends away. Maybe I'll keep this game going a bit longer.

Darting toward the heavy pines, the needles crackle in the dry heat of the evening. Passing a boulder taller than me, it radiates the stored warmth of the afternoon sun as I run past.

"I know you're close, tigritsa. I can hear you." His heavy footsteps follow mine.

My pulse spikes as I push between two thick trunks and sprint towards a playground.

Fighting the giggle trying to escape my throat, I duck under a wooden bridge and hide behind a long, enclosed slide.

I try not to breathe too loudly so I can listen for him.

The soft rubber matting makes it impossible. All I can hear is the voice in my head screaming at me to lose and let him catch me.

A flicker of movement catches my eye. I can see his feet beneath the wooden beams as he walks away from me.

Slowly, I work my way around the slide to the open end and push myself inside.

My work sneakers grip the smooth plastic surprisingly well, and I shimmy up the dark tube to the small alcove at the top.

Where is he?

I thought for sure he was heading to the jungle gym.

Raising myself slowly, I peer over the short wall to see if I can spot him.

A hand lands on either side of me and his broad chest presses against my back.

"Thought you could run?" His warm breath bathes my sweaty neck as his lips brush my ear.

"Yes," I stammer. I'm more winded now than when I was running.

It's like I'm suffocating in his presence.

"Now that I've caught you, does that mean I get to eat you?" he growls, his body vibrating against mine.

The round ball of his tongue piercing drags across my collar, sending a shiver of electricity down my spine.

"Because I can still taste you after all this time."

My fingers tighten into the wooden grip as I take a deep breath.

And throw myself back into the shadows of the slide.

I can't stop the laughter that escapes as I fall away from him.

When my shoes hit the ground, I gather myself to run, but his powerful legs wrap around me from behind and we both tumble to the earth.

I get up before him and squeal as I run towards the shade of a pirate ship playhouse. The massive sails snap in the low breeze. They cover my gasp of surprise when I feel his hands surrounding my waist.

He picks me up, my feet dangling in the air, and sits me on a big concrete cannon so I straddle it.

Pushing his hips between my knees, his burning palm works to my throat and he tilts my face up to look at him.

"It seems I've found a pirate's treasure." His thumb traces my jaw as he stares at my lips.

Damn, I want him to kiss me.

A buzz interrupts us.

The hand on my neck stills as he pulls out his phone. His face darkens as he looks at the screen. "Fuck. I have to go."

I cover his fingers with my palm. My pulse is so fast, I can feel it through his knuckle.

My teeth roll my lower lip between them. "Jax, I—"

How do I tell him I don't want him to go? That I like how much he wants me, but I worry it will change once he knows what I'm hiding.

"I like this game, sweetheart. Let's see what happens when I catch you next time." He flashes a mischievous grin before he takes off in a sprint.

A cool evening gust pushes my sweaty shirt against my skin, making me shiver.

"Just leave me here then, dickhead!" I call out after him.

What the hell just happened?

Doesn't he know I was just about to give in?

Is there such a thing as a boxing emergency?

The more I think about it, the crankier I get as I stalk back to my car.

He left me panting and practically begging for more. Why did he just leave?

Maybe next time, I won't let him catch me.

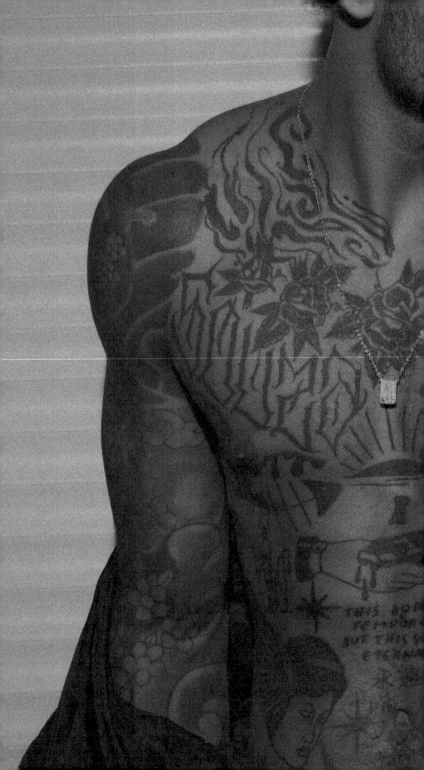

CHAPTER TWENTY-EIGHT

JAX

My fingers still ache, wanting to touch more of her.

But Nikolai's text was urgent.

I should have kissed her. But I want the next time I claim her lips to not be a goodbye.

Mikhail's office is packed when I get there.

Nikolai gives me a slight frown and points to the clock over his head.

Yeah, I know. Vegas streets are packed in the evenings. I had to take my motorcycle onto the sidewalk a couple of times to bypass lines of cars.

Mikhail stands behind his desk, his large hands spread over the oak surface. "This is the third club where they have harassed the owners and demanded payment. They have pushed us too far. It is time to shove the Reapers back into their hole." His fist slams hard enough the papers drift away.

"Which club?" Alexei pipes up from the far corner.

I can't see Mikhail's mouth beneath his balaclava, but his eyes narrow without turning. "El Coño."

Shit. It's one of the biggest dance bars in the city.

He raises his muscular arms towards the ceiling. "Don't kill. We don't have a cleanup team big enough for that place. But, boys—" He drops his gaze to where it feels like it's burning into me. "—fight like your father is watching."

Abruptly, Mikhail turns on his heel and disappears through a side door.

Nikolai steps forward and begins pairing us up.

Alexei is my beat-up bro tonight.

"Aw, looks like we're a couple. Hotty and Toddy. What do you think?" He loops his lanky arm over my shoulder and grins. He points his thumb towards his chest. "I'm the hotty. That makes you a stiff drink. What do you Americans call it, a Shirley Temple?"

"What? That's a virgin drink, man. No alcohol." My curls fall in my eyes as I shake my head.

I never know when Alexei is being serious or fucking with me.

"Ah, yes. Virgin. Like you?" His silver tooth flashes as he ducks my half-hearted punch.

"Like your asshole before I throw you to the Reapers?" I chase him down the hall and we both jump into his Maserati.

Our mood grows more serious as the cars gather in the dark parking lot.

"This place is packed." There's a line out the door of people looking to gain entrance.

One of the bouncers touches my shoulder as we push past the line. "They're tearing hell, man. I'm glad you and your boys are here."

Alexei and I exchange a look before stepping into the dark room filled with dancing bodies and pounding music.

It's hard to see anything wrong through the gyrating

crowds and the fog machines expelling mist in a thick layer.

A tiny waitress wearing a g string and silver stickers over her nipples pushes closer to us. "They're in the back. They have Roscoe trapped until his brother gets back with the payment." Her eyes are nearly black in the dim light.

The large shape of Nikolai and several more of our guys appear around us. We push our way through mostly naked women dancing against hordes of college aged guys who have no idea they're being hustled.

Two Reapers stand outside of the office. Their foreheads glisten with sweat.

It isn't overly warm in here. The air conditioning is keeping up.

Watching their eyes and their twitchy hands, I think I know what's going on.

"They're high as fuck," Alexei yells over the deep bass of the music.

"So we can hit them twice as hard." I ball my fists, and we both launch together.

I land four solid blows before the tank even realizes that he's been hit.

Alexei launches himself to kick his guard squarely in the head.

They both drop, but Alexei bounces up and stomps the fallen guy's face.

We leave the two unconscious men and push through into an expansive room.

That's completely trashed.

Papers and books cover the floor. The desk has been flipped and thrown against the far wall. A throng of leather vested Reapers gather around the back.

Every head turns to face us as we bust in.

"Time to teach some lessons," Nikolai grumbles behind me before charging forward.

Everyone erupts into limbs flailing, yells, and cussing.

Wading through, my knuckles bleed from beating the shit out of every one that stands in my way.

Alexei and I regroup and find Knox in the center. He's holding a long blade to the throat of the very battered club owner, Roscoe.

"Put down the knife." I don't want to get any closer. Blood is already dripping from where the blade is pushing into the skin.

"Fuck no. You don't own this town. Not anymore." Knox's beard is coated with spittle as he talks, matching the glisten of sweat on his bald head.

"You're wrong there, asshole. We beat your pack down." I gesture to the room of brawling men around us. Mikhail's guys are prevailing.

Knox points the knife at me as he talks. "Your days are numbered. We have the funds coming to shut you down." He tilts his head back and yells, "Boys!"

The door in the back flies open and a new throng of Reapers rush into the crowded space.

Brody leads them and freezes when he sees me.

His shiny vest betrays his loyalties.

"Well, brother. Seems we have a situation." He raises his fists and stalks towards me.

Is he kidding? Does he know what the fuck I do?

A loud hiss fills the room, and the smell of gunpowder permeates the air.

Nikolai stands with a silenced smoking pistol while a red stain spreads across Knox's shoulder.

"The next one hits your heart." Nikolai waves the barrel at Knox to back away from the beaten owner.

Brody stops, his brows knit as he looks from Knox,

slumping to the floor, and back to me. "You don't know what you've done," he growls before jumping to his father's side.

His hand juts out, finger pointing at me. "You and the people you care about are going to pay for this, *brother.*"

All the standing enemies drag their battered friends out through the back.

My stomach tightens.

Why did it feel like it wasn't just a threat against me?

Sofia.

Shit. He knows I've been there. And now he knows I work for Mikhail.

"Niki, I need to go." Panic races through my body.

This urge to protect her consumes my thoughts.

Nikolai looks at me with his expressionless face. "Is it more important than this?" He gestures to the room full of groaning and unconscious men from both sides scattered around.

"Yea, I'm sorry." Most of the injured are getting help.

But, none of them matter as much as her.

"Alexei, please. I have to go." I grab his arm and tug him to follow me.

Pushing through the front of the club, we jump in his car and ride in silence.

"She must be something." His accent is thicker when he isn't talking smack. "Nikolai always says women are a distraction. But—" He pauses and turns to me, wagging his finger. "—don't forget he married first."

Blood is spattered over his neck and jaw, yet he's giving me relationship advice.

He slams the brakes, lurching us both forward.

"I'll cover your rounds this week. That waitress in Vox is hot as fuck, anyway." His hand sticks out of the driver's window and flips me off as he speeds away.

Crazy ass, but he means well.

My phone pinpoints her location.

Getting to Sofia is all I can think about as I wind my way through the streets of Vegas.

I just hope Brody hasn't gotten to her first.

CHAPTER TWENTY-NINE

SOFIA

"Sof, I'm not here just to be your personal babysitter." Anna stands over me with her hands on her hips. "I have shit to do, too. Is it a stretch to think maybe I have a date tonight? She isn't my kid."

"You have plans? Sorry, I didn't know it was a secret." My voice comes out a little cranky, because I am.

The daycare called at the last minute and said they were full for this evening. They've been at capacity with a huge convention being in town and everyone working extra shifts.

Including me.

"Well, maybe I do." Her tone softens as she leans against the counter. "It's just exhausting always worrying about who's going to take care of her, ya know?"

"Um. Yeah. I get that. I'm her mom. Look, I'll call Mrs. Wilson. She told me that if I get in a pinch, she'd watch Maeve. So go have fun."

She's right. She isn't responsible for my daughter. Anna already helps so much.

I just wish she had warned me. But, she's been acting kinda weird lately, more distant.

There's a little knot in my belly that tells me something isn't quite right, but I don't know what.

"Fine," she says with a dramatic sigh. "I'll pick her up when I'm done. But, next time, some warning?" Anna says before disappearing into her room.

Sure.

"Come on, baby girl. Aunty Anna is busy. Let's get that nice old lady on the phone." I pick up Maeve and carry her to my bed, letting her crawl around on the comforter as I make the call.

Thank God she says yes.

Mrs. Wilson lives four doors down and is standing outside of her door in the warm evening breeze when I show up.

"Thank you again so much!" Sliding the diaper bag from my shoulder, I hand it to her first before Maeve.

"Oh, honey. I know how it goes! I raised four babies. Sometimes things just happen." Her kind smile is framed by curly gray hair.

A brown-eyed toddler runs up and hugs her knees from behind.

She laughs. "This is my grandson, Nate. He is excited to have a baby in the house tonight."

He gives me a toothy grin and a shy wave with jelly-covered fingers.

I'm feeling better about this already.

"I'm going to do a short shift tonight, but if Anna gets done early, she said she could pick her up." I give Maeve a soft kiss on her forehead and hand her to Mrs. Wilson.

Maeve doesn't fuss, thankfully.

Traffic is horrible. It's like every single car in Vegas is on the road.

I can't even imagine how busy tonight is going to be.

Pulling into the big parking garage, my headlights sweep past the entrance into the casino.

And over Jax, leaning on his motorcycle.

How does he always seem to know where I'll be?

The clock on my dashboard is leaving me very little time to make it inside.

I park and gather my stuff, half expecting him to wrench my car open.

But, he doesn't.

He waits for me near the door to the stairs.

"You need to come with me," he says without moving.

"Is this your attempt at a date again? You really don't understand this, do you?" What ever happened to dinner and a movie?

Jax can't seem to do anything by the rules.

He pushes himself away from his leaning Ducati and falls in step next to me. "I'm serious. It's important." His warm palm finds my elbow, and he tugs me closer to him as we walk.

"Jax. I have to work. Maybe later?" My fingers are just brushing the handle when he twirls me around to face him.

His lips are thin and his jaw set. "I'm worried about you, okay? You might be in danger."

My thoughts jump to Maeve.

"What kind? Tell me!" Panic makes my heart race as every possible bad scenario begins to rush through my mind.

His curly hair sways over his brow as he shakes his head. "It's hard to explain. You really should just come with me. You can stay at my place for a few days."

Anger begins to replace the panic.

"Is this a joke? You're fucking with me." I wrench my arm away from him and pull the door open.

His hand flattens over it, shoving it shut out of my grasp.

"No. This is more important than slinging margaritas, Sofia," he growls, reaching for me again.

"You're scaring me, Jax." I stumble backwards, trying to create some space from his intense presence.

His chin dips and the corner of his mouth rises in a smirk. "You should be scared." His arm snakes out.

But I shove my purse at him and turn, running through the opening to the outside path that surrounds the casino.

His deep voice follows me. "You want to run, tirgritsa, that's fine. I'll give you a head start. If you really don't want to come with me, then don't let me catch you."

CHAPTER THIRTY

JAX

Song- Formaldehyde Footsteps, BertieBanz

I don't want her things to disappear, so I take a moment to toss her purse in the saddlebags of my bike and text the security here to send someone out to watch it.

She has a solid thirty second lead.

Should I let it go for a full minute?

No.

I've waited too long. Part of this is driven by my overwhelming need to have her with me.

To take her home and have her to myself.

I crave the taste of her pussy on my lips again.

My cock twitches at the thought.

It's been long enough. If Kai taught me anything, it's that life is too short not to go after what you want. And Sofia is at the top of my list.

Taking off in a slow jog, I follow the only walkway that winds around the expansive building and backs onto the golf course. There isn't anywhere to hide here, so she must really be running.

It may be cheating bringing up the cameras on my phone, but I know when I catch her, we'll both bask in the victory.

At the first tee, I pause.

Which way would my little tigress have gone?

The flicker of movement on my screen tells me to the left, right towards the line of trees. Exactly where I want her.

Enzo has a hell of a network set up. I have access to the cameras not only in the casinos, but all the traffic and exterior ones as well.

My only question is, how long do I let her think she can hide?

Biting back the grin, I head in her direction, trying to be as light on my feet as I can. Reaching the tree line of a sweeping golf course, I press my hand against the rough bark and strain my ears, hoping to detect any hint of movement.

Fuck, nothing.

Pressing forward, I notice a flicker to my right, prompting me to increase my speed and fix my sights solely on her. With a quick flick of her head, she shoots me a sly grin that freezes me in my tracks.

As she breaks out into a sprint, I feel the adrenaline rush through my veins, propelling me forward. She's quick. But not fast enough for me.

The closer I get, the stronger her strawberry scent grows. I'm fucking feral for her at this point. In a split second, I lunge towards her, my arms encircling her waist as I bring her down with me, landing on the ground in a tangled heap.

"I told you not to let me catch you," I growl in her ear, rolling us over so I am on top. My body presses on hers to keep her in place.

Her head tilts to the left. In a split second, I sink my teeth into her throat, relishing in the sensation of her struggling against me.

I'm so distracted by her taste, her body against mine, that without warning, she swiftly brings her knees up, crashing them into my gut before I even have a chance to react. As the pain shoots through me, I instinctively let go, giving her the opening she needs to roll over and leap up.

"Try harder next time!" she calls out as she sprints off.

I've never gotten up so fast in my life.

She takes off out of the tree line and heads back to the greens. My breath comes out in ragged gasps as I close in on her, but she manages to evade me by swiftly ducking out of the way.

Fuck.

As I look up, I can see where she's heading. What she doesn't realize is there's a pond just on the other side of those pines. I'm done. I need her.

I stalk behind her, but I can't hear her footfalls. So she's hiding from me.

"Given up yet, sweetheart?" I call out, glancing to each side for her, hitting my palms against each trunk as I pass.

"When I catch you, you're mine, and I'll fuck you until you accept that."

From my right, I hear the sound of rustling leaves, causing me to swiftly turn. I catch a glimpse of her ponytail swaying in the breeze. Closing the distance between us, I seize her by the hips. In response, she twirls around, gripping my t-shirt tightly, causing the collar to rip. My fingers tighten around her throat as I push her against the rough bark, my thigh finding its place between her legs.

"Fuck, Jax," she says breathlessly. That has my cock throbbing for her.

"Mine," I say with a smirk.

Her chest heaves as her hot breath beats against my face. Her eyes dart around before focusing on me with a darkness in them.

Her hands push against my exposed chest, and I tighten my grip on her throat. She has driven me to this level of obsession with her.

"You've got one chance to stop this, Sofia." I lower my tone, feeling her heart pound against my palm.

Her arms wrap around my neck, and her legs around my waist, as her lips crash over mine. The shift causes me to stumble back while holding onto her ass as I devour her mouth.

Just like I've fucking dreamt of doing for years.

She claws at the remains of my top, ripping it from my body, making the air brush against my sweaty skin.

She tastes just like I remember, like strawberries and mint. With her lips pressed against mine, her fingers tangled in my hair, I lean in closer to intensify our kiss.

She consumes me, lighting a fire within me.

Breaking our touch, she backs away with a mischievous glint in her eye. I lunge towards her before she can turn and grab her by the waist, tucking her against me as we fall to the ground. She backs away on her ass, her eyes never leaving mine as I crawl towards her on my damn hands and knees.

There is only one thing I can do.

Catch her and claim her as mine.

CHAPTER THIRTY-ONE

SOFIA

Song- Bite Marks, Ari Abdul

FUCK. THE WAY HE'S CRAWLING TOWARDS ME, STALKING ME like I'm his prey, has me all kinds of turned on. But, I like this game. So before he can grab me again, I jump to my feet and run as fast as I can. The forest blurs past as I run. My lungs are on fire as his footsteps are relentlessly closing in. I keep going.

I want him to catch me. When I admit it, all of my worries disappear.

I am alive.

With the blood pounding in my ears, I swiftly duck over a low hill and find myself facing a tranquil pond of water.

"Shit," I hiss.

My body instinctively leads me to the right.

I know he's close.

My lips tingle with his lingering presence, and the anticipation of his strong arms around me quickens my heartbeat.

As I hear him approach from behind, a giggle escapes my lips. He growls in my ear, lifting me effortlessly into the air. My legs kick as I let out a squeal.

With a swift motion, he spins us around before we fall down on the ground. I'm pinned beneath him with my wrists securely held by his strong grip.

He tears off my jeans and tosses them aside, then climbs up my body until his erection presses against my pussy.

His lips claim mine and I hear the zipper of his pants.

"Fuck, sweetheart," he mutters against my lips.

"More," I pant out, arching my back.

Inhaling sharply, I lift my hips, my body responding to the sensation of his finger sliding along my slit.

"I'll chase you around wherever you want if this is how wet it gets you."

He slams his hard length inside me and I squeeze my eyes shut. I seize his shoulders, my nails sinking into his flesh, a mix of pain and determination in my grip.

"Oh my god, Jax."

He grunts in response, thrusting deeper. He lifts me up until I straddle him. When he tilts his head back, baring his throat, I can't resist leaning forward to bite him before planting a kiss on his lips.

His fingers dig into my ass as he guides me to following the pace of his relentless fucking.

"So damn good, Sofia," he groans against my mouth.

I push on his shoulders so he lays down on the grass, and he stifles a small groan. His eyes lock onto mine, filled with such burning desire that it makes me blush.

Dragging my nails down his chiseled abs, I press hard enough to leave angry red marks in their wake. I glide up and down, skillfully grinding my hips against him, hitting that sweet spot.

With another soft moan, his hand extends, encircling my throat and exerting pressure against the sensitive bite mark he had left me with earlier.

"Fuck, I need more," he pants out, taking me by surprise by wrapping his arms around me and rolling us over so he's on top. He tightly grasps my thigh and forcefully guides it towards my chest. His head tilts back as he whispers my name while sinking deep inside me.

Leaning down, his tongue traces a wet path from the base of my throat to my chin. My fingers tangle in his curls.

"That's better, isn't it, baby? I can feel your sweet pussy strangling my cock. You're close, aren't you?"

His husky voice sends thrills through me.

"Come on, sweetheart, come all over my cock like a good girl." He slaps my ass, and with one final thrust, his lips crash over mine as an orgasm shatters through my body. I'm shaking in his hold and he keeps fucking me, kissing and biting me.

I scream out his name, and the sound reverberates through the air.

He pulls out, sitting back on his feet and strokes his cock, not breaking eye contact with me. He jerks forward, with my name on his lips and his warm cum hits against my bare stomach.

"Holy shit," he mutters to himself.

With a smirk, he leans forward and scoops up his hot seed from my skin with his index finger.

"Open up, baby."

"Jax!" I shouldn't be turned on again, but I am.

I do as he says, and his finger slips inside my mouth. I bite down until I feel bone and suck the salty liquid off.

"We'll be here a while doing that to clean me up," I giggle.

With a mischievous sparkle in his eyes, he looks behind us. I follow his gaze and see the pond, its surface shimmering like a mirror under the starry night sky.

"Come on," he stands, his cock standing to attention in front of my face. I accept his outstretched hand, and with a gentle tug, he helps me up and leads me towards the glistening water.

"Jax." I let out a laugh as he bends and scoops me into his arms. I pull the cami top over my head and he unclasps my bra with one hand.

I raise my eyebrow at him, and his laughter fills the air.

"What?" he asks, giving me a boyish grin while clicking his tongue bar against his teeth.

I shake my head, sliding the straps off my shoulders and tossing it to the ground.

"Shit, it's cold," he says as he walks us into the water.

"Great, can't wait."

"I can think of a way to keep you warm, tigritsa," he whispers against my cheek. My body shivers against his. As he gently lowers us into the water, I cling to him tightly, feeling the icy embrace of the freezing fluid against my overheated skin.

"Fuck," I hiss out.

I shift in his arms, positioning myself to straddle him, wrapping my arms around his neck, and pressing my nose against his.

My body trembles as he playfully splashes my stomach, and then I feel his hand sliding down, his fingers caressing my belly button in slow, circular motions. Just that gentle touch alone has me ready to go again.

Wrapping my ponytail around his fist, he yanks my head back and sucks on my neck as his other hand ventures lower, settling between my legs.

"You want more of me already?" I tease.

"You have no idea how much of you I want, baby."

My heart quickens at his words. As guilt starts to form, I force myself to swallow it down. I have to tell him the truth before we get any deeper. He's made it clear. His persistence tells me enough.

"Is that right?"

Without a word, he silences me with a deep kiss, his fingers slipping inside me, igniting a fire within.

"Looks like you want me just as bad, sweetheart."

As he captures my lips again, a warm blush spreads up my neck.

"Give me one more and scream my name, baby," he whispers against my cheek.

He quickens the pace, stealing all the air from my lungs with his kisses. Enough to have me trembling against him, letting another climax rock through my body. He brushes his hands across my face, forcing me to look into his eyes.

I know what I have to do. He deserves to know, even if he never wants to speak to me again.

"Jax," I whisper.

"Yes, baby?"

"I need you to come home with me."

I can't go into work like this. I'm going to have to call in sick and hope they don't fire me.

A smile lights up his face and I take a deep breath.

"I couldn't possibly say no to that offer," he replies.

We dry ourselves off with his ripped shirt and then continue to walk hand in hand through the course. Jax, with his bare chest, is incredibly distracting. As we approach the lot where my car is, Jax digs out my purse from his bike and shoves on another black top.

Shit. I glance down at my shaking hands, nervously fumbling with the zipper of my purse. I finally manage to retrieve my apartment keys and extend them towards him.

Looking at them quizzically, he furrows his brow in confusion.

"I need to go and get something first. Let yourself in. I won't be long."

"Everything okay? You don't need to be nervous, not around me."

Tears sting in my eyes. I'm going to turn his life completely upside down tonight. I can't speak, so I just nod. Just as I try to leave, he reaches out and firmly clasps my hand, gently guiding me to face him, his hands tenderly cupping my cheeks.

"I'm so fucking happy I found you again, tigritsa."

With one last kiss, I back away. With a heavy heart, I climb into the car, and as soon as I shut the door, a sinking feeling settles in my stomach. I watch as he puts on his helmet, not before blowing me a kiss. Watching him speed away, I feel my hands tighten around the steering wheel.

I can do this.

Maeve deserves this. And so does Jax.

If I end up losing him because of that, I can live with my decision.

CHAPTER THIRTY-TWO

JAX

ONCE INSIDE SOFIA'S COZY APARTMENT, I SWITCH ON THE lights and head straight for the kitchen. Opening the fridge, I search for a beer to quench my thirst.

Nothing.

Just a load of kid food. Maybe it's for the kid she babysits.

I decide to go to the coffee machine and make one for each of us instead.

I have no idea what spooked her. The fact she gave me her keys was a relief to me.

She wants me here. That has to be something, right?

Taking my steaming cup, I sit on the couch, and a spring digs into my ass. It's another reminder that I need to dig and find out what she spent the money on.

Pulling out my phone, I chuckle, reading the messages from Alexei.

Alexei: Nikolai is pissed at you.

Alexei: I told him to shut up. He's just jealous you're getting some.

Alexei: Wait? You are getting some, right?
Or did she tell the king of chaos no again?

I quickly type back a reply.

J: I'll speak to Nikolai tomorrow.

His response comes through instantly.

Alexei: I don't care about that. You ignored
my other question...

J: I don't kiss and tell.

Putting the cell on the table, I rest my foot on my knee. I have this burning need to protect Sofia. Brody and his gang can't touch her when she's with me. I just need to figure out a way to tell her without her freaking out on me.

As the door creaks open, I feel a rush of anticipation and push myself off the couch. With Sofia's arrival, my heart starts pounding, and I'm immediately drawn to the sight of the little girl in the pink sleepsuit, snugly cradled against Sofia's neck.

Every time I try to make eye contact with Sofia, she averts her gaze. I blink at her. What the hell is going on here?

With quick, silent steps, she hurries past me towards the door on the right. I can't drag my eyes away from the little girl's dark mop of curly hair.

I cautiously follow, my footsteps barely making a sound, and lean against the sturdy frame. I watch as Sofia gently lowers the sleeping baby into the soft padded crib.

"Momma."

My heart stops.

Sofia has a kid? Who's is it? Brody's?

Chaos

As I back away, my palms become clammy with sweat. The small living room feels suffocating as tension mounts, my restless pacing amplified by the echoing click of the door as Sofia steps in.

She looks like she's about to burst into tears. Despite my own confusion, an overwhelming desire to hold her close overtakes me, and I rush towards her, wrapping my arms around her in a tight embrace.

She pulls away, her nails digging into her skin as she anxiously picks at the rough edges.

"I need to tell you something, Jax," she trails off, looking at the floor. I step forward, tipping her chin up with my finger.

"I gathered that, gorgeous. You have a kid?"

She nods.

"Are you worried that will change things between us? Because it won't."

She sucks in a shaky breath and I ask the one question I'm dying to know. Because it could change everything, especially with how Brody is acting.

"Is she Brody's?"

As her face turns pale, she vigorously shakes her head.

"Well, that's something," I say, trying to lighten the mood. But she's still the same color as the fucking wall behind her.

"Sofia? Talk to me. I'm always around kids. It doesn't bother me. Stop worrying."

She nervously chews her lip. She links her fingers through mine and leads me back towards the little girl's door.

Opening it up just a crack, I can see the sleeping baby in her cot. The name Maeve in pink letters on the wall above.

"She's yours, Jax."

With a rush of adrenaline, my heart jumps into my throat, leaving me breathless. Am I hearing things?

"Repeat what you just said." I can barely get my words out.

"Jax, that little girl in there, she's yours. You are her dad."

I drop my hand from hers, running my fingers through my hair. I stumble backwards. Dad. I'm her dad.

Those dark curls are now vividly in my mind.

My brain works overtime to do the math, two years ago, nine-ish months after that. She would be just over one.

I've missed over an entire fucking year of my daughter's life.

"Jax, are you okay?" Her voice is hoarse, like she's about to cry.

I snap my head up. She's shaking, her eyes welling with tears.

Fuck.

"I-I-Yes. Just give me a second."

There's a glass door out onto a small balcony. Sliding the packet of cigarettes out of my pocket, I offer one to Sofia. She holds up her hand and shakes her head.

I have to use a lot of force to push the damn door open. The railing is so close, it could hardly fit two people.

I light the cigarette and let it burn into my lungs before tipping my head back and exhaling. I had to get some air. The last thing I want to do is say something wrong and fuck this up before I even get the chance.

Sofia and my daughter have been living cramped up in here, fuck.

I want to slam my fists against the iron railings, but I stop myself. Somehow. I just got Sofia back in my life. How the hell am I supposed to be a father?

My heart starts to race and I don't know how to react. I'm furious with myself for letting her go the first time. For missing so much. Yet, I'm petrified.

Everyone around me dies.

What if I can't protect her? What if me being in her life ruins it, like it does for everyone else? I can't do that to her.

To either of them.

Taking one last drag, I flick it over the railing. Sofia remains motionless as I step back into the room. I can sense her hesitation to even come near me. I'm messing this up.

"Sofia."

"Jax." Her voice is barely a whisper, and it hurts.

Striding towards her, I firmly grasp her face, guiding her attention to meet my gaze.

"I'm so fucking sorry, sweetheart," I whisper before closing my eyes and resting my forehead against hers.

"Sorry for what?"

"Leaving you to do this all by yourself."

"We did okay, Jax. She's a little angel, really."

I nod, a lump forming in my throat.

"Did you want to stay with me tonight, meet her in the morning?"

The nerves are clear in her tone.

That little nagging voice in my head tells me that they don't need me. My hands start to shake as I pull her tiny frame against mine. The walls feel as though they're closing in on me. My chest tightens, and I struggle to take in a breath.

I know what I need to do. What I should do.

I just need some damn air.

CHAPTER THIRTY-THREE

SOFIA

My face nestles against his chest, feeling the rapid thump of his heart against my cheek. I can't work out what he's thinking. That tortured look in his eyes before he walked out for a smoke worries me.

He went to a dark place, and I have no clue why.

"I understand if it's too much, Jax. If you need time—"

He shakes his head as I pull out of his tight embrace. I need some space, too. My feelings for him confuse me, they consume me.

"Let me go to my apartment, grab some clothes, and then I'll be back."

His voice drops, and I simply nod my head and give him a small smile. I wouldn't be able to hide the disappointment from my voice if I spoke.

As I look into his dark eyes, I know exactly what he's doing. He can't hide the pain on his face.

He's running.

Even if he might not want to. That's what he's doing.

Hugging my chest, I take a step back to watch him.

His curls fall into disarray as he runs a hand through his hair, his lips flatten with a hint of sorrow.

"Go, then. I'll leave the door unlocked for you."

He shakes his head. "Lock it. I'll use the key you gave me."

"Okay." I'm pretty sure I'll find it in an envelope in my mailbox in a few days.

He steps forward, pressing a soft kiss to my forehead, and I fight the sob that threatens to erupt.

Why does this feel like the end?

I can't look. His heavy footsteps vibrate on the floor beneath my feet. The second I hear the click of the latch, I fall against the wall, smothering my face with my hands.

Was this too soon?

Did I drop it on him the wrong way?

Have I ruined Maeve's chance to have her dad?

My shaky hands wipe the tears flowing down my cheeks. I kind of thought he would be different. That maybe I would be enough for him.

Tipping my head back, I hit it against the sheetrock, taking deep breaths to bring down my blood pressure.

Maybe there's a chance he'll be back. Or that is just a stupid fantasy.

I've dreamt of this day since I gave birth to her. No one seems to bring me to life quite like Jax.

All I can do is wait for him to show me the man he is. I've survived on my own for long enough, except this time, he might just leave my heart broken.

CHAPTER THIRTY-FOUR

JAX

Slamming my front door shut behind me, I head straight to the refrigerator and grab a cold beer.

I almost turned around on my way here in a sudden panic that Sofia might think I'm just walking out on them both.

I'm not.

There's no way I would do that to her. I couldn't break her heart like that.

She didn't do any of this to spite me. In fact, what she has done for me is nothing short of incredible.

And I need to show her that.

I need some space to gather myself. I'm on my own now. I don't have Kai guiding me out of causing chaos in my life.

I didn't trust myself back there, in the heat of the moment, not to ruin everything. So, I did what I do best, get on my bike. It's the only way I know how to think.

Grabbing a bag from the wardrobe, I shove in some clothes.

If I fuck this up, I lose them both. That isn't a possibility.

And that little flutter I get in my chest, just thinking about waking up and cuddling my daughter, tells me everything I need to know.

That I need to get my ass back there. Yet I can't shake that nagging voice in my head telling me I'd be a useless father.

Sliding out my phone, I hover my finger over Nikolai's name, but pause. There is one other person that I look up to that will kick me into gear.

I scroll down to find Frankie Falcone's number and hit dial. I need someone to tell me that I can fucking do this. That I won't ruin them.

"Ah, Mr. Carter. Everything okay?" His deep Italian accent comes through the speaker.

"Uh-Yeah. You?"

"Don't bullshit me with small talk, Jax."

I blink a few times. He was never one to beat around the truth. A moment of silence passes while I find the words to say without sounding like a complete asshole.

"I-I just found out I'm a dad." It feels weird, like I just admitted it to myself.

"Shocker."

I frown. "What do you mean?"

"You knocked someone up in Vegas? What does she want, money?"

"No, Frankie. She's already had her. I have a daughter." I pause. "With Sofia."

"Oh, shit. Jax. When did you find out? You sure she's yours?"

I immediately get defensive. Sofia would never lie about that.

"Yes. She's mine, and about half an hour ago."

"Where are you?"

"Back at my place."

He mutters something under his breath in Italian. "Please don't tell me you found out and ran."

"No? I came back to get some clothes. I'm going back. I just needed a minute."

"Does she know that?"

I can sense the irritation in his voice.

"Well, yeah, I told her."

"What the fuck are you doing calling me? Get your shit and get back there, Jax."

I wince, holding the phone away from my ear. I don't get why he's so pissed.

"Jax, do me a favor. Sit and think about it for a minute. I know you didn't run. I know you'll be a brilliant father. Sofia, she doesn't know any of that, does she?"

There's muffled noises coming from the speaker. I rub my hands across my beard.

Shit.

Zara clears her throat. "Jax Carter, get on that fucking bike right this second."

"Oh, hey, queen Zara."

"Jax. I mean it." She scares me sometimes.

"Okay, okay! I'm going."

Her biting tone calms. "Congratulations, though. A little girl. We can't wait to meet her. What's her name?"

I swallow past the lump forming in my throat. That suffocating feeling is coming back into my chest.

"Maeve."

That was the name above her crib. My little girl is called Maeve. My eyes sting. I'm a dad and I know nothing about my daughter.

"Beautiful." Zara's soft voice knocks me back into the real world.

"Thank you guys. I'll see you soon." I cut the call. Grabbing my bag from the bed, I throw it over my shoulder. Kai would punch me square in the jaw if I didn't go back there and try to be the best dad I could be.

Fuck.

I wish he could meet Maeve, too.

CHAPTER THIRTY-FIVE

SOFIA

Song- Home, Good Neighbours

A SMILE CREEPS UP ON MY LIPS. I CAN SMELL HIS STRONG aftershave before anything else.

My heart races as I open my eyes, rolling over on my bed to face the door.

"You came back?"

Concern flashes across his face as he strides to the edge of my small double bed.

"You've been crying?"

I chew on my bottom lip. My puffy eyes probably give me away.

He kicks off his sneakers and crawls onto the bed, pulling me into his embrace. I rest my head on his chest.

"Why the tears, sweetheart?" he whispers, stroking my hair away from my face.

"I thought I'd scared you off, that I'd messed this up for you and Maeve."

He tuts, sliding himself down the bed while keeping one arm around me.

"You didn't mess anything up. I shouldn't have just left like that. I'm sorry. I was always coming back, I just... panicked."

I blow out a breath as the relief washes over me.

"So." He pauses, and I sit myself up to look at him.

"You would have missed me if I left?" he says with a boyish grin. I playfully tap his chest and he grabs a hold of my hand.

"I might have." I pout at him.

He strokes my face, and I lean into his touch. Suddenly, with him, my worries start to disappear.

"You're not mad at me?" I ask, drawing small circles with my nail on the fabric over his pec.

"What? No? Never. You had my baby, all on your own. You've brought her up and done everything you possibly could for her while I dicked around Vegas. I could never be mad at you for that."

"I tried to find you, you know. It was pretty hard considering I had no last name, and, apparently, you don't exist on social media."

"Well, I do, under the King of Chaos. But I don't even run that shit."

I trail my hand up his neck and frame his face. "I'm happy you came back, Jax. Thank you."

"Your roommate didn't look too thrilled to see me."

Weird. She's the one pushing for me to tell him the truth. I heard her come in a while ago, not that she checked to see if I was okay.

"Ignore her."

I have no idea where this actually leaves us. Jax doesn't seem like the settling down type, the one woman forever kind of guy.

"What are you thinking about in there?" he whispers, moving a tendril of hair away from my temple.

"Nothing, everything. I don't know," I say honestly. "This changes a lot for us, Jax."

My body shivers as his large hands slide down my side, resting on my ass in my shorts.

"Does it?"

I squeeze my eyes shut as he rolls on top of me until his nose is touching mine.

"I disagree. I'm never letting you go again, tigritsa. That doesn't change."

He nudges open my thighs, settling between them.

"Give me a chance to show you, well, both of you?" He tilts his head, his eyes searching mine.

"I think for you, I can break my rules, Jax Carter."

He presses his lips against mine. It's slow and sweet. It's everything. A taste of what our future could be.

Before we can go any further, I break the kiss. He raises his eyebrow at me, running his tongue along his lip.

"We need to get some sleep."

"Fine." He pretends to whine. I bite down on my nail as he sits up, pulling the black top over his head, leaving me staring at that 'v'. Once his jeans and socks are off, he snuggles back into bed, pulling the cover up under my neck.

"Turn around. I'm the big spoon," he teases.

I do as he says, wiggling my ass against his dick. "You might regret that."

"I definitely already do," he replies, sliding his arm over my belly and pulling me flush against him.

"Good night, gorgeous," he whispers, pressing a kiss onto my shoulder.

I wake up to the smell of fresh coffee next to my nose. As I blink my eyes open, I panic, rolling over and finding an empty, yet warm spot next to me in bed.

Grabbing my robe, I rush out of the room. I never oversleep. Ever. I didn't even hear Maeve's usual loud screaming of 'momma' from her room.

I stop as I round the corner to the kitchen, a smile breaking out on my face. Jax is there, sticking his tongue out at Maeve, whose giggles fill the room. He's trying to feed her yogurt in her highchair. I glance over and Anna is standing behind them, resting on the counter with her hands on her hips, a stern look on her face.

"Morning," I call out, and all three faces greet me.

I head straight over to Jax and Maeve, who holds out her arms, doing her little grabby hands.

"Morning, tigritsa," Jax says, with a smile that makes me all fuzzy.

I stop in front of them, not knowing what to do. I can feel Anna's hard stare from here.

Jax makes the decision for me, leaning over and planting his lips on my cheek.

"She doesn't seem to want to eat the yogurt, just play with it," he says, holding up the spoon, which makes Maeve start clapping.

"Yeah, she prefers the making a mess part. She likes feeding herself. She's an independent little madam, our girl." I give him a shy smile.

"Aren't you?" I coo at Maeve, giving her a kiss on the forehead.

"Hey, where's mine?" Jax pouts.

I roll my eyes. He raises his eyebrows, making the blush spread on my cheeks.

Grabbing a book from the floor, I put it on Maeve's

table and turn my attention to Jax, pressing my lips to his, keeping it as PG as possible.

"Much better," he smirks, giving me another peck as he runs his hands through my mess of curls.

"Book," Maeve says behind me.

"She's adorable, Sof," Jax whispers. I can sense the hint of sadness in his voice.

"She really is. Just wait till she learns how to push all your buttons." I wink at him, trying to lighten the mood.

His hand smooths Maeve's hair in a mimic of how he had touched mine. "My tigryonok can do whatever she wants to me."

Tears threaten to spill. He's being perfect. This couldn't be going any better.

"Tigryonok?" I tilt my head.

"If you're my tigritsa, that makes Maeve my tiger cub." He grins.

"Well, that's cute."

I step back as Jax's phone buzzes.

"I gotta grab this," he says, heading for the balcony door. As soon as he slides it closed, Anna clears her throat behind me and I spin around.

"Well, looks like baby daddy took it well."

"Yes, he seems to."

"Good." She pushes herself away from the counter, flipping her blonde hair over her shoulder.

"Maybe he can help us get this place fixed up better."

"He's her dad, not a bank account, Anna." I glare at her.

She rolls her eyes dramatically. "You better get back to work, then."

With that, she walks past me and slams her bedroom door. What the hell was that about? Shaking my head, I pick up Maeve from her seat and give her a cuddle.

"That's your dadda," I say to her, looking at Jax out the window.

She doesn't understand yet. I'm sure it won't take her long.

Putting Maeve down on the floor with her collection of brightly colored toys, Jax beelines towards us.

"I have to work this morning for a few hours. Are you at the restaurant today?"

"No, today is my day off." Crossing my legs, I sit on the rug next to Maeve.

"Good. I'll be back in a few hours. You'll both be here, right?"

I eye him suspiciously. That look on his face tells me he is up to something.

"We will."

He stops as he's leaving with his palm resting on the handle. "Good. I'll see my girls soon."

My stomach flutters. *My girls.*

That is something I could get used to.

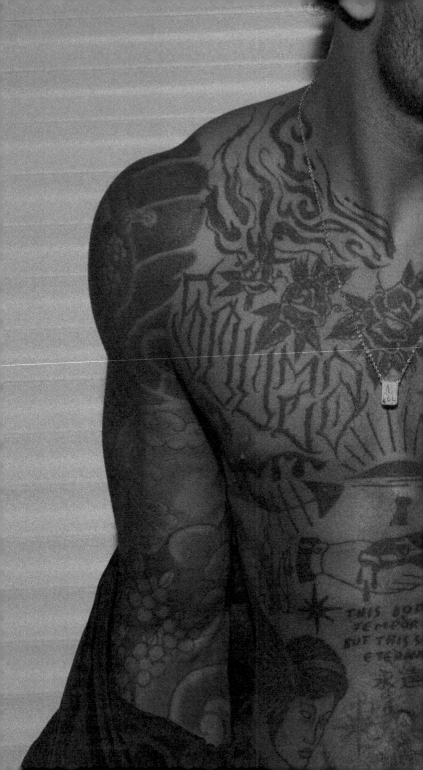

CHAPTER THIRTY-SIX

JAX

"WHERE THE FUCK IS 'SLOT F'?" I GRUMBLE AS I DIG through the pile of pieces on the floor. One wooden dowel and a slab sit closest, but neither of them matches the drawing in the instructions. Painting the wall pink was the easy part.

The driveway alarm on my phone dings. Swiping to bring up the camera, a blacked out Range Rover pulls into view.

I'm just about ready to jump up and rush to the door when I see Nikolai step out of the driver's side, and Alexei from the passenger.

Pushing the mic button on my screen, I can talk to them through the speaker. "I need help!"

Frustrated, I toss my cell aside and pick up the diagram again.

A loud slam reverberates through my house as they rush in.

Nikolai carries a rifle, and Alexei two ivory-gripped pistols. Both have wild eyes and are panting, swinging their barrels around the room.

"What the hell, Jax?" Nikolai drops the end of his gun to point at the floor, his blue eyes narrowing.

Helplessly, I hold up the creased paper and shrug my shoulders. "I can't figure this shit out. I know you have a kid, so thought you would know."

Alexei slides his Colts into the empty holsters under his arm. "You called us here for furniture?" He rolls his 'r' in his thick accent. Shaking his head, he steps over to the kitchen and digs through my cabinets until he finds a bottle of vodka.

"Let's hope we never have to build children things for you, Alexei," Nikolai grumbles as he tosses his AK on the couch. "Fine, Jax. We will prepare your house for your *malysh.*" His thick legs fold under him and he snatches the directions out of my hand.

Alexei slumps into an overstuffed chair across from us with the bottle propped on his thigh. "This is so much trouble. Now, you'll be like Niki. Boring." He lifts the liquor and takes a long swallow.

"I think I'd like that," I admit quietly.

Nikolai looks at me from the side, his lips purse slightly as he gives me a small nod. "It's good." He drops the pamphlet on his lap and picks up an oblong shape and threads it into a long rectangular one.

"No, I don't think—" I hold my hand out to stop him, but shut my mouth when I see him join the two pieces to match the drawing perfectly.

"See? Women are a distraction. Once the novelty wears off, some of the blood leaves your dick and you'll be able to think again." He holds out the base of the crib to me. "Put the screw in those holes. I know you can do that, or we wouldn't be building baby things." The corner of his lip turns up in a wry smile.

"Ha. Ha." I hate that he's right. Obediently, I work on fastening everything together that he gives me.

"Alexei, put that swing together." Nikolai points to the long metal bars leaning against the wall.

Alexei sits up with a frown. His tousled hair falls over his eyes as he lets the bottle droop in his grip between his knees. "And if I don't want to?"

Nikolai glares and throws a ball of tape from the packaging at him.

"Think of it as birth control. Get those built." Nikolai's thick finger points again.

Alexei grudgingly stands and wanders over to pick at the parts. "It says I need a screwdriver with the little X on it." He turns in a circle and sits cross-legged. "I guess I'm off duty." He takes another long pull from the vodka.

I have the tool he needs sitting next to me. "Here." I toss it gently to him.

He catches the end in the palm of his hand, and it punctures the meat below his thumb. "Fuck!"

"Shit, man. My bad." I didn't think I threw it that hard.

He pulls the metal out of his flesh and caps his fingers over it. Standing, he pours a splash of alcohol over his oozing wound. "I'm bleeding!"

"You could have done that over the sink. Go clean up. Then your mess." Nikolai doesn't look up, but continues to assemble the jigsaw pieces of the crib.

Alexei throws up his hands. "When I was in Siberia, I fought a great bear! See this scar?" He points with the bottle to a thin white line on his upper arm. Turning, he saunters down the hall.

Nikolai turns to me. "That is a bicycle accident when he was ten."

Alexei's voice carries from the back of the house. "When I was in Moscow, I killed two men who were trying to mug me! I got a scar on my stomach from it!"

"He ran into a post when he was fifteen because he put a bucket on his head," Nikolai whispers, a smile dancing over his lips.

Alexei arrives back in the living room with a cloth over his thumb and a towel. "But what will this scar be? What bragging rights do I have that I was stabbed while building a swing for an infant?"

I'm trying not to laugh. "Maybe it can be a rattlesnake from the deserts of Vegas?"

Alexei's eyes light up. "Oh, yes. Perhaps you can skewer me again, right next to it?"

"I would volunteer if it stops you from whining." Nikolai hands me the last piece for the crib.

Snapping it into place, I step back proudly. "Hell, yeah. Look what I built."

Nikolai's heavy hand lands on my shoulder. "Careful, or a snake might bite you in the ass for that one." He waves another screwdriver in his hand menacingly.

"We. I meant 'we'." I busy myself with picking up the empty cardboard boxes.

Alexei laughs. "Nikolai doesn't like to share the credit. Well, nothing." He saunters over and hands the bottle to Nikolai. "Remember that one girl in Novosibirsk? She was begging for both of us? And you kicked me out of the room, you bastard." Alexei's silver tooth glimmers in the sun from the window as he grins.

Nikolai settles himself next to the swing and begins bolting the legs together. "She would have been asking you all night if it was in yet. I didn't have patience for that." He waves his hand in an idle gesture, then points to the cradle. "Be useful. Bring that here."

Alexei nimbly avoids stepping on parts to pick up the seat. "It worked out. I found two women at the bar to come back with me."

"*Da.* They both asked that same question all night. Did they get bored and finally just play with each other?" Nikolai gives the swing a test push and watches it rock back and forth.

His eyes unfocus, like he's looking a long way from here.

"I remember doing this before Elena was born." He shakes his head with a frown. "It was a better time."

Standing, he towers over me to hand me my tools. "We have to go, since your 'emergency' is taken care of."

"Yeah, I saw you have the Rover. You guys look like drug dealers in that thing." I jerk my thumb towards the front of the house where they're parked.

Alexei picks up Nikolai's gun from the couch and hands it to the large Russian. "We are today. There's sixty kilos of coke in the back that we took out from under the nose of a Reaper," he giggles. "Like, he was doing a line when Niki stepped out. He looked like he saw a ghost."

Nikolai walks towards the door and shrugs. "He got his fill when I shoved his face in it until he stopped breathing."

"I noticed at the rally the other night those guards looked high. I didn't think Reapers dealt that shit?" I always thought they were just running guns and gambling. They're always lurking around the fights, both in the ring and behind the ropes, taking bets.

Alexei pauses on the porch, letting the sweltering heat roll into my entryway. "You know, the bags all had a 'V' on it, but it isn't like Mikhail's mark."

Nikolai nods. "I have an idea, but will need to run it by my brother."

I follow them outside. "Mikhail might know? Who else runs with a 'V'?"

Nikolai's jaw clenches as he looks at me. "My father."

CHAPTER THIRTY-SEVEN

SOFIA

Jax has been here more than he hasn't for the last few days and seems to be getting a little more comfortable with the new dynamic.

Being a daddy looks good on him.

Maeve seems to adore him already. She shrieks and giggles when he walks in the door, her chubby fingers clasping the air, begging him to pick her up.

But I haven't seen him since yesterday.

It shouldn't make me doubt anything, but it's hard not to. So soon in all of this, my own worries seem to pop up so easily.

Maybe I should start doing things differently. I don't want to spend the rest of my life flitting from one crappy job to the next.

What if this thing with Jax doesn't work out? He's a famous boxer. I know he has women throwing themselves at him.

How long before he gets bored?

He makes me feel so amazing.

But so did Brody, for a while.

A tendril of fear winds through me. I need to prepare myself. So, I spend the morning researching schools and financial options to see what I can qualify for to go back to and finish my degree.

With a bachelor's, it will open the door to get a job in a clinical office while I work on my master's.

There's even a grant application on one site.

What the hell? Might as well fill it out.

It looks like if I take only a class or two per semester, I'd be done before Maeve is old enough to go to kindergarten.

I could give her a better life, even without Jax.

A heavy knock startles me before the door swings open.

His smiling face locks on mine before searching for Maeve, playing on her mat on the floor.

"Hi, my beautiful girls." Jax reaches down and scoops his laughing daughter into his arms.

He's every bit the perfect-looking dad.

It hurts to think this could be temporary. But when he leans over and kisses me, the fire that spreads through my body covers any doubts.

"I have a surprise for you. Well, two. I was wondering first if I could take my girls out on a date?"

His brown eyes light up as he watches me.

A butterfly of excitement flutters in my belly. "That would be nice."

Maeve knots her hand in his hair, making him wince.

"Easy, baby girl. I'll take that as a 'yes' from you, too." He carefully untangles her fingers and slides her down so she's sitting on his hip.

Getting off the couch, I start walking to my room. "I need to change. Where are we going?"

His gaze burns down my body. "You look amazing.

We'll be inside and outside. What you're wearing is perfect."

I glance down at my stained tank top and holey shorts. "Um. I'll be right back."

Swapping into a light green sundress, I brush out my ponytail and throw on fast makeup before meeting him back in the living room.

He's sitting on the floor with Maeve, reading her a book. I think my mascara is running already. He's so adorable.

"Oh, tigritsa…" he groans when he sees me.

A flame ignites in my chest. "Well, let's go before she needs a nap." I wink at him, hoping he gets my hint.

He clears his throat and stands holding Maeve. "Does she have a bag? I'll grab it."

When he slips the strap over his shoulder, I swear I'm dreaming.

A deep purple Land Rover sits in the driveway. It almost has an iridescent look when I walk closer.

Jax walks to the rear passenger door and opens it.

"Let me get the car seat out of my—" My words choke as I see him settling her into a brand new pink one.

He's thought of everything.

"You won't need that one anymore, sweetheart." Jax sticks out his fist, knuckles up. "Hold out your hand."

Hesitantly, I flatten my palm beneath his.

He drops a key fob with a tiny purple tiger charm. "It's yours."

I freeze, staring at him.

"Jax." Words disappear.

His fingers curl mine around the black plastic before he gathers me in his arms. "I want to take care of you. Both of you." His soft lips touch the tip of my nose. "Now, let's get going. It's already getting hot out here." Spinning me, he guides me around the front to the driver's side.

"Jax, I…" I'm still speechless.

He laughs and helps me slide into the cool leather seat. "Push the brake and hit the button."

The engine purrs to life and cold air hits me in the face, shocking me back to reality.

"I can't accept this." My hands rest on the steering wheel.

Is it cooled?

"Don't be silly. It's the very least I can do. You gave me a *daughter*. You should have something safe to drive." He shuts the door.

My throat tightens. I'm his baby-mama.

I guess he did want to be a dad. But does he want me?

Not knowing is hard.

"There's a big kid zone in the casino next to where you work. I thought we could go there?" Jax slides his seat back and stretches his legs out.

"Okay." This thing drives so smoothly. I don't have to slam the shifter into reverse twice to make it stick.

There aren't any warning lights on in the dash, either.

It is a lot better than my car.

I've barely parked when Jax hops out and opens the back, pulling out a new stroller that fits the car seat.

"That's fancy." I sold the one I had to move to Vegas and haven't had the money for a new one.

He grins as he pushes Maeve. "Only the best."

I'm overwhelmed when we get inside by the whirring lights and tinny music playing from every arcade game.

Jax buys a fistful of tickets and pushes us through the crowd to a merry-go-round.

I've heard about this place, but have never been here before. It's too expensive on a waitress's salary.

Maeve is one lucky little girl.

Watching her legs kick out in joy as he holds her on top of the bobbing horse makes my heart feel full.

She'll have everything she wants.

It's uncanny how much they look alike. Same curly brown hair and eyes. Even their smiles are identical.

I do feel a little more at peace now that they are in each other's lives.

Whether or not I'm in his doesn't matter.

"Hey, check it out!" Jax weaves Maeve through a group of people and stands triumphantly in front of a punching game. "I'm gonna win you a prize." He tugs the rings off of his right hand and shoves them into his pocket before handing the man working the booth his ticket.

Jax gives me a wink, pulls his arm back, and hits the bag so hard it sounds like a gunshot.

Maeve startles and starts to fuss, so I hoist her out of her pink ride and hug her to my chin.

A loud buzzer and lights erupt from the top of the machine, pushing her into a full-blown meltdown.

Cradling her teary face into my neck, I coo her as Jax rushes over.

"Shit. I mean, dang it. I didn't think of it." His brow furrows as he rubs her shuddering back. "I messed up. I'm sorry." He clenches his jaw when she pulls away. "Is she okay?" he asks softly, dropping his hand.

"She'll be fine. She's just tired. Nap time comes often when they're little." My lips press against her temple.

Maeve rubs her nose into her hands and across my collar until her sobs lessen into small whimpers.

Jax watches, a look of helplessness on his face.

"Sir? You won. Did you want to pick your trophy?" A bored looking older man with a thick beard calls out to Jax.

Jax reaches out and strokes Maeve's head before walking over to the operator.

Who proceeds to pull down the biggest teddy bear I've ever seen in my life.

It's taller than Jax. His sheepish smile peeks out beneath the giant fluffy nose. "Think this will make her happy?" He raises one oval paw in a wave.

Maeve turns to look, then buries her face back against me.

"She's just tired. That's enough bear for the whole neighborhood!" I tease him, hoping to lighten his mood.

Frowning, he gathers the stuffed arms around his neck like a backpack, and pushes the stroller with his other hand. "Let's go. I have that second surprise, anyway."

By the time we get back to the Range Rover, Maeve is asleep. She shifts easily to her car seat.

This time, Jax takes the wheel.

He's quiet as we wind through the streets. I can feel the Nevada heat pushing through the tinted windows of the mid-morning sun.

Another hot one.

"I feel crappy for scaring her," he mumbles. His knuckles pop as he squeezes his fist on his lap.

"It's fine. She's only one. That's what they do. They startle, they cry, they forget. Next time, it won't be so bad." I'm not used to seeing him brooding.

We haven't really spent a lot of time together. Seeing him withdrawing makes me wish I could comfort him, but I don't know how.

This is all new for him. He's being thrown into parenthood.

I've had a lot longer to get used to it.

A heavy gate blocks our path. Jax pushes a button near the mirror and it slides open before us.

"Where are we?" The house is almost the size of one of the casinos. There's a sprawling yard with a dark modern building placed stylishly in the middle.

"My, I mean, our house." He presses another spot, and a wide bay door garage opens.

I can feel the temperature change as he pulls into the dim space.

"Who else lives here?" There's at least six cars here.

Is that a Lamborghini?

My heart races. I didn't know a boxer could make this kind of money.

"No one else." He gets out quietly and pulls a sleeping Maeve out in her car seat. "I want to show you something." He clicks his tongue piercing against his teeth.

I'm learning he does that more when he gets nervous.

What does he have to worry about? By the looks of this place, he has everything he could ever want.

Or, whoever.

My stomach knots.

He leads me into a foyer that ties in with the front door and into a spacious living room.

Is that a playpen? And a toybox?

"Jax? Why is there foam on all the corners?"

His smile grows as he sets our sleeping baby on the floor and pulls her from the seat. "It's for her. Nikolai helped me make it safe for her."

I spin around, taking it all in. "This is very sweet, Jax."

He reaches out and takes my hand, pulling me with him down the hall.

A nursery, decked in pinks and purples, is filled with a new crib, a changing table, even a rocking chair.

This is too much.

"Oh, wow, this will be great when she stays with you." I withdraw my hand and hug my belly.

"'Stays with me'? Where do you think you're going?" He lowers Maeve onto the crisp sheets of her bed and turns to me with dark eyes.

"I don't think it's right that I'm here. What if you meet someone else? You want your baby mom cramping your style?" I try to wave nonchalantly, but the emotions are getting too hard to hold back.

His palms wrap around my upper arms and he makes me face him. "Why the hell would I want to do that? And you're not just my baby momma, you're mine."

"Am I really?" Searching his eyes, I can't find any shred of doubt in them.

"Damn right. Mine, all fucking mine. I told you, I wasn't letting you get away this time. I meant it." His lips crash against me, silencing any argument I may have had.

It's strange going back to my place, knowing I'm emptying it out.

Jax offered to come with me, but I thought it was better for me to go alone so I could talk to Anna.

"So, that's it? He shows up and you just run to him?" She pushes her blonde hair behind her shoulder.

"You know it's more complicated than that. He's Maeve's father. He needs a chance to get to know her." The good thing about being broke, there isn't much to pack. "Besides, I thought you'd be happy I'm leaving. You've been, well, distant lately."

Anna leans her tall body against the counter and crosses her arms. "Well, I think you should take him for everything you can. Sue him for child support and run."

It's like I don't even know her anymore. "Why would I do that?"

"Just think of everything you can do with his kind of cash? It's the perfect situation. You don't have to stay with him." Her eyes widen and a smile spreads over her face. "Remember, we always talked about buying a villa outside of Cabo? We could do that now, with his money."

I shake my head.

"It's more important that Maeve gets to know her dad. For me, too." Pushing the last of Maeve's toys in my stretched duffel, I set it next to the door.

"You know, it was supposed to be *my* shift that night, Sof. If I had ended up with him, I would have made sure you were taken care of. I've supported you through your wedding disaster, your pregnancy, and now this?" Her hands land on the back of the couch as she lowers her face to be even with mine.

"He has a *Lamborghini*. He can afford whatever you ask of him." As if to emphasize her word, she peels a torn corner of fabric from the upholstery to reveal a spring sticking out. "This is what you're leaving me with?"

I shouldn't have told her about his cars. But I had to when she asked about the new Land Rover I drove.

I'll have to ask him to come over with me next time to pick my old car up.

It will be almost embarrassing parking it with his other expensive vehicles.

"Fine. Whatever. Just don't forget your friends, Sof." She holds out her hand, palm up.

"What? I don't have any cash." Does she think he just threw money at me?

"The key, Sof." Her blue eyes narrow. "I have to find another roommate now."

Shit.

I hadn't thought of that.

"I'm sorry. I'll make sure I cover my share through the end of the month." My lip trembles.

Is this the end of our friendship? Over a guy?

"That'd be nice. You can just cash app."

I drop the worn brass key into her hand and leave before the tears start to fall.

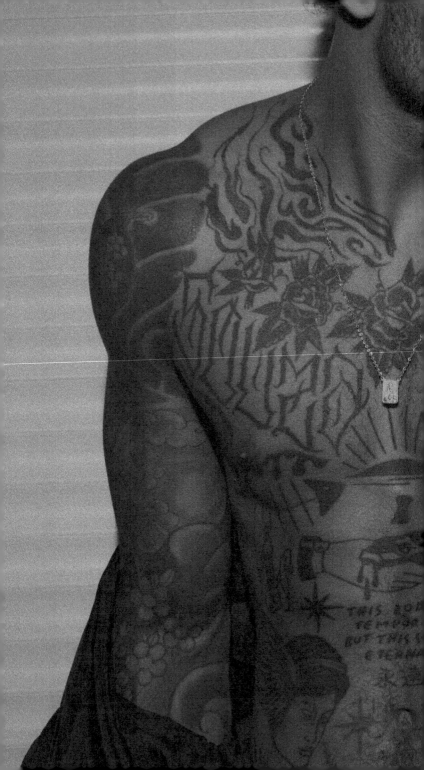

CHAPTER THIRTY-EIGHT

JAX

Song- Mine, Sleep Token

WHILE SOFIA PUTS MAEVE DOWN FOR THE NIGHT UPSTAIRS, I get busy with my 'date night' plans. It's not so easy to organize this when you have a kid, so I thought I'd bring the experience to our home.

Sofia was upset yesterday. I've never wanted to punch a woman before. But hearing how nasty her roommate is, I'm glad she got away from that toxic bitch.

So I thought, tonight, once Maeve is down for the night, I'll cook her a nice dinner and treat her like a damn princess. She deserves it. She might not like being spoiled, but that won't stop me.

My girls will have everything they could ever dream of, I'll make sure of it.

After lighting an obscene amount of candles to illumi-nate the dining room, I dim the lights and scatter yellow rose petals over the table, then place the chilled cham-pagne in the center.

I clap my hands together, admiring my handiwork.

I want to know every single thing about her. Now I have her in my life, I can never let her go.

I'm plating up the pasta into fancy ass bowls as I hear Sofia creep down the stairs. I'm giddy excited, anticipating her reaction.

"Mr. Carter. What is this?"

"This, sweetheart, is our first official date."

I sense her behind me without even turning. She slides her hands under my top, running them up my abs. I'm about ten seconds away from tossing the pasta across the room and jumping her. But I won't. I want this to be special.

"We've done all of this a bit backwards, haven't we?" she giggles.

I drop the spoon in the saucepan and turn to face her.

The smile that lights up her face makes my heart race. The entire reason for my existence is this moment.

"There's no right way to do anything, baby. I'd say the way we've done it is pretty damn incredible, don't you think?" I press my nose against hers and grip her hips.

"I think so. Being here, with you, makes me happy. You really are one of the good ones, Jax."

My eyes close. I'm not. I'm far from it. I never will be. But I'll try my hardest for her.

"No, tigritsa. I'm not a good person at all." I glide my nose along her smooth cheek, down to her neck.

"But that doesn't matter. I will always be your good boy."

She giggles as I suck on her throat and pat her ass.

"Now, it's your turn to be a good girl for me. Go and sit down. We eat. We talk. And then…" I trail off.

She plants her hands on my chest, and her dark green eyes meet mine.

"And then, what?" she asks, biting down on that full bottom lip.

"I fuck you so hard you won't be able to walk tomorrow."

Her lips form an 'o'.

"Or do you want it slow and sweet?"

She taps her chin, pretending to debate which one. I tug her towards me, flush against my body. "Let's do both. Either way, I'm tasting every single inch of you tonight."

She shivers against me as I release her.

"Sit." I follow behind her with the food and pull out her chair for her and then sit in mine. After a day of training for my next fight, I'm starving.

I watch as she takes her first bite, letting out a little moan that has me shifting in my seat.

"Good?" I ask, taking my own mouthful.

My dad used to make this all the time growing up. I thought I'd get sick of it. But, as time has gone on, it reminds me of him, so I keep eating it.

"Mm, yes. Very." She smiles. "So, you like to cook?" she asks.

I twirl my fork in the pasta as I contemplate the answer. "Not really. I was never really home enough to cook."

She nods slowly. "Will you still be away from home a lot?" She starts poking at her food.

I lean over and place my hand over hers. "No. I have a reason to want to be here now. Although, my work does have some less than social hours. I can't help that."

"Boxing? You train in the day, right?"

Leaning back in my chair, I bite down on my tongue. I suppose now is as good of a time as any. Drop the bomb and hope she doesn't run.

"The boxing, yes. I do that during the day. The stuff

for the mafia can be any hour that Mikhail or Nikolai needs me." I watch her closely.

She coughs, dropping her fork. "Excuse me? You are joking, right?" She fixes her gaze on me.

"No, baby. I am not joking. I've done this for years. Back in New York, I was with another family. It's what I do, what I'm good at."

She frowns. "Is that how you've got all of this?" She waves her hands in the air dramatically.

"No. Not all of it. My father died when I was younger. He left me everything he had. Turns out, it was a fuck ton. Between that, the boxing, and the mafia, I've got enough for anything we want."

A few moments of silence pass.

I stuff in another mouthful despite my appetite leaving me rapidly.

"Well, fuck." She blows out a breath and slumps back in her chair.

I can feel the cogs in her brain turning, and it's putting me on edge.

"I don't want to hide shit from you, Sofia."

She fidgets with the hem of her blouse before looking up. "Is Maeve safe?"

"Yes." I don't hesitate in my answer. No one would get close enough to even breathe in her space.

"You promise me?"

"I swear it. Mikhail's operation is solid here. I would never let anyone close enough to hurt either of you."

I keep the issue of Brody's biker gang to myself for now. It'll be taken care of soon.

Picking up her fork, she stabs a piece of pasta and eats it. "What about you?"

I raise an eyebrow at her. "What about me?"

"Are you safe? Should I be worried about you not coming home to me?"

"I'm fine, baby."

"Make sure it stays that way. Jax, I mean it. If I, at any point, feel it's unsafe for Maeve, I'll have to take her away."

I drop my fork and it clatters against the table as I stand.

"No."

"No?" She pushes out her chair and stands in front of me, a grin twitching on my lips.

"It's my job to protect you and our daughter. Let me do it. You don't run from me, Sofia. You know that I will chase you. I'll never stop. But you need to understand something—"

"Oh, do I?" She tips her chin up to me and I lace my fingers around her neck, my thumbs framing her jaw.

"Yes. That I'd give up my own fucking life for you and that little girl upstairs. Without even blinking, I would do that for you. I'll keep you safe. I'll give you everything. Just never, ever, threaten to leave me like that again." It would break me to pieces. I've just found them, yet they consume my every thought.

They are providing me a lifeline I never knew how badly I needed.

"I've lost people who meant everything to me before. I'll never let that happen again." My voice almost shakes as I say the words.

I couldn't protect Kai. People I love die.

But this, I won't fuck up. I can't.

"I hear you, Jax."

Relief washes over me. I release her and step back.

It's not until I look up that I find passion in her eyes as she stares back at me.

"I trust you. Don't break that."

My heart is pounding in my chest, my brain spinning at the dark places it just sent me to.

I run my hand through my hair, trying to regain some sense of control over my own damn mind.

"Never."

She loops her arms around my neck and drags me down, pressing her lips against mine. "Now eat. You promised me a date night."

Stealing another quick kiss, we sit back down and finish off the rest of our food. It's followed by strawberry cheesecake and the rest of the bottle of champagne.

I sit back in my chair, just taking in her beauty as she speaks. Her favorite color is yellow. Her dream is to be a psychologist. Her parents died in a crash when she was eighteen. How can she talk about it so easily? I'm almost jealous. I can barely say Kai's name still. She craved cherry yogurt when she was pregnant with Maeve. She used to do ballet, which explains why her stripper moves were so damn good.

She pauses in her talking and looks down at her hands. "I was thinking, we need to get Maeve's last name changed–to add Carter."

I open my mouth to speak, but the words don't follow. I hadn't even thought about that. Ideally, I want them both having my last name.

"I-I didn't know your last name, so I gave her mine."

She's nervous, shifting in her seat. I nudge closer and rest an arm over her shoulder.

"Hey, it's okay. I'd love that, sweetheart."

"Maeve Garcia-Carter." Her gaze rises to meet mine with a hopeful look. "I kinda assumed you'd have a Russian last name, seeing as you seem to speak it? Tigritsa and all that?"

"Want to know a story?" I whisper into the top of her head.

"I do."

"My real last name is—well, was—Kuznetsov. My dad was Russian, my mom, as you know, half Armenian. So I was Jax Kuznetsov. When my parents split and my dad took me to live with him, he told me I needed an American last name. It was safer that way. So I became Jax Carter."

"Legally?"

"Yep. So Maeve will be a Carter, too."

"A proper family." She looks up at me and beams. "To think, all of this started with a game of never have I ever."

"Best game ever." I lean in, my fingers digging into her exposed thigh. That little black nightdress has been teasing its way up every damn time she crosses her legs.

"Never have I ever eaten out a woman on my dining table."

"Oh, that's good. Seeing as I've been having dinner off of it."

I smirk at her, running my tongue along her jaw. "I've got a better one."

"Hmm, hmm."

"Never have I ever had a woman back in this house."

She pulls back, eyeing me suspiciously. "I don't believe you."

I hold up my hands.

"Truth. I haven't slept with another woman since New York. Two damn years ago."

She blinks at me in disbelief. "There is absolutely no way. You're gorgeous. You're, well, you. Girls must be falling at your feet for the King of Chaos."

"Well, the King had a pretty high standard set by this beautiful, unattainable little redhead. Who left the next morning and took part of his broken heart with her. I've simply been existing. Those women, they didn't spark me back to life like you did. So, I didn't want them."

That night was the first time since Kai's death I felt anything. I clung onto it. I've tried to get this woman off my mind. I've fucked around, but I never go through with it. They do nothing for me. That night with Sofia was all I needed to get myself off.

"No wonder you chased me if I had that effect on you." She sips her champagne, hiding her smile behind the rim of the glass.

"Life changing and unforgettable, sweetheart." I wink.

"It is starting to blur in my mind, Jax. I think I need—"

I don't let her finish her sentence. I knock my chair over in my haste to stand and lift her into my arms, dropping her down onto the table.

"I've had your taste on my tongue for two years. Spread those legs and let me hear how much you love me eating you," I growl in her ear and step between her thighs.

CHAPTER THIRTY-NINE

SOFIA

I can hear Maeve fussing downstairs and Jax telling her that her bottle is coming. I can't help but laugh as I do up the buttons on my blouse.

Another day at the restaurant, but I have managed to get a few applications filled out in the last couple of days. Hopefully, I'll hear back from one of them soon.

Dealing with the hungry general public is not what I want to be doing for the rest of my life.

My chest swells as I walk down into the lounge, finding Maeve settled on Jax's lap, looking up at him as she drinks her milk.

They are too damn cute.

"I wish I could stay here with you two." I fake pout at Jax.

"You don't need to go back there. Quit, stay home with us. You know you want to." He wiggles his eyebrows with a smile.

I roll my eyes. "Jax, unfortunately, I don't have a choice."

He picks up Maeve and props her up on a cushion next to him and starts rifling in his jeans pocket.

As soon as I see the shiny black card, I straighten my spine.

"No, Jax."

If Anna was here, she'd be yelling at me to take it and spend every dime I can. But I'm not like her. I want to work and build something I can be proud of, that Maeve can look up to.

And I certainly don't want Jax to think I'm just some money grabber. I might have birthed his child, but he's already done more than enough to make up for that year he missed.

That wasn't even his fault.

"Tigritsa, take it." He waves the card in the air as I walk away, into the kitchen.

Reaching into the cabinet, I pull out my thermos. If I can save up for a little while longer, I can pay for those college courses.

It's just a matter of time.

"Jax!" I yell as he spins me into his arms. A giggle escapes me when I see the card between his teeth.

I pluck it out and slide it into his back pocket.

"Not happening, Jax. I've got this. I have a plan."

"I bet that plan would move far quicker if you quit that job you hate and could actually focus on it."

That smirk tells me he knows damn well he's right.

"It would. But, still not happening."

I try to turn around, but his hands come down on the counter on either side of me.

"Sofia. I have more money than fucking sense right now. Use it, please, baby. It would make me happy."

He gives me those puppy dog eyes, retrieving the plastic and holding it between us.

"It's nothing. Seeing you doing something you love is everything. Quit. Spend whatever the hell you need to finish your degree. And then, today, instead of working, go and buy you and Maeve a whole new wardrobe."

"We don't need new stuff, Jax."

"Well, how about for my fight tonight?"

"I have clothes," I say sternly.

"You have an argument for everything, you mean." His lips hover above mine. "Take the damn card, Sofia. I'm not joking."

He pulls me into him, circling my waist with his strong arms. "In fact, the more you spend, the better I reward you tonight. How about that?"

I let out a sigh.

Anna's words nag me. I won't become that woman. The first thing I'll do is enroll in that college.

But the reward he's talking about has me clenching my thighs together.

I take the card from between his fingers. The smile that lights up his face makes me feel better.

"Good girl," he mutters against my lips. "And even if you bankrupt my card, which, to be honest, would impress the hell out of me. I'll just sell a couple of my Lambo's."

"You are completely reckless, Jax."

"I prefer the term *chaotic*. It's my quirk."

CHAPTER FORTY

JAX

"Jax, get the fuck back over here!" Grayson shouts across the gym. He flew in for a pre-match training session. After chewing my ass about losing my license, he's now working me until I pass out, it seems.

I glance up from my phone just as Alexei makes a run at Nikolai. I brace myself, sure Niki could pin him to the ground with one hand. But Alexei ducks out of the way, jumps on his back and puts the big fucker in a headlock.

"Tap out."

Alexei's bicep strains against his throat. Nikolai, now red faced, grabs hold of Alexei, who is finding this whole thing funny.

"I got the big one!" Alexei calls out to me and I chuckle.

Grayson watches on, completely unamused. Another notification comes up from my bank and I grin.

She's being a good girl, spending my cash.

A loud thump catches my attention as I find Alexei now on the mat with Nikolai standing on his chest.

"I let you think you'd won."

I shake my head, typing out a text to Sofia.

Not that she's spending anywhere near the amount I'd want her to. But I see that she enrolled in her course, and by the looks of it, bought some shoes.

> J: Keep spending, it's making me horny.

> S: Be a good boy and get back to training.

I bite down on my lip, my cock now pulsing. I can imagine the blush on her face just typing out that text.

"Oooh, you sending spicy messages?" Alexei calls out, walking towards me with a wild smirk, wiping the sweat from his forehead.

> J: Are you trying to get me killed? I'll see you at home...

It's quite possible she will be the death of me.

Locking my phone, I toss it back down on the bench.

"None of your business. You given up? Got your ass beat already?"

He jabs my arm in response, and I chuckle.

"Didn't even feel that."

It's probably the fact I'm numb to most things. Physical pain is nothing to me.

"Jax, let's go. We've got one more hour. You wanna get

yourself killed in the ring? You decided to fight with no fucking rules," G shouts and the room goes quiet.

I swallow, taking in his words. Before Sofia and Maeve, I wouldn't have given a shit. I live, I die. Whatever.

But now, I have a purpose. There's a glimmer of hope for me. Something I am clinging on to. The world isn't as black as it once was. And that is because of my girls.

So Grayson is right. I don't wanna die in the ring, I can't. I have to see my daughter grow up.

"Calm down, I got this."

I duck under the ropes with a new sense of determination.

There is no option to lose this fight. Not anymore.

CHAPTER FORTY-ONE

SOFIA

I MAY HAVE SPENT A LOT OF HIS MONEY, ALTHOUGH MOST of it was on new sneakers for Jax and clothes for Maeve. I did, however, buy an outfit for his fight tonight. With a pair of dream shoes. I'm hoping it is enough to earn my reward. The first thing I did, before I even went shopping, was pay for the enrollment tuition for the next semester. Once I graduate, I'll be paying him back every dollar. Contrary to what Anna may think, he isn't my walking bank account, and I don't want it. But, it is nice, for once, to be taken care of and not have to panic about being able to afford everything for Maeve. For the first time in years, I can actually think about myself for once.

Yes, I'm a mom. But, it's felt like since her birth, that's all I am. I know I'm much more. I love that little girl. I love being her mother. Finding Jax has meant I can claw a bit of myself back.

Laying out my new outfit, I look down at a pair of leather jeans and a lace bodysuit to match my new Louis.

I may have searched for an underground fight on the internet and, after seeing some of the grisly pictures, I'm petrified. For Jax, more than anything. No rules. Just two men beating the shit out of each other. I don't know if I can watch. He wants me there, so I will be there for him.

The door slams shut and loud male voices carry up the stairs. Jax was dropping Maeve at Nikolai's with his sitter, which in itself is giving me anxiety. But if Jax trusts him, so do I.

Heavy footsteps pace up the stairs and my heart races. I've steamed and pressed his shorts and his outfit is out on the bed, with the new high tops I bought him.

"Hi, baby," he growls as he enters the room.

I spin to face him. He has that boyish grin on his lips as he stalks towards me and lifts me into his arms.

"Everyone is waiting downstairs to meet you," he whispers in my ear.

I met them briefly when I was waitressing, but this is different. They know I mean something to him.

"Who is 'everyone'?" My lips purse in doubt.

"Nikolai, Alexei, and Lara."

"Lara?" That provides me some relief, another woman to talk to rather than two scary looking Russians.

"Nikolai's sister. She's fun. You'll probably get along."

"Fun?" I raise a brow at him.

"She has a dry sense of humor like Nik. That's what I mean. So, put the claws away. I'm yours."

He sets me down on my feet. My hands thread beneath the thin fabric of his shirt and rest them on his hard chest.

"I'm not jealous. I was just wondering what you meant by that. Like wild or just a sense of humor." I bite down on my lip and bat my lashes at him. Pulling on his silver chain, I yank him down to me and kiss him.

"Mmm, more," he grumbles, capturing my lips again.

"I need to get ready." I nod towards our clothes on the bed.

He glances over and his eyes narrow. "You didn't spend enough today, and buying me stuff does not count."

"I tried, okay? Look at my shoes. They're more expensive than my rent!"

"Put them on for me."

He pushes the robe from my shoulders and it pools onto the floor, leaving me in just my new red panties and matching garter belt.

"Holy fuck, Sof." His finger slides under the thin strap to my thigh. "How am I supposed to concentrate knowing you're wearing that for me?"

"The soles of my shoes match my panties." I lick my bottom lip, backing away from him, and open the heels out of the fancy box.

I bend over and put the first one on facing away from him.

As I slowly stand and turn back to him, he's running a hand across his face.

"Wow. Look at you, tigritsa. Good enough to eat."

"You think?" I spin to give him a full show. The way he looks at me makes me feel truly beautiful. Something else I'd lost after giving birth.

It's like Jax is slowly rebuilding parts of me I hadn't even realized had tumbled away.

"Stunning. Perfect. Fuck, I'm a lucky man." He closes the distance, his rough hands gripping my hips.

"Are you nervous?" I ask.

He grins. "No, baby. I love fighting. It helps me."

My fingers stroke along his cheek. "Helps you? With what?"

"Just dealing with stuff." He stops and clears his throat. "When I'm in the ring, I forget everything."

"Oh, Jax. I had no idea. Do you want to talk about it?" My hands still, framing his jaw so he looks at me.

He stiffens, so I press a soft kiss on his neck. I don't want to push him, especially not before his fight.

Maybe changing the subject is a better idea. "Hey, we need to get ready. I wanna see my man win tonight. How are we celebrating?"

"By fucking on every single surface in this house, sweetheart."

"You better be victorious, then."

He leans down, running his tongue along my jaw. "Just make sure you don't leave Nikolai and Alexei's side tonight, okay? I can't be distracted in there."

"I promise."

"That's my good girl," he taps my bare ass, making my pussy ache for him.

He looks past me to the bed and cups my cheeks. "You got my stuff ready for me?"

I nod.

Call it instinct, I bet no one has really looked after him. I want to be that person.

"You didn't have to do that, sweetheart. I'm here to take care of you."

He presses a soft kiss to my nose, and emotions swirl in my chest.

"Hey, we're here for each other, Jax. Let me do this."

I'm at home here. We're building a family. With every day that goes by, Jax owns a little bit more of my heart. He's sweet, and he wants to protect me and Maeve.

As my new heels click on the wooden floor, he spins to face me, and leans against the wall, which shows his bulging muscles. He bites down on his knuckle.

"Damn, baby. You're the knockout here tonight."

I giggle, feeling the heat of the blush on my cheeks.

He holds his hand to me and I take it, feeling that spark shoot through me as I do.

Nerves pit in my stomach as he leads me down the stairs, where the strong Russian accents are filling the room.

They all stop and turn as we walk into the kitchen. The big one doesn't change his neutral expression, but the other man does, revealing his silver tooth and the pretty girl next to him, with long straight blonde locks. They both smile at me.

"Guys, this is my girl, Sofia," Jax announces.

"Ah, the girl who turned Mr. Chaos down changed her mind."

"Alexei." The big one scolds him. Jax laughs as he places his arm on my shoulder, pulling me against his side.

"What? Our boy Jax loves the chase." Alexei winks at him. Heat rises into my cheeks.

"They have no idea," Jax whispers in my ear, and that only makes me blush harder.

The blonde woman steps forward after slapping Alexei in the back of the head.

"Pleasure to meet you. I'm Lara." She extends her perfectly manicured hand, covered in diamond rings.

Shit. Is she some sort of Russian royalty?

Awkwardly, I extend my arm and grasp her palm. She bursts out laughing, pulling me in for a hug. "Ignore those asshats. Just stick with me. You'll be fine."

God, is it obvious I'm so nervous?

"Thank you," I whisper back, as she pulls away with a smile.

"Hey, you didn't give me a hug today." Alexei fakes a pout towards Lara. Nikolai glares at him.

I can't help but laugh at their interaction.

"Don't pout, sladkiy. It's not a good look on you," she replies in her thick Russian accent.

I almost jump when Nikolai claps his hands together, announcing our departure.

"We're going in the Lambo. You guys can park next to me when we get there," Jax says. He laces his fingers through mine and squeezes.

Alexei storms forward, and Lara drags him to a swift stop by grabbing onto his shirt.

"Keys. I'm driving," she says, holding out her hand.

CHAPTER FORTY-TWO

JAX

Song- Limits, Bad Omens

WE'RE IN THE UNDERBELLY OF VEGAS. WHERE THE PUBLIC doesn't venture, but where the darkest money comes to play.

There's no weigh-ins, no referee. This is a blood sport, and the crowd is already thirsty for more.

Cash and drugs change hands as I wrap my palms with athletic tape. We don't use gloves, just enough to hold our knuckles closed when we try to bash each other's faces in.

She watches me, her lower lip tucked between her teeth. Sofia's been silent most of the night, staying close, but so distant.

I know she's scared. But she shouldn't be. I'm not.

Some days, I don't care if I win or lose. Dying wouldn't be that bad. The last few years, I fought like I had nothing to lose.

That's changed.

I have my purple-haired tiger, and a baby with my eyes.

There's no doubt I'll win for them. It's a fire inside of me.

Nothing can stop me.

"Remember what you're supposed to do, Jax. No matter what he says." Nikolai's grip is tight on my shoulder as he smears Vaseline on my eyebrows. His thick finger points at me, inches from my nose. "Don't let him get to you. I know you're making this personal. Emotions are—" He turns his head in an obvious glance to Sofia. "—distractions."

I nod as he slides my mouth guard between my teeth.

Mikhail told me to win. But, it's so much more than that.

It's for her. To show the Reapers I can protect her. Brody will be out there. He needs to see that I'm not to be fucked with.

A chant floats over the stands and covers any other noise.

There's a buzz in the air walking towards the ropes. Everyone walking with me slips away as I find the bottom step and slide into the ring.

I recognize the man on the other side. He's the asshole she was dancing for at Brody's party.

It was the night I found her again.

Maybe I should thank him for being such a jerk she came back to me?

I'll repay him in blood. Finally, I'm getting to take out my fury at his hands touching her, when deep down, I knew she was always mine.

The thought tightens my fists in front of my chest as a scantily clad woman walks between us with a placard.

First round.

I catch a glimpse of Sofia standing between Nikolai and Alexei, then send her a wink as the bell dings.

The Reaper stalks forward, his oiled body towering over mine. His arms weave, guarding his chin as we start to circle.

Tossing a few jabs, I start to see his weakness. He drops his elbow to his ribs just before he swings.

Stupid fucker.

The next time he does it, I make my first move. Ducking from his punch, I land three hard blows to his stomach and a solid hook to his jaw as he gasps.

Screams rise from the crowd. Some cheering, others groaning.

His eyes narrow and his nostrils flare as he regroups. Pounding his hands together, he comes back for more.

"You won't win," he grunts before his arm drops.

Landing another volley on him, his dazed look flies around the arena as he backs away.

"That looked like it hurt," I jeer at him.

A tiny cut begins to ooze over his left brow that furrows into a glare. Charging at me, he wildly swings.

When I dance out of his reach, he doesn't relent, but manages to hit me in the stomach a couple of times and a glance off of my temple.

"If you don't drop, we know how to get to you," he grits past his mouth guard. Backing away in long strides, his right arm points out at Sofia.

That motherfucker.

Rage clouds my vision.

How dare he?

I've been playing nice, but that's over.

Raining vicious punches on his head, he falls to the ground, covering his ears with his hands.

It doesn't stop me.

Blow after blow finds its spot.

"Jax!" Brody appears at the edge of the mat, banging his palm.

When I look up, terror etches his features.

"Please! Don't! He's my friend." Brody's fingers stretch out to me as he begs. "For me? Brother?"

I pause, my arm cocked above my head, and I meet his gaze. "I had a brother. He's dead." Dropping my fist, I can feel the skull of the man beneath me cave in with a crunch.

His limbs fall limply with a gurgling exhale.

Brody's yell climbs louder than the crowd, and he claws out, trying to drag himself into the ring.

Knox, his arm still in a sling, grabs him by the belt and holds him back.

"You're going to pay!" he screams, red faced with spittle flying. "And your fucking bitch!" His guys wrap around him and pull him back into the crowd.

"Jax!" Nikolai bellows from behind me. "Time to go!" His foot braces on the bottom rope as he gestures for me to hurry.

Alexei is ushering a wide-eyed Sofia out ahead of me.

Beer bottles fly past us, thrown from the stands.

"I guess I took care of their favorite," I mumble as I duck another empty, narrowly missing my head.

"That was the idea." Nikolai propels me in front of him. I can feel his hand twitch as he's hit by the makeshift projectiles, but the pressure never changes.

"Get your shit, get your girl, get the fuck out. We got your back." Alexei shoves my duffel in my hand that holds my street clothes, then drags Sofia up.

She's walking stiffly, like a wooden doll.

I think she's in shock.

"Go. My turn to fight." Alexei's silver tooth glimmers in his wide grin. His hair falls in front of his wild eyes before he turns away to stand next to Nikolai, blocking the hall from the arena.

"Sof? Come on." When I tug her to follow, she moves like her legs aren't working.

Shit.

"I'm going to carry you if you don't hurry!" I dip my shoulder to pick her up, but her hands brace against me.

"Don't touch me. You're covered in…" Her words trail off as she stares at me.

I glance down. Blood and gore is splattered across my chest and arms.

Nasty.

"Fine, I'll clean up later." Wrapping my hand around her wrist, she lets me lead her outside to the car.

"I'll drive while you wipe yourself off." She snags the duffel from me and begins to rush around the front of the Lambo when she stops.

Brody and two of his buddies appear out of the shadows.

"You fucked up, Jax." Brody's voice cracks. "First my girl, then you shot my dad, then you kill my best friend. We could have been family, man. You took so much from me." Tears well and spill over his cheeks.

Grabbing Sofia, I pull her behind me. He's broken. I know what men like that can do.

I am one.

Now he knows how I feel.

Losing a best friend is an agony I'll never get over.

Kai should be here.

Maybe there's a fucked-up piece of me that thinks he deserves to feel that pain, too.

Brother.

A fate worse than death. For the pain he's inflicting on

people. He broke Sofia's heart. And the dead man in the ring threatened her.

To my face.

"You're a piece of shit, Brody. I don't treat people the way you do. Using them. Betraying them. Your buddy threatened my girl. If you think I'm not gonna bash his head in for that, you can be next." My body quivers with adrenaline as I watch the two guys next to him.

"She's a whore." His sadness shifts to anger. "I'm glad she's not my wife. It would have been the biggest mistake of my life."

Her hand tightens on my arm.

"I'm going to reunite you with your dead fucking friend if you don't shut the hell up," I growl. Every nerve ending in my body feels like it's on fire.

Brody pats his companions with the back of each hand to their chests. "Not now, boys. I have other ways." His brown eyes narrow as he focuses on me. "You're going to wish you stayed on my good side, *brother.*"

CHAPTER FORTY-THREE

SOFIA

Song- Give, Sleep Token

"Jax," I hiss, yanking his arm and notice the tension in his muscles.

Brody's smirk sends a warning signal, and I can practically hear Jax's boiling rage about to explode. I know Brody well enough to see he's doing this on purpose. He wants me to think Jax is a monster. I need to get Jax away from this.

With a firm grip on his forearm, I use all my strength to pull him back towards me.

"Look at me, Jax. He isn't worth it. Take me home."

His nostrils flare as the gym door crashes open behind us. Out barre the Russians, Lara sandwiched between the two men. Alexei's hair is a wild mess as he stalks over to Brody, his eyes filled with a manic intensity.

And, of course, Brody and his friends run toward their bikes.

"Fucking pussies!" Alexei shouts after them, wrapping an arm over Lara.

"Get in the car, Jax. Now." I keep my tone firm, and point to his Lamborghini behind us. I don't want to sound like a mom, but he needs a kick in the ass.

Ignoring the anger clouding in his eyes, I go up on my tiptoes and press my lips against his, disregarding the blood and whatever else stains him.

It's enough for him to relax against me.

"I'm going, I'm going." He smirks. His voice is filled with playfulness as he opens up the driver's side door for me and then smoothly settles into the passenger seat.

"If I crash this, it's on you," I say, pressing the ignition and it roars to life.

"Cars can be replaced, baby. Just be careful with her. There's a lot of power."

Great, that gives me confidence as I tap the accelerator and it shoots forward.

After a few minutes, I get the hang of it as Jax is wiping his chest with a t-shirt.

I don't know what to say to him. He killed a man with his bare hands in the ring. Hell, he would probably have done the same to Brody if I wasn't there.

But, as I glance over and see that he's watching my every move, it changes nothing about how I feel about him. I just want to know how his mind works. What made him snap?

I saw it happen. After the guy pointed at me, Jax flipped.

"Why'd you kill that guy?" I ask, keeping my eyes on the road.

"He threatened you," he replies, clicking his tongue bar.

"So, let me get this straight. A guy simply says some things about me and you cave his skull in?" I blink, shaking my head, trying to wrap my head around his thought process here.

"Yep, and I'd do it again. I told you I'd protect you, that you're safe with me, that means from anyone. I think I made that clear."

I chew on the inside of my mouth. "Yeah, I think they got the message, Jax." I pause. Still reeling from his words in the ring.

"What did you mean you had a brother that died? Brody never mentioned another brother?"

I sense him stiffen beside me. I glance over and his jaw is tight.

"Kai. He was my best friend. My only real brother in this life. He died just before I met you in New York."

It's almost as if he stopped before his voice broke and everything starts to click into place. His grief is still eating at him.

"I'm sorry, Jax. That must be hard."

With a sharp nod, I sigh as he places his bloodied hand on my thigh.

"Are you mad at me?"

"I'm not, Jax. I guess it might take me a while to get used to this. As long as you always tell me the truth, we will be fine. Okay?"

"Always, sweetheart. No secrets. I'm sorry if I scared you."

Cutting the engine, I pull into our driveway and turn to face him before responding.

"I'm not scared of you. Don't get me wrong, that whole thing was terrifying. I know you'd never let anything happen to me."

As he strokes my cheek, I feel a wave of relaxation wash over me.

"Never."

He takes us inside our home, and without hesitation, I head straight to the freezer to find ice. I can feel his eyes on me as he stands by the counter, his gaze never leaving my movements.

"Let me see your hand."

With a wide grin on his face, he proudly displays his bruised and battered knuckles. I pick up the left, pressing the ice over the swelling already starting to show.

He lets out a hiss, which makes me struggle to suppress a giggle.

"This hurt?" I touch another open cut with the cool cloth.

"I'll heal," he grits.

I nod, picking up the other hand, which is even worse than the first. "Both of them, seriously?"

"Why? You worried I can't get you off with them for a few days?"

My cheeks instantly burn. "Don't try to distract me, Jax Carter. I'm looking after you."

As he leans closer, his mouth glides along the curve of my throat, igniting a tingling sensation.

"It's my turn to look after you, sweetheart. My tongue and dick work just fine."

"Remember what you promised me earlier if you won?" I bat my lashes at him and bite down on my lip.

I squeal as his chair goes flying, and he throws me over his shoulder, making me bounce with every step he takes. "I've got a fuck load of adrenaline running through me. Are you ready for me, tigritsa?"

I playfully smack his butt and slide my hand under his boxers as he jogs up the stairs and takes us into the bathroom.

Before he sets me down, I slide my finger between his ass, making him jump.

"Oh, you're going to get it for that."

My back presses against the tiles as he switches the shower on, which pours over us from every angle in the ceiling.

"Bring it." I tip my chin up, watching as the blood that covered him fuses in the water and washes away.

A darkness flashes across his eyes before he slams his lips over mine and his fingers curl around my throat. "I've been so bad, Sofia. Want me to be bad for you, too?"

I nod, my chest heaving as he unbuttons my leather jeans, sliding his hand under my panties.

"Good girl."

CHAPTER FORTY-FOUR

SOFIA

Song- Slow Down, Chase Atlantic

As I CLICK THE FRONT DOOR SHUT BEHIND ME, THE SOUND of a woman's gentle laughter reaches my ears, causing me to pause. As I stomp through the hall towards Jax's voice, my heart rate quickens with each step. I had my enrollment day to finish my psychology degree, which has just about fried my brain. All I want to do is cuddle up to Jax and Maeve and relax.

I blow out a heavy breath when I see Jax with Maeve on his shoulders, bouncing her around with Lara and Alexei laughing on the couch.

A smile grows on Jax's face as he spots me and rushes over, causing Maeve to erupt into a fit of giggles.

"Let's get Mommy," he growls.

Playing along, I act scared and start to run, my footsteps echoing in the room. I can't resist turning to see Maeve's delighted expression as she pretends to chase me around the couch.

As he gently lowers her onto the floor, she sprints

273

towards me. Without hesitation, I scoop her up and tightly embrace her.

"Hey, you two." I kiss her head as Jax's hand slides around my waist and he pulls me close, dropping his lips to mine.

"I didn't come here to watch porn," Alexei whines before Lara slaps him on the back of the head, causing him to spit his lollipop out of his mouth.

"It was just a kiss. Maybe if you upped your game, you might get some of those," Jax shouts back.

"I prefer their lips on my dick. Thank you." Alexei's wild laughter erupts.

With Maeve on my hip, I sit on the couch next to Lara.

"You guys want a coffee or something?" I ask, bouncing Maeve up and down on my knee. Jax steps in front of me and lifts her up into his arms.

"You need to go get yourself ready, sweetheart," he says with a mischievous grin. Running my hands through my hair, I already feel the heat spreading up my chest from the way he's watching me.

"What for?"

I trail my gaze up his clothes and furrow my brows. He's in his leather pants, boots, and a tight black tee.

"A date."

He looks proud of himself. There is no way I could say no to that face.

I look over at Lara and Alexei, who are both grinning at Jax.

"I'm babysitting," Lara confirms.

Alexei clears his throat. "We, you mean, no?"

She laughs. "No. I have no idea why you followed me here. I'm babysitting you and Maeve."

He huffs, pulling out a pack of cigarettes, offering one out to Jax.

"I'm good," Jax says, holding up his hand and shaking his head.

I stand and go up on my tiptoes, lightly brushing my fingers along the smooth leather on his thigh.

"Does this mean I finally get to ride the biker tonight?" I whisper.

As I push away, he chokes on a cough. I can't help but laugh at Jax's open mouthed expression while I make my way towards the stairs.

Holding on to Jax as tight as I can, now that we've been on the road for a few minutes, I'm way more relaxed. There is just something about seeing him on his bike, and being pressed up against him, that has me all kinds of turned on.

The roads are clear as we speed along. I slide my hand under his jacket and shirt, trailing my fingers along his abs, traveling south towards the hem of his tight riding pants.

Pushing my chest harder against his back, I start massaging his thigh.

"Unless you want us to crash, you gotta stop." His voice comes through the speaker in my helmet.

He would never put me at risk. He's just going to have to concentrate for me.

"Just keep your eyes on the road. Don't tell me this isn't a fantasy of yours?" I reply, working my way to the zipper and cupping his hard dick.

His groan comes through the headphones, which only spurs me on. He leans back, his hand gripping behind my knee, which gives me access to release him in the tight space and wrap my palm around him.

"This is a really fucking bad idea." He trails off as I start pumping his cock a couple of times.

"A bad idea? Or a really, really hot one?" I tease.

"Both," he grunts.

I can hear the frustration in his tone. I know it's killing him, not being able to get to me. He can't take his eyes off the road. Right now, he's at my mercy. And it's the sexiest thing I've ever experienced.

"You're being such a good boy."

A growl escapes him. I can't even miss it on the speaker and excitement rushes through me, thinking about what he's going to do to me.

"As soon as we stop, you're going to pay for this, sweetheart."

I pump him harder, running my thumb over the tip to wipe up the pre-come.

"That's exactly what I'm counting on," I reply, squeezing my thighs tighter around him.

He comes to an abrupt stop at the edge of the lake and kicks out the stand. On shaky legs, I hold on to his shoulders and get off the bike. I don't even have a second to take in the sunset as his arm shoots out, and he tugs me back by the elbow.

A gasp escapes my lips as his palm glides down the bare skin of my stomach, effortlessly unbuttoning my jeans and slipping beneath my panties.

He tugs me towards him by the pussy and flips up his visor and then mine. His dark eyes are filled with one thing: pure passion.

"You thought I'd let you get away that easy?" he says in a low tone.

I swallow, looking around. My eyes are drawn to the rug on the ground, where a bottle of wine and two glasses are arranged amidst scattered yellow flowers. The candles dance in the breeze. He did all this for me.

"Here? What if someone sees us? Anyone could turn up!" I protest.

My heart races with a mix of fear and excitement. I shuffle my legs apart and his finger slides along me and as he pushes it inside, a moan escapes me.

"That's what makes this so hot, baby. The fact you're already soaking and fucking my hand tells me you want it, too."

I look down and realize that my hips are already grinding against his grip, like a complete slut for him. With a slight shift, he adjusts himself and lifts me onto the bike, so I'm sitting on it, facing him. I wrap my legs around his waist, feeling his strong muscles beneath my touch.

As he helps me out of my helmet, I hold my breath.

With a firm grip on my chin, he forcefully pulls my face towards his.

I scoot my butt so I'm closer to him, wrapping my arms around his neck. He thrusts his fingers deeper inside me and curls them to hit the spot that has me panting.

His dick presses against my core, and a grin twitches up on my lips. There's no one here. Just us.

"Never have I ever had sex with a biker on his bike before," I say with a grin.

"And I'll be the only one."

I nod slowly, feeling a slight tingle on my bottom lip as I bite down.

"I've heard there's three ways to ride a biker?" I slide my hands under his leather jacket and down the front of his body, cupping his hard cock. His groans being muffled by the black helmet only spurs me on more.

My breath catches in my throat as his hand suddenly

tightens around my neck, the sound of rushing blood drowning out all other noise.

"There's five ways to ride a biker, sweetheart. I'm going to show you all of them."

I blink a few times, I'm so caught up in him, my brain doesn't give a crap about numbers.

"Five?" I question. "So, fingers, face, cock, bike, and what?"

I'm completely blank on the missing one.

"Thigh, baby. On my lap. You're going to rub that perfect cunt all over my leathers until you get yourself off. And do you know what the best part is?"

"What's that?"

"There's no one around *yet*, so you can scream my name as loud as you like." His eyes squint as he smiles beneath his mask.

I'm completely turned on. I can't say I've ever got off on someone's leg before. But with Jax, I'm pretty sure he could get me off without even so much as touching me.

"Let me get those jeans off."

I do as he says, lying back on the bike. As he pushes up my top, a burning heat spreads as he runs a finger along my stomach and swiftly undoes my pants, peeling them down my legs with my panties. Leaving me completely exposed to him.

A deep growl rumbles from under the helmet. "So fucking beautiful, Sofia. And all mine to enjoy."

He leans over me, lifting me under the arms so I'm back on his lap. I shift into position to straddle his thigh. As my pussy connects with the smooth, cool leathers, I let out a little moan.

Holding myself upright around his neck, I roll my hips, and his fingers dig into my ass.

"Look at you, making a mess all over my thigh."

He gently lifts my chin and then removes my leather jacket, allowing the gentle breeze to caress my sensitive skin. As his fingers lightly trail down my arms and he looks into my eyes, any shred of embarrassment I could have had disappears.

Not when he's looking at me like I'm the hottest woman he's ever laid eyes on.

"That's it, baby. Such a good fucking girl for me, come all over my leathers," he praises and slaps my ass. I tip my head back and he places his hand around my throat, but doesn't tighten his hold.

That alone puts me on the edge of exploding.

"J-Jax, I need more." I sound like I'm begging, but I am. I need more of him. I need him to consume me completely.

"Damn, Sofia. You're like a fucking dream."

With a hand on my hip, he maneuvers me so I'm wrapped around him again.

"Hold on to the handles, on your stomach, legs on mine," he commands.

I do as he says as best I can, tightening every muscle to stay in position with my ass in the air and my stomach resting on the seat.

I search behind me. It's even hotter seeing him still in his helmet as he has his way with me. His palms travel up my thighs. The anticipation is nearly killing me. I'm aching for him.

"Please, Jax, baby."

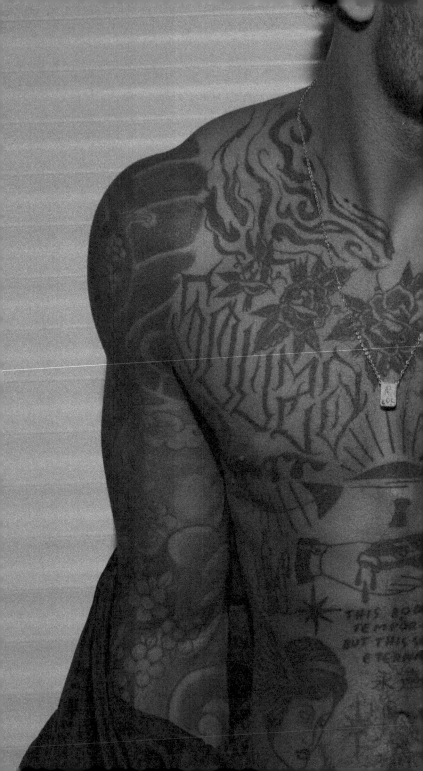

CHAPTER FORTY-FIVE

JAX

Song- RIDE, Chris Grey

WITH A VIEW OF HER ASS, AND HER RESTING OVER MY BIKE squeezing the handles, I swear this is my every fantasy come to life.

As I tease her entrance, her legs quiver on me and I have to bite back a moan.

I slowly sink two fingers inside her, all the way to the knuckle, and she cries out when my thumb circles her clit.

"Holy shit, Jax."

Every time she moans my name, I lose another bit of control.

"Go on, sweetheart. Ride my hand. Let go for me."

She drops her head down and I thrust harder inside her.

"Don't hide from me. Tell me how good they feel inside you."

Her words come in breathy gasps. "So good, Jax. You're too good."

I grab her ass in one hand, sliding my soaked fingers out and up to circle her tight hole.

"You ever done this before?" I really hope she says no, that I can be the first one to do this.

"N-no," she says almost breathlessly, and my dick is so fucking hard I can't think straight. No way is she ready for me to fuck her there today. Soon, but not now.

"Are you going to let me eat your ass, baby?"

She nods. As quick as I can, I pull off my helmet and drop it onto the ground, shaking out my sweaty hair. Collecting a good amount of saliva on my tongue, I bring her butt back to me, spread her open, and spit. Grabbing her under the thighs and taking the weight of her body, I bend down and with one slow lick along her pussy; I work my way back and circle around her puckered hole.

Her legs are shaking violently in my hold, and I can't help but get a thrill at how she's falling apart.

"You like that?" I ask.

I can't make out her answer, so I lick again with the tip of my tongue. "Words, baby."

"Yes, Jax. Fuck," she says through gritted teeth.

Her hips buck against my face, and I suck on her pussy. She's so sweet. So perfect.

I'm desperate to be inside her. I want to watch her come all over my dick, and feel her pussy milk me for everything I have.

With one final lick and a slap on the ass, I flip her around. Her flushed face and sparkling eyes have me moaning.

"Time for you to ride my cock, tigritsa. Show me what you've got," I say with a smirk, knowing full well I could very well come as soon as I sink inside her. I'm that pent up and ready for her.

She uses my shoulders to lift herself up, aligning herself with me, and then she lowers herself down.

"Fuck," I hiss.

My body tenses instinctively as her fingers grip my neck tightly, and I can't tear my eyes away from her hooded gaze.

"This is what you want?" she purrs.

I pull her closer, wrapping my arm around her back, and my lips find the smooth skin of her throat. "Yes, baby. Just like that."

Her rhythm intensifies, and she leans on my chest for stability, her body weight pressing against me as she rides me. As her nails dig into my flesh, I feel myself getting lost in the pure ecstasy that is Sofia.

"Kiss me," I groan.

Her legs tighten around my hips and she lowers herself all the way to the base. Fuck, I nearly see stars as her lips find mine and I deepen the kiss.

"Come in me, Jax. I want to feel you."

Holy shit. Her words cause me to lose control completely. Wrapping her burgundy curls around my hand and gripping her hip, I thrust up into her and push down on her shoulders so I'm as deep as I can go. Over and over again. Her screams fill my ears. Nuzzling my face against her neck, I erupt inside her harder than I've ever come before.

It's like I've just died and gone to heaven.

My lungs burn as I lift her to keep milking everything I have out of me. I want her so full of me it drips down her thighs.

I hold her close, her head pressed against my shoulder, and I savor the feeling of her in my arms. And we just stay there, my cock twitching inside her warmth.

I pull back and frame her beautiful face with my hands. "You are perfect, sweetheart."

It's like without her, I can't breathe.

She is the one who anchors me, gives me a reason to claw my way out of the dark. When I am with her, the world is calm.

It's like everything stops screaming inside my mind. The second she touches me, it dissipates into nothing but her.

Stroking her flushed cheek, she smiles at me and my heart races.

Yep. She's the one.

"I don't want to move," she whispers.

"Then don't. But all your favorite snacks are down there. I know I could do with something before I take you again."

She giggles and I tighten my embrace.

I could stay like this forever.

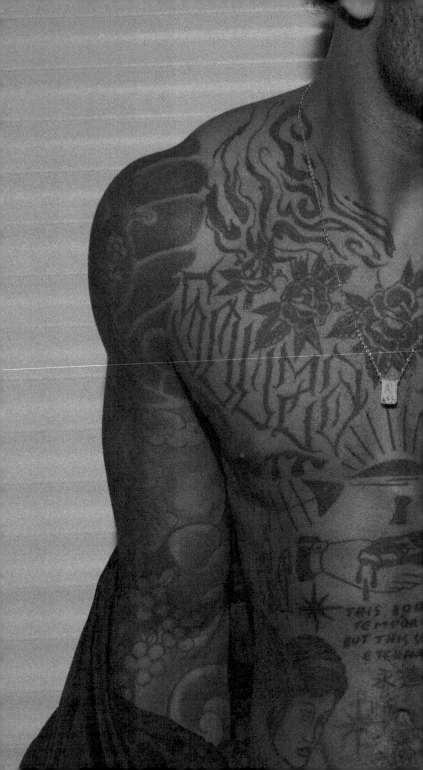

CHAPTER FORTY-SIX

JAX

Song- Godzilla (feat. Juice WRLD), Eminem

Nikolai lets his wrist hang over his steering wheel as he stares at his phone. "Looks like Enzo has a project for us." He flips the screen around so I can see the texts. "We'll pick up Alexei, first."

Reapers have been spotted with another load of coke. Enzo sent a picture of the truck and license plate.

The cell dings in my hand as Nikolai pulls out in the street. An update from a traffic camera spotted their vehicle heading north through Vegas.

"Didn't your brother say he wanted more info the next time they got drugs in?" I wasn't with them the last time they took some from the Reapers, but I was there for the ass chewing that Mikhail dished out for not taking advantage of the information they could have gathered.

Nikolai grunts.

None of us liked getting scolded. But, I see the point. He needs to know who's pushing the narcotics to the

287

Reapers when we've effectively blocked most of their income sources.

I guess it's why they've been acting more bold lately.

Alexei cackles as he crawls in the back seat. "Finally! I can't wait to slice and dice some of these fuckers."

Nikolai holds up a finger, pointing towards the ceiling of his Hellcat. "Only *after* we find out where they are getting their supplies."

Alexei leans forward, his head jutting between our shoulders. "Okay. But when is the time up? Ten minutes? Twenty? I need to know how long I have to wait before I can cut out their hearts." The car bounces as he jumps up and down, his back pressing against the roof.

"Knock that shit off," Nikolai growls. "Or I'll make you stay in here while Jax and I have a discussion with them."

"Talking?" Alexei stills. "Is that what it's called in English?" He leans away, his arms stretching across the backrest. "Then I can't wait to exchange words."

I can hear Alexei muttering under his breath. It almost sounds like he's reciting the dictionary.

"Turn here." I direct Nikolai while watching the updates from Enzo.

We're in a section of Vegas most people don't see. Dilapidated buildings, potholes, and overgrown lawns pass us as Nikolai slows down.

Watching the driveways and alleys, I spot the rear of the truck sticking out of a rundown building that looks like it used to be a mechanic's shop.

Nikolai parks a block past so we can sneak up on them.

Darting behind worn fences and forgotten, broken down vehicles, we manage to work our way close enough to look in the windows.

Waving to Nikolai, I hold up two fingers. That's all the men I can see inside.

He nods and disappears around the corner.

A scream rips through the hot afternoon as Alexei barges through the front door, startling the two men bent over the crates.

He leaps onto a box, pointing his pair of pistols in their faces, all while keeping up his deranged keening.

"Alexei," Nikolai says as he walks in calmly behind him. "You're going to shatter the windows if you don't stop."

"I got them, Niki! Time to talk!" He leaps up and down like a chimpanzee before landing on the dusty floor. "On your knees, motherfuckers!" Alexei screeches, pressing the muzzle of his gun into the forehead of the closest wide-eyed Reaper.

Nikolai shakes his head and steps closer to me. "Jax, make a quick sweep. I'll get these two tied up before Alexei makes us deaf." He winces as Alexei makes another hawkish sound from behind him.

It only takes me a few minutes to clear the area before I'm back inside.

"Well, at least you stopped yelling." I look at Alexei as he is opening up the boxes.

Cellophane wrapped bundles are stacked inside. Each one has a sticker with an embellished letter "V" on it.

"Vacation. Visitor. Various," Alexei mutters, pulling the packages out and stacking them in our duffel bags. He turns to me, his silver tooth gleaming. "I'm practicing my English before I take it out on them." His thumb jerks over his shoulder at the two bound and gagged men kneeling on the concrete.

"Did they tell you where it came from?" I ask Nikolai.

He's working on tying a rope over one of the old car lifts. "*Niet.* They seem to want Alexei to do all the babbling." He paces over and grabs the taller of the two captured and drags him over to his makeshift noose.

He loosens the tie around the biker's mouth and slides the lanyard beneath his chin. "I'm not going to give you many chances to talk since I have your buddy, too." Nikolai tightens the slack on the line until the guy's toes are just barely touching the floor and his eyes bulge manically.

I whip a chair over and straddle it so I'm leaning on the back. "So, who's supplying you?"

Sputtering, the Reaper tries to answer. "I don't…know."

Alexei saunters over. "Where did you pick these up?" He waves one of the tightly wrapped kilos in front of the strung up man's face. "No answer? Let's start with the clues…" Alexei pulls out a long knife. "I want to teach you words. V is for violence." He lunges forward and drags the tip of his blade from the left shoulder to the middle of the chest. Then, from the right side, to meet his mark in the middle.

The scream echoes inside the cavernous room.

"See? What other things start with the letter V?" Alexei's voice takes on a sing-song quality as he dances in front of the sobbing man.

Blood drips down to puddle beneath his feet, struggling to keep his weight off of his neck.

Nikolai wanders to the other kneeling Reaper, brandishing a weapon that looks identical to Alexei's. "I want to see if I can make you cry as loud. Do you think I can?" He wiggles the gleaming edge beneath the chin of the older enemy.

"Fuck you," he spits. "Knox is going to kill you all for what you're doing."

"Knox is a pussy. I made him fall like a child with one teeny tiny bullet." Nikolai leans back and thumps himself on the chest. "I've been shot with a bear gun and still stood and fought."

My eyes flick to Alexei, who nods enthusiastically.

Jesus.

"I need to know who is supplying. Or I'll ask for Alexei to assist me." Nikolai squats and rocks forward.

"Jax? Can you soften this one up a little?" Alexei steps back from his hanging victim and gestures at the sopping belly.

"Gladly." My first punch cracks a rib. The next hits him hard enough that he stops breathing for a moment.

He gasps like a fish as his lips turn blue.

Nikolai slices into number two, but that one doesn't make nearly as much noise. "Alexei, I need your help. I think this guy knows more than yours."

Alexei grins at me. "I can do that." With a wild look, he reaches behind his unconscious mark and saws loudly with his serrated edge.

Tossing something at Nikolai, it takes me a moment to realize what he's done.

A dismembered hand floats through the air and lands with a messy thump next to Nikolai's foot.

The kneeling man starts to hyperventilate, fixating on the lifeless limb.

"Alexei, is this an English thing?" Nikolai raises an eyebrow as he looks down.

Giggles erupt. "I gave you a hand." Alexei is laughing so hard he's bent over, clutching his knees. "English is fun."

Nikolai picks up the body part by one finger and dangles it in front of the man's paling face. "You will end up in pieces. Do you want to be alive when it happens, or a fast death?"

Vomit spews from the guy's quivering lip, making Nikolai jump back.

"You're not making a very good case for yourself. Maybe I should make you lick my boot clean first?" Dropping the chunk of flesh, the giant Russian wraps his palm around the back of the man's neck and shoves his face into the fetid stomach contents. "Tell me the name of the contact, and I will end this."

"Kirill," he grunts into the frothy bile against his mouth.

Alexei lets out a groan. "Oh, damn. Time for cleanup." He runs his knife over the throat of the hanging man at the same time as Nikolai stabs his blade through the skull of the Reaper at his feet.

The red puddles merge into the old oil drain in the middle of the floor.

Nikolai stands, wiping the steel before sliding it into his sheath. "Jax, let's get this loaded while Alexei works. He gets messy."

As we finish loading the drugs into Nikolai's Hellcat, Alexei shoves the last of the pieces of body into the back of their vehicle.

Following Alexei through the streets of Vegas, he heads directly towards the club that the Reapers call home. Leaving the truck in drive, he dives out the door and then runs to where we wait, diving into the backseat just as it crashes into the side of the building.

"Go!" he yells, still laying down.

Dirt and rocks fly as we're thrown back from Nikolai accelerating us away.

"I'll drop this off with Mikhail. He will be happy with a name." Nikolai rolls to a stop outside my house.

Alexei crawls over the seat as I get out, then plops himself down.

"Alexei? You got blood and shit all over the inside of my fucking car!" Nikolai growls before the door slams shut.

I can hear Alexei laughing through the glass as they pull away.

It was a productive day. A month ago, I'd be heading towards one of the bars to have a few drinks to unwind.

But, *my family* is waiting for me.

CHAPTER FORTY-SEVEN

SOFIA

Song- Home, Good Neighbours

JAX WRAPS ME UP IN HIS ARMS AND LIFTS ME OFF THE FLOOR as soon as he gets through the front door.

I've been waiting for him to come home to tell him the news.

"You're in a good mood," I say, blushing as he sets me down and runs his fingers through my hair.

"Just happy to be home with my girls for the rest of the day."

"Dadda, dadda, dadda."

Jax's eyes go wide as he looks down at Maeve hurtling towards his legs.

"Baby girl, come give dadda a hug." He scoops her up into his arms and nestles her into his chest.

My eyes sting as he looks at me with the same emotions I'm feeling.

"She just said it, Sof."

I step forward and squeeze them both. Resting my head on his shoulder while stroking Maeve's back.

"Momma," Maeve babbles and I choke on a sob. This moment is perfect.

Our own little family.

"Yes, beautiful?" I whisper.

She just giggles and looks up at her dad. The complete love in his eyes as he looks at his daughter is enough to make my pulse skip a beat.

He leans in and presses a kiss to her cheek. "I love you, tigryonok."

That's it. My heart explodes in my chest.

I wonder what it would be like one day hearing him say those words to me. Because with every passing moment with this man, I seem to be falling deeper and deeper.

When I'm with Jax, I can take on the world. Our souls were meant to find each other, I'm sure of it.

He looks down at me with that same look in his eyes as he presses his lips softly to my temple.

"You girls have a good day?" he asks, setting Maeve down on the couch with a book.

"We did. We did some grocery shopping, and I had a call—"

His strong arms wrap around my stomach from behind, and he brushes my hair away from my neck.

"What call?" he mutters against my throat.

"I have an interview scheduled for tomorrow. I get to train and do my classes. If I get the job, that is."

He spins me around to face him, and I'm met with a smile. "I'm so proud of you, baby."

He hugs me tight and I can't hide the grin on my own face.

"Are you able to watch Maeve in the morning? I should only be gone an hour or so."

"Of course, as long as you trust me on my own." He wiggles his brows, but I can sense a hint of unease.

Maybe he is doubting himself a little bit.

My hands find their place on his chest, and I look up at him.

"I trust you with Maeve, Jax. You are an awesome dad. She loves you. Don't ever think otherwise, okay?" I give him a stern look to let him know I'm being serious.

"What could possibly go wrong?" He tilts his head.

"Nothing. You will both have a great time. Now, I was thinking about heading out to a park with Maeve. You coming?"

"Damn right."

———

After we put Maeve to bed, Jax helps me tidy the kitchen up before our movie night. As I bend down to put the last plate in the dishwasher, a crack comes through the air and my ass stings, causing me to jump in the air with a scream.

"Jax!" I shout. He's red faced laughing with the towel he just whipped me with wrapped around his fist.

I run towards him, and he darts out of the way easily and takes off.

"Get your butt back here!" I call out and chase after him through the hallway. He stops just before the front door, turning to face me, so I barrel into his chest. With a squeal, he lifts me by the waist and my back slams against the wall, his hand covering my mouth.

"Shh, you'll wake up Maeve."

My eyes go wide as he licks his lips.

"I have something for you, tigritsa."

Holding me in place by pressing his hips against mine, he pulls out a small black box from his back pocket. I tighten my legs around him and he removes his hot palm from my mouth so I can catch my breath.

I eye him suspiciously, but my heart is in my throat.

"What is it?" I ask quietly.

"Open it." He takes a sharp breath and holds it as he watches me.

I can't stop the tears that well in my eyes when I open it. I run my finger along the thin silver chain, onto the diamond heart that has three silver letters entwined in the center, J, M, S.

"Jax, it's beautiful," I gush.

"So you always have us with you," he whispers.

I've truly never been happier in my life than I am right now.

"Thank you, for everything, Jax."

Carefully taking the delicate necklace from the box, I hold it up between us and he covers my hand with his.

"Let me." He threads it around my neck and puts it in place.

I look down, and it sparkles in the light. Bringing my gaze back up to his with a grin, I grab the thick silver cord that sits around his neck and pull him forward to kiss me. His hungry mouth takes my breath away. I twist the chain around his throat so it tightens and his fingers find their place on my neck.

"You really know how to turn me the fuck on," he says in a low voice against my lips. "Every damn time I look at you, you take my breath away. So keep choking me, baby, and I'll show you just how good it feels, too."

He winks before going back for more ferocious kisses. His hands sliding up my dress send sparks through me. But when his fingers tighten beneath my jaw and he squeezes, I moan against his lips.

"Y-yes, Jax."

"You ready to fall apart for me?" he asks as he pushes two fingers inside me.

"Always," I reply.

CHAPTER FORTY-EIGHT

JAX

IT TAKES ME A MINUTE TO REGISTER MAEVE'S CRYING DOWN the hall.

Shit.

It's just me this morning. Sofia left early for her interview.

"Time to be a parent," I grumble to myself. I've never been alone with my daughter for more than a few minutes. It's both exciting and terrifying that it's just me with her today.

"I'm on my way, baby girl!" My voice makes her fall silent until I push her door open.

Her grabby hands extend over the top of her crib as she reaches for me.

She wants me. I'm *hers*.

It makes my heart swell when she smiles and coos against my chest as I pick her up.

"Dadada." Her babbles might not be what she's actually trying to say, but it makes me feel pretty important, anyway.

I'm so damn proud of her. I want to show her off to the world.

What I wouldn't give for Kai to have met her. "Your uncle Kai would have loved you as much as I do, Maeve-baby." Bouncing, we work our way over to the changing table where I lay her down and unbuckle her pajamas.

Fuck, I hope I do this right.

I wish Sofia was here just in case.

Just as I get the heavy diaper free, Maeve decides to try to roll away, nearly over the side.

"No!" I catch her in a panic, making her start to cry.

Man, I'm screwing this up already.

"Hey… I'm learning. Shh, I didn't mean to scare you." I hate seeing her lower lip stick out like that. "Come on, baby girl. You look just like your momma when you do that."

"Mamama?" She twists again as I try to slide her legs back into her clothes.

Crap. "Not yet. She'll be back soon. It's just you and me this morning."

Buttoning her up, I hoist her back into my arms.

"You know, your grandpa used to make the best pancakes. I wish I had paid better attention…" Another bolt of pain pierces my heart.

She'll never know my dad.

Fighting the knot in my throat, I prop her in her high-chair and tear off a couple of small pieces of banana for her while I work on getting her milk.

Damn. Dad would have words of wisdom. He raised me pretty much on his own. I bet he'd have all kinds of tricks to make me a better father.

What if I screw this up? Looking at her big brown eyes as she fists the mushy yellow food into her mouth, I'd give anything to do things right by her.

"You're my little princess, aren't you?" Handing her the bottle, I pause as a heavy rumble of engines pass the house.

Her dark curls shift on her forehead as she tilts her head.

Pressing her lips together, she blows pieces of her snack all over the tabletop. Squealing, she smears her palms through it as far as she can reach.

Seriously?

Five wet paper towels later, and she's cleaned back up. But also grumpy with me that I had to wipe her face a couple of times.

"Does this get easier as you get older?" I pull her out of the chair and set her down in the little play area I put together, filled with stuffed animals and books.

> Me: How old are kids before they can start cleaning up after themselves?

> Nikolai: Older than you are, apparently.

> Me: Gee thanks, asshole

> Nikolai: you're welcome

That went nowhere fast.

When she starts fussing, it pulls me away from my phone.

"What's the matter, tigryonok?" I pick her up and pull her close. "Should we watch some TV? I might be able to find a cartoon."

Flipping through the channels placates her for a moment, but even with her favorite on, she's still whimpering in my lap.

"Are you hungry? Want some more food?" Carrying her to the kitchen, I offer her a handful of baby cereal that melts in their mouths.

Her head shakes back and forth and her crying elevates. Red faced, she pushes my hand away.

"What's the matter?" I'm running out of options.

Checking her diaper, it's dry. We walk around the room, and I try to show her every colorful item I have.

"Mamama!" She's full-bellied screaming.

My heart races. I don't know how to fix this.

Dammit. I don't want to call Sofia. She's at her interview.

"What, Jax?" Nikolai's voice is gruff when he answers his cell.

"She won't stop—" I don't have to continue. Her sobs are inches from my chin.

"Did you feed her? Check her pants?" He runs down the list of basics.

"Yeah, yeah. I did all of that." Rocking her on my hip doesn't work. "I'm really messing this up, Nikolai. Please, what can I do?"

Her hands clasp and run up and down her face as her back arches away from me.

"Mamama!" She almost drowns out the deep sounds of engines passing by the house again.

"Tell me what she was doing." Nikolai is calm.

I wish I was. I'm ready to take her to the doctor this instant.

"She was sitting playing with her toys and—" I'm watching her writhe away from me and see something strange.

There's an eyeball staring out of her left nostril.

"—I think I figured it out. Thanks." I click my phone off.

Pressing down gently on her nose, I'm able to work the small piece of plastic out.

Her tears dry up almost instantly.

"Oh, Maeve. I need to check your animals more closely, huh?" I'm just glad she's okay.

Her sweaty brow rubs against my neck as she burrows in.

I'm not sure if I feel triumphant. A million worse possibilities of what could have happened run through my head.

Is she really safe with me?

CHAPTER FORTY-NINE

SOFIA

Song- Hypnosis, Sleep Token

OUTSIDE OUR HOUSE, I TURN OFF THE ENGINE and tilt my head, trying to see into the darkness through the rearview mirror. I can hear the rumbling of bikes nearby, but there are no lights to be seen. After what happened at Jax's fight, I'm not stupid. I know there could be repercussions here. Especially knowing Brody is involved.

We ran out of milk again, so while Jax was bathing Maeve, I rushed out to buy some. Now I'm thinking that maybe he should go in the future.

I dial Jax's number and he answers on the first ring, calming my anxiety.

"Hey, sweetheart. I heard you pull up. What's up?"

Maeve is babbling at him in the background.

"I might be wrong, but I think I can hear bikes." I swear I sound ridiculous. Maybe I'm paranoid. But Brody's words have been ringing in my head since. It felt like a threat to me.

"Just stay in the car, keep it locked. I'll put Maeve in her crib, it's probably nothing," he says calmly.

Maeve's cries echo through the phone, making me pinch the bridge of my nose. God, I'm being pathetic.

As the door opens, I spot Jax and I can feel a smile spread across my face. But my joy quickly fades as I catch a glimpse of the glinting silver gun in his right hand.

Maybe I'm not over-reacting.

I snatch up the carton of milk, my hand shaking as I click the unlock button. Jax opens up the door for me, but his eyes are focused at the entrance of our driveway.

"I-is everything okay?" There's a tremor in my voice.

With a sharp nod, he helps me out and steps behind me, putting himself between me and the road.

With a sense of urgency, he grabs my arm and pulls me inside, swiftly locking the deadbolt behind us.

"I'll go settle Maeve," I whisper, stopping halfway up the stairs when I hear his harsh Russian words to whoever he called.

My heart is pounding so hard that my whole body trembles as I scoop up Maeve and hold her close to my chest.

As I sway her in my arms, the floor creaks behind me, and I spin around to see Jax. He leans against the door frame, relaxed, holding Maeve's bottle in his tattooed hand.

"Here you go, baby girl."

Maeve playfully grabs the milk from him. He positions himself in front of us, and we lock eyes, sharing a tender smile. He gently strokes my cheek.

"It's fine, sweetheart. I promise you."

I can hear the pleading in his tone. I trust him to protect us.

Leaning into his touch, I press my cheek against his

palm. "I know. We can talk in a minute, Jax. I think this one needs a story from Daddy before she goes to sleep," I say with a grin.

If this is how it's going to be, I need Maeve protected, always. I'm sure he knows that. He probably already has taken care of that.

After giving Maeve one last kiss goodnight, my stress seems to settle as I watch her snuggle into her dad's chest.

They've built such an amazing bond after a short period. It's beautiful to watch them together. It's like she knows she's safe with him.

I wait on the balcony until Jax quietly closes the door behind him. I can hear her giggling to herself in her bed. He wraps his muscular arm around my shoulders and pulls me against him. I close my eyes as he presses a kiss to the top of my head.

"Are you okay, tigritsa?" he whispers.

"I am. I could use a glass of wine, though."

He chuckles softly, his warm hand lacing through mine as we make our way downstairs to the kitchen. I prop myself up on a barstool and watch him as he taps his rings against the counter while he pours us each a glass. He's hiding something.

I know that because he's clicking that tongue bar against his front teeth like crazy.

"Spill it," I say.

His eyes snap up. "Spill what?" he replies, biting down on his bottom lip.

"Whatever is eating you, just say it." I take a large sip of the wine as he runs a hand through his curls.

"I've upped security on the house. From now on, you'll have either me or one of our men with you at all times."

"Fine with me."

Witnessing the shock on his handsome face, I can't

contain my laughter. "What?"

His brows furrow. "I don't know. I kinda assumed you'd be pissed or be thinking about leaving."

I shake my head and place my hand over his to stop the tapping. "If that's what you think is best for us, I'm not going to argue. You know what you're doing, I don't. I want Maeve safe, that's all I ask."

He lifts my fingers to his lips, softly touching them to my knuckles. "Always, baby."

"And you, Jax Carter. I need you safe, too, please."

"You got it, sweetheart." He winks at me and finishes off his glass.

He moves around the table, tugging my hand with him.

"What do you say, early night?"

As he flashes me his best lopsided grin, I savor the last drop of wine before letting him lead me upstairs. We brush our teeth at our *his and hers* sinks, laughing as we keep making eye contact in the mirror.

He pulls back the blanket for me and taps my side of the bed. I can't take my eyes off of his naked body.

I take off my top and slip beneath the sheets, snuggling up to him. My leg drapes across his body, and I rest my head on his shoulder.

Even just in silence, wrapped up in his arms, everything in the world seems okay. We have our little girl asleep across the hall.

"Do you ever see yourself having more kids?" he asks, stroking his fingers through my hair.

"I think Maeve would love a brother or sister." I think Jax would love a boy. God, I'm getting ahead of myself here.

"Would you get married again?"

I laugh. "What is this, twenty questions?"

His deep breath makes my cheek rise and fall. "Maybe. I just want to know where your brain is, Sof."

I trace the tattoos on his chest with my nail as I contemplate my answer. Although swearing I'd never, ever, get married again after what Brody did, I think Jax may be different. He's special. For him, I would.

"To the right guy, I can be persuaded," I tease.

He pulls my head up by my hair to look into my eyes. "Me?"

"Keep treating me and Maeve like you do, then yeah, I'd marry you, Mr. Carter. One day," I reply with a grin.

"Is that right?" His soft chocolate eyes almost look surprised.

"And what do you want out of life, Jax?"

"To wake up with my wife in my arms, being prodded by our kids."

Kids. As in multiple. My eyes go wide. "How many?"

"Three?" His reply is almost instant.

"What else?" I think he's been mulling this over for a while.

"I'd be back at professional boxing, not that shitty underground stuff. Doing bigger jobs for Mikhail, but enough I get to be home for the people who matter." He lies back, with his hands behind his head, and I push myself up using his chest.

"Maybe a dog? A vacation home. I don't know, is that too much to ask for? Just to be happy," he continues.

"Are you? Happy, I mean?" Staring at him, I try to find any hint that this is a joke.

His lips are firm and his jaw clenches. "Yes. For the first time in what fucking feels like forever, I can honestly say my answer is yes. All because of you, sweetheart."

Tears threaten to spill. I feel the same. I know this man is it for me.

"Now, I seem to have heard that you *might*, one day, want to be Mrs. Carter?"

I can't stop the giggles that erupt when he rolls me onto my back and pins my wrists above my head. His thick thighs nudge mine open as he settles over me.

"You know, I used to dream of this when I was cooped up after having Maeve. That somehow you'd barrel into my life and save me. That she would have her daddy. That I'd find the man who stole my heart and made me her mom. I never thought it would be possible. Hell, even when you did show up, I worried you'd hate me for ruining your life." Chewing on my lip, I wait for his response.

"You made it, baby. You gave me everything I never even realized was possible. You have no idea what kind of hole you dragged my sorry ass from." His warm palm runs up and down along my side.

I wiggle my hips, feeling his dick harden against me.

"I want to see you pregnant with my baby. Fuck, that'll be so hot. You think I'm obsessed with you now? Just wait." He keeps my wrists in one hand and grabs my thigh with the other.

"Well, that sounds good." I smooth a lock of his curly hair and watch his eyes actually light up.

"But I was miserable when I was fat and pregnant. I hated it. I felt so sick, so ugly and useless." My bottom lip juts out in a pout.

"I wish I was there," he says softly. He casts his eyes down. For that split second, I feel his pain and I hate that for him.

"We can't change that, but we're here now. And maybe we can do it again. You can experience all those night feedings, too. It's a ball."

"That sounds like exactly what I want," he whispers against my lips before kissing me.

CHAPTER FIFTY

JAX

Mikhail's mask billows around his nose as he watches me sneak into his office. "Now that Jax has *graced us* with his presence, I'll begin."

Alexei grins at me from the couch and flips me the middle finger.

I bet he's happy. I just bumped him from the top of Mikhail's shit list for the day.

"Enzo has relayed the info on the contact that Nikolai and Jax sniffed out." Mikhail holds up a sheet sized photograph of a dark-haired man wearing sunglasses.

"I was there, too!" Alexei protests, sitting forward while throwing his hands in the air.

Mikhail glares at him, but continues.

"His name is Kirill Yelchin. He was a lackey when I was in Russia, but seems to have risen through the ranks since I've left." He drops the page and picks up another. "This is Knox Leary. He's now target number one. We need to remove any foothold that my father is trying to establish." He waves the closeup of the bearded face I've gotten to know too well over the last few weeks.

"I'm tired of playing. If my father, Ivan, comes to play, it will be a bloodbath. Vegas will burn, and no one will walk away unscarred." His voice raises as he crumples the photograph into a ball between his palms.

"So, a kill order?" Nikolai cracks his knuckles and the very edge of his lip turns up.

I think he's excited. Well, it's the most emotion I've seen him show.

He's like Frankenstein most of the time, completely neutral.

I bet his face cracked.

"Yes. We aren't fucking around any more. I've called in help with clean-up teams from New York. Enzo said that Mr. Falcone will send extra people to try to keep things as hush-hush as possible. But I think we have the manpower here for the front lines." He pulls his heavy rolling chair out and sits, then folds his thick hands in front of him.

He looks like royalty. Acts like it, too. Especially with that balaclava on all the time.

I still wonder if he has scars.

"Dropping off the bodies after confiscating their drugs has pushed them to new levels of aggression." Mikhail continues calmly. "Expect more aggressive resistance. When we've thinned out their ranks, we can organize a coordinated attack on their base of operations." His hand clasps into a fist and the sound of it thumping his desk resonates in the room. "Whatever you do, *do not take them on alone.* We lost two men this week in separate attacks. I don't want anyone else getting hurt."

I see heads bobbing in agreement.

"I can take care of myself." Alexei's voice raises over the murmurings.

"I don't give a shit what you do." Mikhail doesn't even

look at him when he replies. "Everyone else, be safe. Dismissed."

Nikolai veers directly towards me as we start herding through the exit.

"Jax, don't forget Elena's birthday party. It would be nice for another child to visit her." His grip finds my shoulder as we walk down the hall towards the elevators.

"I'll be there. Sofia hasn't let me forget." I step against the back wall while Nikolai hits the button.

Just as the doors are closing, Alexei's hand snakes through the gap, forcing them to open for him.

"Sounds like that girl is the best part of you." The fluorescent lights glimmer off of his toothy grin.

"She really is," I say seriously. "You need someone like that. Are you bringing someone to the party?"

His hair falls away from his eyes as he tips his head back in a full-bellied laugh. "There's no woman crazy enough to tie me down."

"You don't know what you're missing. Being tied down can be fun." I leave him cackling as I head to my bike.

I just can't imagine Alexei with anyone. The kind of psycho that would match him surely doesn't exist.

But he is right about one thing. That woman completes me in ways I didn't even realize was possible.

I can't wait to see the smile on her face when I get in. The entire living room should have enough roses to look like a damn garden. That's why I was late to the meeting. Sofia called me on my way here to tell me she got the job. So I dove into the first florist I came across and gave them enough cash to deal with my 'extreme' request.

Nothing is too much for my girl.

CHAPTER FIFTY-ONE

SOFIA

Song- love me, Ex Habit.
https://lost.exhabitmusic.com/lovemee

"YOU'RE BUSY AGAIN? WHEN CAN YOU NEXT FIT ME AND Maeve in?" I snap back at Anna through my car speaker, looking up in the rearview mirror, seeing Nikolai's Hellcat tailing me. It was certainly strange having to take 'protection' to my new job with me. But none of my colleagues had a clue they were outside.

I hear her tap her nails on the table.

"Well, I have a date tonight and then I'm going to see Stacy about a bar job with her. You know, I have to keep this shitty roof over my head somehow, Sofia."

I roll my eyes. Jax transferred her more than three months' rent to cover my part of the contract. In an attempt to find some calm, I twirl my necklace around my fingers, feeling the smooth metal against my skin. I'm starting to feel like our friendship is slowly disappearing, and it's starting to sting a little. She's been in my life for as long as I can remember. I need to at least try to salvage it.

"What about this Sunday? It would be good for you to get to know Jax, too."

Just as I say that, a text pops up on the huge screen and my mood switches. I told him I was getting out of work early and was seeing if he was going to be home before we pick up Maeve from Nikolai's sitter.

> J: An afternoon for mommy and daddy to get naughty? Count me in. I'm already home, waiting for you.

I hit the gas harder.

"Oh, he's decided to stick around then. Didn't see that coming. Why is he making you work, anyway?" The coldness in her tone throws me off guard.

"I want to work, Anna. I'm finally getting to finish my degree. I'll be qualified soon. Jax supports whatever I want to do."

That riles me back up. How dare she talk about Jax like that? She doesn't have a clue about all the amazing things he does for me and Maeve.

"Let's hope he doesn't do a Brody on you," she says snidely.

"Anna! What is wrong with you? What have I done? Look, I have to go. Maybe call me back when you get that stick out of your ass and want to be my friend again. Because I've had enough of this shit from you." I cut the call, beating my hands against the steering wheel in annoyance. As pissed off as I am, just the thought of being in Jax's arms in a minute brings a smile to my face. Screw what Anna thinks, or anyone else for that matter.

As I kick off my heels in the hall, the sound of a persistent buzzing reaches my ears from the dining room. Intrigue gets the better of me. Knowing Jax, I could be walking into anything.

I stop in my tracks, mesmerized by the unwavering dedication on Jax's face as he skillfully tattoos what looks like the entire back of his hand.

"What's going on here?" I ask, not hiding the amusement in my tone.

As I approach him, I'm almost blown away by the gorgeous art he's created on himself. With a grin, he lifts the needle from his skin and meets my gaze.

"Do you like it?"

My mouth falls open as I take in the sight of a stunning tiger, its black and white ink giving it a strikingly realistic appearance. Leaning over him, I rest my palm on his shoulder to get a closer look.

"Jax, that is beautiful. You're so talented! You never told me?" I blink a few times in shock.

"Wait, is that mine and Maeve's names?" I ask, knowing full well what I'm staring at. Mine is running down his thumb and Maeve's just above his knuckles, all blended into the background of the tiger.

"Damn right. On my skin forever."

"I love it." I press a kiss to the side of his head.

"I've still got a bit of work to do on it, but it's my best work yet," he says proudly.

"So, you're also a tattoo artist?"

He snorts. "No. Me and Kai, we learned when we were younger. Kai's dad had his own shop. He taught us. Kai did most of mine. I did all of his."

He pulls up his shorts, revealing his thick thigh and points to a small skull smoking a joint. "That was his first attempt. Fucking awful," he chuckles.

Jax doesn't mention Kai's name much. All I know is he died a couple of years ago, and he was like a brother to him. I know enough about grief to not push him. He will talk when he's ready to.

"It's different. Looks like he got better, though." I tap his shoulder at a perfect set of boxing gloves.

He nods and swallows hard, making his Adam's apple bob.

I fiddle with the necklace, and an idea springs to mind. "Hey, Jax?"

He places the gun down on the table and turns to face me, his thighs on either side of my legs. "Yes, baby."

"I want one."

"A tattoo?"

I nod. Is this going to hurt?

"Shit, are you telling me I get to be the first one to ink your pretty virgin skin?" he says with a smirk.

"Hey, if you're not going to take it seriously, I'll go to another shop and let a guy put his hands—" I lean in, brushing my lips on the shell of his ear. "All. Over. Me."

A low, guttural growl rumbles from deep within him. As he pulls me closer, his fingers firmly grip my waist, igniting a surge of desire.

"I think the fuck not. I'll do it."

I tap his cheek, looking down at him. "Good boy."

I can't help but notice the way he bites down on his lip, a gesture that makes me squeeze my thighs together. How is he so hot?

His hand trails up my leg and dips under my skirt. "Oh, baby. You have no idea how good I'm about to be for you."

"Now, this tattoo. What do you want and where?" He looks up at me, sliding his hands up my sides.

"This." I point to my necklace, our initials entwined together, surrounded by a heart.

"You want mine there, too?" He looks surprised.

"Yep. All three of us, together. Maybe inside a cute

little heart? Or a tiger paw print? I don't know, get creative. Leave your mark on me." I wink at him.

He licks his bottom lip. He has a new silver piercing in. It's quite an enormous square.

"New tongue bar?"

With a sly smile, he wiggles his eyebrows, teasing me.

"Where do you want this piece of art, then, sweetheart?"

I hadn't thought that far ahead. "Hip?"

Standing above me, he reaches down and effortlessly finds the zipper on the side of my pencil skirt.

"Perfect choice," he whispers in my ear, letting my clothing fall to the floor.

My heart quickens as he steps aside, my eyes lock on his precise movements as he readies the tattoo gun with new needles and ink.

Nerves start to work through my body. "Does it hurt?"

He chuckles. "A little. You might like it. It's addictive."

He takes a seat. He glances at me before returning to the equipment he's still fiddling with. "Dress off, bra off, and lie down on the table."

"Bra off?" I shoot him a look.

He gives me a broad grin. "That's just for me."

"They better not distract you, Jax." I'd hate for a permanent mistake to be on my skin forever because he wasn't paying attention.

He points to the table in front of him. "Lie down."

The cool wood presses against my back. With the tattoo gun in hand, he stands and a chill runs through me. As it starts to buzz, panic takes over.

"Relax, beautiful. It won't take me long. If it hurts, we stop. Just tell me."

His touch sends a wave of electricity through me, and I

nod, trying to steady my breath as he runs his index finger along my skin.

"I'll start with the 'J'."

As the needle touches my skin, I tightly squeeze my eyes shut, bracing for the pain. With clenched teeth, I exhale slowly, trying to ignore the initial sting.

"Relax your fists, sweetheart. One letter down, all good?" he asks over the low hum.

I tense up as he wipes a cool towel over the tattoo.

"Yep, keep going." I rush out my words, trying to relax the tight muscles in my body.

He squeezes on my thigh, and that little reassurance helps. He starts on the next letter, which must be slightly more on the bone as it causes vibrations through my pelvis, which overtakes the sensation of any pain. It's weird but kinda nice.

"Do you trust me, baby?"

As I glance at him through one eye, I'm captivated by the desire that burns in his gaze. "I trust you, Jax."

"Good." His fingers hook under my panties and he slides them down my bare legs. "Spread your legs for me, tigritsa. I'm about to set your world on fire."

I almost jump when he runs his mouth along my stomach. Is he quivering? What the hell? As he gets lower, and it connects to my clit, I confirm that his tongue is vibrating. "Jesus, Jax."

"You like my new toy?"

The intense sensation causes ripples through my entire body, making my back arch off the table. I sit up as he pulls away, but he shakes his head and motions for me to lie back down. "Next letter."

I suck in a breath, my pussy throbbing as he gently guides my right leg down. I can barely feel the machine working. I'm too distracted and too eager for it to be over to get his face back between my legs.

"You think you can stay still?"

Shit. "I-I don't know, Jax."

"Well, I suggest you try, baby." He smirks. His warm breath beats against me, right where I need him.

As his tongue glides along the inside of my thigh, I can feel the intense vibrations resonating through my body.

"Jax, oh my god."

"Good, right?"

"Uh-huh." I dig my fingers into the table as he slowly creates circles on my clit. Even my ass is twitching.

"I-I can't do this," I pant out. The blood is pounding in my ears.

With one hand splayed on my lower stomach, he works on the next section, which causes my hips to move, working against his pressure on my clit.

And, oh my fucking god.

"You're doing so good, baby."

Bringing my forearm over my eyes, I bite down on the inside of my cheek, doing everything I can to stop my body from moving and ruining his work. It's like I can feel the vibrations in every fiber of me. When the buzzing finally stops, I relax.

"We aren't done."

My eyes fly open and I find Jax standing at the edge of the table with a hunger in his eyes. I pull my legs up, and he licks his lips.

"I need to wrap—"

"Jax. Put your face between my legs and make me scream. I need it." I can't take anymore. I'm about to combust.

Leaning over me, he traces a path from my neck down to my belly. The sensation sends tingles of electricity coursing through me. He grips both of my thighs and slides me to the edge of the table. I tangle my fingers in his hair as he drops to his knees.

"I wonder if you'll like this inside you?" With his hands under my ass, he pushes my hips up so I can wrap my legs around his head. I scream out his name as he fucks me with his tongue. I find a rhythm to match and I pull at his hair as I ride his face.

"I'm, fuck, so close."

His fingers dig into my skin, and my knees tighten around him on their own accord. As he works his way back to my clit, I completely shatter around him. I've never come so hard in my life. Though every second of this orgasm ripping through me, he doesn't let up, pushing me open and feasting.

My chest heaves. I don't even have a second to ride out the first one before he brings me back up to another high.

"Again, sweetheart. I dare you. Soak my fucking face."

I can hear the menace in his tone. He slides his fingers inside me and stretches me. He's consuming me completely.

"My tiger loves it," he says before placing his tongue on my clit and letting the piercing do the work while he drives his hand deeper within me.

"Shit, shit, shit." I say it like a chant.

Just as I'm nearly there, he withdraws out of me and back towards my ass.

"Still trust me?"

"Always," I pant out as he spreads my cheeks and his soaked fingers push into my tight hole. Slowly, oh, so fucking slowly. He sucks on me, distracting me from the initial shock.

"Good girl," he groans.

With his mouth back on my pussy, I've never experienced a sensation quite like this. I'm so full, I'm on fire, to the point I can't breathe. Another explosive climax comes over me and I ride it out.

I lift my arms above my head, and Jax swiftly stands, scooping me up by the waist and holding me close to his chest. I blow the strands of my sweaty hair away from my face, then press my lips against his.

"Go look at your new ink, baby," he says, placing me down. With our fingers interlocked, I lead him towards the full-length mirror in the hallway, excitement bubbling inside me.

"It's beautiful," I whisper.

He slides his arms around me from behind and cups my breasts in his hands. It really is, he did a perfect job, despite the distractions.

Meeting his eyes in the reflection, I feel an instant connection.

His grin only intensifies the butterflies in my stomach.

"It is, just like you," he replies, kissing my throat.

CHAPTER FIFTY-TWO

JAX

WITH A MISCHIEVOUS GRIN, SOFIA CAN'T CONTAIN HER laughter as she drops yet another ice cube into my open palm. Turns out, the tongue bar shouldn't be used for that long. Now my mouth is fucking killing me.

"Stop laughing at me." I pretend to pout.

"I'm sorry, it's just so funny. You injured your tongue going down on me. Like, I've never heard of that before in my life." With each beat of her hand against her leg, her laughter grows louder, until she's doubled over with tears streaming down her face. When I pop the ice onto my tongue, it's an instant relief.

I watch her, and the sheer happiness on her face is unmistakable. It's so intense that it sends a sharp pang through my chest.

The moment her streaming eyes lock with mine, it's as if a puzzle piece finally finds its place, and everything suddenly makes sense.

I fucking love this woman.

Love.

There is nothing else it could be. Yet, this dark cloud sits over me, even now. That I'll destroy her, too.

It's the same story with anyone I let get close.

I can't break this cycle. As I rub my hands on my jeans, a sudden tightness grips my throat, like I can't breathe. My phone vibrating in my pocket is a welcomed distraction.

Nikolai's name flashes up on the screen.

"I'm heading to your place. There's been a hit at Enzo's club."

I crack my knuckles. This is exactly what I need. The best way to battle these feelings is to fight. "I'll meet you out front."

The line goes silent.

"Jax… Why do you sound odd?"

I'm never going to live this one down. "I have an injury, that's all I'm telling you."

I hear Alexei's cackle. "Does that mean you've taken that clicking machine out?" Nikolai chuckles.

"Only for the day."

"That must have been a good feast," Alexei yells through the speaker.

I shake my head, cutting the call.

"I've gotta go out for a bit. I shouldn't be long," I tell Sofia, whose laughter has died down. Concern is written across her face.

I pull her into an embrace and inhale her sweet strawberry scent. As she leans back, studying me, I frame her face with my hands. "I'll see you soon, sweetheart."

I almost say it, I'm so close. But what if that ruins everything?

She nods and kisses me.

Just like that, my problems seem to melt away. My mind stops spinning. I'm back where I belong. With her.

"Give Maeve a kiss from me. I'll try to be back by bedtime."

"I will, Jax. Be careful, okay?"

"You got it, boss."

I'm so close to telling her how I feel. But, I don't, not yet.

CHAPTER FIFTY-THREE

SOFIA

Song, I Found, Amber Run

WITH MAEVE DOWN FOR HER MORNING NAP, I HEAD downstairs. The last couple of days, Jax hasn't been himself. It's like something is eating away at him, even if he tries to hide it behind his jokes.

Stopping by the door, I lean on the frame quietly, watching him knock back a hefty measure of scotch and slam it back on the counter. He's tense, gripping onto the kitchen counter with his head down.

It hurts me seeing him like this.

I pad over to him. As I reach him, he flinches slightly when I run my hand softly up his side. I hear him take a deep breath before turning to me.

His bloodshot eyes bore into mine, making me swallow.

"Jax, baby. What's going on?" I ask softly and cup his jaw.

"I'll be fine, sweetheart." He leans into my touch, offering me a sad smile.

I get it. Some things hurt to talk about. But I don't want him to bottle it up and let it fester inside. I let a few moments of silence pass, gently stroking his beard with my thumb.

"It would have been Kai's birthday today," he says quietly.

Grief is something I know well. After losing my parents, I was empty for so long, completely on my own in my pain. I was lucky in some ways. Training in my field of psychology, I found ways to cope. Not everyone has that. Especially men. It's not manly to cry.

"I'm sorry, Jax." I wrap my arms around him and hold him tight, feeling him rest his chin on my shoulder.

"I'll be okay in a minute. We've got enough going on today to keep me distracted."

I pull back, lacing my fingers through his.

"We can talk about him, if you want?" I ask, studying his reaction.

His face pales.

My heart breaks for him as he shakes his head. "I can't. Not today." He runs a hand over his face, letting out a ragged breath.

"Hey, it's okay. There is no right way to grieve. Today is going to be tough. I bet any birthday, event, or memory is. I feel the exact same way about my parents. Sometimes it just takes time."

Hell, it's taken me years to be able to put up some of Mom's favorite flowers for her birthday. I tried the first year and burst into floods of tears every time I looked at them.

His chin buries into my shoulder. "All I can see is his lifeless body, Sof. It's like every other memory fades away and that's all I'm left with. All those years of memories and that is all I see. Today, worse than any other."

My eyes sting with tears, remembering walking in to identify my parent's bodies. That kept me up at night for a long time.

"I struggle to even say his name. I can't remember anything good. All I can see is the blood—" His voice breaks.

I wrap my arms around him, pulling him tight against me as the warm droplets fall down my own cheeks.

"The first couple of years, it's like it isn't real. And then on these big occasions, that sinking feeling creeps back in when you remember you won't get that call on your birthday from them. Or, when I look at Maeve, a pit forms in my stomach thinking about how they never got to meet my beautiful girl. That she will never hear my dad's stupid jokes or bake cupcakes with my mom like I did. And, you think that you'll never be able to speak about them again without your throat closing up on you. But, you can, one day you can. It just takes time, baby," I whisper, stroking my fingers through his hair.

"I just want you to know that I'm here for you, Jax. Whenever you do, or don't want to talk. Being upset, being angry, it's all okay. Just tell me what you need from me. I'm never going anywhere." I pause, remembering what helped me. "Have you ever thought about seeing a professional, to help you with the grief?"

"I don't need help. I just need you, sweetheart. You and Maeve are the fucking light in my life."

I nod, I know I can't force him.

"And you are in ours, too, Jax. We've got you. I promise."

He pulls back and his rough hands frame my face as I sniffle. "He would have loved you and Maeve. He'd be so damn proud of me." He rests his forehead against mine.

"I'm certain he is proud of you. I'll look after you, Jax. I love you."

Those last three words tumble out before I can stop them. But, they are true. I love him with every single part of me.

The first genuine smile appears on his face that I've seen in days.

"I love you, Sofia. You complete me in ways I never even realized I was missing. You are everything. I live for you. I will die for you. You are, and always will be, the perfect in the midst of my chaos."

My heart almost explodes. He owns me completely. I never want this to end.

"We really have created our own perfect, haven't we?"

He nods, tipping my face up to his.

"We have, and we will forever, sweetheart. This family is everything I could have ever dreamt of. I can never thank you enough for bringing me this."

"It was always half you."

He presses his lips over mine and I lace my arms around his neck, pulling him closer to deepen the kiss.

We really have everything.

True love, our little girl and a future we can look forward to. I know, like Kai, my parents will be looking down on me with a smile. I have everything they could have ever imagined.

The echoes of Maeve's usual wake up screams rattle down to us and we both laugh.

"Well, that was a short nap. You wanna go get your little sleepy princess?"

He wipes away a tear with the pad of his thumb. "Always."

With a kiss on the tip of my nose, I squeeze his ass.

"I'll get her stuff ready, then we can leave." As he pulls away, I grab hold of his arm to stop him.

"If it gets too much today, just tell me. We can leave and do something else. Whatever you need, okay?"

"Fuck, I love you, Sof."

A wave of relief washes over me. He knows he can talk to me. He spoke more about Kai than I bet he has since it happened. A sparkle of life came back into him. I just wish I could heal some of his pain.

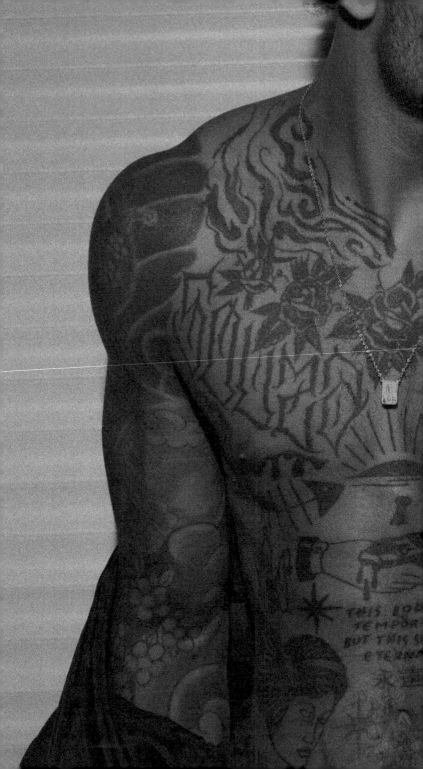

CHAPTER FIFTY-FOUR

JAX

Maybe this is the distraction I needed. The last few years, all I've done on today's date is hide. Wallow. And drink enough that the time slips by.

But, watching my little girl waddle after Nikolai's daughter puts a piece of calm back in my heart.

Alexei takes up the rear of the follow train behind Elena and Maeve.

I swear he's the biggest child. Decked out with a tiara and a smear of lipstick that Elena applied to make him "pretty", he's the loudest of the three.

How can he be so wild, and so good with kids?

It's nice he's keeping them busy.

Nikolai sits in silence on one end of the couch, and I'm at the other.

Sofia and Lara are doing their best to get the decorations set around the elaborate birthday cake that Nikolai bought.

Sofia does look troubled when I ask her for another beer.

I don't want to get up. I don't want to talk.

Today, just existing outside of a bottle is a win for me.

My chest hurts watching Maeve's flushed cheeks as she squeals in excitement when Alexei turns on his hands and knees and chases her.

He's every bit the perfect uncle.

Like Kai would have been.

A knot twists in my throat. He should have had his chance. Not just to meet Maeve, but to be a daddy on his own.

He'd have been better than me.

Remembering how she cried when I punched that stupid bag makes tears well up in my eyes. Kai was gentle. Patient. He'd have done things right.

The girls shriek and run on opposite sides of Alexei before colliding behind him.

Shock blankets both of their faces before they both erupt into tears in unison.

Even their mouths form the same 'o' shape as they cry.

Sofia runs to both of them, gathering a girl in each arm before settling on the floor cross-legged and pulling them onto her lap.

She's so perfect as a mom.

Seeing their curly dark hair bobbing in front of her makes me wish she had two.

Alexei huffs as he collapses on the couch. "Fuck, they'll wear ya out."

Nikolai's hand whips out and smacks Alexei on the back of the head. "Language, idiot."

"Shit, sorry." Alexei's palm works over his scalp as I punch his other shoulder.

"Watch what you're saying, asshat," I scold.

Alexei turns and glares at me. "Is my English not as

good as yours?" Rubbing his arm, he stands and disappears into the kitchen.

Lara gets up and follows him, throwing Nikolai a glare over her shoulder as she does.

"You're cranky." Nikolai doesn't look at me. "You didn't even want to hear Kai's name last year. Too busy finding the bottom of a gallon of tequila."

"So are you. More than usual." I watch Sofia as she consoles the girls. They both rise off of her lap and run down the hall to Elena's room.

I'm sure Nikolai is thinking about his wife. She's been gone almost as long as Kai.

"Does it get any easier?" I ask quietly. I want him to say 'yes'. That I have a light at the end of this black as fuck tunnel.

"No. I am constantly reminded of her." Nikolai glances at me, then back to the girls as they run back in.

Maeve is wearing one of Elena's shirts so that they're matching.

"They almost look like sisters with their dark, curly hair." Sofia nestles herself on the arm of the couch where I can touch her.

Alexei saunters from the kitchen with a handful of cold beers and hands one to Nikolai, then to me. "Well, they should. They're cousins."

"Alexei," Nikolai growls.

"What, does that make us brothers, Niki?" I raise my bottle in the air as a salute.

"*Niet.*" His face is turning red, but he doesn't look at me.

"What does that mean, then? Is that a Russian term?" Sofia sips on her champagne while staring at Nikolai.

His teeth clench. "It means nothing. Alexei has very bad English."

"I fucking don't!" Alexei yells as he leaps out of the way of Nikolai's slap. "I know what the word is." His finger points at Nikolai. "You were married to his sister. That makes them *cousins.*" His hand ends up in front of my face.

My sister?

"I don't think so, Alexei." I know he can be a bit wild sometimes, but he doesn't lie. "What the heck are you trying to say?"

Alexei's eyes narrow and his fist clenches. "Do not make me the donkey on this one. Her father was the same as yours, Sergy. They both died by Ivan's hand." His chin juts triumphantly.

My heart stops.

Darting out my hand, I grip Nikolai's arm hard enough I know it hurts. I don't care.

"Tell me he is wrong. And that you have not been lying to me for two years." The room feels like it's closing in on me.

Nikolai finally looks at me. For the first time, his skin is pale. "I didn't. I just didn't tell you, and you didn't ask."

This hollow feeling inside boils into rage. "How in the hell would I know to ask if I didn't know she existed?" I shout.

Maeve and Elena begin to cry. Nikolai and Sofia both jump up and grab a fussing girl.

"Why would I create pain for no reason? What does it change?" Nikolai hisses as he folds his daughter into his shoulder.

"Your father killed my sister, and my dad? And you let him live?"

I shake my head, trying to wrap my thoughts around this as the anger churns inside of me.

Nikolai gives me a stern glare and nods, looking at his daughter in his arms.

Children's wails fill the room. They're upset because of me.

Lara plucks Elena out of Nikolai's arms.

He stands, crossing his arms formidably across his chest. "He's the biggest crime lord in Russia, Jax. That is why we all left, to build our empire and tear his down. We will get our revenge, the smart way."

My dad was in the bratva. Everyone fucking lies to me.

"How did you know it was me when you came to New York? Is that why you offered me the job with Mikhail?"

My head is spinning. So many unanswered questions and holes in my life. Even my own father had a secret life. A whole other life.

Nikolai clenches his fists.

"We've been watching out for you since his death, Jax. Katerina wanted to meet you. We saw you after Kai's—"

"Don't fucking mention his name," I spit out with venom.

I was starting to think of these guys as family. I guess they really are, but I don't feel any part of it.

My gut sours.

I need some air.

Pushing past everyone to the door, I gulp in the hot Vegas night and try to calm myself down.

Why didn't my dad ever tell me about her? What else was he hiding? He worked with Ivan? I've heard the stories of how ruthless that man was.

My head feels like it's going to explode.

How different would things have been if I had known her?

Nikolai still hates his father for killing her.

Squeezing my own fist tightly makes my knuckles crack with new hatred for Ivan.

Pain courses through me.

I lost someone else. Today of all days.

My whole family. Gone.

How many more around me are going to die tragically?

God, this hurts!

Pacing outside Nikolai's house, this is the first time I've really craved a cigarette.

Kai used to joke that if we had sisters, we would marry each others. That way, we'd really be brothers.

Fuck. He was more family than any of my blood kin.

A cool hand touches my back. "Jax? Are you okay?" Sofia's voice is normally soothing to me. But tonight, I feel like my skin is on fire and I'm a powder keg.

I'm not safe. The tendrils of crimson that keep sneaking into the edges of my vision tell me I'm on the verge of losing control.

"I have to go. I'm sorry. See if one of those assholes can give you a ride home." Shrugging off her palm, I stomp into the darkness to my Lambo.

"Jax? Wait!" She tries to reach for me, but I pull away, slamming the door in her face.

She needs to learn I'm toxic.

A leaking battery of acid that ruins everything around me.

No one tells me the truth.

Except Kai.

Sofia even hid my own daughter from me.

I can't trust anyone.

"Jax!" Her voice is muffled as she beats on my window.

Throwing my hand over the passenger seat, I back wildly out of the driveway.

The road is a quiet place.

There isn't pretending as the asphalt meets my tires.

Purring of the engine is a truth. It tells you immediately when something is wrong.

Speed, distance, time.

That's what I need.

CHAPTER FIFTY-FIVE

SOFIA

Lara gave me a lift home and sent me hers and Nikolai's number, just in case I needed them.

Which spikes my anxiety even further.

Pulling my feet up on the couch, I hold the steaming mug of coffee in front of my face.

I know Jax needs space. He made that clear as he left.

It's a lot to wrap his head around, especially when he's struggling with Kai's death. I can't imagine finding out what having a dead sibling will do.

But, I'm worried. It's been hours. I won't be able to sleep until I know he's coming home.

I just want to be there for him, to help him through this.

Hovering my finger over his number, I hit dial and hold my breath. He might not want to speak to me. I just need to hear his voice. I'll at least know where his head is at.

"Jax?" I whisper as soon as it connects. Relief courses through me that he's not sending me straight to voicemail.

"Hi, sweetheart."

I try to keep the panic out of my voice. "Are you okay?"

I can hear the loud shouting in the background.

"Yeah. I'm fine." He pauses.

I pull my knees up to my chest and hug them before putting him on loud speaker.

"I'm so fucking sorry about earlier. I didn't mean to push you away like that." His words come out in a rush.

"I know you didn't mean it like that. I'm just worried about you. Can you just come home, please?"

He doesn't sound drunk, which is good.

"Yeah, baby. I want to come home. I went on a long ass ride to clear my head, and I feel better. Still want to punch Nikolai in the throat, though."

I laugh. "I get that. You two need to talk."

"Where are you now?"

"Just at some shitty biker bar. I've been nursing a pint for the last hour, just thinking."

"And how is that working for you?"

The crowd in the bar seems to be getting louder. It's hard to hear him.

"Yeah, I ended up thinking about asking you to marry me."

I choke on a cough, making him chuckle. The sound of his laughter washes my worries away.

"You're sure you aren't drunk?" I tease.

He groans. "No, honestly. I'm trying to be better for you."

"Well, it is Vegas, after all. Would be a shame not to."

"You'd seriously still marry me, even after the shit I pulled today?"

I frown. "You did what you thought was right at the time for your own sanity, Jax. There is nothing wrong with that. It's better than kicking in Nikolai's head, in front of the kids."

"True. Didn't think of it like that." There are sounds of shouting in the background. "I'll give you something much better than a crappy Vegas chapel, Sof. I promise. Just you wait."

Butterflies erupt in my stomach as I fiddle with my nails.

I really would marry this man, anywhere. I want him to be mine forever.

"Let's just start with a proposal first?"

"I got you. Let me finish this drink and I'll call Alexei, get him to pick me up and then, I'm going to crawl into bed with you and make up for today."

"How are you doing that?" I blush as I say the words.

"I have a few tricks up my sleeve for you, baby."

"I'll wait up. Get your ass home, Mr. Carter. I miss you."

"And, I love you, Sof. You are the best part of me."

"I love you, too. I'll see you soon."

As we say our goodbyes and the call ends, it's like a weight has been lifted. He hasn't gone into self-destruct mode and he's coming home to me.

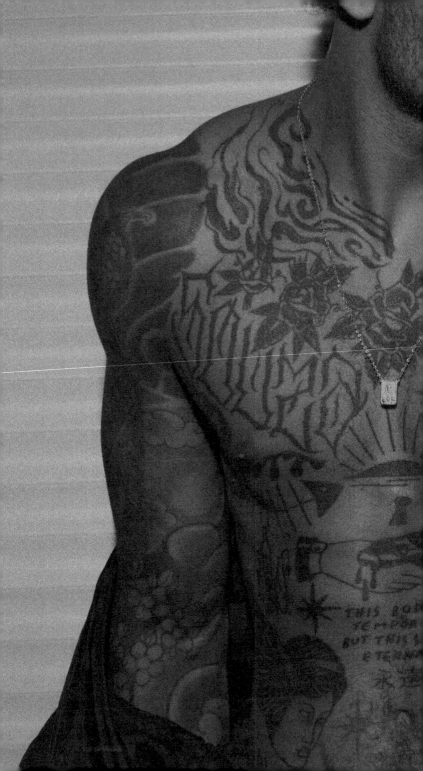

CHAPTER FIFTY-SIX

JAX

How she always seems to settle me is some sort of miracle. Why I pushed her away, I'll never know.

A warmth spreads through my chest. She loves me. I have someone who wants *me*.

The dry Vegas heat washes over my back as the door to the bar opens while a throng of leather-clad bikers pushes in.

I should be worried, but I don't really care. Nothing can kill my high of Sofia wanting me, all of my faults included.

Well, I didn't mind until they start yelling, then pushing at each other.

Fuck. I guess it's time to call Alexei.

One of the bigger ones slams into my side and spills my drink all over my lap. "What the hell?"

He drops me a crooked smile. "Sorry, bro." Turning back to his buddy, he laughs and jumps away from me.

"Don't worry, hun. I have a new one for you." A blonde woman with bright red lipstick appears behind the bar and slides a fresh scotch in front of me.

"This wasn't what I was drinking." I've been nursing a beer for the last hour while talking on the phone.

She gives me a flashy smile. "It's okay, hun. This one is on the house."

The yelling rises behind me, so I down the shot in one swallow. "Thanks."

A different guy barrels into me, pressing me into the hard edge of the bar. I swear if one more of these gorillas runs into me, I'm going to start swinging.

It's time to get out of here.

Grabbing my cell, I work my way away from the rowdy crowd to a small table near the door.

I gotta call Alexei. Nikolai still pisses me off.

Wait. Why can't I unlock my screen? It's like my thumb doesn't want to hit the right numbers.

They blur beneath my fingers. Squinting, I try to focus in on each one, but they swirl in my vision.

What the fuck? One shot and I'm drunk?

The noises around me fade. I only get one more attempt to get into my phone.

But I'm just so... damned... tired.

Maybe I'll just rest my eyes for a minute.

CHAPTER FIFTY-SEVEN

SOFIA

Shit, I think I fell asleep on the couch.

What time is it? Three am? Damn.

Maeve must be sleeping hard. All that time with Elena probably made her tired. Usually she'll wake me up in the middle of the night.

Where is Jax?

I check my phone, but there are no new texts. He said he was going to get a ride.

Did Alexei talk him into something stupid? That guy is a wild card.

After sending Jax a quick message, I make myself a cup of tea and head to the bedroom. Tonight was so crazy. I get why he needed some space.

When an hour goes by, and I still haven't heard anything, a knot of worry starts to grow in my belly.

How do I get a hold of Alexei? At least I have Nikolai's number.

> **Me:** Nikolai, It's Sofia. I'm sorry it's late, but Jax hasn't come home. Can I get Alexei's number?

> **Nikolai:** Sleeping with Alexei is not a good idea.

> **Me:** NO. Alexei was supposed to pick up Jax hours ago.

> **Nikolai:** Standby

My mug is empty after nervously sipping it before Nikolai replies back.

> **Nikolai:** Alexei was sleeping. He never heard from Jax.

> **Me:** What? Where the hell is he?

> **Nikolai:** We will find him

Making sure my phone is plugged in, I stare at it, hoping for some sort of response.

Please, Jax. Tell me where you are. Every time I call his number, it goes straight to voicemail. I want to smash it against the wall.

When he left, he was in a bad place. But when I talked to him, he sounded much happier and eager to come home.

My belly flops. What if he got hurt? Arrested? Do mafia men get arrested? Did some of his old trouble catch up with him?

With a spinning head, I curl up in our bed and pull Jax's pillow close to me. It smells like him. Not like the real thing, but makes it easier to fall into a restless sleep until he's home.

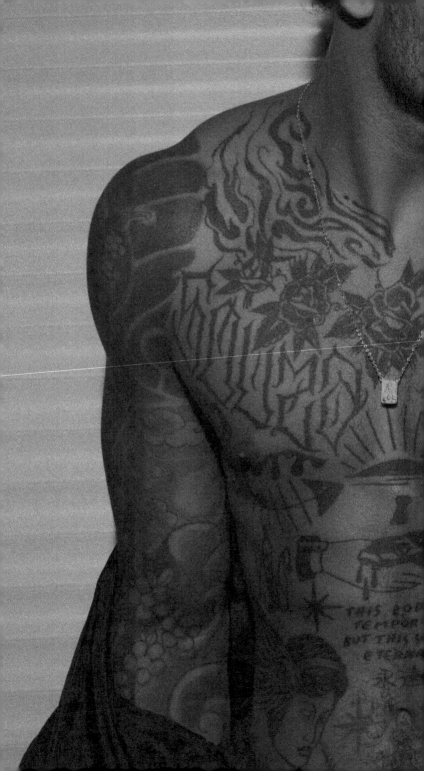

CHAPTER FIFTY-EIGHT

JAX

My heartbeat sounds like the loudest speakers as it thumps in my ears.

Jesus, my head hurts. I try to crack my eyes open, but the brightness sends lightning bolts straight into my brain. Squeezing them shut, I roll over and nestle against Sofia's side.

I must have really gotten fucked up. Even my dick is soft as my belly rolls through waves of nausea.

It's impossible to fight the groan as the room spins behind my eyes.

She shifts against me, turning onto her back.

"I'm sorry, baby. I didn't mean to wake you. I'm just not feeling right," I murmur against her smooth shoulder.

"It's okay. You wore yourself out last night," she purrs.

Wait.

My eyes fly open. Squinting, I take in the blonde hair of the woman who served me a drink last night.

Shoving myself away from her, I fall out of the double bed in what looks like a hotel room.

"Who the fuck are you?" I scream.

She sits up, not even trying to hide her bare breasts as she throws her head back and laughs. "Oh, Jaxxie, you don't remember all the fun we had? They call you 'King' for a reason." Her palm reaches down and flattens the ruffled sheets. "Come back to bed, lover. I'm not done with you."

I catch a glimpse of my boots on the floor. And my pants.

I'm buck ass naked.

"No, no, no. This can't be happening." Bending over, I gather my shit as fast as I can.

"But, it did, baby. Might as well enjoy yourself." She crawls towards me on the mattress, her bare ass sticking up into the air. "Want one more round before you go, champ?"

I think I'm going to be sick.

With my clothes in a bunch in front of my groin, I run to the door and frantically undo the latch.

Stumbling out into a musty hall covered in garish geometric patterns, it takes me a second to get my bearings.

I'm not on a ground floor. I need to get downstairs.

Running until I find a set of elevators, I jab the button as fast as I can, hoping that makes it go faster. How do I not remember any of this? What the fuck am I doing? Sofia and I were talking about getting married last night.

I ruin everything.

Shit. I need to get my pants on. Dropping everything, I dig through the pile and grab my jeans. The elevator dings just as I get my first leg in the hole.

As the doors open, I have one foot in, one foot out, and freeze.

"Jax?" Nikolai's deep voice resonates out. "What the fuck are you doing?"

Alexei starts cackling next to him.

"Alexei? Where were you? I tried to text you…" Where's my phone?

"Sorry, no missed messages from you, man. Did ya get some? Does that mean Sofia is single?" Alexei leans against the wall, watching me with an amused expression.

"Like hell it does!" I can feel the rage surging within me. The need to hit something is becoming overwhelming. Swinging wildly at him, he steps back nimbly as I fall to the floor, my feet tangled in my clothes.

Nikolai takes two giant strides before planting his boot squarely on my neck, pinning me down. "Stop. You did this, not him. What is wrong with you?" His accent is almost as heavy as his weight crushing my throat.

I'm tempted to fight back. But he's right.

I did do this.

My own chaos screwed it all up.

Nikolai lowers his scowling face down over his knee. "Are you done, *durak*?"

I let my arms fall limp. "Yeah. I am a fool."

"A naked one. Your little peepee getting you in trouble?" Alexei points to my dick with the sucker he pulls from his mouth. "If you had a real one—" He grabs his crotch. "—you would not be dipping it all over Vegas trying to grow it like a wax candle."

I'm too groggy for this. "A what?" I ask him as I struggle to pull my pants on.

He squats down next to me and turns his lollipop upside down, bobbing in through the air. "You know, dip a wick, watch it grow. Layer on layer." He tips his head and his nose wrinkles. "Maybe it won't work on you. Too many layers makes your shit burn."

My whole life is an inferno. It wouldn't surprise me if I get some sort of bug that makes it hurt to piss.

I'd deserve it.

There's a knot in my throat, and it isn't from Nikolai's boot.

I'm going to lose Sofia. She's going to hate me. And she should. I had everything I ever wanted and in one night, that I can't even remember, I've destroyed it.

Pushing my head out of my tee shirt, I'm met by a stinging slap against the back of my skull.

Nikolai glares at me. "You have a good woman. Do you know what I would give to have my wife back? And, you just run off and find some whore the second you get your little girly panties in a bunch? Come on." He turns on his heel and stomps back into the elevator. That's not what happened. I'd never go looking for another woman. I love Sofia. What the fuck did I do?

Why the fuck can't I remember a damn thing?

Alexei gives me a push, then follows me in.

"What do I do now?" I whisper. My mind is still foggy, my stomach is twisting, and my heart is shattering into a million pieces.

Nikolai folds his thick arms across his chest, and his blue eyes pierce into me. "You talk to her."

Hitting my head against the mirror, I've done exactly what I thought I would: proved I am a piece of shit, not worthy of anyone's love. This is going to wreck her, but I'll make sure I destroy myself as punishment.

She deserves better. No one needs a fucking train-wreck like me in their life.

"You said you don't remember? Maybe someone slipped you something?" Alexei says, tapping his chin.

I close my eyes, pinching the bridge of my nose. It doesn't matter what the hell happened. I betrayed her in the worst possible way. Excuses don't matter.

I fucked up, and now I have to face the consequences.

CHAPTER
FIFTY-NINE

SOFIA

Song- Hold On, Chord Overstreet

THE BREAD POPS OUT OF THE TOASTER, MAKING ME JUMP.
Even Maeve, clapping to herself, excitedly waiting for her
breakfast, doesn't make me smile.

I feel sick. Jax didn't come home. I haven't heard from
anyone.

I feel overwhelmed as my thoughts are consumed by all
the worst-case scenarios.

Cutting it into little squares, I give Maeve her food and
grab my coffee, dialing Jax for the millionth time.

As the front door opens, I feel a sudden jolt and my
coffee nearly spills from my trembling hands.

"Dadda!" Maeve excitedly squeals.

Jax walks in. His face is pale and his clothes are
disheveled. He's a complete wreck.

With my heart pounding, I rush over to him, feeling a
wave of emotion wash over me. I wrap my arms around
his neck, holding on tightly as tears threaten to spill from
my eyes. I'm grateful he's alive.

His body remains rigid, refusing to return the embrace. "Don't touch me," he says, his voice cracking.

"Jax?"

Taking a step back, he shakes his head, creating a physical barrier between us. As I move forward, he wearily runs a hand over his face.

"Don't," he warns, and my blood runs cold at his harsh tone. "Trust me, after what I'm about to say, you won't even want to be in the same room as me."

Meeting his bloodshot eyes, a surge of adrenaline courses through me, making my heart race.

"W-what are you talking about, Jax?" Is he breaking up with me? What the hell is going on?

"Fuck," he hisses. He can barely look at me.

"Tell me! You're freaking me out!" I can't take much more than this. With every second that goes by, it's like I'm crumbling to pieces.

He looks up at the ceiling. "I slept with someone else, Sof."

My heart stops, and a deafening silence fills the air. As he whispers those words, a sharp pang of pain shoots through my body.

"No," I shake my head rapidly.

He wouldn't do this to me. He couldn't. He was talking about marrying me last night. He wasn't even drunk. This is like he did yesterday. When he's hurting, he pushes away the ones he loves.

"You're lying. You're trying to push me away, aren't you?"

I reach out and firmly grip his face, making him meet my gaze. He's broken, really fucking broken.

This isn't him. This is not my Jax talking. He would never destroy me like this.

"I wish I was lying." He sounds defeated. This isn't him

getting 'caught' like Brody was. This is him, purely devastated. As my heart breaks, I can feel my chest tightening and cracking.

Everything we had is falling to pieces and I can't fix this. I can't save him either. But, as I look into his eyes, something isn't right. This isn't a guy who has gone out and fucked someone to hurt me. The man I love is in there.

I can feel the wetness of my tears as they slowly trickle down my cheeks. The walls are starting to close in on me.

"Why are you trying to make me hate you, Jax?" My voice breaks as I speak.

His own eyes well up. "Trust me, you could never hate me as much as I hate myself."

As I stumble back, my gasps for air become desperate, my chest heaving in an attempt to catch my breath. "Y-you love me, you wanted to marry me. You wouldn't do this. You don't do this shit to people you love, Jax."

"Fuck, I do love you. I love you more than anything in this shitty life. That's one thing I am sure of. But I don't know how good I've got it until I fuck it all up." His eyes snap up to mine and it's like I don't recognize the man staring back at me.

"That's exactly why I think you're doing this on purpose. This isn't you, Jax. You aren't a cheater. I don't believe you would do this to us."

Desperate for comfort, I embrace myself tightly as his harsh words echo in the room.

"Stop making excuses for me! Stop trying to make me into someone I'm not. I woke up, with my dick pressing against a blonde's ass. I called her Sof, for fuck's sake. I thought she was you. I don't remember a fucking thing, but I did it. I broke us. I've destroyed every good thing in my life. Is that what you need to hear? Does that make you believe me? I fucked another woman, Sofia. Listen to what I am telling you."

The impact of his cruel words causes my hands to quiver.

"I am not the man you think I am. Take me off that pedestal. I will never be him. I will only ever be the guy who screws everything up. I am nothing to anyone." He slumps onto the arm of the couch.

My body trembles, but I can't help but shake my head in disbelief.

"Who was she?" I whisper.

He shrugs, lowering his head. Just like his piece of shit brother did to me. Anger rips through me. He wants me to flip. To hate him.

"Look at me, Jax. Break my heart. You want me to hate you? Well, you're getting your wish." My nails dig into my palms as my fists clench.

"I don't know, Sof. I don't know what the fuck happened. But, I can't take it back now. I ruined us."

As my cries intensify, they drown out all other noise. Through the tears, everything becomes a blurry mess. "Why? Why would you do this to us? Did we really mean that little to you?" I'm almost hysterical at this point.

"You mean everything to me."

That's why this hurts so bad. We will never be able to get back this love.

I launch myself at him, beating my fists against his chest.

He lets me. He doesn't even try to stop me until I'm too weak to swing.

Before I crumple to the floor, he grabs my wrists and holds me.

"I'm sorry, sweetheart. I'm really fucking sorry."

Falling to my knees, I feel like I'm in shock. "I can't forgive you for this, Jax. We are done."

His cheeks glisten with tears as he nods slowly. "I know, baby."

Meave's crying shakes me back to reality. I'm numb. I'm heartbroken.

This hurts more than anything I've ever felt.

He ripped not just ours, but our daughter's future from her.

When I look at the pain on his face, I almost feel sorry for him. This is different from Brody. Whatever the hell happened, something is nagging at me that it's not right.

Bile rises my throat as Jax walks over to Maeve and cuddles her into his chest. He nuzzles his head against her, but I can hear his sobs.

Each one shatters me.

This family was his life. He told me so.

I can't watch anymore. It's like I'm a passenger in my own body, watching my future burn in front of my eyes and I can't stop it.

Moving silently, I sprint up the stairs and quietly shut the bedroom door, leaning on it for support as I exhale. With each breath, my chest is tightening.

With burning eyes, I scramble to find a bag and frantically throw my clothes in. Startled, I look up to see Jax standing in the doorway, his face streaked with tears that he hastily wipes away.

"Please don't leave me, Sofia."

I stomp around the bed, creating a loud thud with each step, until I stop right in front of him. I forcefully jab my finger into his chest, trying to make my point clear.

"Fuck you. You really are no different to your piece of shit brother. But, the difference is, you actually shattered my heart." My throat knots as I watch his lip tremble.

"I'll do anything. Please don't do this," he whispers.

I throw up my hands in exasperation. "No. Is this how you'd want a guy to treat your daughter? What would you say to her?"

"I-I…"

"Exactly."

He gave me everything. It was a dream. The kind of love I hope my daughter has someday. Not anymore. It was a lie. I turn and continue packing.

"Stop. I'll leave. This is your home with Maeve now."

With a shake of my head, I ignore him completely and desperately cram dresses into the bag on the bed. I need to get away from here. From him.

He grabs the strap and tosses it across the room, making me jump.

"I'm leaving, Sofia. You need this place for Maeve. Don't argue with me on that, please."

I have nowhere to go. I have nothing.

I can't even move or speak as I watch him stop by the door and turn back to me.

"Can I still see Maeve? I can make arrangements so you don't even have to look at me."

Is that what I want? To never see his face again?

Because even when I don't want to, I still fucking love him. It might hurt me for the rest of my life. But I will never stop loving this man.

I will always belong to him.

"Don't break our little girl's heart, Jax. I beg you. You're still her father. She loves you. Do the right thing by her. If you don't, I'll never forgive you."

In all of this, she is our priority. She always will be.

"You really think she needs a piece of shit father like me around? Honestly?"

As he runs a hand through his hair, a sigh escapes his

lips. His defeated expression is impossible to ignore. He has the weight of the world on his shoulders and he has no-one to blame but himself this time. He did this.

"Yes. I don't care how much you hurt me. Don't do that to her. You aren't that guy, Jax. Whatever it is you have going on, that self-destructive mode, fix it. Before you break yourself. Be better for her." Pushing past him, I go back downstairs, where Maeve is fussing.

His boots echo on the tile as he follows me.

I can't even look at him. Every time I do, another part of me shatters inside. Picking Maeve up from her playpen, I hug her tight. It's as if she is the only thing holding me together.

Jax nervously hovers by the entrance, looking lost.

"Just go, Jax."

My voice cracks as I say the words. With the front door closing, I avert my gaze towards the window, finally allowing myself to let it all out.

With each passing moment, the pain gradually fades, replaced by a numbing sensation that engulfs me completely.

CHAPTER SIXTY

JAX

Song- Never Know, Bad Omens

"WAKE UP." NIKOLAI'S VOICE ANGRILY BREAKS THROUGH the blackness.

I don't want to open my eyes. It's another day. Twenty-four hours longer that I've been away from her.

How many days has it been?

"Jax." His deep voice cracks through again making my head pound.

It doesn't hurt as much as my heart.

Nikolai is big enough, I've seen him crush skulls. Maybe I should ask him to squeeze mine until this pain goes away…

Bitter cold water splashes over me and my eyes jolt open to the blinding light.

"What the fuck?" Sitting up so fast doesn't help the stars bursting in my vision.

I'm soaking wet and have ice cubes in my lap.

"That's the cleanest you've been in a week." Nikolai

throws the empty plastic bucket at me, which bounces off of my shoulder. "Get up. Mikhail has a job for us."

Groaning, I blink at him until some of the focus comes back. "You're a shitty brother-in-law."

Nikolai's thick finger bluntly taps me in the middle of the forehead. "Don't you dare drag Katerina into your bear den. *You* made this mess of your own life." He straightens, crossing his arms over his broad chest. "I'm doing more than your own brother. Remember that."

Brody.

I'm no better than him. Sofia is perfect. But, me? Him? Garbage for ruining her trust.

Dragging myself out of the twisted sheets of his spare room, I walk barefooted down the hall with my shirt in one hand and my boots in my other.

Nikolai shrugs on a black leather jacket then looks down his nose at me. "What are you doing?"

"I'm getting my stuff on." Slumping onto his couch, I glance at the little plastic kitchen set that my daughter and his were playing with together, just a few nights ago.

When I stomped everything into the ground.

"*Niet.*" He waves his hand in a large circle towards me. "You need to delouse yourself before you ride in my car."

I'm pulling on my second shoe, but stop and stare blankly at him.

"I don't know what that means."

"Scrub. Clean. Your. Filth." He sounds each word out and stabs his finger towards me for emphasis. Shrugging his shoulders, he sits down on a chair near the door. "You could have bugs by now, like a street dog in the cesspools."

"You're so damn nice, Niki. Anyone ever tell you what a pleasant disposition you have?" Tugging my feet free, I leave my boots where they lay and stomp my way back to the bedroom.

It seems I'm inconvenient to everyone.

God, this hurts.

Useless. I feel like a burden.

And, I only have myself to blame.

Grabbing a half-full bottle of tequila, I strip off my pants and stumble into the shower.

Just a swallow or two, enough to cut the pain.

I can smell myself as the hot water scalds over me.

Why do I see her face every time I close my eyes? The agony etched across her features when I told her what I did.

Knowing that I did that to her, I deserve every piece of punishment.

No one can be happy around me. I am the destroyer.

The King of Chaos.

Why?

This torment in me grows with every anguished thought. I've lost so many, and each one has torn a piece of me away until I'm hollow.

Used.

Broken.

Loud thuds break through as I lean against the cold tile.

"Stop jacking off in my shower! We need to *go!*" Nikolai's deep voice carries over the streaming water.

Cutting the flow, it's not until I'm half dried off I realize I didn't even soap up.

Giving myself a fast sniff test, at least I cut the grime by half.

Good enough.

I dig in my duffel and find my last pair of clean pants. Damn.

Raking my fingers through my disheveled hair, I pad back into the living room, still damp.

Nikolai wrinkles his nose and shakes his head.

"You need to wake up, Jax. The world is passing you by." He opens the door and gestures me through, then climbs behind the wheel of his hellcat.

How do I do that? Maybe this is all a dream.

Would pinching myself work?

Throw myself off of the roof?

They say, if you die in your nightmare, you wake up.

A horn blaring snaps me back.

Nikolai is glaring at me through the passenger window.

"Sorry." I must have been standing there for a little while by how far out that vein is bulging in his forehead.

His teeth grit, but he doesn't say a word the entire drive to pick up Alexei and then to Vox.

He walks ahead of me through the Vegas heat until he pulls the door open to the club and steps through.

"What did you do to piss him off?" Alexei finally asks. He's stayed quiet the whole time, too. Except for an errant comment about something dying in the seat where I was sitting.

The owner gives us a grateful smile and just points towards the back.

I can hear the yelling from here.

"Remember, if Knox is here, we need him alive." Nikolai tells me over his shoulder before striding through the crowd.

He's a full head taller than anyone else in here, and they part ways to let us through.

The music thumping is making my brain swell in rhythm to it.

I almost want to ask if we can stop for a drink, but I might wait until after we're done.

Two Reapers are standing over what looks to be a

group of frat boys partying. The thugs are knocking them around and stealing their drinks.

Pushing past Nikolai, I don't say a word before swinging and connecting to the back of the first's head.

He falls instantly without a sound.

"You shouldn't be here. This is our bar now." Brody's voice cuts through the fog and leaves an icy chill down my spine.

Glancing up, he's holding a pistol, pointed directly at me.

He saunters closer and waves me away from the other Reaper with the barrel of his weapon.

Wide eyed college kids scurry away from us, abandoning their drinks.

"You look like shit, *brother*. I heard that you're single again. Hmm." He taps the tip of his gun against his lips. "She might need a shoulder to cry on."

Nikolai grabs me just as I'm about to leap forward.

"You stay the fuck away from my girls," I snarl.

Brody's eyes widen before one brow raises higher than the other. "Yours? Are you sure? That cute little baby looks just as much like *me* as she does you."

Three more big guys appear behind Brody, who flashes me an arrogant grin.

Struggling, I manage to break free and dive towards him with my hands outstretched.

A boot lands squarely in my ribs, knocking me backwards.

Shaking it off, I surge again. I want to beat him for every moment of heartache he gave Sofia.

And, in a way, I want him to do it back.

I deserve just as much, if not more.

Another blow bounces off my jaw.

Alexei jumps in next to me, arms flying as he cackles through blows.

My hands lay limply by my sides.

As another fist connects with my eye, and it goes black, Brody laughs.

Just as my face bounces off of the hard concrete, I can feel a big palm wrap around the belt of my jeans and hoist me from the floor.

"Get up. Get out." Nikolai practically throws me behind him.

"No!" Back on my feet, I try to rush back at Brody.

He's standing safely behind a wall of leather vested chests.

"Brody needs to know to stay the he—" I'm cut off by Alexei pushing me backwards.

"Next time. You are acting like a small child. Let's go outside and pout." He grins, but forcefully carries me towards the door.

Nausea rolls in my guts. My ear is ringing and I can't see past the swelling on one side.

"How did Brody know?" Nikolai asks Alexei as they carry me into the sweltering heat.

Alexei shakes his head.

I failed Sofia, again. I can't even protect her when I'm away.

What am I even good for?

Alexei and Nikolai talk in low tones in the front seat.

All I can focus on are the street lights passing by his tinted windows and the feel of the warm leather on my back.

My head is swimming as I fight the urge to puke.

"I need a drink." It'd help kill this pain.

"I don't know why. You have a death wish, Jax. You

should feel the consequences of your choices," Nikolai grumbles.

"This hurts so bad." Throwing my elbow over my eyes, I try to mute the world.

"That one guy got you solid. Did you see his rings?" Alexei turns back.

It sounds like he's screaming.

"I felt them." Pretty sure I'll have a permanent imprint of them.

It isn't long before we make it back to Nikolai's house.

Lara is waiting inside as Nikolai and Alexei carry me from the car. Like a damn invalid.

"Oh my god, Jax!" She gently touches my temple on the swollen side of my face. "Alexei! Nikolai! Why did you let this happen?" She scowls at both of them with her hands on her hips.

Alexei throws up his hands after he deposits me roughly on the couch. "You can't stop a donkey once it decides to run." He flops down in one of the recliners.

"Alexei, what does that mean?" I cough out. My ribs are killing me, and my lip is so puffy it's harder to talk.

He leans back and props his feet up on the hearth by the fireplace. "You. You are the donkey."

CHAPTER SIXTY-ONE

SOFIA

Song- When The Party's Over- from the room below, Sleep Token

ALEXEI IS LATE.

He and Nikolai have been taking turns bringing me back and forth to work since Jax left. They said it's safer for me than going alone.

It's like they aren't telling me something, but I haven't figured it out yet.

When he does knock on the door, it's nearly ten minutes later than normal.

"Alexei! Oh my god! What happened?" He has a bruise on his cheek that's slowly giving him a black eye.

He waves his hand nonchalantly. "It is nothing. Kids these days like to play rough." He scoops up Maeve's car seat and heads towards the back of his car.

"Were you in a fight?" I ask as I follow him out with Maeve in my arms.

He stops and stands, his hair flopping over his eyes as he scratches the tattoos behind his ear. "No, no. It was a donkey." He grins wide enough to showcase his silver tooth, then lifts Maeve out of my grasp to settle her in her seat.

Alexei's Russian to English isn't always very solid, so I let it go.

He pulls up in front of the clinic and lets me out.

"Bye, baby girl. Remember, when Mommy gets home, you get to see Daddy, too." I give Maeve a kiss on the top of her head before I leave.

She's been staying with Lara during the days. It's sure nice to have someone I can trust watching her.

I haven't heard from Anna for a while. She made it clear last time I talked to her that we aren't on the best of terms though.

As the day progresses, I can't tell if it's nerves or dread making my stomach turn.

The girls I work with seem to notice, and make me promise that I'll take a night out with them later this week.

"Hello, lady." Alexei's eye looks slightly better than it did this morning with tinges of yellow around the edges of the purple.

My stomach flip flops knowing Jax will be at the house. But, as we pull in the driveway, disappointment tinges the nerves when I don't see his bike or Lambo parked in front.

"Where is he?" I almost half say to myself.

Alexei squints. "Niki will bring him soon. Jax is too wobbly."

I swear I only understand half of what he says sometimes. "Okay. Thank you for picking me up. Please let Lara know I appreciate her watching Maeve."

My sweet little girl gives me the grabby hands as I pull her and the car seat out.

Every day it's a different vehicle. I wish I knew how long this musical chairs motorcade was going to last.

They all keep giving me vague answers about the Reapers.

I think it still has something to do with Brody after the fight.

Maeve is just settling into her highchair for a snack when I hear the unmistakable rumble of Nikolai's Hellcat pull in.

When the knock comes, I don't know if I want to answer it. It's so hard seeing Jax.

But, I also won't deny him his daughter, no matter how heartbreaking it is.

As the door opens, I'm left speechless.

"Hiya, Sof. Sorry I'm late." His words are slurred coming out of his swollen mouth.

He looks like he's been hit by a truck. The entire side of his face is purple, and I can't even see one of his eyes.

"What the hell, Jax?" Instinct has me reaching forward and almost touching his cheek when I pause.

No. It isn't my place anymore. Curling my fingers until my nails dig into my palm, I let it fall to my side.

He limps as he steps past me, with one arm firmly wrapped around his ribs.

My chest hurts looking at him. "What happened?" Following him into the kitchen, I feel like grabbing him and spinning him around to make him answer me. I know it won't do any good.

"Just work." He starts to squat in front of a wide-eyed Maeve, but stops with a grimace.

She watches him warily like she doesn't recognize him.

"Hi, baby girl. I think you've grown since the last time I saw you." He brushes one of her curly locks away from her temple, making her smile.

"Dadda." Her hands raise, begging him to pick her up.

He groans as he picks her up, then gingerly steps over the couch while talking to her.

Their curly heads touch at the forehead and it makes me nearly cry.

His face relaxes as he tucks her under his neck and holds her tightly.

She stuffs her thumb in her mouth and settles against him, closing her eyes with a look of absolute bliss.

Why did he have to ruin this? He could always have these moments.

My throat chokes up watching them.

I hate that he did this to us.

Wanting to hold him, both of them, brings stinging tears and a knot in my throat that I can't swallow.

When the sob escapes, he looks over and his brow furrows.

I can't handle this. He needs time with her and seeing them together is just too agonizing.

Turning, I run up the stairs and collapse into the bed as shuddering cries fall out of me. Why, even after the damage he caused, do I still miss him so damn bad? That all I can think about is running back down there and covering him with kisses and begging him to stay?

My pillow is covered in mascara and my nose is runny when I hear a soft tapping on the bedroom door.

"Sofia? Are you okay?" He's silhouetted against the hall light, and his arms are empty.

Have I been crying all the way to her bedtime?

"No, Jax. I'm not. I hate this," I sniffle.

I can't even remember a time when I didn't have this ache inside of me. It's like my entire world has crashed and I'm stuck in a loop of reliving this agony over and over.

"Please, Sof. Don't cry over me." His shoulders slump against the pale glow. "I'm not worth it."

"I just, I don't know what to say, Jax. Seeing you with her, it just hurts." Falling back against the comforter, fresh tears dampen the soaked blanket. How do I tell him I just want it to go back to the way it was?

Can we pretend it never happened?

He sighs and rests his head against the frame. "I wish I could fix this. I hate it, too."

Wanting a hug from him, to feel comforted and safe, is all I can think about.

But, I can't. He took that choice away from me.

"Are you, um. Fuck, I don't even know how to ask." Burying my face in my palms, I struggle to regroup what I was going to say.

"Sof… you can ask me anything," he says softly. He sounds just as broken as I am.

"Are you still, um, with her?" I choke out.

"What? Fuck no. I don't even know who she is. I swear." His fist taps against his thigh, almost like he's beating himself up. "I messed this all up for nothing. I'm sorry."

When he grabs the door and pulls it around, I want to scream at him to come back. To hold me. To tell me this is all some nasty prank that will be over.

Why can't it be a joke? Fake?

So we can go back to how we were?

The air changes as he leaves. My phone dings with the motion detection, but I don't check it.

I know he's gone.

CHAPTER SIXTY-TWO

JAX

Song, NUMB, Ryan Oakes

"Where the fuck is this man? He's a ghost and I want him found. Yesterday." Mikhail's thick finger stabs the photograph that he holds so everyone can see. "His last known location was on the north side of Vegas three days ago. Why is my intel more than seventy-two hours old?" He crumples the paper and throws it across the room.

A few days ago, I would have been upset and ready to go on the hunt.

But, that was before my world shattered.

All I can see is Sofia's tear-stained face over and over in my mind.

My injuries are healing, but not my heart.

"Jax! Did you hear a word I said?" Mikhail's deep voice cuts through gruffly.

"Huh? No boss, I'm sorry," I stammer.

Alexei elbows me in the shoulder and points at his own eyeballs before gesturing his fingers towards Mikhail.

"I said, I've talked to Enzo, but he needs a better shot

of this guy for his tracking software. Or a license plate. Anything. I need you to work with Niki on this." His eyes narrow over his balaclava. "And, I want you to stick around after this meeting."

The room erupts in "oohs" and laughter.

All aimed at me.

If I didn't like these guys more, I'd start swinging. But, I guess it's not their fault I'm fucking useless.

Mikhail's arm waves, kicking everyone out until I'm sitting on the stiff leather couch against the wall, alone.

He flips a stout wooden chair around and straddles it, his muscular arms bulging under the taut material of his suit.

"What the hell is going on, Jax?" His dark eyes are nearly black as he stares at me.

But, he doesn't look angry.

"I got, well, a lot going on, boss." How do I tell him I'm just a mess?

He narrows his gaze and stares silently at me until I start to squirm against the cushions.

"Drugs? Are you dipping into the product?" He tilts his head slightly.

"No, never."

"Must be women, then? This town is full of bad ones. They aren't worth getting upset about." His hands grip the back and he stands as if the conversation is over.

"It's just one. And she's the best." Sofia is worth getting emotional over.

I'll never find another like her.

"Then what did she do?" He pauses, one brow raised.

I wipe my face in frustration. "She didn't do anything. It was me that fucked everything up." I let out a long groan.

His mask wrinkles over his nose. "What did you do, Jax?" he asks quietly.

"I slept with someone else."

There. I said it.

He grumbles and moves back to his desk. "She must not have been very special."

My chest aches as I fight to keep the tears from embarrassing me.

"She is the most important person in my life." I love her more than myself. "I'd give anything to fix this."

"Jax. Sometimes we are our own worst enemies." His accent gets thicker. "But, you need to quell that chaos in you and find peace, only then you can find it with her."

He waves towards the door. "Now go. Do not let your distraction get you, or my brother, hurt."

I don't care what Mikhail says, I can't shut down the voice in my head that constantly tells me how badly I messed up.

Or, how much I miss Sofia.

The back of Nikolai's hand smacks me across the chest.

"Did you hear me? Get out your phone and take a picture of him! I'll make another pass." His teeth are clenched as he talks.

Great, I pissed him off too.

"Sorry. I wasn't paying attention. What am I trying to do?" I pull my cell out and am disappointed that there aren't any missed texts from her.

Do I even deserve to have her trying to talk to me? All I do is make her cry.

When I'm near her it's even worse. Every single piece of me wants to hold her and tell her it will all be okay.

I promised to take care of her, and I broke everything.

"Jesus. Fuck. You missed again." Nikolai's hands squeeze the steering wheel hard enough it squeaks in his grip.

"I'm taking you home, Jax. You need to get out of your own head."

Looking around, all I can see is the crowds on the sidewalk as we drive by. Nothing stands out.

"Who am I getting a picture of? I'm ready? Where is he?"

Nikolai growls and leans away. "He's gone. He ducked into that casino." He jabs towards the right.

Shit. That one is run by the Reapers.

Damn.

Why do I keep screwing up? I *knew* this was important.

"Tonight's my night with Maeve. Can you do me a huge favor and—"

"Yes. Just tell me what time you need me to pick you up. My little girl always puts me in a better place. Maybe yours will do the same?" Nikolai glances at me as he turns a corner. He has a sad looking smile on his face when I catch him.

Everyone feels bad for me.

I guess I'm pretty pathetic.

"Thank you." I feel like a kid.

It takes everything in me to walk up the steps to her house. Not long ago, it was *our* place. Together.

My knuckles sound hollow on the door, but she opens it immediately.

"Hi." She chews on her lip when she sees me.

Like every time I see her, my breath catches. She's so beautiful.

I was the luckiest man alive to have her.

"I'm glad you're here. I got called in for a staff meeting this evening. Didn't think it would be a bad thing to leave the house while you and Maeve hung out." Sofia steps back as I step into the hall.

It's like she's afraid to touch me.

Can't blame her. I'm pretty despicable.

"Are you okay, Jax?" I look up and catch her studying me.

"Sof, I—" I don't know what to say. "Yeah, I'm good. Thank you."

At least Maeve doesn't look as scared of me today. My face isn't as bruised and discolored as it was last time I was here.

It feels like years. Each day a decade.

"Hey, baby girl. Daddy's so happy to see you!" Scooping her up, I hug her tightly. Her chubby fingers find the collar of my shirt and clings to it.

"Dadda, Dadda," she babbles.

"I missed you too, *tigryonok.*" Giving her a tender kiss on the top of her curly hair, I meet Sofia's gaze across the room.

My chest aches seeing the pain etched on her face. I don't think I can handle seeing her cry again, so I turn away. "Let's read a book, okay?" Setting Maeve down, she runs to her shelf and picks up her favorite alphabet book.

It's the one I got her, full of motorcycles in the shapes of the letters.

She drops it unceremoniously on my lap and lifts her arms for me to pick her up.

I think we're around letter N or M when I hear Sofia's heels on the tiles clicking closer.

"Mommy has to go. I'll be home at eight." She leans and touches her lips against Maeve's temple, inches away from me.

Close enough I can smell her sweet strawberry scent.

"I love you." Sofia glances at me, tears welling in the corners of her big green eyes, before she pulls away.

Should I tell her I love her, too?

Because I do. More than anything.

But, before I can decide, she's gone.

I guess I must have stopped reading, because Maeve starts squirming and pats the page with her palm.

"I'm sorry. You know Daddy loves you and Mommy? I hope you do." I squeeze her a little closer and continue the book.

Z feels so final.

I hate that it's the end. Picking up story after story, they all do.

There's a last page for each one.

Even the most exciting tales, and colorful pages, have a final scene.

A happily ever after.

Except mine.

I guess I tore mine out. Shredded into a million pieces.

After changing Maeve into a clean diaper and her pajamas, I carry her back to her room.

The giant teddy bear that I won for her is sitting on a small playtable in the corner.

"Oh! Remember when Daddy got this? Wasn't that fun?" Bouncing her on my hip, I pick up the overstuffed arm and wave it at her.

Her cheeks turn red and her mouth drops before she lets out a shrieking wail.

Shit. Fuck.

"Shh. It's okay. That mean old bear can stay in the corner." Turning away quickly, I drag it behind me so she can't see and push it out of her room with my foot.

It doesn't matter what I do, I always choose wrong.

After a few minutes of fussing, she finally settles down

and rubs her eyes tiredly. Giving her one last hug, I lower her into her crib.

"I hope you know how much I love you." When I shut the door, I hear the garage door opening.

Sofia's home.

It's only a moment later that the engine to the Hellcat pulls in.

Sofia comes in through the kitchen to find me sorting the books back onto the small shelf.

"What's with the teddy bear in the garbage can?" she asks as she watches me.

"It's trash. It was a mistake. Every time she sees it, she cries." I don't look at her.

I can't. It hurts too much.

"Jax. She will love it one day. Her daddy got it for her. It's just a bit big for her." She steps forward, almost like she's going to touch me.

But, she doesn't.

I wish, more than anything, she would.

"Kids grow up. They learn to appreciate what they have." Her words are quiet. "We all need to learn those lessons, sometimes."

Is she still talking about Maeve? I can't tell.

"Some of us are too thick-headed. We just make the same mistakes." Brushing past her, I rush out the front and slump into the passenger seat next to Nikolai.

"Did it help?" he asks as he reverses out of the driveway.

"No."

CHAPTER SIXTY-FOUR

SOFIA

Song- In The End, Linkin Park

THIS IS THE FIRST TIME I'VE BEEN OUT WITHOUT JAX, AND I'm nervous.

I know it's just with the girls from work, but it feels like somehow it's admitting that he isn't a part of me anymore.

And, that hurts.

I don't want it to be over. He seems genuinely upset about what happened.

Would there be a way for us to move on, together?

It would be hard to trust him. But, this ache, this pain that stabs me into my chest every single time I think about him, would it go away?

Maybe I'll think about it another night. Trying to get him to talk might be my first step.

If he wants to. He's so hard to read, I can't tell if he wants to come back, or if he's content to stay away.

I didn't want to push my luck with him, since he's been so erratic lately, so I asked Lara if she could watch Maeve tonight for me.

The fact that I'm used to taking care of my daughter alone frustrates me. She should have her dad.

I want him. It kills me every time I pass a motorcycle on the street and I get that flutter in my belly that it might be him.

Maeve tangles her fingers in my hair as I ring the bell at Lara's.

She meets me with a big smile, flips her long blonde hair behind her shoulder and immediately reaches for Maeve. "Hi, curly q!"

Maeve giggles and flings herself into Lara's arms.

"Thank you for doing this on short notice. I wasn't sure if I was actually going to go or not." I pass her the diaper bag and glimpse Alexei sitting on the couch behind her watching television.

"No problem! Where are you going? I'll make sure Alexei and Niki go and keep an eye out." Lara kicks his foot as she walks by with Maeve. "Aren't you, Alexei?"

"Huh? Sure. Yes. What am I doing?" He blinks as he looks between me and Lara.

"You're going to watch Sofia tonight," she calls from the kitchen.

His brows furrow in confusion. "I can see her. She is right here." He gestures at me still standing in the entry.

A roll of paper towels flies over the counter and bounces off of the side of his head. "When she goes to the club!" Lara yells.

Maeve giggles and screeches herself, clapping her hands.

Seeing her happy makes me smile.

"Oh, yea, sure. I'll get Niki." Alexei pulls out his phone and starts texting while rattling what sounds like a piece of hard candy around in his mouth.

"You really don't have to, I'll be fine. It's just a drink with a bunch of girls from the office."

"Don't make me throw something at you, too." Lara steps out and puts Maeve on the floor with a handful of plastic bowls. "You know that you're on the radar for the Reapers. There's no reason to be crazy."

"Fine. We're going to the Shamrock Pub. I have to get going. Thanks again." If I hurry, I should get there in time.

"Say 'bye Momma'." Lara squats next to Maeve and waves her little arm at me.

I blow her a kiss. "Bye, baby girl."

Just like what Jax calls her.

The whole way there I can't stop thinking about him. How broken he is.

Why would he ruin everything if he loved me and Maeve so much?

It isn't fair. He was talking about marrying me. Who cheats when they're supposedly that much in love?

He makes me so mad that he just gave up on us. If only he tried a little harder. I thought he really wanted me, us.

Was everything he said a lie?

It didn't seem to be. There wasn't anyone forcing him to keep chasing me.

God, I loved it when he did.

My friends are already gathered in a booth and wave me over.

They're filled with smiles and polite conversation, but it's hard to stay focused.

I can't stop thinking about just how broken Jax looked last night when he left.

"How about them, Sofia? Aren't they just a hunk of meat that would be fun to bite into?" Lisa gestures past me, pointing to a table in the far corner.

It takes me a minute to adjust my eyes in the dim light, but familiar shapes form.

Nikolai. Alexei.

And, Jax.

He's slumped on the edge of the seat.

"What about them?" I avert my gaze. I don't want to draw attention to them, even if it's impossible not to keep glancing back at Jax.

"Well, you said you are single after your boyfriend cheated on you. They look like an excellent opportunity for a rebound." She giggles into her hand. "Should we buy them a drink?"

"Um. I don't think tonight. Maybe some other time?" Turning back to my margarita, it seems much less tasty than it was a moment ago.

Everything feels sour.

I just want him to come over here, scoop me up, and run out the door with me cradled to his chest and tell me everything is going to be okay.

"Oops. Looks like we missed out." Lisa sighs and turns back to another coworker.

Wait. What does she mean?

Twisting around, I catch a glimpse of the waitress laughing with her hand on Jax's shoulder.

And, he's smiling back at her.

His wicked, sexy, flirty grin.

That's mine.

Not hers.

Was it all bullshit? The tears? The begging? He really is just a dog who chases any bone?

Anger brews in me like a raging storm.

Standing violently, my glass crashes to the floor.

A piece of me hears my friends gasp, but I don't look.

All I can see is *him* with that woman's hand on him.

I barely acknowledge pushing the waitress aside.

"How can you be so happy when I'm fucking breaking inside?" I scream into his face. My palm snaps against his cheek.

He looks up at me in shock, but I don't give him a chance to answer.

To hide my pain and tears, I turn and run past the wide-eyed customers and out the door.

CHAPTER SIXTY-FOUR

JAX

Song- Half A Man, Dean Lewis

THE STING ON MY CHEEK IS NOTHING COMPARED TO THE pain I feel inside.

As she spins on her heel and makes a dart for the exit, that familiar deep ache in my chest resurfaces. When I look at her, I'm struck by the raw agony reflected in her expression.

That I caused. Again.

No matter what I do. I hurt her. I just can't seem to make it stop.

Her words loop in my head. She thinks I'm happy? Doesn't she know that I physically recoiled when the waitress put her hand on my shoulder?

I had absolutely no interest in her. The only woman I'll ever want is Sofia. I won't move on, I can't. My heart belongs to her. Even if I have to rip it out of my chest and give it to her.

That's what it feels like living without her anyway.

Empty.

Dead inside.

"Go after her." Nikolai's voice is stern.

What good am I to her?

Running a hand over my face, the thought of her being upset and on her own eats away at me. I wish I had a fucking time machine and can go back and change everything. Write myself out of her life, take away her misery.

I slam my hands down on the table, feeling the vibrations reverberate through my palms as I push myself up.

"You spill my beer. You owe me a shot." Alexei grins, picking his bottle up.

"Go." Nikolai points to the exit.

As quick as my feet will go, I barge into the door and come to a halt when I hear the unmistakable sound of glass shattering. Her screams echo through the air and I search her out in the dark, finding her bashing the windows of my Lamborghini.

All I can see is the shards flying, surrounding her in a jagged spray that litters the ground around her .

Fuck.

"Sofia, stop!" I shout, launching myself over to her, bracing myself for her to hit me with the jack handle as I grab her by the waist and hold her flailing body against me.

"Fuck you, Jax! Get off me. Of course all you care about is your stupid car," she sobs against me.

Carefully, I unpeel her fingers from the weapon and spin her to face me.

The agony on her face guts me.

She pushes against my chest.

I shake my head and wrap my arms around her, pulling her flush against me, feeling the warmth of her tears soaking my shirt.

"You know that isn't true, baby," I whisper into the top of her head.

With every cry, my heart splinters further. I'm not sure how many more times this can happen before I fall apart.

"Why did you do this to us, Jax? How do you get to sit there and drink with your friends, flirting with women and I cry myself to sleep every night? Why couldn't you just love me enough?"

My throat starts to close in.

My days are darker than even after Kai's death. I can't escape it, it's consuming me.

I pull back, gripping her shoulders and looking into her eyes. They're a painful reminder of what I've done to her.

I deserve every ounce of suffering.

As I glance down, I see the trickle of blood running down her forearm. Fuck. Not only am I torturing her on the inside, she's bleeding, because of me.

With my thumb, I wipe the crimson away. I can't let this happen to my sweet Sofia.

"Smash as many cars as you want. Take it all out on me. Hit me, punch me. Do whatever the hell you want. But, I won't let you ever hurt yourself, tigritsa."

Just saying her nickname out loud is like a kick in the gut. I am numb to any feeling. She should take it out on me. Let me carry it all.

With a head shake, she abruptly withdraws her arm from my touch, creating a physical gap between us. She has no idea how much that space is silently destroying me. With every day that passes without her, wrapped in my own guilt, I'm slowly dying.

She applies pressure to the wound and I feel sick. "You think a little cut hurts me? When you've already destroyed me? This is nothing in comparison, Jax."

I open my mouth to speak and nothing follows. She's

right. That is exactly how I feel. Numb every second of the day.

I can't let her feel anything like I do.

"Let me take you home?" I offer, I need to make sure she's safe. She looks up at me through bloodshot eyes, studying me as her cries have subsided. I can sense her debating what to do, as her face softens, it's like I can breathe again.

She rummages through her bag and tosses her keys at me, storming off towards her Range Rover.

She stares blankly out of the passenger window all the way home. As we pull up into the driveway, she sighs.

"At least you seem to be doing better," she says, turning to face me.

I let out a laugh.

Doing better? I'm the furthest I could possibly be from okay. I don't need to burden her with my real thoughts. So I nod, getting out of the car and leading her inside.

Lara eyes us both suspiciously as we walk in. A frown forms when she sees Sofia's red face.

I keep my distance as Lara wraps an arm around a crying Sofia and walks her to the kitchen.

It isn't until Lara's sharp nails dig into my shoulder I'm back to reality.

"Look after her, Jax," she says to me quietly in Russian.

"I will."

Or at least, I can try. If she will even let me.

The door closes behind me and I slowly approach Sofia.

She doesn't look up as she pours herself a fresh glass of wine. That need to protect her is still in me, it will never go away. Even if it's me I have to protect her from.

"You can go, Jax," she sniffles, turning her attention back to her drink.

I come to a stop on the other side of the counter.

"I just want to make sure you're okay, Sof. You're hurt." I gesture at the drying blood on her arm.

She nods, brushing her fingers over the cut. The silence feels like a heavy weight, suffocating me.

"I'm so sorry, sweetheart. I don't know what else to say. I wish I had answers, or even knew what I was doing that night. But I don't."

I spend my nights trying to remember, something, anything. Why did I do it? How did I end up in that bed? It doesn't make any sense. I love this woman. Why did I fuck this up so badly?

"You can stay in the spare room if you want. At least you can see Maeve in the morning. I have some errands to run anyway."

I scratch the back of my neck. We could have been spending our weekends on trips as a family. As I remember what I've lost, my fists clench. That was the life I wanted. That was the lifeline that rescued me from the darkest corners of my mind.

"Do you think I'll ever be able to fix this?"

As she lowers her head, my hands begin to shake. My last bit of hope in this life is that maybe, she might forgive me. That I can get my family back.

"I don't think you can, Jax. Not while you're like this. The drinking, the fighting, the women. If that's the life you want, there isn't room for me, is there?"

My heart sinks.

"That isn't what I want. That means nothing to me. I just don't know how to make this better."

This is the closest to the truth I've ever spoken. She rises and gives me a smile filled with sadness as she washes out her glass.

All I can see is her pity. Poor pathetic Jax.

She takes her time, drying the clean flute before putting it carefully into the cupboard. When she finally turns to me, she keeps the counter between us. "I can't fix you. Only you can do that. You need to fight. That's what you do best, isn't it, Jax?"

All my fight has gone. I know I can never be the man she and Maeve deserve. All I'll do is fuck them up. They're better off without me. She's right, she can't fix me. No one can.

I can't keep doing this to them. I refuse to be a burden on them any longer.

Fighting to keep breaking the ones I love is no longer an option. The only way they can be happy is without me.

CHAPTER SIXTY-FIVE

SOFIA

Song- Distraction, Sleep Token

"DADA" MAEVE CRIES, HOLDING UP HER ARMS AS I LIFT her out of her crib.

"Dada is here, we can go wake him up." I tell her, but her wails get louder.

Resting Maeve on my hip, I knock on Jax's door. I really need to apologize to him. I can't believe I smashed up his car. I shouldn't have said all of those things to him. It made it impossible to sleep thinking about how hurt he looked when I told him he doesn't have a chance to fix it.

I didn't mean it.

I can't live without him.

When he doesn't respond to my second knock, I cautiously open the door and take a peek inside. The bed is pristine, showing no indication that anyone has slept in it.

I want to make this right.

I was wrong, we can fix this.

Maeve pulls at my hair, still shouting for her daddy.

"Ok, baby. Let's get you changed. Then we can call

daddy, see if he can come back home? How does that sound?"

Her toothy grin lights up her face, and I can't resist running my fingers over her silky smooth cheek.

After a quick diaper swap, Maeve is in her highchair with her bottle. I call Jax and he doesn't pick up. Did he even stay here?

I'm worried about him. Each time I see him, the more lost he seems. That happy Jax isn't there anymore. It's like I'm watching him fall apart.

Something inside tells me that he's not right. None of this is. I can't ignore it anymore. I'm starting to even doubt what happened that night. The fact he can't remember doesn't sit right with me.

He needs to know what I think, he needs to know I still love him. I never stopped, I never will.

I frown, typing out a text to him. Before I can hit send, Maeve erupts into a fit of giggles and throws her bottle across the floor. It sends milk flying everywhere as it hits the ground.

"Maeve!"

She's covered and looking thrilled with herself.

Plucking her back up, I take her upstairs, flick on the lights in her room and sit her with her toys as I rummage for another outfit for her. Closing the drawer, a folded white piece of paper catches my eye.

Curiosity getting the better of me, I pick it up. On the front, in Jax's writing, it's addressed to Maeve.

As I lean against the side of Maeve's crib, I open the letter, my heart pounding in my chest. Transparent blobs can be seen in the top corner where it's gotten wet.

His words pierce through me, filling me with his raw agony. My entire world crumbles around me. I have to physically hold myself upright to stop my legs from buckling underneath me.

I had no idea the depth of his pain.

To my baby girl, my tigryonok.

I want you to know just how much I love you. Even if you only had me in your life for a brief time. Know that it meant more to me than you can imagine.

I hope you grow up to be just like your beautiful mommy.

Kind, brave, a Queen.

But most of all. I just hope you can be happy.

That is all I wish for, baby.

I will always regret not being a good enough father for you. Trust me, everything will be better for you without me. That doesn't mean you don't own my heart and my soul. Because you do.

I hope one day, you can forgive me for leaving you like this.

Even though I might not be here, know that I will always be watching over you. I'm doing this to set you and mommy free.

I'm sure one day she can tell you about the chaos that follows me, I didn't want that for you. It had to stop. The pain had to stop for me.

I wish I could have fought harder and been the man you both deserved. I just couldn't do it anymore.

The smiles I had for you two, they were the only real ones I'd experienced in a long, long time.

Daddy will love you and mommy forever. More than you can ever imagine.

I'm so sorry.

When we meet again in the next life, I promise I'll be stronger for you.

All my love, forever.

Daddy. Xxxx

My vision blurred by tears, I watch as the paper slips from my grasp and floats to the floor. I collapse beside it, the impact against the wooden surface echoing through the room. The full weight of what he's trying to tell me slowly sinks in.

That last line.

Jax wants to die.

He's that miserable, he doesn't see a way out anymore.

I let the man I love believe he is worthless.

How didn't I see this? How did I miss how much torture he was dealing with? How could I let him down like this?

The overwhelming need to throw up takes over. I scramble out of the room and empty the contents of my stomach into the toilet.

I can hear Maeve calling for me, but I need to find him.

With shaking hands, I pull my phone out of my pocket and dial his number again. This time, when he doesn't answer, I call Nikolai, who picks up on the first ring.

"Sofia, is everything okay?" I shake my head, pulling at my hair.

"No. I need to find Jax. Now. I think he's going to hurt himself." I choke as I say the words out loud.

Nikolai murmurs something in Russian, his voice is barely audible. "Hurt himself?"

I swallow down the urge to vomit again.

"He left Maeve a letter."

The line goes silent for a second. "Stay where you are. We are coming to you and then we find him."

"Please be quick. I can't lose him."

"We won't."

As I walk back into Maeve's room, I pick the note up off the floor and more tears stream down my face.

"Please, Jax. Don't do this to us," I whisper, as if he can somehow hear me.

I wish he knew just how much we love him.

I pick Maeve up and cuddle her tightly against me. She looks just like him. She can't lose her daddy. As I wait for Nikolai, I keep calling Jax over and over.

Nothing.

Every failed call threatens to break me.

CHAPTER SIXTY-SIX

JAX

Song- Can You Feel My Heart, Bring Me The Horizon

BROKEN.

Alone.

Hopeless.

I have nothing left to fight for.

My body could go on living- but my brain wants me to die. My heart and soul already feel like they have.

As the rain pours down, I twist the throttle. Even riding has lost its impact. It once was my solace, the place I felt closest to Kai. Now all I can see is his lifeless body, the agony on Sofia's face when I broke us. The blood. Every memory I have shows the truth. I destroy.

Like a relentless illness, I tear through the lives of those I care about. There is only one thing you can do with this kind of toxic; you kill it before it takes over.

I see the red light at the junction. My heart races as I speed up. The scene becomes a blur as horns beep incessantly and water sprays. In that small fraction of time, I find a temporary escape from this torment. My brain stops, I am free.

That is my only way out of this. I have to break this cycle.

Yet, with every dark thought, I have this nagging voice in the back of my mind, screaming at me. What about Maeve? How can you do this to your daughter?

Brody's words are looping in my head. What if she isn't even mine?

I don't know what to believe anymore. In this sick and twisted life, that constantly rips my heart out. It could be true.

My eyes burn making it even harder to see the road. It's too late for me to fix myself, to be the father she needs.

Even if she wasn't mine, I will always love my little girl.

But, no one should have to hold the burden of putting me back together. Not her, not Sofia. I can see in her eyes that she is starting to see through me. I can't let her throw her life away for me. Not after what I did.

I did this to myself.

I got Kai involved in the mafia. I'm responsible for his death.

I slept with someone else and broke Sofia's heart.

I tore my family apart.

I've been a plague on everyone's life since birth. My own mom didn't want me enough to fight for me. My dad lied to me and abandoned me.

I never even had a chance to meet my sister.

Everyone lies to me.

Everyone leaves.

I want to scream. I want this to stop. I need this to end. I can't control it anymore. It's festering inside me, growing and taking me over.

Looking up, I see one of Mikhail's grand casinos, its neon lights illuminating the night sky. I swing into the entrance of the parking lot, ditch my bike, and let the keys fall into a puddle on the ground, making the water splash softly.

"I need a room. Jax Carter," I tell the kiosk woman.

It's all a blur as I stare out into the lobby. Every smile I see sends another shooting pain through my heart.

"Here you go." The woman slides a keycard towards me with a wary smile.

"Thanks," I mutter back, swiping it up without making eye contact.

"Is everything okay?" She asks just as I go to leave.

I turn back, running a hand through my hair. "It will be soon."

I'm so fucking tired of feeling like this. No more battling to claw myself out of the darkness.

Closing the door to the penthouse, I lean against it. With every thought of ending it, I see Maeve and her little mischievous grin. I can almost hear her calling for dada.

The suffocating sensation in my chest is unbearable. It's like my ribs have been cracked open, my heart squeezed, and every ounce of oxygen stolen. Just like how I robbed them of their happiness. With clenched fists, I push myself back up and make a beeline for the kitchen. I head straight for the cupboard, knowing exactly where the vodka is stored.

I grab my revolver, tossing it onto the kitchen counter. I sit up on the barstool, feeling the cool leather against my skin as I knock back the alcohol, its burning sensation engulfing me from the inside. I just want it to numb the pain.

Numb my brain.

With the new pack of cigarettes in hand, I light one up and rest my head in my hands.

More fucking tears run down my face.

I'm pathetic. What kind of man cries?

A weak one.

As I take another drag, the smoke fills my lungs, making it nearly impossible to catch my breath amidst my sobs. The weight of the gun presses down on my palm, amplifying the heaviness of my thoughts.

The ultimate decision rests in my control.

Squeezing my fingers around the handle, my hand starts to shake.

Even now, my mind is at war.

"Kai, just tell me what to do. Shall I just join you? Put me out of this fucking misery?" I whisper into the air.

He can't reply.

He's gone.

And I am so fucking lost.

No one can help me now.

Pressing the cylinder release, it swings open.

Six bullets.

Taking out four, I place them upright on the counter.

Two bullets on opposite sides, waiting to be fired. Closing it up, I spin it.

Maybe in the next life I'll do better. I'll find my sweet Sofia again, and my little baby girl. I can be who they need me to be.

I surrender my life to the mercy of fate for one last time.

CHAPTER SIXTY-SEVEN

SOFIA

I hear the rumble of Nikolai's Hellcat and run to the door. Lara, looking concerned, gently takes Maeve from my arms and comforts me with a soothing stroke on my shoulder.

"Be strong for both of them, Sofia."

The overwhelming need to break down takes over. But, I don't have time for that. I kick my ass into gear and get in the passenger seat before Nikolai speeds out of the driveway.

"Do you know where he is?" I ask. Blood is pounding in my ears making it hard to concentrate.

His jaw remains tightly clenched as he nods, never once taking his eyes off the road.

"Penthouse in one of my brother's casinos."

Why would he?

I cover my face with my hands. He couldn't do it at home, or at Nikolai's. Where we could stop him.

"Jax is still in there somewhere, Sofia. We just have to find him and drag him back out."

"How?"

What do I do to show someone who believes the world would be better without them?

"You do whatever you have to. Anything, Sofia. He won't be rational right now, he's in a fucking dark place. When you find something that gets through to him, use it."

I will do anything for Jax.

As the wipers squeak against the window, I ball my fists, stabbing my nails into my palms. I let Jax down so badly.

"This isn't your fault, Sofia,." Nikolai says softly, I can hear the guilt he's feeling in his tone. We all feel it.

Pulling into the parking lot, Nikolai hands me a keycard and I see Jax's bike. Blind panic starts to set in. What if I'm too late?

He points to the side door. "In there, there is an elevator. It will take you straight into the penthouse."

I clutch the card in my hands like my life depends on it.

"You wait here." I rush out the words to Nikolai and throw myself out of the car before he can even come to a complete stop, paying no attention to the relentless rain beating against my body.

Through my teary eyes, I frantically race ahead, my feet carrying me as fast as they can. Why didn't I see this? How the hell did I miss how depressed he is? Why did I let him get to this point?

I. Should. Have. Known.

As I enter the elevator and hit the penthouse button, a wave of apprehension washes over me. I will give anything for him to still be with us.

Shit, I feel like I'm about to pass out.

The doors slide open and I cautiously step into the room. My cheeks are wet with tears, and I desperately try to stifle my sobs.

Jax is slouched on a barstool with a gun in his grasp resting it on the kitchen counter. He doesn't even look at me. With each spin of the cylinder, it emits a faint metallic sound, adding to the tension in the air.

"Jax," I say softly, tiptoeing to him.

With a deliberate pace, he lifts his head. His gaze is seemingly directed towards me, yet somehow elsewhere. It's like looking at a ghost. His eyes are completely vacant.

"Get out."

I pause, taken aback by the sharpness in his voice. This isn't him. This isn't my Jax.

I shake my head. I have no idea what to do. As my heart races, the sound of my blood pulsating in my ears becomes deafening, and I clutch at my skin, fighting to control the mounting panic. I can't let him do this. I cannot lose him.

How can I show him just how much I love him, how much I need him, when he can't see it for himself?

What I do now can change our entire future. I can't mess this up. I need to do right by him this time, whatever it takes.

He might be breaking. If he is, I have to be our strength to get him through this.

"I can't let you do this, Jax. I need you to put the gun down." I stay where I am, keeping my tone firm but soft.

Jax is the strongest man I've ever met. Now, I'm watching the man with the brightest smile and the ability to make anyone laugh reach his breaking point. His inner turmoil has been hidden from the world for so long, eating away at him without any of us noticing.

"Let me do this, Sof. I can't fucking live like this anymore. I need to stop this cycle before I ruin you, too." His voice breaks as he flips the cylinder open, spins it and snaps it back.

I can feel desperation consuming me, causing my body to shudder with fear. I have to get through to him.

"You will not ruin us, Jax. We need you. We love you. Think about Maeve. Your daughter needs you." I choke out the last words.

"You don't mean that. You shouldn't be here, Sof. Just forget about me, it's for the best." His words almost come out a whisper.

"We can't live without you. I am begging you, Jax. Please don't leave me." I take a careful step forward and watch his grip tighten on the pistol. Shit.

"I mean every single word, Jax." I take another step.

He looks down at his revolver.

"Without you, I'm lost, Jax. I can't survive the rest of my life without you in it. I love you, Jax."

"You're lying. You hate me. I deserve it."

This time, after he spins the cylinder there is a harsh crack as he shuts it. It feels final.

"I swear on Maeve's life. I am not lying to you, Jax. Please put it down. We can talk about this."

"Talk about what? Nothing can fix me! You told me that yourself! I'm broken. I'm already fucking dead inside. I have been for years. What difference does it make? Just leave me alone!"

I flinch as he abruptly stands, throwing his chair to the ground and slamming his free hand down on the counter. Darkness flashes across his eyes. Most wouldn't even recognize this man, but I see him. My Jax is in there somewhere. I just have to reach him.

"You aren't broken, Jax. You have been dealt some shitty cards, life beats you down. You just need some help to get back up, baby. I want to help you. Let me help you. You aren't on your own, Jax. I promise you."

"Leave, Sofia. I mean it," he shouts, pointing the

weapon at the door.

I shake my head and move closer, realizing what I need to do to try to get through to him.

"You really want to do this Jax? You want to put me and Maeve through the heartache you felt after losing Kai and your father?" My voice raises as I speak. I need to be stronger for him, the only option is us both walking out of here, or neither of us.

His face pales. "Don't—"

I cut him off.

This is the only way, with my own pain. I need to show him how much we need him. How much worth his life has.

Nikolai told me to do anything to bring him back.

"How do you think we will cope? By me losing my soulmate? Maeve losing her daddy before she even really got to know him?" I pause, waiting for his reaction.

Nothing.

"What do you think Kai would say about you abandoning your family?" I shout, throwing my arms in the air out of pure desperation.

I stop at the other side of the counter. He's silent, just blinking at me. I know my words are harsh, but I have to be.

"Answer me, Jax. You think this will take away our pain? It won't. It will kill us all."

He stares at me with bloodshot eyes. "I-It won't. I'm doing you a favor."

My hands violently shake. I can't tear my gaze away from the gun. But, that doubt I just heard in his voice gives me hope.

"No. Jax. If you leave us, you will take me with you."

Glancing over, I notice the assortment of kitchen knives tucked against the cupboard. With shaky hands, I choose one and grip it firmly, extending my palm towards him.

"Sofia, don't," he warns.

As I run the tip across my palm, I feel a sharp sting and brace myself. The physical cut is insignificant compared to the agony I'm sure he is feeling.

I flinch as lightning strikes outside, illuminating the skies.

"This. This is what you will be leaving me with. Complete fucking misery, Jax. Every single day without you will be torture. I can't do it. I can't do this without you."

I remain fixed on him as I swiftly drag the blade from one side to the other. The tremble in his hand intensifies, transforming into a noticeable shake. We lock eyes, it's working.

So I start another line just below.

"Look at me, Jax. Do you believe me now? I fucking love you. I've never stopped loving you. I need you, we all need you. Listen to me. We can get through this. We can get you help. I can show you your life is worth living."

I'm on the verge of hysteria with my heart pounding in my chest. I saw a flicker of something behind his eyes, I can't stop.

"Is this what you wanted? To hurt us? You want to kill us all? Fine," I say as calmly as I can. He needs to believe I am completely certain in my decision as I raise the knife to my own throat.

I don't care what it takes. I won't let him leave us. I'll hurt myself to save him from himself. That is how much I love this man. I need him to understand he is the center of my world.

I owe him this. For missing the signs. I let him down, but that will never happen again.

"If you go, I go." I will not fail him.

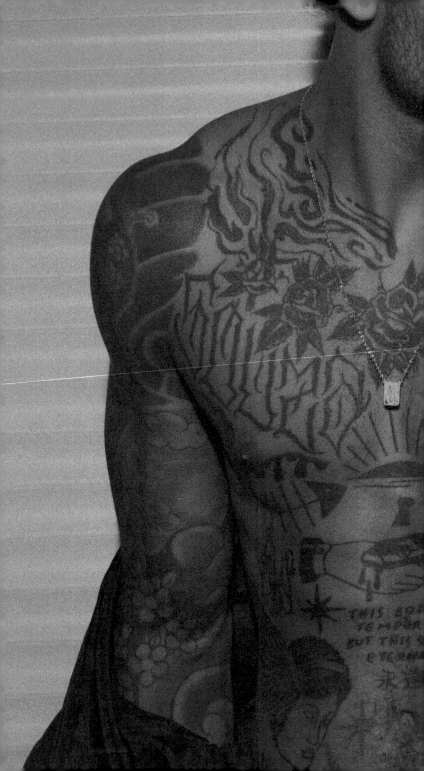

CHAPTER SIXTY-EIGHT

JAX

I LEFT MY LIFE IN THE HANDS OF FATE, AND ASKED FOR A sign.

Here she is.

Prepared to jump with me.

Like hell am I letting her do that.

But, the more I hurt her, the more it kills me. How can I make this stop?

I didn't think losing me would do this to her. I didn't know she still loved me after what I've done to her.

The pitch black hole I am trapped in is slowly ebbing to gray.

Could there be another way for me? I hear her words, I feel her here with me.

I'm not alone. But, I'm still breaking her.

It's exactly how I imagine Kai would react if he were here. The helplessness in her voice, the raw pain in her eyes.

I matter?

As the blade grazes her skin, the blood drips down her throat and instinct takes over.

Sofia matters to me more than anything else. With a sudden release, the gun slips from my fingers and crashes onto the granite countertop, causing the room to fill with the sound of its echoing impact.

"Sofia, no!" I shout.

In a burst of adrenaline, I knock everything out of the way, propelling myself to reach her in record time.

Without hesitation, I seize her wrist, causing the knife to fall to the ground with a loud clatter.

Fuck.

"You don't hurt yourself because of me, Sofia. I told you this," I whisper as I wrap my arms around her, feeling her warmth against me.

I'm clinging to her as if she is the lifeline that keeps me from drowning. With each moment that passes, some of the shattered pieces of my soul mend.

That moment of peace I felt earlier when I thought it was all over is back now. Because of her.

She's my solace now. As I press my face against her neck, I can smell the faint scent of her perfume, and tears stream down my cheeks.

I'll let her in. As much as I can.

My mind is still swimming, but maybe I can show her the broken Jax and she won't abandon me.

She holds me close. Maybe she can accept me for everything that I am. It's enough to give me hope that there is something more for me in this life.

CHAPTER SIXTY-NINE

SOFIA

Song- Lovely, Billie Eilish, Khalid

His body shakes against mine as he sobs uncontrollably. We become one, sharing the weight of our emotions. I don't know which of us is holding the other up.

"Don't leave me, Jax." I whisper, but he doesn't respond.

In a desperate attempt to make him listen, I push myself back and firmly hold on to both sides of his face, forcing him to make eye contact with me.

"I love you, Jax. I love you so fucking much. I can't let you do this to yourself. Please, Jax. Come home, we can have another chance. I forgive you."

He nods and I wipe away the tears from his cheeks as he rests his forehead against mine.

"I'm so sorry, Sofia." He whispers.

"Feeling how you are, Jax, is nothing to apologize for. I'm sorry I didn't see this earlier. I let you down, baby." I sniffle, bringing my nose to his.

"I will never, ever, do that again, Jax. I promise you. Let me help you? Let me love you?"

I'm desperate. I need some indication he is still with me.

He stays quiet and his jaw clenches and relaxes where it rests against my temple. "I don't deserve you, sweetheart."

"You deserve the whole world, Jax. You have so much to live for, so much love to give. I know it might not feel like it now, but it will get better. You'll get through this and I'll be by your side every second. I'll never let you go."

His head drops slightly as he nods.

"It's fucking embarrasing, Sof. I'm a man. I should be stronger than this. I shouldn't feel so weak all the time. I'm supposed to protect you and Maeve, not be like this. You shouldn't have to watch me crumble apart and put me back together. I'm weak and I don't know how to make it stop."

I shake my head and press a soft kiss to his cheek.

"You are not weak, Jax. You are so incredibly brave. You've battled this for so long on your own. You put everyone else first before yourself. You're an amazing man. We can find the best way for you to heal, baby. There is a way through."

"I don't feel it," he whispers.

"I know, baby. I'll show you. We'll do this together. Okay?"

"Okay."

He straightens, and I step back and lace my fingers through his.

"Let me take you home? Tonight, we can just sleep. Tomorrow, we will talk through every hard piece you can offer me. We can rebuild."

I watch as he swallows nervously and my heart splinters.

It's going to take a lot more than talking, but it's a start. I can help him. I can be his safe space. I can bring him home to us.

"Thank you, tigritsa."

He steps towards me and tips my chin up. There is life in his eyes, love in them.

"I've got you, Jax. Always. You are my person in this life, the other half of my soul. I love you for exactly who you are and all of your chaos, no matter what."

He inhales sharply, pulling me closer in one swift motion.

"I love you, so damn much. I will never stop. I will try to be the man you and Maeve need. I promise I will win you back and I will make you proud. I just don't know how long that will take or how I'll get there."

I shake my head, a small smile tugging at the corners of my mouth. "We can figure all of that out together, Jax. I've got you, baby."

There is a glimmer of hope for us and I'm going to hold onto that as tight as I can.

I will do what it takes for him.

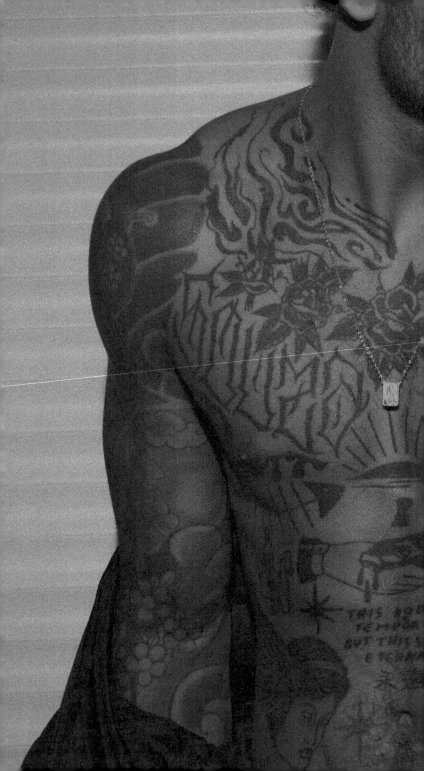

CHAPTER SEVENTY

JAX

Song- Telomeres, Sleeptoken

My head is pounding as I wait for the machine to finish pouring Sofia's coffee. I tossed and turned all night, trying to form the words to tell her what's been going on inside my head.

How do I explain to her that I hate myself?

Can she seriously forgive and want to be with someone as fucked up as I am? How can she even trust me again?

I still don't have a clue what happened. What if I black out again?

Sofia's eyes light up with a smile as I hand her the steaming mug, and she promptly sits up in bed. She takes a small sip and sets it down on the nightstand as I crawl across the mattress next to her, resting my back against the headboard.

"Did you sleep okay?" she asks softly, like she's walking on eggshells.

"Once I had you in my arms, I seemed to." I answer honestly.

She shuffles herself closer to me and rests against my shoulder. Her sweet scent of strawberries fills the air, momentarily distracting me from my restless thoughts.

"We need to talk, Jax." Her voice is full of concern.

She sits herself back up and I'm already missing her touch. Running my hands over my face, I fight the fear that I'll lose her.

Is she going to push me away?

She might have just been saying all those things to stop me, not because she meant them. The more I delve into my own mind, the more my palms grow clammy.

I feel her soft touch on my cheek and I open my eyes to find myself looking right into her beautiful green eyes.

"What's going on in there, baby? Remember we talk, no more side stepping. Speak to me. I want to listen. I want to help you, we have to get you through this."

I swallow.

She's right. I just don't know where to start, or how much to even tell her without scaring her off. There is only so much fucked up one person can handle. But, I need my family back. It hits me with a pain in the chest. This is my home. Even if Kai were here, this would still be my home.

"I honestly don't know where to begin," I say, it's a half-truth. I kinda need her to drag this out of me. Prove to me that whatever fucked up stuff I have going on in my head, she isn't running.

My mind is a swarm of death and destruction. One after another, piling on top of me until it crushes me.

"Let's start with last night," she breathes.

She positions herself in front of me, cross-legged. She reaches forward and laces her fingers through mine. I look down at our entwined hands and smile.

"I saw what the damage I was doing to you, I spiraled. I thought you'd all be better off without me."

Fuck. The words burn as they come out of my mouth and I see the sadness on her face. She's trying to hide it, I know. She wants to protect me from the pain I cause.

I release my hand from hers and twirl the rings on my fingers.

"There is more to this than just what happened between us, isn't there?" she asks.

I'm shutting down. I can feel it happening. She moves closer, shifting onto her knees so that our faces are just inches apart.

The softness in her touch as she runs her fingers through my hair soothes me.

"I know you're holding back on me, Jax. We can't keep running from this, it won't work. So I'm going to say something. Is that okay?"

I look into her glistening eyes and nod.

"Jax, I love you so much it hurts, in the best possible way. I meant everything I said last night. You are home now. We are your family and we fight this together."

Her hands find my cheeks and she wipes away a tear I didn't even know was falling.

"Fight for us, baby. Let me in. Please let me help you. I want to. I need you with me. Maeve needs her daddy."

I suck in a breath. Brody's words echo doubt in my mind, yet again.

She pulls back and tilts her head.

"Jax, what?"

"Is she mine? You promise she is? I mean, I'll love her either way. She will be my daughter no matter what, but—"

Her brows furrow as she looks at me, tears forming in her own eyes making my heart race. I want Maeve to be mine more than anything.

"There is absolutely no doubt Maeve is your daughter, Jax. I swear on my life. What made you ask that?"

The seriousness on her face says she isn't lying. Why did I even doubt her?

"Brody, said—"

"She sure as hell isn't Brody's. Not even mathematically possible. I didn't sleep with him for three months before the wedding. There's no way."

As she sniffles, I reach out and tightly grip her hand.

Fuck, I've hurt her again.

"I'm sorry, sweetheart. I shouldn't have even asked."

With a gentle shake of her head, she reassures me by squeezing my fingers.

"No. I bet that killed you hearing him say that. That isn't fair." Her tone is laced with anger.

It did. Amongst everything, that was a spear to the heart.

"We can pick our baby girl up from Lara's later. I bet she'd love a daddy cuddle."

A smile creeps up on my lips, just thinking about having my little princess in my arms again.

"I'd like that. I love her, Sof. It killed me not seeing her every day."

"Well now, you're home, Jax. No more of that."

For how long though? Before I fuck it all up again.

A moment of silence passes. I don't know what to say. I'm scared I'll get it wrong. I'll lose her again.

Her thumb moves rhythmically over my knuckle. "I forgive you, Jax. The past is in the past. We move on, together."

As I look into her eyes, I believe her.

"I want to be here, Sof. This was never about wanting to leave you two, not like that."

Her lips purse as she stares up at me. "Then tell me, what was it about? How long have you felt like this?"

"Since Kai's death." Fuck. Even saying his name, all I can think of is finding his body in the rubble. That guilt takes over, I can't shake it.

I might not have killed him, but I pulled him into this life. I'm responsible for that. He would want to beat the shit out of me for being like this. For not living when he was gone.

"Hey, baby."

I can hear Sofia speaking and I struggle to find my way to her. I'm just so fucking lost.

The moment she embraces me, I lean in and rest my head against her shoulder. How many times does she need to see me fall apart? This isn't fair for her.

"I'm so sorry I didn't see this earlier."

I don't know how long I cling onto her. But, I do until I don't feel like I'm drowning anymore.

"Jax, I really do love you, I hope you realize that." Her voice is hoarse, as if she's been sobbing for hours.

"I love you, Sof. I will never stop."

"I know." She leans back and wipes away my tears. At the same time I brush hers away with my thumb.

"Quite the pair, huh?" I joke. When she smiles, it makes my heart flutter.

"How about we go make some breakfast? I'm starving. Then we can talk some more, get Maeve, and then we can stay up all night if we have to? We get this out. Does that sound okay?"

I hesitate. I want to scream "yes". I know I need to get this off my chest. I just don't know if I can physically do it. But, I want to try.

"No matter what you tell me, I'm never leaving your

side. I've got you, we are a team, a family. Please let me love you, Jax. Will you let me do that?"

She presses her nose against mine.

For her, I'll do just about anything. "I can do that, sweetheart."

It feels totally natural cooking in the kitchen with Sof. So much so, I forget about everything else, other than us, for a few minutes.

As we sit on the couch with our food, she rests her legs on my lap and gives me a playful smile.

I know she is the one to get me through this. I'm not alone anymore. Nikolai reminded me too as I went to get out of the car last night. We are family.

When I finish my sandwich, I place the plate down and rub small circles on her calf.

"What's wrong with me, Sof? How can I think like this when I have you and Maeve? What kind of man does that make me?" I shake my head, almost asking myself the question. I don't understand what is going on in my brain.

"Because you aren't well, Jax. You can't help it, just because we can't see what's going on up there." She taps her head. "Doesn't mean it doesn't exist. You're the strongest person I know. Just admitting how you feel is proof of that. Men have feelings too. You shouldn't be afraid to speak about them, not with me."

It doesn't mean I'm not ashamed of it. I close my eyes. Trying to compose myself, maybe I can finally talk about Kai without my throat feeling like it's about to close in on me. It was at that moment, the turning point in my life, when everything shifted, and I knew I would never be the same.

The day I descended into a dark place that I never truly left.

I keep my eyes fixed on the wall in front of me. I can do this.

"It started after Kai died. Not long before I met you. That night with you was the first time I'd felt alive since I buried him."

I know she knows how that feels with her parents' death.

"Loss can do some awful things to you, did you ever stop and grieve for him?" she whispers.

"No. I distracted myself. I've been numb for two years. Fighting, killing, whatever I can do to get through the day. When I sleep, all I can picture is his body crushed under the rubble. And, the blood pouring from his head."

I take a breath as the words tumble out of my mouth and run my hand over my face.

"It's like I died with him too that day, except I wasn't the one put into the ground."

Sadness engulfs me.

"That was until I found you again, and Maeve. You gave me something to want to live for. I was happy, I loved every fucking moment."

We make eye contact and she sniffs.

I lower my head, shame creeping back over me at what I've done.

"And then I ruined it all. I hurt you, I lost myself. I didn't see a way out. I thought you'd all be better off without me. You would be happier if I was dead."

I gulp down the lump in my throat.

"Oh, Jax. I know it might feel like that, but I'd be so lost without you and so would Maeve. The world would be so black and grey."

She propels herself towards me and jumps into my lap, holding me tight. Keeping me together.

"How do I fix this, Sof? What if it happens again?

What if next time I can't claw myself out and you aren't there to help me?" I whisper.

She pulls back, I can feel her brain working as she studies me.

"I think you need to talk to a professional, Jax. We can find someone who can keep it confidential. Do you still want to, umm…"

She pauses, like she's struggling to say the words.

"No. I don't think so." I say it with all of the confidence I can muster. This second, it's true. But, she's right. I do need help. I can't do that to her again.

She blows out a breath. How the fuck did I get this bad?

"Do you ever talk about him? Remember him?" she asks, tilting her head.

"I try my hardest not to. It works best if I bury it."

She runs her hands through her hair. It's too real, too final when I speak about Kai out loud in the past tense. So instead, I let it gnaw away at me for years and fester inside.

Her palm works up and down the length of my arm. "Do you want to try? With me? What about one funny memory?"

Part of me wants to run away, but then I remember her face last night. The torture in her eyes as she desperately tried to save me.

She put a damn knife to her throat to stop me from hurting myself.

She deserves this. So, I tell her the first thing that pops into my head.

"Probably the time when he crashed his bicycle and flew over the handles. We'd just got our bikes, well, stolen them, and were trying to get away from the cops. It was always me that found the trouble, and Kai was there behind me cleaning it up."

"Like a brother." She looks up at me.

"Exactly."

Okay. That wasn't so bad. The memory replays in my head and I feel myself smile.

I reach out and touch her cheek. "He would have liked you."

"You think?"

"Yep. You keep me in check. Would have saved him a job. And you are the purest, most amazing woman on this earth. It would be harder not to love you."

"You know I don't mind keeping you in check." She smiles.

"You shouldn't have to. Hell, he shouldn't have had to either." My breath catches, and I tip my head back against the couch as tears sting in my eyes.

"You are mine, Jax. Just as I am yours. We're a family. And do you know what families do?"

I open my mouth to speak and can't find the words. I lower my chin so I can look at her.

"I-I don't know, Sof. My own mom didn't give a shit about me. I lost my dad." I shrug, trying to keep down the anger brewing inside of me. I'm upset at people I can't even take it out on.

She pulls my face to hers, like she's reminding me of where I am.

"We never give up on each other, baby. We are all we have in this life, we take on the world… together. I can't fix you. But, I can be there through everything, walk side by side with you to take on the bad."

"I'll talk to someone, sweetheart. I'll do it."

I never want to feel how I did last night.

"You aren't on your own anymore. You don't have to fight this alone. I am right here and I am not going anywhere."

My heart hammers in my chest.

"You really mean that? You want me and this life for you guys? You still want forever?"

"I mean it. We draw a line under the past and we move on. I know you would never intentionally hurt me. I know you love me. I want my family back, I want *you* back."

I stroke her hair away from her face, and her nose presses against mine. I'm finally home.

I am where I need to be and where I need to fight to stay, forever.

Her love hauled me out of the depths of hell. She deserves the world to be delivered to her feet and I'll do that.

"I'll make you the happiest woman on this planet, I swear. I will love you with everything that I am and ever will be. No matter what, from this day on, I will do right by you and Maeve. Starting with therapy."

The thought might make me itch. Talking about my feelings with a stranger, but I trust Sofia. She's training to deal with people exactly like me.

I admire everything about her.

No one should feel as hopeless as I did.

"I'll get it all taken care of for you, Jax. But, you talk to me, whenever, whatever it is. No more holding it in, can you promise me that?"

"I promise you," I say. "Thank you, baby," I whisper, nuzzling my face into her neck.

Gently, she lifts me up by my hair.

"Can I have a kiss now?" she whispers, her breath hitting against my cheek. I can practically sense her smile.

"Is that what you want, baby?"

And like that, my heart races, my body ignites. She brings me to life.

Our lips meet, and I give everything I have in that kiss. All of my love, my truth, my forever. I am hers.

"Now, shall we go get ready and pick up our little girl? The last piece of our puzzle," she asks.

Another reminder of the life she has given me that I have to fight for.

CHAPTER SEVENTY-ONE

SOFIA

THE DRIVEWAY ALERT DINGS ONTO MY PHONE, AND I GET UP to meet Lara at the door.

She's becoming a good friend, and it's nice to have someone to talk to who is familiar with the work that Jax, and the rest, do.

"Hey! Come in, I have coffee going." I give her a quick hug as she enters.

Her blonde hair is pulled back in a tight braid today, it makes her look younger than me.

"That is the biggest smile I've seen from you in a long time. Things going better?" She drops her bag by the couch and squats next to Maeve to give her a light kiss on the top of her head. "How is my May-May?"

"La-la!" Maeve's drooling grin brightens her face. She grabs the book she was reading upside-down and hands it to Lara.

"Okay, I'll read while I talk to your mommy." She sits cross-legged next to Maeve and starts slowly turning the pages.

"I think things are going better. Jax is out picking up his

449

Lambo from the shop, but he should be back in a bit." I pour two cups and carry hers over to set on the table.

"Oh, yea. I heard you did a number on his car. He deserved it. Men. They can be so *tupoy.*" She turns another page and looks down at Maeve. "If you get a brother, make sure you keep him in line like I keep my brothers, okay?" Her Russian accent is nearly lost in Maeve's curly hair.

"What does that mean?" I forgot to add milk, so get back up from the couch and head to the kitchen.

"Dense. Men have such a hard time seeing what is in front of them. Now that you've knocked some sense into Jax, he should be better. I had to knock Niki and Mikhail around a few times. Niki I know is better with women. He was very good with Katerina. But, Mikhail, it remains to be seen." She takes a careful sip from her coffee and sets the mug back down where Maeve can't reach it.

She's so good with Maeve. I wonder if she plans on kids?

I'm almost tempted to ask, but my phone rings, vibrating across the kitchen island.

It takes me a moment of staring at it to register the caller ID.

No way.

"Hello?" Do I really want to do this?

"Hey, stranger! How are you?" Anna's voice comes across extra chipper.

I haven't talked to her in weeks.

"I'm fine. What's up?" Definitely a mistake to answer. All I feel is awkward.

"Well, I feel bad for how things went down the last time I saw you. I was out of line. So, I was wondering if I could take you out for a drink? You know, catch up?" There's a hopeful lilt in there.

A knot of doubt forms. Maybe she wasn't as bad as I remember? I guess she really was trying to make sure Maeve's financial needs were met.

"Yea, I guess we could maybe next month? I'm kinda staying close to home." I want to stay near Jax. It's taking a lot to keep him out of his darkness, and I don't want to leave him alone too long.

There's a pause. "Oh. Why keep yourself locked up all alone? Come on, it'd be fun to go out. You can bring Maeve."

"I'm not by myself." That's weird of her to say. "I just want to spend some extra time with Jax. I can meet up with you, but later."

I can hear her take a deep breath. "You're still with him? I thought you guys split after he slept with Stacy? That's why I was thinking maybe you would need someone to talk to."

"We had some things to work out, but, no, we didn't break up." Why would she care? I'm not asking her for money.

"I can't believe you'd go back to him after he did that. You left Brody for the same thing." Her snide attitude is starting to piss me off.

"Brody fucked around on me for a year. Jax got messed up once and doesn't even remember her—"

What?

"Wait, how the fuck do you know her name?" I can feel the heat of anger growing in me.

Jax had no idea who the girl was.

But, Anna knows?

"I-I think it is just a rumor. I mean, I don't know for sure," she stammers.

"What else aren't you telling me, Anna? If our friendship has ever meant anything, you need to spill it." I practically scream into the phone.

Lara's eyes widen from the living room floor and Maeve stops to watch me.

"Nothing," she says quietly. "I have to go."

The click as the line goes dead echoes through me.

"Dare I ask?" Lara looks up at me.

Slumping into the chair, my hands are still shaking as the rage courses through me.

That bitch *knew*.

"I know where Jax was that night. I wish there was a way to see the camera feeds." I remember Stacy bragging about big tips one night at the bar she worked at when she wasn't dancing for Gil.

Lara looks lost in thought. Maeve crawls away to her pile of books and starts digging through for a new one.

"I have an idea." Lara seems to snap out of her reverie.

"I'm all ears."

"The boys all talk about this Enzo guy. He has access to everything. I can talk to Niki and have him do the research. What do you think you'll learn?" Lara leans back, her head tilts with her brows furrowed.

"I want to find out exactly what happened that night. Something hasn't sat right with me that Jax couldn't remember anything. When I talked to him, he was saying he wanted to marry me, and sounded completely sober. Definitely not drunk enough to lose track of what he was doing and wake up in a strange bed. If you had just seen how broken up he was—"

Lara holds up her hand. "I know. I smelled him. Men who are fine with being dogs don't go a week without a shower." Her nose wrinkles like she's remembering. "Let me text my brother."

CHAPTER SEVENTY-TWO

JAX

As I park my Lambo in the garage, completely repaired with new tinted blue windows to match the metallic paint, I spot Lara's G-Wagon parked in the front.

It's nice Sofia and Maeve have her in their lives too. They love her. Lara is a better person than that bitch, Anna.

Lara is just like her brothers, fierce and protective.

Rubbing my temples, I try to relieve some of the tension in my skull. Apparently my first week of therapy is supposed to gently break me in. Well fuck, if that was easing, then I have no idea what I'm in for as this goes on.

I won't give up though. I made a vow to myself and to Sofia that I refuse to break. I never want to go back to that dark place and put the people I love through that again. I'm one of the lucky ones. I had Sofia to drag me out of the depths of hell. A lot of men, they don't have that.

It's drilled into us as kids, you don't cry. You don't show weakness. You must be strong. When you fall, you don't cry, you brush yourself off and do it again. Over and over until you can't take it anymore.

I never had a mom to help me. I lost my dad. All I had was Kai.

I rub the skin on my throat trying to force myself back to reality.

As the front door closes behind me, I rush into the living room when I hear Maeve's cries and find Lara bouncing her around on her hip.

"Where is Sofia?"

Her lips purse, and it makes my heart beat erratically.

Did she leave? Did I fuck up?

I shake my head, and try to bring myself back.

"She's upstairs, Jax. I need you to do me a favor..." She trails off.

"What?" I frown, taking Maeve out of her arms and cuddling her against my chest. She grabs my cheek and giggles.

"When you go up there, just keep calm."

"You do realize telling me to do that will usually have the opposite effect?" I mutter as my heart starts to pound. I settle Maeve on the couch and double take up the stairs. The open office door allows a soft glow from the computer screens to spill into the hallway.

"Sof?"

She spins in my desk chair to face me, tears stream down her cheeks. I dash towards her and lift her gently into my embrace.

"Baby, what's going on?"

As I look at the screen on the left, my blood runs cold.

The woman from the night I ruined everything.

It makes me sick to even see her.

Sofia forcefully redirects my attention from the computer to her, gripping my jaw.

"You need to watch the footage, Jax."

I swallow the bile rising in my throat. "I-I can't."

She shakes her head, her long hair swaying with the motion.

"It's not what you think, baby. Sit down." Her tone is firm and I sink into the leather chair and position her on my lap, clasping her tightly.

As I squint at the screen, the feeling of dread intensifies, causing a sinking sensation in my stomach.

She clicks play on the video.

I can feel my body growing numb with shock as I helplessly watch two large men dragging my unconscious form down a dirty hallway. Leaning forward to get a better look, I can't make out their faces. I'd bet my life they're Reapers looking at their leather vests.

The blonde bitch saunters behind them, flicking her hair over her shoulder as they fucking pull me across the floor.

My jaw is so tightly clenched that it feels like a vice.

"Motherfuckers," I spit out.

Sofia clicks the next video. This one is from earlier, showing me at the booth on the phone to her. The bar is full of bikers.

She points to the woman in the background, who is watching me.

"That's her," Sofia says softly.

I blink a few times as the scene unfolds, and she hands me a glass. I remember this. I told her I was having beer.

I hit my palm against my forehead.

Why did I take the drink from her?

"Fuck," I mutter.

I lean back on the chair, feeling the heat of the inferno raging within me.

I was fucking drugged.

What the hell happened in that room?

And why?

I need answers, and I need them now.

My head spins. I don't even notice Sofia twist around in my lap to face me.

"Jax."

I flinch as she shouts trying to get through to me.

Squeezing my eyes shut, adrenaline pumps in my veins with a need for blood.

"Back with me, baby. We need to talk about this before you do anything."

Her sweet voice drags me back to reality, away from envisioning me ripping these guy's heads from their shoulders.

"Where did you get the footage?" I ask, tapping my fingers on the arm of the chair.

"Enzo. Lara got his number."

She averts her gaze and I pull her chin back to face me. She's holding back.

"The rest. What made you look into this?"

She takes a shaky breath.

"I-I had a call from Anna. It was really weird. She knew the name of the girl that you, umm."

Fuck.

The pain on her face is still there. Even knowing I was drugged, I still feel disgusting.

Unworthy.

Tears sting in my eyes.

I'll never be able to remember. I will have to live with this forever. It is always in the back of my mind.

"I never told her anything, Jax. It got me thinking, maybe there is more to it. It never sat right with me. I never believed you would willingly do this to us. I always knew how much you loved us. This proves it."

A small smile creeps up on her lips, but I don't understand why. And, what the hell does Anna have to do with this?

Would she really be involved in hurting Sofia? Is she a threat to my family?

"Why do you seem happy about this?"

She shuffles on my lap and loops her arms around my neck.

"Because it proves what I knew all along. You didn't do it, Jax."

I rest my head against her chest. Why do I still feel so shitty about it?

"I take it there is no CCTV in the hotel room?" I ask.

"No, Jax. But, now we have a lead. We can get to the bottom of it, if that will help you?"

I snap my head back up and look at her beautiful face, her smile.

"Don't you need to know, too?"

She shakes her head.

"You were drugged, Jax. Unconscious being dragged across the floor. I want these people to pay for what they did to you, yes. But, what happened that night does not impact our relationship. You did not cheat on me, Jax."

"Fuck." I hit my head back against the rest.

I am going to kill these assholes.

Sofia presses a kiss to my cheek. I'm not sure what the hell I did to deserve her love.

Running my fingers through her hair, I crash my lips over hers.

"I'll find them and make them suffer for all the pain they've caused us, sweetheart."

She pulls back, giving me a naughty grin that has my cock twitching.

"Good."

"Can you email me the footage?" I ask.

"Yep, one sec."

She climbs off my lap making a distance I hate. But, I have to get to the bottom of this, to move on and give Sofia all of me. Without it eating away at me every day.

"Done."

My phone pings, I slide it out and forward it straight to Nikolai with a simple message.

> J: We find them and we end them.

His reply is fast as I'm messaging Enzo, asking for information on Anna and anything he can find on these guys involved.

> N: Fuck, Jax. Yes. I'll see you at Mikhail's meeting?

Shit.

I look at the time.

As I glance up, Sofia is watching me intently, leaning against the desk.

I stand up, feeling the warmth of her body as I place my hands on either side of her.

"I have to go. Mikhail's called us in."

Before I pull away, she surprises me by grabbing the chain of my necklace, holding on tightly.

"I love you, Jax."

"I love you, tigritsa. You have no idea how much."

"I have some bad news." Mikhail clasps his hands in front of him on his desk as he looks around the room. "We lost three men last night in a clash with the Reapers. They were sporting high end weapons we haven't seen them use before and tracking tech that almost exceeds our own. There seems to be more money coming in, and until we can figure out how and where it's coming from, we need to kill on sight." His fist balls and bounces against the oak surface with a thud that echoes through the room. "I'm done fucking around. They're being spotted outside of homes now."

Shit. I remember hearing the engines. "Yeah, boss. I think they've found my place, too."

Nikolai turns and one of his blonde eyebrows raise before he mouths the word "shit" in my direction.

Even if I am pissed that he lied to me, I understand why he did it, he's grieving his wife. I know he's got my back. He is family.

"That does it. Get your families to the casino. We will post extra guards. They aren't brave enough to come in here. It is time to exterminate those filth like the *parazit* that they are." He stands quickly, knocking his chair backwards against the wall. "I'll offer a million dollar bonus to anyone who can bring me the head of their leader," he growls into the crowded room.

Murmurs and jostling spread through the gathered men.

It's a hell of an incentive.

I just want to find the men I saw in the video. Those two assholes nearly cost me everything.

My rings dig into my fingers as I squeeze them tight.

Knowing I didn't cheat on her soothes the anguish in my soul, but it's been replaced with fury.

They need to pay for what they almost took from me.

The loves of my life, my girls.

But, now, it's time to keep them safe.

"You're with me, Jax." Nikolai's giant palm rests on my shoulder briefly as we leave the meeting. "I'm glad you're back." A tiny smile turns up the corner of his otherwise serious mouth.

"Thanks. I can't wait to beat a few of these fuckers to death." Jabbing the button for the elevator, it's hard to just stand still as the boiling blood rushes in my veins. Bouncing on my toes like I'm in the ring, I catch Nikolai grinning in the reflection of the silver wall.

"Get your family packing. I'll pick you up in an hour and send Lara to pick up Sofia, we will get your revenge," he says as we part ways in the lobby.

"Sounds like a plan." My bike is parked near the entrance. Within seconds, the hot Vegas wind is cooking past me as I speed through the streets.

Sofia is radiant sitting with Maeve on the couch, reading through a book. Her maroon hair tucked behind her ear, and the light in her eyes when she looks at me, makes me feel like the luckiest man on the planet.

"You're home fast. Meeting go okay?" Her lips thin slightly. I know she was worried.

"About as expected. Well, maybe a little worse. The Reapers got some of our guys last night and—"

Her gasp interrupts me. "Who?"

"No one you know, baby. But, because of that, Mikhail wants us to bring our families into the safe house. So, you'll need to pack a bag for you and Maeve. Lara will be here soon to pick you up. I'll grab one later." I let my lips linger for an extra long time on her sweet mouth. Then press a long kiss to the top of Maeve's head.

Sofia's fingers wrap around my wrist before I back away. "Where are you going?"

"I'm going to make them pay for what they did to us."

CHAPTER SEVENTY-THREE

SOFIA

Song- Make Up Sex, SoMo

I QUICKLY ZIP UP MAEVE'S LUGGAGE AND BRING IT downstairs, ready to start packing my own. She's been sound asleep for the last ten minutes in her crib. She must have gotten bored of watching me fold her clothes. As much as I hate the thought of leaving, I have to keep Maeve safe and let Jax do what he needs to do.

The thudding noise resonates through the air as I make my way down the stairs. I head down the hall towards the home gym, and as I slide open the door, the cool air-conditioned breeze brushes against my face. Jax doesn't even notice me to start with, he's red faced punching the shit out of the heavy bag. With each blow that lands, the chain's rattling intensifies.

Clearing my throat, he abruptly stops, clutching the leather on both sides and leaning against it to catch his breath. Slowly, he turns his face in my direction, a subtle smile playing on his lips.

I saw it in his eyes, he's scared of us leaving him again.

I need to show him, remind him of how much I love him and that I'm not going anywhere. That he can speak to me whenever he wants, about anything.

I lean against the doorframe, captivated by the way his muscles protrude, enhanced by the shimmering sweat reflecting the light. I clench my thighs, we haven't had sex since he moved back home. I didn't want to press it. In his head, until yesterday, he believed he cheated. He has a lot to work through.

I need to bring him back to me. I quickly gather my hair into a high ponytail, securing it with the scrunchy on my wrist. Shamelessly, I let my eyes roam over his sculpted frame.

"See something you like, sweetheart?" he says in a low tone.

I step inside and slide the door, leaving a gap so I can still hear if Maeve wakes up.

"Not sure yet." I tease, watching as he pushes himself away from the bag and rips off the gloves with his teeth.

I stop opposite him, adjusting my black slip dress to lower my knees onto the mat.

His intense gaze consumes me, igniting a fire within that only he can create. As I slip one strap down my arm, he takes a step forward, but I quickly raise my finger to halt him.

"What's the impromptu punching session about?" I ask.

His gorgeous face contorts with confusion, and he responds with a boyish grin, playfully shaking out his curls.

"Well, if you must know. I've been told to try to channel some of my thoughts, my anger, into my boxing. Focus on my goals and use it as an outlet."

I slide the other strap down. He's not finding therapy

as atrocious as he thought it would be. Even if this is something we battle for the rest of our lives, it's worth it.

"And, what has you needing that?"

His eyes fixate on me, and he licks his lips greedily as I seductively lower my dress, revealing the black lace bra underneath.

"I-I, fuck." He shakes his head.

"Come on, baby. Look at me."

As he obediently does as I ask, I use both hands to unclasp my breasts, maintaining eye contact with him to signal that he can speak.

"God, it sounds so fucking dumb out loud."

"I promise, it won't." I quickly counter.

His tongue bar clicks against his teeth and he takes a deep inhale.

"I'm scared to fucking death of you leaving me. Even if it's just to a safe house. The thought of coming home and my girls not being here, it hurts. I just got you back."

Removing my bra, I drop it on the floor beside me and feel the cool air against my nipples.

"I'm never leaving you, Jax. Ever. I promised you that and I meant every word. I love you."

"Deep down I know that, but my head—"

"It's completely valid, Jax. I'll be counting down the hours until I'm back home with my man." I lean back, propping myself up on my forearms, and lift my hips to slide out of my dress.

"Jesus, Sofia," he hisses.

"You've been such a good boy, Jax, opening up to me," I say, batting my lashes at him.

Sitting back up, I catch his eyes widening as I sensually cup my breasts in my hands.

"Is that right?"

"Yes." Resting up on my knees, I delicately slide my fingers under the lace of my panties.

"Do you want me, Jax?" I ask, tilting my head to the side.

I start to lower them slowly. His eyes darken and it makes my pussy throb.

"Fuck, yes. Sof." His voice is hoarse.

He licks his lower lip and I can't take it anymore. His dick tents his red shorts. The air crackles with electricity around us.

"Show me." I almost whisper, removing my panties.

He shakes his head, causing my eyes to widen in surprise. Then, he swiftly pushes down his shorts and kicks them across the floor. I find myself unable to look away, my mouth watering as I stare at his throbbing erection.

"Crawl to me, baby. You said I've been a good boy. Now it's only fair I get to hear you gagging on my cock."

There he is. My Jax.

I get on all fours and slowly crawl towards him, my heart pounding in my chest. Positioning myself in front of him, my fingertips trace a path up his thighs, eliciting a deep groan from him.

As I wrap my hand around his shaft, he groans and pulls me back by my ponytail, keeping my lips just inches from tasting him. He slides to the side and sits on the padded floor, pulling me between his legs.

"Spread your knees wider. Ass in the air. I want that pretty cunt on full display in the mirror," he commands and it sets me on fire.

I get into position and lick the tip, watching his jaw clench as I take him to the back of my throat. With my hair wrapped around his fist, he controls my movement, fucking my face.

"Well, isn't that the perfect sight? Your pussy is begging to be touched. Be a good girl and do it."

I moan and close my eyes as I slowly circle my clit. My whole body tingles.

"No, baby. Finger yourself."

Shifting my waist, I smoothly slide two fingers in, stealing a glance at him in the process. His eyes never leave the mirror behind me.

"You can take more than two. I need you soaked for me." He jolts his hips up, and I gag on his cock as I add the third for him.

Holy shit.

"Yes, fuck, Sofia," he groans, and it only turns me on more.

I can hear my wetness as I thrust in and out. Getting closer and closer, tears stream down my cheeks.

"I need to be inside you."

Before I can register his words, he sits up and lifts me under the arms to straddle his lap, his cock pressing against me.

With my arms wrapped tightly around his neck, he grins and crashes his lips over mine for a ferocious kiss. I use his shoulders to lift myself while feverishly still tasting him, and line him up with my entrance. His fingers dig into my hip as he tugs me down hard, causing me to moan into his mouth. Breaking the kiss, I look between our bodies, watching as I ride him.

"Look how perfect you take me, tigritsa."

With one hand firmly on my waist, and the other around my throat, our eyes lock. That spark of raw desire within his almost sets off fireworks in me. Rolling my hips, I mimic his hold, squeezing my fingers on either side of his throat and slam my lips over his.

The sensation has my head fuzzy. All I can feel is his

cock relentlessly pounding into me. With each kiss, he steals the air from my lungs, leaving me breathless. I can feel the blood roaring in my ears, drowning out everything else.

"I. Fucking. Love. You," he grunts out between each hard and final thrust.

I cry out his name when he releases my throat and I collapse into him, riding out my orgasm on his pulsing length, while I'm sinking my teeth into his neck and he's spilling into me.

Holy shit.

He lays down, pulling me with him, his dick twitching inside of me. His rough hands frame my face and I sink into his touch. I am finally home. He is back where he belongs.

"I love you, Jax Carter," I whisper against his lips.

He gives me a genuine smile that mends my heart.

We lay in each other's arms, in silence as he cuddles me tight against him. It's like he doesn't want to let me go.

I push myself up.

"You do what you have to do. Once this is over, we have a lot of time to make up for." I tell him, biting back a grin.

"I'll make everything up to you, Sofia." He strokes my cheek and presses a delicate kiss to my temple.

I can't wait for this to be over, so our family can finally be back together again, forever.

CHAPTER SEVENTY-FOUR

SOFIA

"Dada!" Maeve screams, throwing her doll across the floor with her bottom lip quivering.

Jax left a few minutes ago with Nikolai, and Lara is running late. Nikolai's daughter is upset because she forgot to pack the blanket that was her mom's, so Lara had to make a U-turn.

Picking up Maeve, I bounce her on my hip and turn on the TV.

"We will be back with daddy in no time, I promise." I soothe her, kissing the top of her hair.

The doorbell rings. I rush over and open it, expecting Lara.

As I swing it open, I'm met with a puffy-faced Anna, sniffling as one of my guards tightens his grip on her arm.

"She said she knows you. I have orders not to let anyone in. But she is, how do you say it? Insistent," he says with a thick accent.

Tears cascade down her fearful face.

"Sofia, I really need to speak to you." There is despera-

473

tion in her voice. She looks like a damn mess. Since we last spoke, I've tried to call her. I need answers for her involvement. She has cut off every call.

I take a step back, my grip tightening on the door as I look at my guard.

"She can come in. Tell Lara I will meet her outside when she gets here."

He gives me a swift nod and releases Anna.

She brushes past me, looking at the two bags packed on the floor.

"Let's go in the kitchen," I tell her, pointing out of the room.

I place Maeve down in her playpen. She claps as she spots the cartoons on the TV.

Crossing my arms across my chest, I watch as she places her bag on the counter with shaky hands.

"Are you going to explain how the hell you knew about Jax?"

She wipes away her tears with the back of her finger.

"I-I fucked up. Brody, he—"

My heart almost stops.

Brody.

"Brody, what?" I raise my voice and step towards her.

"I've been sleeping with him, Sof. I'm sorry."

I pinch the bridge of my nose. I am so done with her. "Really, Anna? What the hell is wrong with you? You know he's getting married right?"

"He promised me things." She shrugs.

I straighten my spine, looking at her new clothes and her designer shoes.

Of course. She's only ever been interested in one thing; money.

"What does any of that have to do with me? Fuck who you want, Anna."

Anna's gaze fixes on Maeve and I can't shake the feeling something is wrong. I position myself in front of her, obstructing her line of sight to my daughter.

Her lower lip trembles. "He's scaring me. I need help."

I sense she's lying to me.

"What is he doing?"

I jump back as she abruptly gets up, her hands shaking. Instinctively, I stay where I am, stopping her from getting anywhere near Maeve.

"I need a coffee. I'll make you one." She pushes past me and starts looking through the canisters on the counter until she finds the pods.

What the hell?

After she puts a cup under the spout, she looks at her handbag and chews on her nails.

What if she's in deeper than what I thought? Could Brody be behind all of this? To hurt Jax?

How far is he willing to go?

I'm not taking any risks. I know what Jax is out doing right now.

I slide my phone out of my back pocket.

"Ouch," Anna cries out, doubling over, clutching onto her stomach dramatically.

I look up from my phone.

"What's happened?" I ask, keeping my voice calm.

"Period pains, shit. Can you get me a tampon?"

"They're in the cupboard in the bathroom, Anna."

Does she seriously think I'm that dumb? She straightens herself as I step towards her bag. Her eyes go wide and she starts breathing rapidly.

"You need to tell me the truth or get the fuck out of my house," I say.

Something is in her purse. The closer I get, the more her hands tremble.

"I-I can't."

"Oh whatever, Anna. I'm calling Jax."

Her face pales. "I can't let you do that."

I don't recognize her voice. As the cell rings, Anna launches herself at me. With a sudden snatch, she takes the phone from my grip and tosses it forcefully, causing it to soar across the room.

With my hands raised, I take a step back and assume a protective stance in front of Maeve, ready to defend her if necessary.

"I have to do this, Sof. I'm sorry. Brody wants her." Her eyes are wild and her smile twists with malice as she stares past me at Maeve. "Would have been easier if you just took the drink. I wouldn't have to hurt you."

Despite the burning tears in my eyes, an overwhelming need to fight consumes me.

She isn't going to touch my daughter.

I block her path and get in her face.

"Get out!" I shout.

"Not without Maeve. I have to save myself."

A surge of rage overtakes me when she makes an attempt to push past. Without hesitation, I snatch her by the hair and forcefully jerk her in the opposite direction.

"You aren't taking my baby anywhere, you bitch." With a swift motion, I hurl her down, making her face crash onto the floor. With a groan, she sits up and uses the back of her hand to clear away the blood that trickles from her nose.

"You'll pay for that," she spits onto the tiles and launches herself up like she's possessed.

With a burst of energy, I shove her as hard as I can, and time seems to stretch as she stumbles backwards. With a resounding crack, her head strikes the corner of the kitchen island, sending a powerful vibration through the house as she thumps down onto the floor.

Holy shit. What have I just done?

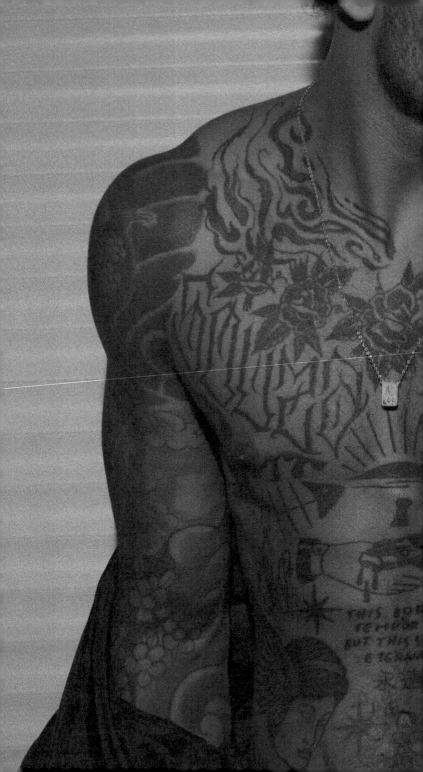

CHAPTER SEVENTY-FIVE

JAX

"ENZO, TELL ME WHO THE FUCK IS AT MY HOUSE!" I put him on speaker as I slide on my helmet and get on my bike.

Sofia called and it got cut, now I can't get through and my fucking security system isn't working on my phone.

I look behind and motion for Nikolai and Alexei to follow, leaving the others to clean up the four dead Reaper's we've left bleeding out on the rubble.

I accelerate onto the main road,

"Hold on, Jax. It looks like a blonde woman, small build."

"Anna?" I ask through gritted teeth weaving through the traffic. I'm only a few minutes from home.

"Yes. It looks like it. The guards got back to me, Sofia is fine. But, be warned, you may need to do a clean up."

Oh fuck.

"That's fine, I've got Alexei and Nikolai with me. I'll sort it. Thank you."

He cuts the call and I pull into the drive just as Lara pulls up. I pull off my helmet and hold my hand up to her.

"Stay in the car," I order, rushing into the house.

The first thing I see is blood, all over my floor and a shaking Sofia standing over the body.

I carefully approach her.

"Sofia, baby. Are you hurt?"

I softly cup her cheek and scan her body for marks, feeling less murderous when I fail to find anything.

"I-I think I killed her," Sofia whispers, her trembling hands now covering her eyes. I pull her against me and hold her tight.

"Shh, it's okay, sweetheart. Let's go sit down."

I guide us towards the couch and help her sit.

"Dadada," Maeve claps from her playpen, completely oblivious to anything. I pick her up and turn my back to the body on the floor just as a wide eyed Alexei walks through the door.

"Oh shit," he turns back to look at a stern Nikolai.

"Is she okay?" Nikolai asks me and I nod.

I take a seat next to Sofia with Maeve cuddled against me and wrap an arm around her shoulders.

"I need you to tell me what happened, baby. It's important."

"S-she's with Brody, he told her to take Maeve. She came at me, I pushed her and she hit her head. Really hard, Jax. I swear I heard something crack,"

Good I think to myself.

Wait. What did she just say?

I hold Maeve tighter as she snuggles into me.

"Brody tried to steal our daughter, is that what you just said, sweetheart?" I try my hardest to keep the rage from my tone.

She lets out a sob and nods.

"The bitch isn't dead!" Alexei calls out and I look up and he's prodding her arm.

"Nik, get some water, ice cold," he orders.

Sofia's head comes up as she watches Nikolai pour water over Anna. I press a kiss to Sofia's cheek.

If she's alive, she can fucking answer us.

"Can you take Maeve upstairs while we deal with this,"

"Y-yes, what are you going to do?"

"I'm going to get some answers," I place Maeve in her arms.

"I'll send Elena up with you."

Anna groans as I stand.

"Get a chair and tie her to it, she's not going anywhere," I say, cracking my knuckles as Sofia takes Maeve.

"Alexei, you tie the whore."

"Normally that sentence has a much sexier meaning," he grins at me.

The front door flies open just as Alexei gets the last knot tied.

Lara puffs through with a guard trailing helplessly behind. "It looks like a parking lot outside. I thought you men were supposed to be out chasing bad guys." She stops when she steps past Nikolai. "Who is she?"

"This—" I grab Anna's blonde hair and tilt her semi-conscious head back. "—is Sophia's bitch of an ex-friend, Anna." I let go, and her chin falls back against her chest.

"Why is she tied, Alexei?" She turns to him.

He backs away, holding up his hands. "Just doing what Jax asked."

Anna groans, her swelling eyes blink rapidly as she looks up at us. "Shit."

Fury swells in me and I grab her shoulders, shaking her violently. "Tell me everything before I beat it out of you!" I yell into her face.

A small hand taps on my shoulder hard enough I glance back.

Lara has her arms crossed over her chest and she shakes her head slowly. "Jax, that is not how you torture a woman."

"What? Yea, pain makes even the biggest men talk." Looking back at Anna, she's not very big. It wouldn't take much to break her.

And, as angry as I feel, I could tear her in half.

"Women are made to endure agony. What hurts the most, is to damage our hearts." She flits her hands, shooing me away. "Let me show you."

Stepping past Anna, she picks up the oversized bag on the counter and begins to rifle through it. "Hmm, what is this?" She tosses out a plastic baggie filled with a pale yellow powder.

Alexei picks it up and opens it. Sticking his finger in, he puts a tiny bit on his tongue.

Nikolai slaps him in the back of the head. "Fool. What if that was poison?"

Alexei shows off his silver tooth as he grins. "Not deadly, but I might sleep well tonight."

Lara pulls Anna's cell from the depths of her purse. "Here we go. Look, even opens with a thumb." She glances at me. "A little help?"

Prying Anna's hand open takes more effort than I thought it would before Lara presses the phone to her pad.

"Let's see what we can find." The tip of her tongue sticks out as she scrolls through the unlocked device. "Oh. Here we go, messaging your boss that you want to fuck him. And, here, is this your new bff?" Lara flips the screen so Anna can see it.

Anna doesn't answer.

Lara types furiously. "Well. Guess what, you just fucked her husband. Naughty girl."

Anna's eyes open wide. "No! You didn't!"

There's a thump as Alexei slumps onto the floor against the cabinet.

"Don't worry." Nikolai lays him flat. "He's still breathing."

"Oh, girl. Your friend is so mad at you!" Lara giggles as Anna squirms, making her chair shift. "I will make it better." Her thumbs fly in a heated response. "Oops. Sounds like she's calling Brody to tell him about some guy named Mike?"

"Stop! I'll talk!" Anna whines through her split lips. "Brody is the one who drugged you. He wanted to get back at you by faking a paternity test and taking Maeve. He promised me diamonds and a free ride if I just got her."

My vision starts to cloud red. Knotting my fingers in her tangled blonde hair, I jerk her to face me. "He did *what?*"

"Brody set you up to make it look like you slept with Stacy." Tears stream down her cheeks as she looks up at me. "He wanted to get back at you." Her eyes flick to the stairs where Sofia went. "He's still mad you got her. Which, honestly, pisses me off. Please, just let me go, you'll never see me again."

My arm raises. I want to drive my fist through her snotting nose so badly, I—

Nikolai's giant hand grabs my elbow, holding me back. "She might be more useful alive. I want to hear more about these diamonds."

"Fuck them. Where's Brody?" Grabbing her jaw, I make her see the anger seething in my eyes.

"I, I don't know. He said he would meet me back at their club in an hour when I had Maeve."

Alexei snores loudly with a ribbon of drool running down the corner of his face.

Nikolai pulls me away. "Go. We will follow."

"Tell Sof where I went." Digging out my own phone, I pull up Enzo's number.

"Yes, Jax?" His gravelly voice sounds like I interrupted him.

"Enzo, I need a favor. It's an emergency. I gotta track someone down."

CHAPTER SEVENTY-SIX

SOFIA

"Jax! Wait!" I shout down the stairs just as he opens the front door.

With a sudden halt, he pivots towards me, his eyes filled with a chilling rage, while I swiftly descend the steps to meet him.

With each step I take towards him, his fingers tighten on the handle. To my left, I catch a glimpse of Lara slapping an unconscious Alexei on the floor, and Anna, in a state of panic, tightly bound to a chair while Nikolai ominously watches over her.

"Are they going to—"

Jax shakes his head.

"She is learning her lesson. She knows not to come back to Vegas."

That's one thing off my conscience, I suppose.

"Where are you going? What did she say?"

The muscles in his jaw constrict, like a silent manifestation of his inner turmoil.

"It was all Brody. He had me drugged and it was all a set up. He paid her to take Maeve from us." I can hear the

487

fury rising in his deep voice with every word, and I close the distance between us.

I'm angry they did this to us, and that I've lost a friend.

I'm devastated this happened to Jax.

That unmistakable look in his eye reveals his clear destination.

"You're going on your own?" I tilt my head as my heart races.

Roughly, he cups my face and tilts my chin up, his intense gaze locking onto mine.

"I'm going to finish this, Sof. No one threatens our daughter. He tried to take everything from me. It's time I returned the favor. I'll be fine, sweetheart."

My bottom lip trembles. "Just make sure you come back to us, Jax. Please."

He presses his lips over mine to silence me.

"I can't stop until he's gone. I'm doing this to protect our family, baby. Our baby girl. You two are all that matter to me. I'd sacrifice everything in a heartbeat for you two. It would be the easiest decision I'd ever have to make."

As I shake my head, his grip on my cheeks tightens.

"But, I *will* be coming home. I love you," he says and kisses me again, this time harder, before he pulls away.

He cuts off any chance for me to respond as he slams the door shut. Leaving me staring at the wall with tears streaming down my face.

CHAPTER SEVENTY-SEVEN

JAX

Song- Like A Villain, Bad Omens

EVERYTHING THAT HAPPENED, IT ALL BOILS DOWN TO *HIM*.

His shitty way is what gave me Sofia. And, almost took her away.

Because of him, I nearly fell into a hole I would never return from.

No more.

I don't even remember the first mile from the house, my Ducati accelerates so quickly, I can barely hold on. Weaving between the cars, I know I look like a black blur to the people on the sidewalk.

They better stay out of my way, because I'm not stopping until I find him.

"Which way?" I'm nearly at an intersection. "Did you find him yet?"

"Hold." Enzo's deep voice is soothing. He knows how important this is.

How he always stays so damn calm in any situation boggles me.

"Left."

I follow his command instantly, my knee nearly dragging on the hot asphalt as I make the tight turn.

I hear him curse quietly. "Okay, got him back. He's about eight blocks ahead, riding north with two other bikers." His fingers click on his keyboard. "I have Mikhail notified. He said he will send reinforcements once you have him stopped."

Makes sense. None of the rest are as fast on a motorcycle as I am.

I have Kai to thank for that. All of those years racing with him is going to pay off tonight.

"After this stoplight, turn right down that alley," Enzo says matter-of-factly.

Fuck stopping. I blow through the red and dodge a car crossing in front of me, then dart down the small street.

Nothing is going to keep me from getting to him.

The cops can pick up what's left if they even catch me.

"You might be able to see them ahead. Your guy is in front." He pauses. "It looks like they're heading in the direction of one of their locations. If you engage, expect reinforcements."

I know where they're going. Their main club.

That's fine with me. He's gonna be a statement.

The three motorcycles appear in front of a couple of cars waiting for green.

It's hard, but I wait until they're moving again.

Jetting past the sedans, I get just behind the closest.

Grabbing my helmet by the lower edge, I swing it as hard as I can into the back of the head of the first Reaper.

He falls limply, his Harley wobbling and crashing into the sidewalk.

The second doesn't notice his buddy, but I can see him do a double-take when he sees me pull up next to him.

"Surprise!" Throwing my weight into it, my Ducati weaves as the blunt top of my makeshift weapon slams into his face spraying blood across my visor.

Shit, his tire almost clipped me before it's thrown into the oncoming lane.

There's a satisfying double thump as the passing pickup runs over him.

Now, all that remains, is my wonderful brother.

Brody glances over his shoulder. When he sees me, his motorcycle wavers within his lane, then he twists the throttle to shoot forward.

There's no way his hog is going to outrun me. But, the panic I saw in his eyes tells me he doesn't care.

"I know what you did!" I scream at him as I rocket faster.

His arm leaps up to block my blow. "Fuck you, Jax!" he screams as he tries to veer away from me.

Slamming on his brakes, he falls behind me and cuts across the oncoming traffic, swerving between two heavy duty cargo trucks.

Fuck. There's a concrete divider.

I barely catch a glimpse of him turning off.

Nope. Not happening.

Pulling back as hard as I can, I yank my bike into a wheelie and land the front tire up on the median, then hit the throttle, gunning for the spot I last saw him.

Gotcha. His rear end disappears down the far road two intersections down.

Dodging headlights and horns, I weave past several wide eyed drivers before jumping onto the sidewalk. Screaming at people to get out of the way, I finally find the cut-off and hit the gas.

There he is.

Asshole thought he could lose me.

One more time, I pull my Ducati up on its back wheel, this time letting my legs dangle as I twist the throttle.

Letting go, I let myself roll and bounce on the hot asphalt as my beloved bike crashes over Brody's head and throws him off of his own ride.

I'm already on my feet before he even lands.

It's the best feeling in the world when my fist lands against his face.

"You. Fuck. You. Drugged. Me." Each word is punctuated by my knuckles slamming into him.

He tries to throw his hands up to fend me off. "You deserved it!" he screams before his teeth crack with my next strike.

I sit back on my heels. "Why? What the fuck did I do to you?"

He pushes himself up on his elbows, touching his bleeding lip gingerly. "You grew up with everything. I grew up with nothing," he spits. "My whole life was mom telling me how much she regretted leaving your dad to marry mine."

When he tries to sit all the way up, I land another hard hit to his cheek, knocking him flat again.

"Fuck," he groans, twisting to lay on his side.

"You better give me a damn good reason not to stomp your face into this curb." I stand and kick him in the ribs.

"She's mine." He curls and coughs blood. "You have everything I wanted. I deserve her back."

My boot finds his stomach. "You worthless asshole. You *had* her. It's your own fault she left." I'm having a hard time feeling sorry for him.

All I can think about is the pain on Sofia's face when I told her I had cheated on her.

He did that. He made me do that. I hurt her, and he almost ruined me.

My foot connects again, and I feel a crack.

Well. Look at what parking lot we ended up in. His clubhouse.

"Isn't this convenient. We're at your homebase, brother-boy. Let's get a little closer, okay?" Grabbing him by the back of his shirt, I drag him across the sweltering concrete.

There's an old fashioned hitching post in the front of the tired western themed bar that frames the big main doors.

Dumping him next to one of them, I grab a hold of his torn shirt tail and pull, ripping off a length as long as my leg.

Perfect.

When I extend his arms above his head and tie them to the base, he screams, writhing in the dirt.

"Aww. Sore? How about I even you out?" Stepping over his twisting torso, I kick him, shattering bones with each blow.

"There? Better?" My adrenaline is starting to wear off. I can see the front of my motorcycle buried in the bushes nearby and decide to dig it out.

Let him suffer for a while.

Heaving my bike up, it doesn't look like it took too hard of a hit, thankfully.

I barely got my Lambo out of the shop.

Fucking Brody. It's his fault for that, too.

Pushing the Ducati closer, I'm just lowering the kick-stand when I hear him muttering something.

"What's that?" I let the wheels roll a little closer so I can hear him.

"I said," he coughs, spitting up blood. "She's a whore. She'll leave you like she left me."

"See? You just couldn't leave it alone, could you?" I knock the peg back up and climb on my motorcycle.

It starts right away. Must not be too beat up.

Revving the engine, it still sounds perfect.

Locking the front brake, I push and pivot the back end of the high end machine so the tire rests on Brody's stomach.

"I'll see you in hell, brother." Twisting the throttle, I release the clutch and let the rear spin.

It's been a while since I've heard someone scream like that.

Piercing, like a warning siren.

The rubber tread rips through the last of his shirt, then the flesh of his stomach until the main door of the Reaper clubhouse is spattered with flesh and bits of intestine as the weight of my high speed machine eats away all of the soft tissue beneath it.

His wail turns into a gasping gurgle when my bike chirps on the asphalt beneath him.

Through him.

Headlights appear from either end of the parking lot and rush towards me while Brody takes his last breath.

Nikolai climbs out of his Hellcat. "I missed the fun. I had to get Alexei's sleeping ass loaded. Do you know how hard it is to wrestle a limp Russian?" He walks over to Brody's body and kicks the lifeless foot. "One less Reaper. Well done." He claps me on the back.

More cars pull in and our guys unload with weapons ready.

"We clear these buildings. Start with this one." Nikolai gestures at the men to go into the main hall that I just finished painting.

"Do you want to stay? Or, go check on Sofia?" Nikolai's brows raise as he asks.

"I'll stay. He's not the only threat to her. Let's wipe them all out." I take the pistol he offers, and follow him inside.

I can hear sporadic gunfire throughout the building as our crew pushes through, but Nikolai and I don't encounter anyone alive.

"Hey, I found the office, I think." I push into a room with a big desk and piles of papers.

The picture of Knox on the wall is a dead giveaway. I can't resist raising the barrel and pulling the trigger at his bald head.

Expecting a ricochet, Nikolai and I look at each other in surprise when it makes a hollow thunk.

"No shit?" Pulling the gaudy frame away from the brick, there's a gap with a safety box sitting in it.

Nikolai grabs it out and sets it on the shelf below it. Popping it open reveals at least a dozen small black velvet bags.

He picks one up and tosses it to me, then pries another, dumping the contents into his wide palm.

"Jax. These are diamonds. There's at least a hundred in this one." They glisten under the fluorescent light.

And, they're big. Some are several carats.

"Holy crap. You gotta tell Mikhail." I put the soft pouch back with the rest. "This will put a big hole in their resources."

Nikolai nods slowly, gathering the box under his arm. "They will want this back. We need to find out who gave it to them, and for what." He frowns. "I have a feeling I already know. Let's go. I'll have the boys burn the rest of the buildings. Let's leave this one whole, so they can feel the full loss of their precious treasure."

"I like that idea. Think we can ask Mikhail to show his face in exchange for what, millions of dollars in diamonds?" I ask as we step back into the dark parking lot.

Flies are already gathering around the smear of Brody.

Nikolai laughs. "It would take more than money for that." He looks me up and down. "You don't have the right equipment to bribe him."

He swings the door to his Hellcat wide, and tosses the box in the backseat before climbing in. "Go check on Sofia. All that's left here is ashes."

Alexei stirs in the passenger seat. "What are we burning?" He wipes the drool from his chin.

"We're going to find some sage and expel those impulses from your stupid brain that tells you to try yellow powder in baggies." Nikolai rolls his eyes up at me before slamming himself into his car.

I feel like a weight has been lifted off of me.

Brody nearly ruined everything for me and destroyed me in the storm he created. But, Sofia's love pulled me through.

She's my lifeboat.

My anchor.

CHAPTER
SEVENTY-EIGHT

SOFIA

Song- on your knees, Ex Habit
https://ffm.to/onknees

SITTING HERE IN THE DARK KITCHEN, I CAN HEAR THE SOFT ticking of the clock. My home is surrounded by armed guards. Lara has already taken Elena to the safe house with her. I'm waiting here for Jax. Maeve is sound asleep without a care in the world, she has no idea what is going on.

Behind me, a soft warm light flickers, casting a gentle glow.

The taste of the wine lingers on my lips, a bittersweet reminder that all I can do is sit here until the other half of me comes back home. My head is filled with a whirlwind of wild scenarios.

What keeps me going?

Knowing the power Jax has, that fire in his eyes. He won't lose. He can't.

The sudden click of the front door shutting startles me, causing me to jump back in my seat. The room is filled with the echoing sound of his heavy footsteps. Without hesitation, I sprint towards him.

He cuts the distance in half and we crash into each other in the middle of the room. Without a word, he lifts me into his arms and crashes his mouth over mine. My hands tangle in his hair, his tongue explores my mouth as my back slams into the wall behind.

His powerful embrace supports me as he kisses me with an intensity that takes my breath away. With anticipation building, I slide my hands down, skillfully undoing his belt.

"Is this how you want it?" His deep voice sparks me further.

Just as I free his cock, I look up and meet his dark eyes boring into mine. He's home. He's mine.

I want him to own me.

His dick pushes against my aching pussy. My fingers trace along the defined contours of his abs, slowly making their way up until they reach his throat.

"I want you to completely consume me, Jax. Let go and fuck me until I'm yours." As I squeeze my fingers tighter, I feel his body tense up.

"Remind me of how good we are."

I run my tongue along his jaw.

"Bite me, mark every inch of me."

A growl erupts from his chest, starting a fire only he can put out.

His hand tightens around my hip, anchoring me firmly in place.

"Dig your nails in deeper, baby. Make it fucking hurt," he hisses.

When I do, he groans. Holy shit. He leans in, biting down on the flesh on my shoulder, and I cry out.

"You want me to mark you? You want me to lose

control? Baby, you have no idea what you've just let your-self in for."

His nose gently grazes the line of my neck, reaching up towards my ear. I can feel his warm breath on my skin as he firmly grasps my ass through my shorts.

"Run," he whispers, dropping me to my unsteady feet. That raw, animalistic passion lies behind his eyes and I spin on my heel and sprint.

My heart racing, I grip the wall to prevent myself from slipping on the tiles before darting around the corner. I head towards the patio doors, grabbing the closest chair and throwing it over to slow him. I'm fighting the urge to burst into a fit of giggles. As my fingers barely graze the handle, a sudden jerk at the back of my neck makes me cry out.

He lifts me from behind, and everything becomes a blur. Suddenly, I find myself on top of the dining table. As quick as I can, I attempt to crawl away.

"Jax!" I cry out, the cool air hitting against my hot skin as he rips my shorts and panties from my body and drags me back to him.

"That was too easy, sweetheart." He slaps my ass so hard I bite down on my forearm to muffle my cries. Fuck, I want him. When I hear his zipper opening, I push my hips towards him. I'm flipped over with my back pressing against the table. A smirk spreads across his face as he towers over me.

As his hands slam down on either side of my head, his dick presses against my pussy.

"Jax, please."

He bites down on his lip as he slides his cock along my slit. Seizing the silver chain around his neck, I forcefully bring him closer until our lips are tantalizingly close.

"Fuck. Me. Now."

I don't even recognize my voice it's so full of need. My fingers work frantically at the hem of his tee. In one swift motion, he tugs it over his head and thrusts inside me.

"Such a perfect tight cunt. It's all mine, sweetheart. All fucking mine."

I cry out his name, my back arching, as he bites down hard on my shoulder. The pain and the pleasure battle against each other.

But, I want more. I want him feral for me. When he pulls himself out, I quickly nudge myself backwards and roll off the table, dashing towards the stairs.

"You know nothing can stop me getting to you, sweetheart," he calls out from behind me and the thrill sets me alight.

His heavy strides draw nearer. I can sense the surge of adrenaline flooding through me, heightening my awareness of him. I can practically sense the warmth of his breath as it grazes my skin.

My heart is pounding when he lunges forward and seizes a handful of my hair, causing me to whirl around and collide with him. My fingers scratch down his chest as he shoves me up against the wall, kicking open my thighs at the same time tugging my head to expose my throat.

The sensation of his body pressing against mine makes my blood roar in my ears, while the searing pain in my scalp intensifies.

"You're being naughty, tigritsa," he growls into my ear, sliding two fingers inside me and I cry out.

His hand abruptly detaches from my hair and tightly covers my mouth and nose.

He fucks me with his fingers relentlessly, to the point I'm so stretched around them. My legs open wider on their own accord and I lose myself.

I can hear how soaked I am for him with each thrust.

With a wicked look in his eye, he slides them out and steps back, but his other hand remains tightly secured around my throat.

"One."

With his eyes fixed on mine, he slowly opens his mouth and sucks his index finger clean.

"Two."

He smirks as he repeats the process with the second one, popping it out of his mouth.

"Three."

My jaw drops open and my cheeks burn. I watch as his tongue traces a path along his ring finger.

I feel my breath tremble as he leans in closer to me. In front of my lips, he extends his pinky finger.

"Four. Now open and taste how sweet you are."

What the hell? There were four fingers inside me?

Doing as he instructs, I bite down and use a sucking motion to thoroughly clean it.

"Good girl," he says, before slamming his lips over mine.

I claw at his hair to deepen the kiss. As his nails dig into my ass, I can feel myself being lifted up the wall. I wrap my legs around his waist, clinging to him tightly.

"I'm going to feast on your delicious pussy until you pass out."

That light in his eyes, it hits me in the heart.

I open my mouth to speak, but before I can, he grabs me by the ribs and spins me upside down against the wall.

As soon as it happens, all the blood surges to my head, creating an instant sensation of pressure.

"Wrap your hands around me," he commands.

I feel his arms, strong and secure, effortlessly supporting my weight as my back presses against the smooth wall.

"Bend your knees and spread them as wide as you can."

I do as he says. My foot collides with a frame, causing me to flinch. The sound of shattering glass resonates through the room.

"Shit," I hiss.

But, then I feel his breath hitting against my pussy. A fuzzy feeling takes over my head, causing my muscles to quiver.

With a last nudge, he pulls back his hips so I'm level with them.

"Wrap those pretty lips around my cock, baby."

Gladly.

I suck the tip just as he runs his tongue piercing along my pussy. My moans are muffled by his thickness in my mouth.

He switches, like the artist he is, between licking, sucking and biting all while grinding his hips into my face.

My head feels weighed down, but every inch of my body is pulsating with an intense desire.

"You better come on my face before you pass out, sweetheart."

Oh fuck.

He flicks on my clit. I squeeze his ass as my whole body begins to shake violently. An orgasm rips through me so hard I see stars.

Holy shit, my toes curl, I come so hard on his face. But, he continues to eat me like he's starving, taking everything he can from me.

Carefully, he takes my weight in his arms and spins me around the right way. I let in a shaky breath and blink until the world stops tilting and I feel the pressure leaving my head. When I come into focus, all I can see is his dark eyes staring at me with love.

He kisses me like he means it, with everything he has. He steals my soul from my body and I don't care.

He pulls back and strokes my hair from my face softly.

"Do you remember now, tigritsa?" he whispers, his voice hoarse.

I reach out and stroke his short beard.

"I'll never forget, Jax."

I catch that darkness flashing across his eyes. I can sense him losing himself, even if it is just for a split moment.

"What do you need from me, Jax? Tell me."

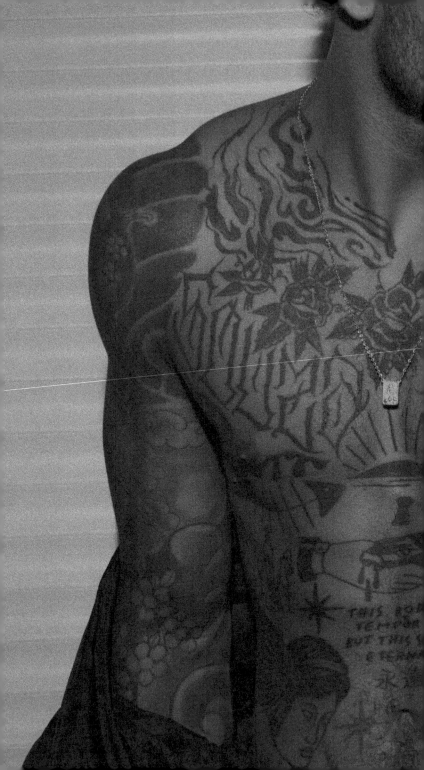

CHAPTER SEVENTY-NINE

JAX

Song- PLEASE, Ex Habit
https://lost.exhabitmusic.com/please

WHAT DO I NEED?

To sink so deep inside her, claim her as mine, and never let her go. I don't want her to ever forget how perfect we are together.

She needs to know how much life she breathes into me.

I just fucking need her to love me forever.

Holding her tightly against me, I take us to our bedroom and quietly close the door behind me.

I let out a groan as she rolls her hips, her soaking pussy smothering my shaft. She sensually nibbles on her bottom lip, enticing me.

"Is this what you need, baby?" She purrs and I nearly explode on her.

I stumble backwards, and my back collides with the solid door.

My grip on her waist tightens as she skillfully twists my

chain around my neck, applying just the right amount of pressure.

"Choke me and call me your good boy."

Her eyes light up, and everything else fades away. I love what that does to her. The feeling of her having control over me is fucking electrifying. This has and only ever will be for my sweet Sofia.

She slips her hand between our bodies, wraps her dainty fingers around my dick, and starts to move it up and down her pussy. Those soft little moans are turning me the fuck on.

"Use me, Sofia. Claim me."

She licks her lips and uses the tip of my cock to press on her clit as her mouth falls open.

"Please, baby." I trace her bottom lip, pulling it back.

She slides her legs down my thighs until she is on her feet. Her eyes are sparkling as she presses down on my shoulders and I drop to my knees before her.

With her fingers tangled in my hair, she lowers her gaze to meet mine, a small smile slowly spreading across her face.

"Is that what you want? To be used like my own personal fuck toy, Jax?"

Tilting my head back, I relish the sensation of running my hands along the softness of her calves.

"I don't just want it. I'm down on my knees begging for it, baby." I need this. I want to feel how much she loves me. Mark me as hers again. Bring me the fuck back to life.

"You haven't really been a good boy though, have you?"

I swallow, I haven't. Tonight, I murdered my brother in cold blood. With no remorse, or an ounce of sadness. I will never grieve for that bastard.

She grabs hold of my chin, directing my attention back into those big beautiful eyes.

"Maybe I should make you work for it," she teases.

She releases her hold on my face and saunters away towards the bed. I watch the way her hips sway, that curve above her ass. Fuck, she is perfect.

She twirls around and perches on the edge of the mattress. Slowly and, oh, so fucking teasingly, parting her legs as she places her hands on her knees.

"Damn, baby," I groan.

"You know what to do, Jax. Crawl to me and then you can fuck me as hard as you want."

I clench my jaw to suppress the moan that's trying to break free.

Holy shit.

Her swollen, soaking cunt is begging for me and I am just as desperate for her. To fill her with me, to watch as my cum spills down her thighs.

To make her mine.

"I'll stay on my damn hands and knees for the rest of my life, sweetheart, if it means I can sink into that pretty pussy."

Crawling silently, my eyes are fixed on her as I watch the blush slowly making its way up her neck. Reaching her feet, I indulge in the feel of her smooth skin as I sensually lick up the inside of her calf. Pulling myself up to climb on top of her, she tugs me closer and presses her lips to mine.

I flip us over onto my back, hooking my arm under her body and bring her hand to my neck.

"You wanna ride me, sweetheart?" I smirk.

She doesn't answer with words, but by lifting herself up and guiding the tip of my dick into her. With a tight grip on my throat, she lowers herself. Her mouth makes the perfect little 'o' and her eyes flutter closed.

"Halfway, baby. Keep going,"

I slap her thigh to spur her on and her gaze locks onto mine. With my hands grabbing each ass cheek, I lift her up and down to ride my dick, pushing her down all the way to the base.

"Shit, Sof. You feel so good," I grunt.

"Harder," she cries out.

That turns me completely feral for her. I push my hips up and drive into her without stopping, feeling the tension build in every muscle of my body.

"I'm so close, so close, Jax."

Sweat beads on my forehead, my head goes fuzzy as I surge towards my release.

"Squeeze my neck, now!" I grit out.

With the blood rushing in my ears, I seize the opportunity to wrap my fingers around her throat, so we can share the overwhelming sensation that consumes me. I keep fucking her until every drop of my soul has left my body.

She collapses against my chest. I wrap her in my arms, pressing a kiss to the top of her head as I try to regain my breath.

"I love you, Sofia. I love you so damn much," I whisper.

I feel the soft stroke of her fingers on my cheek as she lifts herself up, her eyes meeting mine.

I hope she realizes one day how deep my love truly runs for her, and that I can show her just how special she is.

"I love you, Jax. More than life itself, always remember that."

Softly, she kisses me, and I am completely absorbed in her touch, shutting out the world.

"You're safe now, Jax. We got through the storm and now we live."

Holding her tightly, I let her words resonate.

We have been dragged through hell, and she has seen me at my worst. She took my broken pieces and put them back together.

She loves me for who I am.

I am home.

CHAPTER EIGHTY

SOFIA

One month later,
Song- My Home, Myles Smith

"COME ON YOU TWO!" I CALL OUT AS JAX IS ON ALL FOURS chasing a giggling, screaming Maeve around the yard. With a playful grin, he catches her and pulls her close, his arms wrapped tightly around her as she giggles with delight.

"I've got you," he growls, and lays her down on the grass to tickle her.

Her infectious little laughs fill the air, bringing an overwhelming joy to my heart. Just watching them completes me. I can't hide the bright smile on my face.

Our family.

He puts her back on her feet, and she spots me with a wide grin.

Jax sits up on his knees and whispers something in her ear. The next thing I know, she's full speed doing her wobbly run at me. With my arms open wide, I pick her up and spin her around. I close my eyes, savoring the moment, as Jax walks towards us and gently kisses my cheek, his touch sending shivers down my spine.

I can feel the cool evening breeze on my skin as the sun slowly dips below the horizon.

"Dinner is ready and we all know dinosaurs like daddy have to have their food, don't we?" I say to Maeve, who enthusiastically nods.

"I'm more looking forward to my dessert," he whispers in my ear and my cheeks blush.

I look up at him. The admiration in his eyes sends a rush of warmth through my veins. But, what makes me happier is the life that shines in them.

He's getting there. He hasn't missed a single appointment with his therapist. We talk, every day, whether it's small things, or the heavy stuff.

It would have been his dad's birthday last week. He opened up and told me about him, and his life growing up. We even cooked one of his dad's favorite dinners.

I'm so damn proud of this man. He fights his mind every day, but he lets me in more and more.

After we finish up dinner, I start tidying up Maeve's books from the floor and I can feel the weight of their gaze on me. Jax leans against the counter, his arms relaxed as Maeve sits comfortably between them.

"What are you two up to?" I raise a brow.

Jax chuckles, shaking his head. "Nothing, Momma."

I can tell he's up to something by the way he bites down on his bottom lip.

Maeve gets her bath, and I go to grab a set of pajamas out of the drawer just as Jax hands me a white one.

"Thank you, baby," I say, taking it from him.

Putting a wriggly Maeve into the onesie, I start on the snaps. As I start with her legs, I can sense Jax's presence lingering behind me.

After popping the last one under her chin, I blink a few times and my eyes are drawn to the cute pink text on the front of the outfit.

And, my heart skips a beat, as if time momentarily stands still.

As I sit her up on the changing table, a sob catches in my throat.

It reads: *Mommy, will you marry my daddy?*

"J-Jax?" I stutter.

"Turn around, sweetheart." His voice is soft, yet full of anticipation.

I pick her up into my arms and turn around, tears blur my vision. Jax looks nervous as he kneels down, a small blue box clasped tightly in his hands.

With a flick of his wrist, he opens it, and my breath catches in my throat. Tears stream down my face as I admire the magnificent princess cut diamond, shimmering brilliantly in the light.

"I-I" Words fail me.

"Sofia Isabelle Garcia, will you be my wife?"

I don't need to think about my answer. I know it in my bones. I want to be his forever.

"Yes. Jax. A million times yes!"

When he stands up, a look of relief spreads across his face. He reaches out and pulls me towards him, our lips meeting in a passionate embrace.

"You've just made me the happiest man to walk on this earth, sweetheart. I promise I'll love you for the rest of my life," he whispers against me.

"I love you, Jax. So much."

"I love you, tigritsa. More than you could ever imagine." He presses a kiss to the top of Maeve's head. "And I love you too, *tigryonok*. My girls."

Nuzzling my forehead against his chest, I close my eyes

and immerse myself in the comforting sound of his heart pounding in my ears.

"I'm so proud of you, Jax. I know Kai would be too," I say, stroking his cheek.

He is the best daddy, the best partner I could ever have wished for.

"I hope he is. I couldn't have done any of this without you, baby. You saved my life."

My gaze shifts upwards, and suddenly he moves in, his nose gently touching mine.

"And I'd do it again in a heartbeat. I would do anything for you, Jax Carter."

Despite every storm life throws at us. We will always have this.

Our perfect little family.

A love that can survive anything.

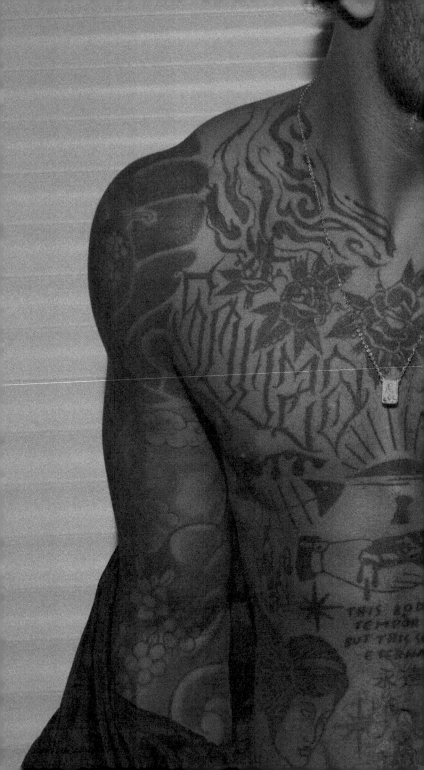

CHAPTER EIGHTY-ONE

JAX

Song- I Get To Love You, Ruelle

FOR THE FIRST TIME ALL MORNING, I FINALLY HAVE SOME time to myself. Nikolai and Alexei have gone to greet my New York family. All of them have flown in for our wedding. I took Sofia and Maeve to visit the crazy bunch last month. I've missed them. It was nice to get back in the ring at King's Gym. Now I have my boxing license back. Grayson and Keller are working on a plan to get me my title back.

Finally, everything seems to piece back together.

It's only a matter of time before I fuck it up again. Things never run this perfectly in my life. It isn't possible to be this calm.

I step in front of the full-length mirror and run a hand through my curls.

An entire room full of people are waiting for us in the ceremony room downstairs. What if Sofia gets cold feet?

Or, realizes that I'm not enough for her?

Fuck.

521

Am I even good enough for her?

My mind races, thinking about the night we met when I caught her running from her wedding. How beautiful she looked in her dress, even with black make-up streaming down her cheeks.

I clench my fists, trying to practice those stupid breathing exercises my therapist drills into me. I can't beat the shit out of anything in Mikhail's casino penthouse. I shouldn't need to do that either.

What the hell is wrong with me?

Today of all days, I can feel myself slipping back into that gray place. And, this time, I'm on my own.

A light knock at the door jerks me back to the real world.

It's funny how fine you can look on the outside when on the inside, you are breaking. No one can see the silent battles. Except for me, I have someone that can.

I don't want to talk or see anyone right now. I just want Sofia. I want her to hold me and tell me everything is okay.

It's bad luck to see her before the wedding. I've been warned and we sure as hell don't need anymore of that. We've had enough for a lifetime.

But, I need her.

The tapping continues. Reluctantly, I swing open the door and all the air rushes out of my lungs.

My perfect, sweet Sofia is standing there.

Her long red hair is curled and hangs over one shoulder. And, damn, that tight lace, white dress that dips between her breasts certainly has my head spinning, in the best possible way.

I trail my gaze back up, and concern is written all over her face.

"Jax, are you okay?"

As she takes a step forward, I welcome her inside. Her

sweet scent invades my nostrils as she brushes past me and spins back to face me.

My breath hitches as she places her palms on my chest and adjusts my navy tie.

"You look absolutely stunning, sweetheart."

When she blushes, I feel my heart start to race.

"I thought this was bad luck? You're the one who told me that," I say with a grin, trying to push down the negative shit swirling through my thoughts.

She shakes her head, her eyes narrowing as she pulls back to study me.

"I was sitting in my room, on my own and a wave of nerves hit me. All I wanted was you, Jax."

I slide my hands down her soft arms and hold my hands over hers on my chest.

It's like she is so in tune with me and my emotions. She just knows what I'm thinking.

I love her for it.

"Were you worried about me, baby?"

She nods.

"I know you hate being away from me, Jax. It's the first night in a long time we've been apart. I just wanted to check in, make sure everything was okay. And tell you, I love you and I can't wait to be Mrs. Carter."

She looks up at me through her lashes and those doubts from a few minutes ago, they start to fade away. She's here, telling me exactly what I needed to hear.

She claws me back to her, she is my safety.

"I had visions of you running out on me, or not even turning up. That you realized I was no good." I have to be honest with her.

"You know that isn't true, right? I'm not going anywhere. In fact, in a few minutes' time, I'll legally be yours. No getting rid of me then."

She pouts at me, and I chuckle.

"Same goes to you, sweetheart."I stroke the top of her hand and press a kiss to her temple. She wraps her arms around me and hugs me tight.

And, sometimes that is all you need. Men, like anybody else, sometimes just need to be held tight and told that everything will be okay.

There isn't a cure for a mind that works against you. There is no magic button to press to make the dark thoughts go away.

I'll have to battle this every day, probably for the rest of my life.

And I will.

I will continue to fight for us.

For me.

For our daughter.

And most of all, for this beautiful soul in front of me.

I will never stop, and with her by my side, I know I can do it.

She is my strength in this life.

My forever.

Now the good days outweigh the bad.

I have a radiant light in my darkened world.

And in spite of everything, **there is always beauty in chaos.**

THE END.

EPILOGUE

SOFIA

I FIDDLE WITH THE RINGS ON MY FINGER AS I JOG DOWN the stairs back to Maeve's second birthday party. Our home is filled with familiar faces. Nikolai has Elena on his shoulders trying to get the balloons on the ceiling. Lara is chasing Alexei round the room, trying to snatch back her phone.

Even Mikhail is here, petrifying the kids with his mask. Jax's New York family are all here too and their kids are running wild. He was right. There are so many of them. They're cute though, and Maeve loves playing with them.

Elena eagerly grabs a balloon, it pops when she squeezes it too tightly, right as I stop in front of Nikolai. She jumps and bursts out into tears.

"It's okay, princess. Daddy can get you another," Nikolai says softly, lifting her into his arms.

"Do you know where Jax is?" I ask, looking at the bouncy castle in the yard, but I still can't spot either of them.

"Went to the garage," he says while soothing his daughter.

"When are we doing the food?" Alexei calls out behind me. I spin to find him holding the two-tier princess castle cake in his hands.

"I'm not telling you again. Put the damn thing back," Lara hisses, slapping his arm.

He grumbles, but does as she says.

I can't help but laugh. "Soon, let me go get the birthday girl."

I stop by the door and lean on the frame. Tears of joy threaten to erupt. Jax has Maeve on his bike, with her facing him and sporting a brand new pink helmet.

"When you're old enough, you can have a motorcycle to match. Well, we might have to ask Mommy." He turns to face me with a grin on his lips. "Isn't that right, Mommy?"

With his arm outstretched and palm facing upward, he signals for me to approach. I gently take his hand, caressing his wedding ring.

Anxiety creeps in, but it's mixed with excitement.

"Is there room for one more on there?" I ask quietly.

Jax's brow furrows as he nudges himself back, signaling for me to take a seat by tapping the chair.

"Here, put Maeve on your lap, maybe?"

I laugh. He's just so cute sometimes.

Shaking my head, I raise my eyebrows, trying to get the message across. "I don't mean me, Jax."

His mouth just drops open. His eyes dart to my fingers splayed out on my belly.

"You're pregnant? We're having a baby? Is it really happening?" The exuberance in his voice has me on the verge of crying.

I grin as he wraps his arms around me.

He bends down and places a kiss on my stomach. When he leans back I grab his face and press my lips over his. I wanted to give him this. A chance to not miss a single second of their life. Just like he deserves.

"I can't believe this. This is amazing,"

His smile is so bright as he picks up Maeve.

"You're going to be the best big sister. What do you think? Is there a little brother in there?"

I kinda hope so. I'd love to see Jax be a daddy to a little boy. He would be completely in his element.

"Baby!" Maeve shouts, and we both laugh.

"Are you ready for more chaos, Mr. Carter?"

His tongue glides over his lip as he clasps my hand.

"Always, sweetheart. I am the king of it, remember?"

"I do, and I wouldn't have it any other way."

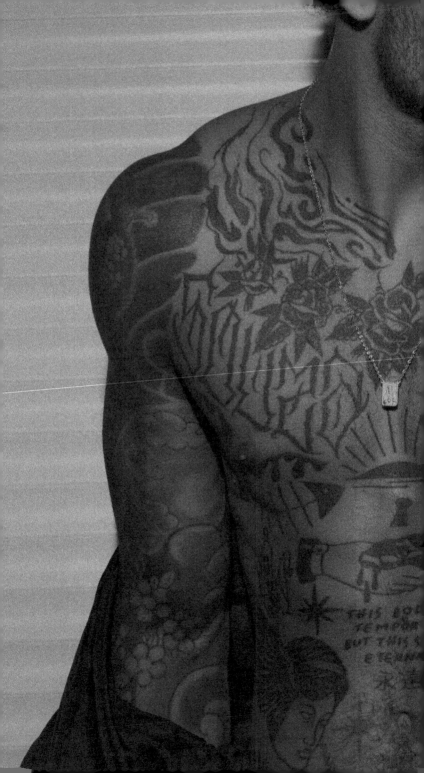

EPILOGUE

JAX

I can't believe it.

I'm going to be a dad again. And, this time, I'll be there for all of it.

I get to see Sofia growing my baby. Fuck, it's going to be perfect.

I can't wait to look after her, to spoil her.

Grow our family.

We walk hand in hand back to the party, a house filled with our friends.

"She needs a little nap, then tell Alexei we can do the cake." Sofia drops a kiss on my cheek. I tug her wrist before she can leave and kiss her properly.

Frankie lands a hand on my shoulder. "You've done good here, Jax. We're all proud of you."

"Thanks, *Dad.*"

With a chuckle, he gives me a friendly slap on the back of my head. "Enough of that."

Just like old times.

I look over and notice Nikolai gripping his glass of vodka so tightly that it seems on the verge of shattering

"I'll be back in a sec." I tell Frankie and head over to Nik in the corner on his own, vacantly watching on as the party continues.

"You okay?" I ask, taking a seat next to him.

He pours me a glass and slides it over.

"Fine." He clicks his ring against the table. "What's got that grin on your face?" he asks.

"Sofia is pregnant."

"Congratulations." With a smile, he raises his glass to me before downing the contents.

I look at his wedding ring. He rarely wears it, and I never question him about it. We all deal with grief differently.

"You ever thought about finding someone again?" I ask, already regretting the question when his face morphs into fury.

"No."

I wonder what my sister was like to put up with his grumpy ass. Can't be many people in the world to do that.

His face softens and I follow his line of sight to his daughter playing with Lara.

"What was she like? My sister?"

He stiffens before resting an arm on the chair next to him.

"Katerina. She was funny, like you. She could even make Mikhail crack a smile."

"So, the opposite of you?"

He raises one eyebrow and nods.

"Yes. Probably in every way. She was kind. She was an incredible mother. She saw beauty in even the ugliest places. She deserved better."

I'm sad for him. Bringing up his little girl on his own. No wonder he is the way he is. If I lost Sofia, I don't know how I would cope.

The thought makes me click my rings against my glass. "So, when are we getting revenge?"

He looks up and his jaw clenches. "Soon. Let's see where these diamonds take us."

I quickly sit upright, my senses heighten as I notice Mikhail making a beeline towards us.

"We need to go." He squeezes his tattooed hand on Nikolai's shoulder, who stiffens.

He shoves his phone in front of Nikolai's face.

Nikolai's eyes widen as he watches whatever footage is on there. "That's interesting. Know who she is?"

She?

"That's where you, Lara and the donkey come in."

"You need me?" I ask, hoping he says no. I don't want to leave my daughter's party.

As Mikhail shakes his head, his intense, dark eyes lock onto mine.

Oh, he's pissed. I'll keep my mouth shut.

"Today is family day for you, Jax. You're good to stay here." Nikolai orders as he stands, shrugging on his leather jacket and nods to Lara and Alexei, pointing towards the door. The three siblings, and their crazed donkey, storming out of the door, like they're ready to take on the world.

Sofia comes over to join me, sitting herself on my lap. My arm snakes around her waist as I protectively stroke her flat belly.

"Where did they rush off to?" she asks, leaning her head back against my shoulder.

The sight of her full lips is impossible for me to resist.

Mine.

My beautiful wife.

"Work, I've got the day off. I'm sure I'll find out tomorrow."

"I've got you all day, huh?"

As I kiss her again, a mischievous grin dances across her mouth.

"And night," I whisper in her ear and feel her shiver under my touch.

The chaos can wait for another day, because right now, I am exactly where I need to be.

Home.

NEED A LITTLE MORE CHAOS?

You can sign up to my newsletter to receive a bonus honeymoon chapter. It's spicy with a bit of breeding kink, which may or may not have resulted in Sofia's second pregnancy.

www.lunamasonauthor.com

ARE YOU READY FOR NIKOLAI?

CAGED is coming soon!

She is on a mission to take down the Volkov's and he believes he's protecting her.
It's a battle for blood.
A story driven by revenge.
But what happens when they steal each other's hearts?

You'll find out on June 27th.

Bodyguard x Spy.
Enemies to Lovers.
Single dad.

You can pre-order CAGED now.

And we can't forget our Alexei and Lara. CRAVE, A brother's best friend x stalker romance. Coming September 20th.

Their pre-order is also available now!

MORE BY LUNA MASON

Some of the characters from series one, Beneath The Mask, made appearances in Chaos. If you haven't had a chance to read the series, they are all now live on Kindle Unlimited.

Distance, book one, Keller and Sienna
Detonate, book two, Grayson and Maddie
Devoted, book three, Luca and Rosa
Detained, book four, Frankie and Zara

Roman Petrov, a marriage of convenience novella, part of the Petrov Family Anthology will be releasing in early 2024. You can pre-order ROMAN now!

ABOUT
LUNA MASON

Luna Mason is an Amazon top #20 and international best-selling author. She lives in the UK and if she isn't writing her filthy men, you'll find her with her head in a spicy book.
To be the first to find out her upcoming titles you can subscribe to her newsletter!

You can join the author's reader group (Luna Mason's Mafia Queens) to get exclusive
teasers, and be the first to know about current projects and release dates.

Acknowledgments

I am lucky to be surrounded by such supportive, inspiring and hard-working people. I couldn't do what I love every single day if you all weren't there to help me.

If publishing a book has taught me anything, it's once you find those people, you hold them close.

So, Jan, Nalleli and Melissa. You have been on this author journey since the start. Honestly, out of everything that has happened, meeting you guys is right there at the top of my list. I would be lost without you and I am incredibly lucky to have friends like you.

Jay, the glitter in my life. The beta reader who found me right at my very, very first Tik Tok and has stuck with me ever since. I cannot tell you how grateful I am for you. From beta reading and never being afraid to push me out of my comfort zone. For pushing me to write a MMC to beat Keller off the top of your list. For always being there when I need you. The fact that I get to see you FINALLY at RTD is so exciting. Thank you for being you. For sharing your experiences with me and trusting me. <3 You.

Katy, Jas and my PR guru, Kasey. Thank you for putting up with my chaos. I will never change, so please continue to whip me into shape and shout at me. Thank you for everything you do for me.

Bobby. The guy who works behind the scenes, no matter what time of the day, I know you have my back. Your knowledge and guidance honestly impresses me every day. I adore working with you, I will always be thankful for you taking a chance on me at the start and I can't wait to see where we take this.

To the author friends I have made along the way, this job can be lonely in our little fictional worlds. It can also be scary. But when I have you guys behind me, cheering me on, I couldn't ask for anything more.

Last but by no means least, to my family and my boys. I do what I do for you and I couldn't do it without your support. I love you all, very much.